ABOUT TH

Jim Crossley read modern history at Cambridge and has written six successful books on military history. Retired from a career in industry, he lives in Norfolk and enjoys sailing and country living generally. He has always been fascinated by the relationship between Britain and Germany, two nations united by many common values and family connections, yet torn apart by two world wars.

By the same author:

Something Wrong With Our Ships	2008	Published privately
British Destroyers 1892-1918	2009	Osprey Publishing
Bismarck: The Epic Sea Chase	2010	Pen and Sword
The Hidden Threat	2011	Pen and Sword
Monitors of the Royal Navy	2015	Pen and Sword
Voices from Jutland	2016	Pen and Sword

Jim Crossley

The Perils and the Prize

Jim Crossley

The Perils and the Prize

Vanguard Press

VANGUARD PAPERBACK

© Copyright 2020
Jim Crossley

The right of Jim Crossley to be identified as author of
this work has been asserted by him in accordance with the
Copyright, Designs and Patents Act 1988.

A CIP catalogue record for this title is
available from the British Library.

ISBN 978 1 78465 787 1

*Vanguard Press is an imprint of
Pegasus Elliot MacKenzie Publishers Ltd.*

www.pegasuspublishers.com

First Published in 2020

**Vanguard Press
Sheraton House Castle Park
Cambridge England**

Printed & Bound in Great Britain

Dedication

This book is dedicated to my wife, Anne, who has supported me in my writing and tolerated the associated ill temper and frequent absences.

Chapter 1

It was a bleak wintry afternoon. The last shafts of daylight filtered through the skylight onto the reclining model in the centre of the room. William contemplated a wet, dreary walk home to his little room in Chelsea. His painting was not going well. It was never going to go well. The Slade School, under the direction of Henry Tonks, still insisted on the highest standards of anatomical accuracy in every student's work and William just couldn't get it right. Looking at his attempt at a male nude, even he could see that the flesh did not clothe the skeleton as it should. The muscles did not seem to be consistent with the posture, but fought each other in little distorted knots around the joints. He couldn't get the left foot to rest convincingly on the dais. Landscapes, seascapes and pictures of boats came naturally to him but he simply couldn't draw people as the Slade demanded. After his first year there, he knew he was an unsatisfactory student. Eventually he would have to do something about it. Eventually…

The truth was that he enjoyed student life in London, in an idle, uncommitted sort of way. When he had come to London the previous autumn, he had been a somewhat gawky country boy, his tall, athletic frame giving testament to a rigorous routine of games and exercise at school. Exposure to the Chelsea set, however, prompted a rapid transformation in the middle-class provincial lad. His clothes and demeanour had become those of a typical art student. His long, dark hair flopped down over his ears and collar. His face was paler; he secretly hoped more "interesting" looking. Although above average height, he gave an impression of vulnerability, almost of weakness. His grey-blue eyes seeming always to be probing for an escape route from whatever situation he might be in. He wore a loose-fitting corduroy jacket and the fashionably floppy trousers known as "Oxford Bags". Great care was taken in the selection of loosely knotted ties and scarves, so as to look casual yet chic. He smoked strange Balkan cigarettes. Better off than most of his contemporaries, and with no parent to moderate his expenses, he could afford long evenings in the fashionable arty pubs and eateries around Chelsea, and drifted aimlessly among a group of like-minded friends. They gathered noisily together for animated discussions of art, politics and the human condition generally. Mostly scions of wealthy families, he and his set were not greatly affected by the depression then blighting less fortunate people all over the civilised world, but this did not stop them from adopting fashionable Marxist views and languid drawing room pacifism.

That evening he remembered he had promised to go with some Slade friends and a few would-be actors from RADA to a lecture by a Mr Markwitz entitled *The Wondrous Achievements of Soviet Russia*. He was looking forward to it, not because of the lecture, but because afterwards they were going on to a private club in Pimlico which had a seductive reputation for scandalous goings-on. He was dreaming about this when the bell rang for the end of the session and it was time to pack up his things and go home. The model ambled off his stage, modestly wrapped in a towel. The janitor began his regular litany of complaints about the mess the young ladies and gentlemen were making of the wash room. The students looked despondently at their latest creations and stowed them away to be worked on later. Gradually the Slade shut down for the night, disgorging its denizens into the wet, cold, colourless streets.

By seven William was at his lecture. The little hall was full, the audience consisting mainly of students like himself, but with a smattering of rougher-looking types – trade unionists, Communist Party members, even the odd genuine worker. It was difficult to tell whether Markwitz had ever actually visited Russia or not, but he certainly seemed enthusiastic about the place. It was a veritable paradise, he said, for working people. There was a universal free health service, no unemployment, and everyone helped his neighbour as there was no economic competition. Women had equal rights. Art, cinema and poetry flourished. He showed lantern slides of factory workers eating happily together in works canteens, of peasants, transformed into collective farm workers, smiling at each other as they raked together piles of hay, of earnest students studying engineering in magnificent lecture halls. He waxed lyrical about the development of Soviet arts and theatre. Above all he praised the liberation of people from the stultifying influence of superstition, of the church, and of cruel domination by their feudal landlords and their capitalist bosses.

"All the people of the Soviet Union," he declared, "are fellow workers, each receiving what he needs, each giving what he can. Nothing can resist the force of this movement. It falls to you, workers, students and activists to bring these blessings to our own poor country."

It wasn't quite clear what Markwitz meant by "our own poor country". His accent and name did not exactly identify him as a true Brit. German? Polish? It wasn't clear, but that didn't matter. He had made his point. He sat down, looking pleased with himself, and invited questions from the floor. There was some desultory questioning about foreign policy.

"How," he replied, "can a country free of religion and capitalism not be peaceful?" About trade unions: "They are the organ of the workers' control." Someone tried to ask something about freedom of the press. This produced a little scuffling at the back of the hall and two large men appeared shouldering their way towards the questioner, but Markwitz was equal to the situation.

"All Soviet newspapers are entirely free to express the thoughts and the wishes of the people. They are not controlled by the ruling class as they are in England."

This seemed quite satisfactory. The meeting broke up amid polite murmurings of approval and the audience filed out, whispering to each other in awed tones, rather as so many non-conformists might leave from a revival meeting. There were people at the door handing out leaflets and news sheets, but William and his little group pushed past into the street and towards a pub.

"Well, what did you think of that?" asked Guy, a fellow Slade student.

"Not much new really, but he spoke well, didn't he?" replied William. "I wonder what it's really like in Russia though? You know, I don't believe that fellow has ever been there."

"It's certainly difficult to get in. I tried but they wouldn't let me as I was not a Party Member. Oh well, I'm on for a drink, Will; how about you?"

They drifted into the Royal Dragoon and chatted happily there for the duration of a round or two until it was time to go on to the Café des Artes.

The club was in a Chelsea back street on the top floor of a dreary-looking grey building, the rest of which was taken up by a shabby antique shop. You entered by going up an outdoor fire escape and opening a red leather-covered outer door. Behind the door sat Boris, the doorman, who checked membership cards and took coats in grumpy silence. You then pushed through a heavy velvet curtain into the club itself. You had to blink several times before your eyes adjusted to the dim light and the haze of strange-smelling smoke.

There were several little groups clustered round tables drinking the "house special" cocktail which, that evening, was a bitter mixture of absinthe and vodka, laced with Worcester sauce. The clients were mostly students but there was a sprinkling of older arty types of both sexes, hoping perhaps to revive the pleasures of their youth, or perhaps to pick up a young girl or boyfriend with whom to misspend the night.

William's party grabbed a vacant table and ordered drinks. There were eight of them, four aspiring actors from RADA, and Rosie and Camilla, two fellow art students, who both affected the vague, languid manner then fashionable in arty circles. Camilla was a talented painter, and was to become well known for her family group portraits painted in great houses for wealthy clients. She put a pale arm around William.

"Willie, darling, do find me some cigarettes I'm positively gasping for a smoke." William gave her one of his Balkans.

"Thanks, you're *such* a dear, but isn't it too *too* dull in here, same old lot? Oh, I do get so tired of it."

William tried to think of a suitable reply when a disturbance arose near them. Jacky, one of the RADA boys, a youth so handsome that it was hard to draw your eyes away from him, stood up quickly and glared at an elderly man who had somehow found a place at their table.

"Take your hands off me," he hissed. "You are a disgusting old man. Get out of here, or I shall have to ask Boris to throw you out."

The interloper, a little the worse for drink, shambled away. Jacky flushed scarlet, but Rosie comforted him.

"We all know what you're really like, sweetie, so don't take offence. Anyway, I bags the first dance with you and we'll show 'em all. I hear there's going to be a Charleston."

Sure enough, at that very moment, a band struck up and soon the little dance floor was crowded with couples drifting and swaying to a slow waltz, the air above them a cloud of blue cigarette smoke. After a few dances the compere announced the start of the floorshow and the audience settled round their tables to watch the usual mediocre performances leading up to the high spot of the entertainment. After the conjurors and a man who told dubious jokes, two girls in short dresses and with fashionably bobbed hair appeared on the stage. They were announced as "Barbara and Cassandra, the Amazing Charleston Sensation". As the first notes of the dance sounded, they seemed at first to freeze, then they were off, incredibly alive and vigorous, throwing themselves into the rhythm of the wild dance, seeming to understand and react together perfectly, like two puppets violently motivated by a single puppeteer. Limbs whizzed faster and faster, legs kicked higher and higher, and as the music rose to a level of intensity worthy of its dark African origins, the girls threw themselves at each other, parted, kicked high, twirled, came together again, all the time shivering and shimmering to the music. Sometimes the band paused, and the pair was statue still, looking fixedly at a point above the audience's head. Sometimes the pace was so frantic that arms, legs, skirts and faces seemed to blur into a single mad mass of colour.

The band stopped. "Now all Charleston!" shouted the compere. The floor thronged with dancers, strutting, kicking and shimmying to the music until it seemed that the floor and walls of the old building must burst with the sheer energy of it all. William sat mesmerised at his table. He could Charleston all right, but he had no partner, as Camilla had drifted off with Guy. Conversation was impossible with the din of the music and the shouts and laughter from the dance floor so he just smiled vaguely and carried on drinking the venomous cocktails. It was late now and his head was struggling with the assaults of the music and the alcohol. The dance finished and his party started to drift away. He found himself left alone at the table with Jacky. Exhausted by dancing, Jacky had managed to shake off Rosie, who had been becoming boringly amorous, and was relishing a final, well-earned drink.

The two young men left together; they both lived near The World's End at the end of Chelsea High Street, and they strode a little unsteadily down the shining wet pavement, where old newspapers whirled past them on the bitter wind. All at once a figure stepped out in front of them. He was a tall man in a shabby greatcoat fastened with string around his waist. In the dim light of the street lamps they could make out a hollow, pallid face and William noticed that one arm of the greatcoat was empty.

"Good evening, gentlemen," said a surprisingly cultured voice. "I don't suppose either of you can spare a few coppers for a wounded soldier?"

Jacky seemed to want to walk on, after all, these unfortunates were common enough in 1920's London, but William held back, as if mesmerised by the figure in front of him. He was suddenly ashamed of himself, unable to face the reality that the stranger represented, the injustice, the tragedy of his own humiliation. In his dazed, inebriated condition, the man's words had somehow awakened him to the stark, desperate reality of life in depression-hit London. He was suddenly appalled by the contrast between his frivolous evening and that of this poor, broken creature wandering homeless and alone in the damp, joyless streets of the great city. He dug in his pocket and found four half crowns – ten shillings – which he thrust into the outstretched hand, then, unable to face the thanks of the stranger, or even to speak to him, he hurried on his way, scarlet-faced with embarrassment. Jacky had seen his friend's generous gift and sensed his discomfort. They were now only a few steps from William's door.

"For God's sake, Jacky, come in," he muttered. "I need to talk to someone."

The two climbed the stairs and William lit the gas fire. Jacky slumped in one of the armchairs and watched as two whisky and sodas were produced.

"Well, what is it, old chap?" he asked. "Was it something that fellow said?" William thought for a moment. Jacky was not one of his close friends, but suddenly he felt an urge to talk to someone seriously, and Jacky it would have to be.

"Do you ever feel your life is utterly futile?" he began. "From what I hear you are going to be a fantastic actor, but I know I'll never be much of a painter and here I am dawdling about in London pretending to be a serious art student. I'm spending the money my father earned by hard work and couldn't use himself because he was killed in the war. My mum and my brother and sister too, blown up in a ship. I survived, and here I am wasting time on a useless life of sham art and sleazy nightclubs. I've got to find something useful to do, and I think it will mean getting out of London. That fellow in the street, it's a damned disgrace; he'd been a soldier, probably an officer, and look at him now, poor chap. That really brought it home to me, that and the things the lecturer was saying about Russia. I feel so utterly useless! I hate this life we lead. God, Jacky, I might as well have blown up with the rest of the family."

Jacky sipped his whisky and thought for a while. He was no fool and he had always liked William, sensing his unease in the shabby bohemian world which they both inhabited.

"Well I suppose we all feel like that from time to time. You say I will succeed on the stage. Believe me, I love acting more than anything, but I know I'm not half as good as some of the others in my year. I get the good parts because people say I'm good-looking, but as for talent that's another thing entirely. I think we just have to take life as it comes. Unlike that old soldier we're both lucky. There's no point in worrying about it. But if you really don't like the Slade, try something else, that's my advice. You'll be happy enough when you get your teeth into something which really suits you. Good God! Is that the time? I must get home."

"Don't go," said William. He simply couldn't bear the thought of being alone that night in his miserable little rooms. "There's a spare bed in the other room, do stay."

So the two sat in front of the gas fire. Jacky was a good talker. Like many stage people he was self-absorbed and deeply interested in the impression he made on those around him. He loved talking about himself and letting his unbridled imagination soar into all sorts of improbable scenarios. That evening he dwelt on the possibilities of getting in to the movie business, maybe in America, and fantasised about the career that he might create for himself, making films with gorgeous women. "I have even got a sort of audition soon," he announced, "but I am sure it will come to nothing." His host slumped moodily in his chair. He hardly listened to what Jacky was saying but dwelt gloomily on his own prospects and the miserable, useless life that he was leading. Eventually a pause in the flow of words enabled him to announce that he was going to bed. Jacky's optimistic conversation had only emphasised his own depression. He slept badly and woke with a hangover.

The cold light of a winter morning, coupled with a throbbing headache and a churning stomach did little to cheer him. He could not touch the egg and bacon breakfast which his old landlady had prepared downstairs, and the sight of Jacky, elegant, graceful and fresh as a daisy eating heartily, made him more nauseated than ever. Somehow a plan for the day formed in his brain. He would not go to the Slade today. He would go down to Walworth and talk to his guardian. As soon as his visitor left, he grabbed his things and set off.

In the yard at the back, William kept his AJS motorbike. Hoping that a spin might make him feel better, he put on his greatcoat and flying helmet and wheeled the machine out into the street. His breath made great clouds of mist in the cold air as he kicked at the starter. The engine made a few pathetic pops then died completely. He swore to himself as he fiddled with the mixture control and the throttle. Not a sign of life. He resorted to push-starting, running down the street, pushing the machine and then letting go the clutch so as to spin the engine. After two or three tries, he was leaning exhausted against a wall, panting and cursing to himself. By this time half a dozen urchins had appeared as if from nowhere and were making helpful remarks such as "Won't she go, mister?" or "Like yer 'at, gov."

All of a sudden the audience melted away as a London bobby appeared round the corner.

"Trouble, sir?" he said, glancing briefly at the licence plate.

"Well, yes, actually she won't seem to start."

"I don't know much about motorbikes, sir, but if you were to ask me I would say you could try switching the petrol on."

William glared at him furiously. Of course the petrol was on; he wasn't a fool. To prove the point, he glanced down at the little brass tap under the fuel tank. Impossible! It was off. He remembered turning it and remembered pressing the button on the top of the float chamber to flood the carburettor. Then the revelation came to him. Idiot! He must have forgotten to turn the tap off last time he used the machine. So now he had turned it the wrong way. It was all those bloody little urchins' fault for putting him off. Red-faced and angrier than ever, he turned the tap and kicked the starter again. The motor burst into life, and soon settled down to a steady tick-over. Thanking his saviour profusely, a shamefaced young man rode off over Battersea Bridge and along Nine Elms Lane towards a mean little house in the poorest part of London, which served as a rectory for the Rev. James Tullow, known to his friends as Flopsy.

Flopsy had been a close friend of William's father. During the Great War he had served as a chaplain in a Guards regiment and had earned an MC and bar for outstanding bravery in rescuing wounded men from no man's land. Always slight and frail, he had lost a lung to a German gas attack during the Somme battle and had come out of the army physically wrecked, but had nevertheless plunged himself immediately into one of the toughest, poorest parishes in London. William drew up outside the house and was pleased to find that Flopsy was in.

"Just a moment, old chap, I've got to try to find somewhere for Betty here to go. Been beaten up again at home. Can't go back there. See what I can do."

William caught a glimpse of a filthy-looking young woman, obviously pregnant, with a livid bruise on her cheek. He sat down to wait. There were various comings and goings at the rectory. At last it seemed that Betty had been suitably accommodated, then Flopsy came through into the little dining room to talk to William. He looked pale and exhausted, but he smiled and did his best to make his young visitor feel at home. It was difficult to imagine this frail, flustered and faintly absurd-looking clergyman as a member of a crack regiment. His hands fluttered as he spoke and he kept looking about him and seeming to remember something he had forgotten. His sparse, unkempt, sandy hair fell untidily over his forehead. He was apt to knock things over when moving about and to lose his train of thought when speaking. He was constantly out of breath. William, however, knew that he had been one of his father's staunchest friends and it was to him that his dad had entrusted his only surviving child as he went to war. For as long as he could remember, William had been able to speak easily to him on any subject and be certain of a sympathetic hearing.

After the usual formalities and a tray of tea and biscuits, William got down to the reasons for his visit.

"I'm sorry, sir," he began. "I feel awful troubling you with my little problems when you have so many desperate people to deal with, but I just don't feel I'm on the right course. I'm never going to be even a competent artist – that's certain and I feel I'm wasting my life. Oh, I enjoy London and the parties and everything but something happened last night which made me feel so vain and inadequate" – he described the evening and the encounter with the old soldier – "I just feel as if I was on a road to nowhere." (This phrase had occurred to him as he was riding over Battersea Bridge. He was rather pleased with it.)

His guardian studied him closely. He noted the long hair, the rather foppish clothes, the unmistakably studied demeanour.

"Oh, dear William," he said. "I can't tell you what to do, you have to work that out for yourself, but do tell me, have you any ideas?"

William was about to answer when a furious knocking interrupted their conversation. A grubby little boy burst into the room.

"Please, Mister Reverend, I'm to tell you Aunty May is taken queer and she can't do the soup today, maybe not for a week. Sir, can I have one of them biscuits?"

The plate was passed over and, to William's horror, the brat grabbed, not one, but a handful, and was gone out of the room at a run.

"Blast it," said Flopsy. "What am I going to do about the soup? There will be twenty or thirty at the hall in an hour and it's the only hot food most of them get in the day. Now I'm going to let them down. What on earth can I do?"

"What about tinned soup?" suggested William, struck by a sudden brainwave. "I passed a big grocer's shop on the way here. We could dash there on the bike and get it. Then we could warm it up here."

"Oh, brilliant!" cried the clergyman.

So off they set, William and Flopsy on the AJS, Flopsy nursing a large suitcase. They managed to get two dozen cans of oxtail and buzzed unsteadily back to the rectory. Flopsy dug out his largest saucepans and soon he had William stirring them on the stove while he went around to the hall, which was only a few steps away, to set out the bowls and spoons. Luckily, there was plenty of bread left over from the previous day. As soon as the soup was hot, the two struggled out with the brew to where their first customers were waiting in line. Some had brought a bowl or mug, to take a helping to some friend or relative. A sorry lot they looked, thought William, as he ladled out the soup. They were of all ages, thin, drawn and mostly dirty. Above all, there was an air of helplessness about them. These were people who had given up on life. No prospect of work. No joy, except perhaps when they could scrounge a bottle of something, and only cold, dirt and misery to be certain of. They didn't seem particularly grateful for the soup, and they looked at him, he fancied, with sullen contemptuous expressions. Few said "Thank you," and none returned his smile as he doled out the oxtail. Who was this precious-looking young man, come down to gawp at them? It was him or the likes of him that ratted on the workers during the general strike, and they hadn't forgotten. It occurred to William that these were exactly the proletarian masses whom the communist lecturer had been talking about. Victims of the injustice inflicted by capitalism. But something else struck him strongly. They obviously respected and trusted Flopsy. He seemed to know many of them by name and he had a word for everyone.

"Hello, Mrs Carver, and how's young Billy liking school?"

"Good to see you on your feet again, Reggie, soon have you running a mile."

His little quips and kindnesses brought a rare smile to careworn faces and even, sometimes, a laugh.

Flopsy managed to delegate the washing-up to two of the local ladies and he and William returned to the rectory. Somehow, William couldn't return to the conversation about his own woes. His guardian told him a little about the unemployment and squalor in the poor parts of London. About the crime and fear of crime which stalked the streets. About the miserable lives of his parishioners.

"Hot soup here five days a week, and that's all the decent food some of them get – and to think that we fought a war to make a land fit for heroes."

Somehow, William found that he had been talked into coming again the next day to help – Aunty May was unlikely to return to the foray for several days. It would have to be tinned soup again;

neither of them had any idea how to make the proper stuff. Tinned was expensive but somehow William couldn't bring himself to ask for the money he had spent at the grocers, and Flopsy never mentioned it. So, the next day, he arrived again at the rectory, this time wearing a haversack stuffed with tins. The procedure was the same as the day before, except that, of course, Flopsy had forgotten to get any bread. Once again, the motorbike had to be used to collect loaves from the bakers. This time the passenger on the pillion was a young street urchin who clearly had never done such a thing before and disguised his nervousness by whooping and yelling at the top of his voice and using language which made William blush. He discovered afterwards that his passenger had managed to purloin a shilling from the baker's change.

After the soup routine, William and Flopsy got into a discussion about communism. Flopsy was not nearly as hostile to the idea as William had expected.

"Honestly," he said. "I look around me here and I see a whole mass of people who have no chance, no hope at all and they have almost no opportunity to get out of it. Now, I am no admirer of Marx but I have to accept that he has a point. Ownership of the means of production really does seem to give a few people – increasingly few, actually – a disproportionate share of the good things in life. I'm not the only priest drawn to communistic ideas. We've got to face the fact: traditional Christianity means nothing whatever to most of these people. They come for the soup, OK, and they come to me if they are in trouble, but a church service? Never. The only people who come to my church are a handful of shopkeepers and middle-class types. Not the masses. You must have heard of William Temple?" William had. "Well, you know he only just managed to get ordained because, like me, he wasn't in line with all the dogma they stuff into you at theological college. But he's really bringing Christian socialist ideas home to people. If Christianity means anything, it's caring for our neighbours, even if they do smell bad and swear often. Maybe all of us clergy ought to take a lead at least from the Labour Party, if not from Marx. What about you?"

Before William could speak, Flopsy remembered that he was already late for his planned round of visits that afternoon. Once again, his young visitor found he had been manoeuvred into another day of the soup run. It occurred to him that he had missed two whole days at the Slade already, and his friends would be wondering what he was up to. That evening he made for the Royal Dragoon to see if anyone was around. Sure enough, the usual group turned up and were soon engaged in a noisy free-for-all argument about the French Impressionists. William hung around on the fringes of the conversation, feeling somehow that he was now a stranger to all this and that he had nothing to add to the chatter going on around him. He was only a few miles from the Walworth he was coming to know, but this seemed like a foreign country. The party was interrupted by the entrance of an excited and exuberant Jacky.

"Well, how did it go?" asked Guy. William wondered what "It" was.

"Fantastic! I met this American. Funny-looking cove, a bit fat and greasy actually. Something to do with a studio in Hollywood. He made me do a little scene out of Hamlet, you know the "To be or not to be" one, then he telephoned someone else – we were at the Savoy you know – and I had to do it again with both of them watching. Then they sent for a girl, I think she was French, and I had to do a little love scene with her. That was quite fun actually. They asked me to wait outside and I could hear them chattering through the door, then they called me in again and I had to stand around posing for lots of photos. At last he asked me if I had an agent. Well, I said I hadn't and he said he would send a contract direct to me, and I should sign it and be ready to sail for America in three weeks' time. Just like that. On the Queen Mary too. Then he said, "Oh, you'll need something to be going on with," and gave me a hundred pounds. New five-pound notes. Just look!"

So Jacky was bound for the States and films. William was glad for him, but somehow his friend's success made him even more insecure about his own future. As the pub rang with celebrations and the film-star-to-be stood one round after another, he sunk gloomily into his own thoughts. Several times people tried to drag him into the midst of the celebration and everyone wanted to know where he had been and when he was going back to the Slade, but he answered evasively and kept sullenly to himself.

It was soup again the next day, and this time, at last, he got a chance to have a proper talk with his guardian. Eventually they agreed that William should abandon the Slade and return home to Tyneside; he would write to Flopsy as soon as he had some concrete plan as to what he should do. Flopsy emphasised that he must look at all options and make a serious decision within eight weeks.

"You can't hang around for ever," he said, "but you must give yourself time and space to think things through properly. I think a little time at home is a good idea."

At the same time as William was studying art in London, another young man, – in fact a relation – was coming of age in a divided and strife-torn Germany. Hans von Pilsen had been sheltered by the wealth of his family and his father's international connections and overseas income from the hardships caused by the collapsed German economy. The family still lived in the castle in Prussia which had been its home for centuries, although economic circumstances had enforced the closing off of many of the rooms. In spite of this, Hans could not ignore the misery which surrounded him and the hopelessness which dominated the lives of so many of his countrymen. He himself had successfully passed the first phase of his law examinations and it was assumed that he would soon find a comfortable place as a corporate lawyer. It seemed that a safe and prosperous life was awaiting him, if only the country could emerge from its economic woes, but he could not enthuse about the prospect. He was an active and adventurous young fellow, never happier than when shooting game on his father's estate or setting off in his sailing dinghy to camp on some remote island with a few friends. A lawyer's office seemed a miserable place to spend one's life when there were deer to be hunted, fish to be caught and grilled over a camp fire and fearsome wild boar to be found and shot in the forest. But there was a ray of hope. He had joined a sailing club with premises on the Baltic, not far from his Prussian home. Most of the other members seemed to be smart young fellows like himself, recently graduated from university. The previous month they had been addressed by General von Seeckt, the chief of the miniscule armed forces which Germany had been allowed to retain after 1919. The general was a daunting figure, stiff, reserved and formal in his approach, but he spoke eloquently about Germany's shame of 1918, the injustice of the peace settlement and the need for all Germans to unite and work together to restore the honour of the nation. It was stirring stuff. As a finale von Seeckt dropped some hints about a new organisation taking shape somewhere to the east. An organisation which somehow would change the fortunes of the nation and make it great and respected again.

Around the time of von Seeckt's visit, subtle changes seemed to be taking place in the club. Sailing races in small keelboats was soon supplemented by "voluntary" runs through the nearby forests. A new physical training instructor appeared from no one knew where and somehow talked the young men in the club into stricter and stricter regimes of fitness and endurance. It was even rumoured that some members had been invited to take a test, but no one was quite sure what had happened, as those who took it either clammed up or somehow ceased to appear at the club, leaving mysterious excuses. What was happening? Well, Hans would soon know. He had been invited to "Spend a day with Otto" – that meant taking the test – in a few weeks' time. After that he'd know all about it.

The test was gruelling. Six young men had to jog along soft, sandy tracks in a dark, hot, airless forest, singing lustily. This went on, not for half an hour, like their usual runs, but for a full hour and a half, then, when they were ready to die with exhaustion, the instructor halted them at the edge of a lake. They had to strip and plunge into the water then swim a quarter of a mile to a small island. Two of them gave up and had to be rescued and immediately sent home while the other four floundered half dead onto the island. There a sergeant from the army was waiting for them. Still stripped to the waist and barefoot, they next had to run along logs laid across trenches while the sergeant pelted them with fir cones and whatever else he could find. Anyone who fell off was immediately sent back to repeat the exercise until he succeeded. Next the four had to work together to move some large tree trunks across a clearing, and manhandle them over a wall. Another soldier, an officer this time, watched them, making notes on each man's performance. More such team tests followed. When they had finished, a third member of the party was sent home, and the remaining trio were given a drink and told to put on army-issue overalls. Then they were marched to a hut where they thankfully sat down to rest. The respite was brief. A sheaf of papers was placed in front of each man and a written test commenced, probing into mechanical understanding, mathematics, literacy and ability to reason logically. Finally, each one had to give a brief talk on a subject chosen by the directing officer – Hans' subject was "Should Germany respect the terms of the Versailles treaty" – then to submit to criticism of his argument by his fellows. Exhausted as he was, Hans found this difficult, but managed to struggle through it, making a few points he had heard from his father. As soon as the classroom tests were completed, the party was off to the lakeside again and had to swim back and reclaim their clothes. Hans was relieved to see a truck waiting for them but instead of picking the exhausted party up, it sped off in front of them, leaving them to stumble back to their assembly point where they lay down more dead than alive and waited for the bus which would take them back to the yacht club.

A week later, Hans and Claus, one of his fellow participants in the tests, were asked to present themselves in Otto's office. Otto and one of the officers who had monitored the testing were waiting. The officer spoke.

"Gentlemen, I have to congratulate you. You have been successful in some gentle testing to see if you are fit for service as officers in a new organisation which is going to restore the honour of your fatherland. You have a choice now. You may join us and, if you prove yourself during your training, you will become a member of an elite new unit of the nation's armed forces, or you may leave this room and never say another word about what I have told you or about your experience with us so far. You may discuss your decision only with your parents, making it quite clear that they also are bound to secrecy. If you, or they, break this confidence you will be sorry for it. Now you have two days to decide. Return here and let Otto know your decision."

Hans did not take long to make up his own mind, but what about his parents? His father, Albricht, was not a military man. He had been a diplomat and senior civil servant in the Kaiser's government and had excellent connections in the German industrial hierarchy. His career had survived the fall of the imperial regime, and he was now dabbling on the edge of right-wing politics. He had been especially keen to encourage his son to become a lawyer and often tested him by arguing political and legalistic points with him. How would he react to this dramatic change of tack?

Hans approached the subject with trepidation after dinner on a Sunday evening. He need not have worried. To his immense surprise, Albricht knew all about von Seeckt's lecture and about the selection process which Hans had undertaken. "This has always been a military family," he said. "Your grandfather and your uncle were distinguished soldiers of the Reich in their time and it will be an honour to us all if you follow them in your generation. Join with our blessing."

"Join with our blessing?" said Hans to himself. "There is something fishy there. I have never heard of Father talking about blessings before."

He was not particularly close to his father but he did know that he had connections with some nationalist politicians and members of the German Officer Corps. He had also talked from time to time about restoring the privileges of the Prussian aristocracy, an idea which seemed to Hans' generation totally absurd. Come to think of it, his father's unexpected familiarity with the goings-on at the yacht club wasn't the only strange thing which seemed to have been happening recently. There had been unfamiliar visitors to the house, some of them seemingly important political figures. Even Hindenburg, the revered president, had once visited and spent an afternoon closeted with Albricht and a suave gentleman called Herr von Papen, another visitor, in the study. Then there was that red-faced fat man who talked so loudly and was not at all the type whom his parents normally associated with. He had actually deigned to spend a few minutes talking to Hans, and had seemed delighted to hear that he was a member of the sailing club. There were assorted senior military officers and the occasional ambassador. Strangest of all was a vulgar fellow wearing a sort of khaki uniform. Hans had quickly made himself scarce when this horrid creature unsubtly began to caress his thigh when they happened to be standing close to each other in the hall. Rohm – that was his name. Why on earth was his father entertaining such oddities? His mother too seemed deeply involved in whatever it was that was happening. It was quite embarrassing how she had made up to the fat red-faced man – what was his name? Hermann something, Goering – that was it.

Hans was uninterested in affairs of state and blissfully ignorant of the political developments going on around him. In fact, his father was helping to put together an alliance between the National Socialist Party, Hitler's fearsome and brutish political vehicle, and the old-fashioned, militaristic Nationalist Party. It would help his father's cause and enhance his reputation with both sides if his son was to be a member of the armed forces. The army particularly had an almost mystical status in German imaginations and a revived German Army was the Holy Grail of all true German nationalists. Albricht had once caught himself thinking that he, like Abraham, was prepared to sacrifice his only son at the command of the Almighty – but Albricht's "Almighty" was certainly not Abraham's God. He quickly dismissed the thought.

Chapter 2

William made his somewhat inglorious return to Tyneside on his faithful AJS, following the old Great North Road all the way from Charing Cross to Newcastle. It had been a solid ten hours bumping along amid the lorries, motor cars and farm traffic. Mrs Wellibond, the housekeeper, who had been with the family now for twenty-five years greeted him warmly at Stonebeck House, the family home. She had prepared one of her famous dinners and sat down at the table herself to make the most of the return of the only surviving member of the beloved family which she had served so long and so well. Not a day passed by without her recalling those two awful events of 1916, the loss of William's mother and two siblings when their ferry hit a mine, and the death of his father in an unexplained flying accident only two months later. Since then she had treated William virtually as a son. She was secretly glad that the idea of the Slade had been given up and dared to hope that he now planned to settle on Tyneside and try to make his living there. It was 1929, and things were, she said, a little better than they had been, although the shipyards were not too busy the coal mines were working hard and people had a little more money to spend. She was keen to show William the changes she had made to his old family home. Two large flats had been made out of the two wings of the house, and in each of these respectable tenants had been installed, an engineer working for Parsons and his wife and "a very untidy young man who fiddled with radio sets and suchlike". Their rent was enough to cover the cost of keeping up the house, and they contributed towards the wages of Mrs Wellibond herself and some extra help in the house. The redoubtable housekeeper was delighted to hear news of Flopsy, who had been a regular visitor to Stonebeck before the war. By the time they had finished talking, William could scarcely keep his eyes open. There was a coal fire in his own little bedroom, looking over the front garden, and as he climbed into the familiar bed, all his old forgotten things were around him, each in its proper place.

His first task the next morning was to pay a visit to Mr Walder, the solicitor who was trustee of the family estate and was to remain so, according to his father's will, until William reached the age of thirty. He had arranged the meeting by letter before leaving London, and had told his trustee a little about his plans. Walder's office was in Whitley Bay. He looked more like a prosperous farmer than a lawyer, red-faced, plump and domineering in manner. His attitude was, William thought, a little too patronising. He produced a file of figures, which William stared at. They meant nothing to him. "Let me explain, young Portman," he began. "Your father's estate was worth altogether about a hundred thousand pounds, a tidy sum, mostly coming from the bonus shares he got over the years from Parsons. Apart from some small bequests, this has all been held in your trust fund. On top of that there is the house, of course, and personal possessions. The house just about covers its costs, and your income, five hundred pounds per year, is paid out of the trust fund. Now the fund actually produces about three thousand pounds per year, and we have been investing the surplus income, so it's now worth about a hundred and thirty thousand pounds. We've been very cautious about our investment policies. No American trusts, no foreign bonds, good old-fashioned gilts and a few reliable British equities. I've a bad feeling about the stock markets, especially in America, and although we could have grown the sum faster, we have taken the most cautious approach we could."

William nodded his approval.

"Now, you told me in your letter that you were thinking of setting up some sort of business up here," continued the solicitor. "You must understand that my duty is to safeguard your funds until 1939 when you will be thirty, but the will does not preclude us from financing a modest private business venture. What had you in mind?"

31

"Well, sir, I thought I might rent some suitable premises on the Tyne and go into boat building. There are plenty of skilled workers around here looking for work and costs would be less than in the south where most yachts are built. I've a little experience in boatbuilding myself and I think I could make a go of it."

Walder looked dubious. Boatbuilding didn't seem like a very good prospect and he knew that this young man had no commercial experience whatsoever. He spoke slowly and deliberately.

"I know boats are fun, William, and you do know a bit about them, but boatbuilding is like any other business – all about money. You can pour it into an enterprise like that forever and finish up with nothing but debts. I've seen it too often. I don't know much about boats myself but I do know that any manufacturing business needs hard graft, experience and the ability to sell products at the right price. I can't let you spend your inheritance on something like that until I can see that you can manage it properly. Now I suggest you go away and think again. I'm sorry."

William had never liked Walder much and now he hated him. There he was sitting in his office laying down the law. What did he know about boats anyway? How dare this man question his ability to run a business. He hadn't even asked about William's admittedly rather sketchy ideas about a range of small ketches designed for the family sailor, but it was no good arguing with this stubborn, opinionated man. He mumbled something about coming up with a plan, made his excuses and departed.

William's next call was much more to his liking. Freddy Seal had been his father's boatman and companion on many pre-war yachting adventures, and then been his mate on a wartime minesweeper. He had saved his father's life after a mine exploded accidentally and was utterly devoted to the family. Since the war he had married and settled down, working on various gentlemen's yachts in the summer, and repairing and looking after small boats during the winter months.

"Aye, Mr William, right glad I am to see ye, and they say as you'll be with us for a bit now." A powerful hand pumped William's, and Freddy's leathery face broke into a wide grin. "I've a done something maybe I shouldn't when I heard as you was a' coming. I've put the lad 'ere on getting old *Columba* ready for the summer, she ain't sniffed water since 1914, but she's a good old boat and right as rain, and I thinks to myself – Mr William he'll be wanting her in the summer."

"Quite right, Freddy, and how do the sails look?"

"They'll do a season maybe."

The two chatted for half an hour or so and then it was time for William to get home for lunch. An astonishing sight greeted him at the house. A young man, dressed in overalls, was squatting on the front lawn entangled in an impossible mess of wire and rope. His hands were bleeding in several places and there was a large bruise on his forehead. He was muttering and cursing to himself, and looked embarrassed and guilty when William walked up to him.

"What the duce?" began William.

The man tried to struggle to his feet, but tripped on a wire and tumbled headlong onto the soft, damp grass. He managed to sit up. Tall, thin and dishevelled, he presented a sorry picture, but even as he struggled to free himself from his entanglements a broad grin lit up his face and soon the grin transformed into an uncontrollable guffaw.

"Good morning," he stammered, "I'm Hugh Wesley, your tenant in the west wing; that is if you're William Portman. I hoped you wouldn't mind if I put this aerial up on the lawn here, it's a dipole – two masts and one hundred and fifty feet of wire – but I seem to be making a bit of a mess of it. Never was much good with this sort of thing."

William suppressed his own laughter and helped his tenant to disentangle himself. When he stood up, William could see that he was a thin, gangly fellow with long limbs and untidy hair. He wore thick horn-rimmed glasses. As he looked at the muddle around him, his shoulders again began to shake with peals of infectious laughter.

"For heaven's sake, Wesley," said William. "Let's go into the house. I'm sure Mrs Wellibond will have enough for both of us and we'll fix your dipole or whatever it is after lunch."

William was not the most organised or methodical of people, but being a sailor, he at least knew something about masts and ropes, and he was a hundred percent better at the job than his tenant. Using some old fence posts driven into the ground as strong points, he soon had the masts ready to haul upright, while Hugh struggled with insulators and wire. In a couple of hours the masts were vertical and the whole contraption seemed reasonably secure.

"Come and have a look at this," said Hugh, after he had coupled the aerial to a wire leading into the front room of his flat. Inside, William found an indescribable jumble of valves, wires, condensers, speakers and other such gadgets, some of which glowed and hummed quietly as Hugh turned on the power. He spoke into a microphone. A crackly voice with a distinctly foreign accent replied.

"Come in Hoopoe."

"Testing testing," said Hugh, "you are loud and clear."

"Loud and clear, out to you," said the voice.

Hugh turned down the volume. "Wonderful!" he cried. "That was Marc in Belgium. This is an HF set you see, almost unlimited range in the right conditions and a broad enough bandwidth to carry voice. I never managed that before, but this is the first time I've had a proper aerial. You know, we're really getting somewhere." He positively glowed, just like one of his radio valves, with happiness.

From that moment on, Hugh became a firm friend. It was astonishing to see that a man so clumsy and impractical was transformed into a neat, dextrous worker when faced with small electronic components and a soldering iron. Also, he was brilliant at explaining what he was doing and why.

"Look, if we put another capacitor in the circuit here we'll change the critical frequency; now I'll show you how we work it out." Or "You see this valve? We've got a problem because its connection to the grid battery is faulty somewhere. Have a look and see if you can find what's wrong."

William became fascinated by the technology of radio. He had never been a great mathematician but had been taught the basics and he soon picked up the calculations he needed to work on simple circuits. There was a satisfactory combination of logic and, it seemed, artistry, about the design of them which appealed to him. He and Hugh would often struggle with a system long into the night, unwilling to be beaten.

Most days William would go down and talk to Freddy about how *Columba* was getting on. Recommissioning an old wooden boat is quite a task. Keel bolts have to be inspected, seams filled, old paint scraped off and new coats applied, standing and running rigging overhauled and sails patched up. Occasionally, William would lend a hand himself. He enjoyed working with Freddy and the lad who helped him; there was a constant exchange of humorous comments as they worked and it was great to see the old boat gradually looking as if she might soon be fit to go to sea.

Hugh's circuits were not just a hobby. He was well known in the radio world, and earned his living by providing a contract design service to manufacturers and operators. It was a somewhat precarious existence but he enjoyed the work so immensely that he could imagine doing nothing else. William envied his enthusiasm and the way in which he had found a role in life which exactly suited his talents. If only he could do the same himself. Since the interview with Walder, nothing in the way of a business idea had occurred to him and, when not working on the boat or with Hugh, he gloomily tried to paint local landscapes and seascapes, producing nothing that satisfied him.

He was still at a loose end when a conversation with Mrs Wellibond started an entirely new train of thought. William knew that his grandfather on his father's side had been a German nobleman, and his own father had been proud of his German roots, insisting always that his offspring should be bilingual and respect their ancestry. He had reluctantly changed the family name from von Pilsen to Portman during the war to prevent the boys from being persecuted at school. William's grandmother had married for a second time, after the death of her first husband, again to a German, a successful naval officer. William vaguely remembered his grandparents and how kind they had been to him and his siblings. Mrs Wellibond happened to mention in conversation that William's father, Max, had often mentioned his elder brother, Albricht. William wondered if this German uncle of his was still alive and dug around in his father's papers until he found an address. He determined to write a polite letter, in German of course, and see what the situation was as regards the German half of the family. More quickly than he had expected, a reply came from Uncle Albricht himself with an open invitation to visit, either at the family's estate in East Prussia, or at their house in Berlin. William determined on a visit in the very near future. He would meet his uncle in Berlin, where he was engaged in government business. William would stay in the house for a few days, then take himself off for a tour around the country, bringing his painting things with him. Albricht was apparently the only surviving relation of his generation. He had one son, Hans, about William's age. It might be fun to meet this Hans.

The von Pilsen Berlin establishment proved to be a good-sized town house. A servant met him at the door and explained that the master of the house was expected home shortly. There was very little sign of the privations which Germany had suffered in the starvation after the war and the terrible inflation of the early 1920s. The house was richly decorated with some interesting English landscapes. In the drawing room William recognised two Constables. A bloodthirsty collection of battlefield pictures adorned the hall, showing, according to the captions, various members of the von Pilsen family triumphantly trampling French, Danish and Austrian adversaries under their horses' hooves. The servant brought in an evening paper which was full of economic gloom. Stresemann, the chancellor and Foreign Minister, who had successfully rescued the German economy and had got some way towards integrating the country back into the society of civilised nations, had died in October 1929. However, the papers were saying that the cheap credit from the US which had financed German industrial expansion was disappearing, unemployment was on the rise again, and "new political elements" – whatever they were – were looking for more radical solutions. William leafed through the papers without much interest until his host was announced.

Uncle Albricht strode into the room looking like the cat which had got the cream. He was sleek, well-groomed and expensively dressed, and he greeted his young relation very warmly in slightly laboured English. William returned his good wishes in German and implored his host that this should be their medium of communication.

"My dear, sir! How good of you to make this concession. I do wish my dear wife – she is detained at our place in Prussia you know – such an Anglophile – was here to see you. My dearest William, your father and I were the firmest friends. Do make my home your own while you are here. Unfortunately my son, Hans, is eh… abroad at present, I would have so loved you to meet him. I flatter myself that he has all the best qualities which have made our family useful to our fatherland. Now I'm afraid it is only me, your old uncle, you will be meeting here. I hope my man has attended to you well? Good, now let us have dinner and talk."

William was immediately on his guard. From what information he had gained from letters and from talking to Mrs Wellibond, his father and Albricht were certainly not close friends, and something about this polished, over-polite and rather dominating man aroused his suspicions. However, he proved an attentive host, listening with interest to William's news, and the dinner was excellent. Over a glass of port, his uncle asked him what he knew of German affairs. On hearing that he took little interest in politics, his host launched into an animated resumé.

"The enemy we all face is Communism. It destroys loyalty, property, decency and religion. In Germany, after the events of 1918 we narrowly avoided a Communist takeover, and of course even I have to admit that the creed has its attractions to workers who have no reason to be loyal to their state. It also appeals to – forgive me – naïve students. But it rots all noble, decent, human instincts. And there is another enemy of humanity – an element which does not share our values or our loyalties – I refer of course to the Jews. Do you have Jewish friends, William?"

William thought for a moment. He honestly didn't know which of his friends were Jewish and which were not, so he shook his head.

"Excellent! Well, let me tell you that in England, as here, they are parasites, gnawing away at the fabric of the state and of society. Here in Germany we have recognised this perhaps before you have. As you may have heard, Walter Rathenau, the Jew who managed to become head of the giant engineering and electronics company AEG, and then to insert himself and his disloyal tribe into political circles, for example, got what he deserved." (Walter Rathenau, a highly intelligent and loyal German Jew, who had been a minister in the wartime German government and a very effective member of the post-war administration, had been murdered by racist fanatics in 1922.) "So we have two enemies to contend with; we must defeat the Communist and the Jew. Now, I am a member of a small group of loyal Germans who believe that a solution can be found to these problems. Only this afternoon I was meeting with Herr Hitler, head of the National Socialist German Workers' Party – the man's a fool and a rabble rouser – but he does have a way of galvanising the workers and leading them away from Communism. If we can get him to work with us established industrialists and with the army, we will have a force which can sweep away our rotten republican government and the corruption which is destroying us… but I am sorry, I am talking too much politics. Tell me, William, how well do you remember your father?"

"Well, I was only seven when he was killed, but to me he was the kindest father imaginable."

"Yes, yes, I can believe that, and he was a brave sailor too. I believe he won a medal, but really it is so interesting to understand a man's motivations, is it not? Tell me, how did he feel about the war? We in Germany thought it was so tragic that our two great nations should be fighting each other. Maybe he thought the same way?"

William didn't like the turn of the conversation. He was not going to discuss his father with this man, of whom he was instinctively suspicious. He answered evasively.

"Well, I can tell you," continued his uncle, "people like ourselves in Germany never understood why England made war on us in 1914. We had our differences, of course, but we are of the same blood and we have the same values. The real danger to civilisation lies elsewhere, to the east, and we should have fought together against that. I think your father might have agreed. We were very close, you know, your father and I. I flatter myself that I now have some influence in German industrial circles and my work in the Chancellery gives me access to all the major political leaders, and I can assure you that never again will Germany fight against our British friends. Together we must fight the godless Communists and we must break the stranglehold of the Jew on our newspapers, the banking system, the arts and sciences. These are the poisons we must face together. But enough of politics, my young friend. Do tell me what you are planning to do with yourself while you are here."

William talked vaguely about a possible tour of the Rhine Valley with his painting things, and the conversation turned to art, to the various galleries he should visit and to the best spots for painting.

The three days in Berlin passed pleasantly enough. Albricht was engaged every day but he had arranged for a friend of Hans, once a fellow law student, Jorgen Kressler, to show him some of the sights. Jorgen proved an amiable enough young fellow and had a comprehensive knowledge of Berlin night life. This was famously lurid at the time, with bars and clubs catering for every imaginable taste and perversion.

It was not in one of these dubious haunts, however, that William became acquainted with the true nature of German nationalist politics.

He and Jorgen were drinking some excellent beer in a bar much frequented by law students, some of whom were familiar with Jorgen and the absent Hans. It was a fine evening and the conversation was lively, with drinkers spilling out of the bar onto the pavements to enjoy the warm, fresh air. For some reason the subject under discussion had turned to the prohibition laws in the US and everyone was deploring the criminality which had come in its train. One particularly loquacious young fellow was cataloguing the murders which had been reported in Chicago the previous week. "It is a shame," he said, "an insult to the very idea of democracy, which we all believe in, that such laws restricting human freedom can be passed in the first place, but that is nothing compared to the callous destruction of life which seems to be part of the philosophy of both the bootleggers and the police. Imagine it. Both sides carry machine guns and move about in armoured vehicles…"

As he rattled on, William noticed a small group of students gathered at a table a short distance from them. Looking a little pale and furtive, they were talking quietly amongst themselves and seemed to be on the lookout for something. Just as they started their meal it became clear what their problem was. Out of a side street burst a party of SA youths, so called "Stormtroopers" wearing quasi military brown uniforms and armed with truncheons. Before the little party could get to its feet the thugs were upon them,

"Juden raus, Juden raus!" they yelled as they set about the defenceless party of Jewish students, kicking and beating the boys and grabbing at the girls, pulling their hair, and throwing food in their faces.

"What the hell!" cried William as he tried to intervene, but his comrades grabbed his arms and held him back.

"Leave it, leave it," muttered Jorgen. "They are only rotten Jews and it's nothing to do with you; you get involved and they'll beat you up too."

One of the Stormtroopers, a big ugly fellow with a broken nose turned towards William and leered at him as he stood with his arms pinned by his friends.

"Oh, we have a Jew lover here, do we?" he snarled. "You do well to hold him back, lads, I'd soon teach your little friend a lesson." He raised his truncheon and thrust it gently into William's face, brushing his nose and tapping his forehead. Then he turned and re-joined his troop. They were dragging the Jews down the street, kicking them at intervals and leaving behind a trail of blood, broken spectacles and vomit.

William slipped away from his party and stood on the pavement by himself, shivering with fury. He had never seen anything so disgusting. It was wanton, vicious, cruelty practised in the open with no provocation whatever. That was bad enough, but even worse was that somehow he couldn't find words to say to his new-found friends. They spouted about democracy and law, then stood by while this was going on. No one thought of calling the police – they would have done nothing anyway – or of doing anything to protect the victims. What was all this about rotten Jews? What was supposed to be wrong with them? Had they no rights like other people? The rest of his party drifted off to another bar but he could not join them. He slunk miserably back to the house, feeling dirty and ashamed of what he had seen, and furious with himself for the feeble part he had played in the squalid affair.

In the morning he made up his mind. He would invent some excuse for not undertaking the little painting tour of the Rhineland which he had planned. He would go home as soon as possible. He was not able to escape, however, without a solemn lecture from Uncle Albricht on the importance of Anglo-German relations.

"I am sure that you will be able to return home now and work for a deeper understanding between our two great nations. You will see soon enough that a new Germany is about to spring from the ashes of this rotten Weimar Republic, a Germany led by men of stature and experience, worthy of standing proudly alongside your British Empire as guardians of civilisation and order in the world. That is our dream."

William felt uncomfortable with this rather formal speech, contenting himself by mumbling a few words about not being much involved in politics, and retiring early to bed on the pretext of needing to depart by the morning boat train. His excuse for his rushed departure was a telegram received from his lawyer, Walder, requesting an immediate meeting. It was true that he had received a telegram, but he had greatly exaggerated the urgency of the request.

William and Walder had their meeting, something to do with a switch in the investment portfolio, but he had other things on his mind. He had become deeply absorbed with Hugh Wesley and his radio experiments. Hugh helped him to build his own receiver and transmitter, and he was ecstatic when he picked up his first Morse code messages from unknown "hams" far away. Hugh told him all about his work for his various clients, and how he was trying to become involved in some experiments for the Air Ministry. Once, when Hugh was late in completing a set for some trials taking place on behalf of Imperial Airways, William packed Hugh and his device onto the back of the motorbike and rushed him to the aerodrome in Lancashire where the tests would take place. While Hugh was with his client, William watched aircraft landing and taking off from the local flying school. As he was gazing at the planes, a vigorous slap on the back almost sent him head over heels. His assailant turned out to be his old school friend, Peter Downes. Peter was a few years older but had always been a friendly presence in the higher echelons of his school. "Thought it was you, William old chap!" he laughed. "What brings you to Ringwood?" In no time it transpired that Peter had recently got his pilot's licence and was waiting for an aircraft, which he had arranged to hire for an hour's practice, to be ready. "She's a two-seater," he said. "Why don't you come for a flip?"

A few minutes later a silver Gipsy Moth was pulled out of the hangar. She was a neat little biplane with two open cockpits and looked eager to be off. Peter told his friend to get into the front cockpit and told him how to strap himself in on top of the parachute which doubled as a seat cushion. He then walked round the machine making a visual check on the aircraft and the undercarriage. Satisfied that all was well, he climbed into the rear cockpit and methodically moved the joystick and rudder bar, checking that the rudder, elevator and ailerons moved as they should, explaining to his passenger carefully the purpose of each control surface. William was excited and highly impressed by his friend's serious approach to the business of flying.

"OK!" Peter called to the mechanic, who had sauntered round to the front of the aeroplane. "Sucking in, fuel on throttle closed, switches off." He held his hand with the thumb pointing downwards out of the side of the cockpit. The mechanic turned the engine over gently three times.

"Fuel on, throttle one and a half inches open, switches on. Contact!" An upwards pointing thumb. The mechanic swung the prop once vigorously and the engine burst into life. A little puff of smoke issued from the exhaust, and in a moment the hundred horsepower four-cylinder DH Gipsy engine was idling smoothly. Peter let her warm up, checking again on the control surfaces and the instruments showing oil pressure, temperature and fuel contents. After a couple of minutes he opened the throttle wide and checked the engine revs. "Two thousand one hundred, that's OK!" he shouted into the speaking tube. "Now I'm going to check each magneto by cutting off one at a time. Revs shouldn't fall by more than three hundred." The check confirmed all was OK. The airfield had a control tower, but there was no radio in the Moth so, after looking round carefully, Peter waved the chocks away and taxied to the end of the runway, the engine burbling away gently as she bumped over the grass.

William was thrilled by the whole business; he admired the smooth methodical procedure of checking and starting the machine, so different from the unstructured carelessness of driving off in a car or a motorbike. He relished the regular, healthy throb of the engine, and the purposeful elegant structure of the machine. Somehow he had got to become a part of this business.

A green from the tower, and Peter pulled onto the runway. The little plane came alive and trembled excitedly as the throttle was opened wide and she sped over the smooth grass and soared clear of the boundary fence and away into the sky. There were a few high white clouds but otherwise it was a perfect, clear day so you could see the ground spread out below like a subtly coloured map. Cars and lorries wound their way along the roads, trains, each one trailing a plume of smoke sped along neat rails, and two merchant ships were crawling up the Ship Canal. Away to the west the mud of the Mersey Estuary glistened like highly polished shoe leather in the sun. They banked and flew south and then west along the north coast of Wales. The motor beat steadily and the magnificent panorama of hills, woodland, yellow beaches, white surf, green fields and blue sea spread beneath them. Peter dived low to get a better look at a big liner – a Cunarder by the look of her – steaming majestically towards Liverpool Dock. After half an hour they turned around and flew low along the shore line, causing commotion among some dogs running on the beach, and sending a family of seals squirming and tumbling off their sandbank into the water.

Peter's landing back at Ringwood was less than perfect. He came in too high, instinctively put the nose down and picked up so much speed that he had to gun the engine and go around again, swearing loudly into the speaking tube. The second time he got it right, and the Gipsy Moth bounced gently on the grass and taxied slowly back to its hangar.

William felt he had never experienced such intense joy and excitement, or seen anything so beautiful. He had been entranced by the flight and had fallen in love with the little aeroplane. As soon as he could he took out his pad and pencil and sketched the aircraft on the field, they were mostly Moths, but there was a Percival Gull, an old Avro and a handful of other types. Each had its own character, its own way of squatting on the ground, its own particular line of beauty. Somehow William's pencil, so clumsy in drawing figures, managed to capture them perfectly. As soon as he got home, William checked his bank statements. Yes, he could afford a few flying lessons.

Chapter 3

Cousin Hans had an altogether more serious introduction to flying. Shortly after the interview with his father, he received his call-up papers and found himself in a basic training barracks not far from his home in East Prussia. Every German soldier, sailor or airman had to start his service with basic infantry training. This was no pushover. It tested men to the limits of their mental and physical endurance, each day presenting a new and more demanding challenge. It comprised an initial year with the Flieger Ausbildungs Regiment in which there was no smoking, no drinking, and no home leave. There were a few lectures and courses on military history and tactics, otherwise it was all demanding physical work – marching, singing, assault courses and field exercises. Physical fitness and mental toughness were everything. Unlike most armed forces of the time, German instructors taught infantry soldiers to think for themselves as well as to obey orders and the soldiers who emerged from the training process were not only physically tough, they were also self-confident and decisive. Hans, on his first leave home after basic training was a much-changed young man. Physically he had put on weight and muscle and mentally he had changed from an easy-going, likeable youth into a confident, motivated young soldier.

Only after the gruelling year of training were recruits introduced to flying. Officially Germany was still banned by treaty from having any sort of air force or military aircraft, but a special arrangement with Russia enabled the country to lay the foundations of what was to become the most formidable fighting machine in history. The initial flying training was conducted at Lipetzk, close to Moscow. Here, in secret, potential flyers were taught their craft in a selection of obsolete biplanes, salvaged, somehow, from the havoc of 1918. The instructors were a small band of aces who had survived the Great War and were dedicated to the establishment of a strong new German air force.

In this atmosphere Hans excelled. He was a natural pilot, and immediately related to the rhythm of each aircraft's movements, its virtues, its vices and the tricks it might play on the unwary. He adored every moment he spent at the controls, especially when he was alone over the frozen Russian countryside, diving perhaps towards some unsuspecting Russian farm building, playing hide and seek among the clouds or picking a route through stormy weather back to his base. The wind whistling past the cockpit was music to him, the throb of the engine poetry. By the end of 1931 he was a superb flyer, one of the best which the system had produced. Sometimes, however, even Hans realised that this life among comrades in barracks was profoundly incomplete. Shut away in training camps and then in Russia, he had had little opportunity to develop a social life and, while singing patriotic songs with his mates was all good fun, there seemed to be an important part of life on which he was missing out. Of course, during his rare home leaves, he was idolised by girls. For them a tall, handsome aristocrat engaged on a secret mission for his country was a prize indeed, but his romances never got very far. Leaves were too short, the demands of his parents too pressing ("Oh, Hans, you must be home this weekend, I have promised that you will open the produce show in the village on Saturday") and his experience with the other sex was too limited for him to form any intimate relationship. A certain arrogance, developed in his military training, was impressive enough to his fellow recruits and instructors, but it was not the way to any maiden's heart. Besides, what were his prospects? He had no idea what he might do after his training was over. Officially the Luftwaffe still did not exist. There were now several hundred trained recruits, but with no air force, what could they do? Certainly they could not stay in Russia forever.

He need not have worried about his career. As he was due to pass out of Lipetsk, he received a letter asking him to join the German national airline, Lufthansa, as a reserve pilot. The letter was less of an invitation than a command. Lufthansa was in fact a thinly veiled training ground for potential Luftwaffe flyers, and, among other projects, it operated a fleet of fast mail planes which darted about the country every day carrying priority mail. It was to this service that Hans was attached. Flying a Heinkel biplane, Hans soon learnt to cope with the hazards of all-weather flying in winter and summer through thunderstorms, ground mist, downpours of rain and fogs. If you couldn't handle such hazards you didn't last long with Lufthansa. After a little over a year of this life as a civilian pilot, his activities were interrupted by a peremptory demand to report again for military duties. To his astonishment, Hans was issued with an unfamiliar uniform and ushered in secret onto a train which took him across the Alps and into northern Italy. There, Goering had arranged for German airmen in disguise to train with the perfectly legal Italian air force. Delightedly they spent the summer diving at roof top level over Italian soldiers crouching in trenches, shooting at toy balloons in the sky and revelling in pretend dog fights with their comrades. This was real flying and all the Germans seized every opportunity to be in the air as long as there was light. Their machines were the sturdy little He 38 biplanes, developed in secret and already superior to most British and French fighters, agile, fast and a delight to handle, especially in the warm, clear blue sky of northern Italy.

There were also lectures to attend. At one of them, Goering himself addressed the flyers. Already the man was becoming flabby and dissolute-looking, and insisted on dressing himself up in absurd-looking uniforms, but there was still something of the old spark. "Men of the reborn Luftwaffe!" he bellowed, "within a year the shame of 1919 which has humbled the name of Germany will be avenged. We will have strong forces of every kind, but especially our Luftwaffe. You men will be the new Teutonic Knights, the cavalry of the new Germany. One folk, one state, one leader." Everyone cheered him to the echo. Hans had his doubts. This was the same slimy fellow who had seen endeavouring to charm his mother only a few years ago. The cheap-jack salesman who his father had secretly laughed at. Could he really be part of a regime which might renew the Fatherland?

There was another speaker who was more to Hans' taste. Ernst Udet was a hero to every German flyer. An ace pilot during the war, and a celebrated stunt flyer after it, he had been given responsibility for developing the capabilities of the nascent air force. A recent visit to America had convinced him that the dive bomber was the weapon of the future. Seated at the controls of a Curtiss fighter-bomber, he had been mesmerised by the sensation of diving vertically at his target, the aircraft practically a missile in itself, placing his bomb accurately from the lowest possible level, hauling the plane out of the dive and zooming away at maximum power. No other method of air attack was anything like so accurate, so difficult to combat or so terrifying to the enemy. In front of the young pilots, he waxed lyrical about the potential of modern dive bombers. Udet was a superb flyer and a convincing speaker, revered by any German with an interest in aviation. He concluded by telling his audience that in a short time a suitable dive bomber would be available for them to use; in the meantime, if they wanted to be the true heroes of their country, they could make some practice dives in their Heinkels.

Hans could hardly wait to be in the air again, but when he was, he found the dive-bombing operation was not as easy as it seemed. Firstly, not having dive brakes, his aircraft would easily get out of control in a steep dive, gaining so much speed that the airframe was in danger of coming apart. Secondly, there was a grave danger of blacking out as one pulled out of the dive, and indeed of pulling up so hard that the wings were torn off the plane. One of his comrades was killed in this way on his first attempt. Eventually the unit commander had to ban dive bombing practice until more suitable machines became available.

There was another learning experience waiting for Hans in the sunny groves and in the elegant cities of Tuscany. The Germans were in theory confined to their barracks in order to keep their presence secret, but the guards were Italian, relaxed and accommodating for the price of a little tobacco. One young flyer,

Karl Lenz, actually had his own private Mercedes brought down to provide convenient local transportation. They found the locals easy going, welcoming and hospitable. Plates of delicious pasta and bowls of fruit would appear as if from nowhere. The local wines lifted the spirits and lubricated budding friendships, and late at night a glass of grappa often instilled boldness into the most timid hearts.

Sonia lived with her family in a small, square town house built around a little central garden. The house was battered and unkempt on the outside with paint peeling off the green shutters and great lumps of plaster missing from the walls. Inside, however, there was that dash of elegance which only an Italian household can achieve. All the downstairs rooms opened onto the garden, a blaze of colour, always cool and always beautiful. Besides the profusion of flowers, there were peaches which grew on trellises up a sunny wall and a plumb tree laden with the most delicious, juicy fruit. The father of the family had been killed in 1918, and the head of the household was his widow, Maria, a quiet almost ghostly figure who seemed to spend much of her time whispering with priests or praying silently in the little church down the street. Nevertheless, the aging widow ran her house with surprising authority and efficiency. The two servants were smart and obliging, the house and garden were beautifully kept and the rooms were tidy and cared for. Sonia and her brother Marco had taken over their father's business which dealt in car parts and accessories. Marco handled the parts while Sonia had tapped into a new and expanding market for fashionable motoring clothing and items such as picnic baskets, trunks, rugs and maps.

It was from Marco's office that Hans had first spotted Sonia. Karl Lenz, his fellow pilot, was in search of a part for his Mercedes (Marco eventually got it made locally at half Mercedes' price) and Hans had been wandering around the establishment while the two were discussing technical details. As he looked idly at some elegant leather coats especially designed for motorists, a gentle voice spoke from behind him. "And which one would Signor like to try?" Looking round, he saw the most beautiful pair of dark eyes it was possible to imagine, peering out from under a lustrous fringe of black hair. Taking a step backward, he found he was looking at a figure which seemed perfect in every way, elegant, poised, perfectly proportioned but above all brimming with life and vivacity. The eyes and mouth spoke of humour, the brown limbs of activity and the voice somehow seemed to tease at the same time as it offered service in the shop. Hans had been brought up to be trilingual, having fluent English, French and German and he had quite easily picked up enough Italian to get by, but at first he could only gaze at this beautiful creature. After a few seconds he managed some muttered reply, but Sonia, seeing his difficulty, broke effortlessly into French.

"Oh," she said, "I understand. You are waiting for your friend who I saw speaking to Marco. Well my brother can never stop talking about motor cars, so what shall we talk about, you and I? Oh, don't worry, I know who you are. It is supposed to be a secret but we all know about you German flyers at the aerodrome. Myself, I like to see some new faces. I get bored talking to the same men all the time."

Hans didn't quite know how to handle this unfamiliar creature, so utterly unlike any girl he had met at home. In spite of himself, he felt nervous, almost afraid. He managed to launch into some casual talk about life on the aerodrome, the exercises they were doing, subtly encouraged by Sonia's questions and evident interest. All too soon Karl and Marco joined them and then somehow, after a glass or two of cool white Chianti, the four drifted off to the family house where it had become known that there were to be guests for dinner and a succulent dish of lamb and vegetables was waiting for them. The Germans could not risk being too late back to camp, but before they left, Sonia took Hans aside.

"Listen, my flyer friend," she whispered. "I want to have a flight in one of your planes, can you arrange that?"

"Impossible! The planes are guarded, what would my commander say?"

The dark eyes narrowed and suddenly had a threatening, angry gleam.

"Your commander, bah, I care nothing for commanders, I like men who can do things, make arrangements." Then, suddenly sweet and encouraging again. "Hans, do this thing for me, I want us to be friends."

Hans was so captivated, so bowled over by this fascinating, domineering creature that he could only mutter that he would see if he could arrange something then the two men had to be off. Hans gazed blankly out of the car, daydreaming of what he might do with his lovely Sonia. It could hardly escape Karl's notice that his friend was smitten with their hostess. After some probing he managed to get Hans to tell him about the request for a flight.

"But it's impossible! How could we ever get her into the camp, let alone into a plane?" he moaned.

Karl was more than equal to that problem. "Idiot," he said, swerving expertly round a buffalo cart stopped on the road. "You don't need to get her into the camp. Land somewhere in the countryside and pick her up."

Stupefied as he was with love, this obvious solution had escaped Hans completely. He tried to get his friend to turn around so that he could explain to Sonia right away. Karl had a cooler head. "Let's plan it properly first," he said. "Then we can tell her the full story. A few days waiting will do her no harm."

Hans walked about in a trance for the next few days, which luckily were stormy and unfit for flying, but Karl, who knew more than a little about women, being engaged to be married to a wealthy Belgian girl, had the problem well in hand. He identified a suitable field for a furtive landing and wangled a change in the flying schedules so that he and Hans should take up a two-seater on a couple of occasions the next week to practise map reading on long cross-country flights. So far so good. The next thing was to get the message to Sonia. The two conspirators escaped from the camp one evening and presented themselves. Hans was trembling with excitement, scarcely able to speak, but he need not have been. His love was not there. Marco said that she would not be back until late that evening, but a message was left. The signal for the flight would be the aircraft doing a slow roll over the town. Fifteen minutes later the plane would be on the ground at the appointed place. There must be no delay; they would only stay on the ground for two minutes.

Everything went like clockwork. Karl relinquished his seat and there in the cockpit in front of Hans a trim figure in black leather whooped with excitement as he performed some gentle aerobatics. By the time they had to return, Sonia had looped the loop, spun, rolled and dive bombed her own shop. A brisk wind had got up, blowing across the field in which they were to land. There was no wind sock of course, but Hans knew from the poplar trees around that it would be a tricky landing. His year with Lufthansa had given him plenty of experience of these conditions and he put the little plane down neatly amid a cloud of dust. The two climbed out, leaving the engine running. Hans pulled off his goggles and gazed at his love who was looking radiant and elated by her experience. She kissed him lightly on the cheek, turned and scampered off to her waiting car. She was away and waving merrily before Karl and Hans had started their take-off run.

Hans was so excited that he was quite unfit to take the controls, and his companion had to fly the aircraft as well as marking up the map and inventing a log of their mission. This was his first proper girl, so exotic, so thrilling, so beautiful and he had shown her himself at his best, flying faultlessly yet adventurously, totally in command of the situation, equal to every challenge. And she had kissed him! He felt that kiss a hundred times as he lay on his bunk in the camp, waiting for the evening when a further trip into town was arranged.

This time he borrowed a motorbike, and puttered along the dusty roads, singing to himself. Arriving at the house, he was a little disappointed to find quite a large party assembled. They were all young and seemed to be in high spirits. Marco greeted him affably and introduced him around the party. Sonia was at the centre of the group and although the conversation was in Italian, Hans could tell that she was recounting her day's experience. He swelled with pride. When Sonia finished she turned to him and the company all applauded, but it seemed somehow that their cheers were not quite genuine. Somehow there was a mocking look on the face of several of the Italian boys in the room, and the girls giggled together at some joke which they did not share with their guest. Hans tried to say something in Italian and was rewarded with a peck on the cheek and a brimming glass. He stood there on the fringe of the crowd, watching the Italians as they flirted, quarrelled and joked together. Occasionally someone spoke to him but he felt uncomfortable and out of place among these sophisticated, elegant young people. The merry party continued for an hour or so, then the guests drifted off and Hans was left with Sonia. A little clumsily, he put an arm around her.

"My darling Sonia..." He was roughly pushed away. The figure he saw before him was tense, furious, spitting venom.

"Hans, my little flyer! You are only a boy, a little flying boy. Yes, I enjoyed the aeroplane, but do you really want to know something? I am five thousand lira richer for it. I had a bet with my friend Angelo – you saw him, the small dark boy with the curly hair – that I could get a flight in one of the German planes and now I have. Now, little boy, go away and do what you like, but don't trouble me again. You know nothing, nothing. Do you think you are a man? No! You are a big blond fool who can fly aeroplanes. Nothing more. Go now back to your camp."

Hans stumbled out of the house, blind with frustration and fury. He had been tricked by this girl, made a fool of, laughed at. Furiously he kicked the bike into life and roared off into the darkness, not caring where he went. The machine skidded over the cobbled streets of the town and sped in a cloud of dust down unmade roads in the countryside. It was getting dark but Hans took no notice, twisting the throttle full open and roaring past farmsteads and cattle sheds. As he reached the top of a hill, he suddenly saw a great black form before him. It was close, too close to miss. Slamming on his brakes, he laid the machine down on its side in the dust, slithering towards the obstruction, engine roaring. He felt a stab of pain in his shoulder then nothing...

When he picked himself painfully off the road, he found the bike's engine had somehow stopped. There was no one around, and the obstruction, whatever it was – donkey, buffalo, cow – had wandered off into the countryside. It was completely silent. He lifted the bike onto its wheels. The mudguards were bent and the headlight broken, one tyre had been torn off the rim, but there seemed to be no major damage. Gradually, as his eyes became accustomed to the dark, he made out a tiny crucifix in a wayside Calvary at the summit. Blundering about in the dark, he had almost stumbled over it. Hans was a Protestant, and anyway not a religious man, but he could not help kneeling down before the crude image and mumbling a little prayer of thankfulness that he was not badly hurt. He thought about what had happened to him in the last few hours. Yes, he thought, he had a right to be angry. He had been abominably treated and abused but it was his own fault. He had been a fool and deserved to suffer for it. He had learnt a bit about life and a little about women. Sonia had had a point when she mocked his immaturity as a man. He must learn from it, put it behind him and move on. Above all, never again would he allow anyone to treat him as a fool. Never.

Now it was a question of getting back to camp.

The bike was unusable with a tyre torn off, so, retracing his steps, he pushed it slowly downhill towards a place where he could see some lights. Soon he and the machine were on an ox-cart trundling slowly towards the camp. The pain in his shoulder made him flinch from time to time as the cart went over a bump, but it didn't seem to be serious. To his despair, he was not able to slip past the guards in the normal way but was intercepted by a German military policeman. "Herr von Pilsen? Good! You are to report immediately to the CO." Although it was nearly midnight a light burnt in the administration building, so, tidying himself up as he walked and trying to remember the details of the story about the map reading flight which he had concocted with Karl, he prepared to face the music. The CO was an old ace of the Richthofen Circus and not a man to let a lapse of discipline spoil the career of a talented officer.

"Von Pilsen," he began sternly. "You seem to have been out of camp contrary to instructions, also I understand that your navigational sortie today was not performed as you were ordered. Explain yourself." All Hans could think of was an excuse about trying out a motorbike and falling off. He had nothing to say about the exercise.

"Well, be that as it may, I have good news for you, exciting news. You are no longer a Lufthansa employee, you are now an officer in the new Luftwaffe; furthermore, your instructors have reported to me that your flying is of a high standard, and I have recommended you for a new elite force – the dive bomber squadron. Well done, young man, help to make Germany great again! And next time you go chasing girls outside the barracks don't take a plane with you." With that he reached for a bottle which was never very far from his desk and, pouring two generous measures, clinked glasses with one of the first pilots selected for the fledgling air force.

Unlike Cousin Hans, William was not a natural pilot. His first solo scared him to death when he entered a patch of thick cloud just as he was steeling himself to land. Suddenly he could see nothing and became possessed by a complete fit of panic. Where was he going? Was he about to hit the ground? How would he ever find out where he was? Soon, of course, the little plane shot out of the cloud with the airfield well in sight and he completed his circuit, but he had been so transfixed with terror that he was tense all over and his hands shook violently on the controls. Somehow remembering what to do, he managed to throttle back, drifted in to a bumpy landing and thankfully ran to a halt, sweat pouring down his face. His instructor, a wise old ex-Royal Flying Corps bird, had seen all this many times before and tried to cheer his pupil up, but the damage was done and it took weeks before William stopped finding excuses to put off his lessons and took to the air again.

In spite of the attractions of flying and the delights of occasional ventures to sea in *Columba*, William was acutely aware that sometime he must do something serious with his life. He could not just go on living on his father's legacy but jobs were scarce and with no qualifications what could he hope to do? He still affected the rather arty appearance and clothes which he had cultivated in London and was regarded with some fascination by the young ladies whom he met from time to time at local parties and dinners. In fact he was quite in demand at social events, and had a certain charm and slightly sophisticated air which set him apart from most of the eligible young men among the Tyneside gentry, but with no job and no great estates to fall back on, his attractions had obvious limitations. Cautious parents sought to steer their daughters in other directions. He had yet to find a soulmate of the other sex, and was very conscious that he needed some purpose and direction, a career even, before he could think of developing a serious relationship.

One day, after he had returned to the airfield after practising cross-country navigation in a hired Moth, he sat about in the bar of the flying club, idly sketching aircraft as was his habit. He became conscious of a man in a flying suit who seemed to be taking a lot of interest in what he was doing. Eventually the stranger introduced himself and the two got into conversation. Henry Fosweight – that was his name – was editor in chief and publisher of an aeronautical magazine, *Wings*, and also published books, mostly concerned with aeronautical affairs. He had admired William's sketch and offered him five pounds for it on the spot together with full publication rights. William was quite taken aback, but gladly accepted the money which would pay for his afternoon's flying. Deal done, the two repaired to the bar, and William soon found himself talking freely about his life, his attempt at an artistic career, his love of flying and of boats, and his search for some sort of employment.

"Well, Portman," said his new friend, "we may both be in luck. I can't offer you a job but I can undertake to buy pictures from you regularly, probably three or four a month, and maybe you can do the odd dustcover design as well. There are plenty of people who can draw aircraft accurately, but I've seen very few who can bring them alive as you can. Why don't we give it a try?"

William, now a commercial artist, was, for a while, quite a success. Fosweight was as good as his word, and from time to time other commercial assignments came in on the back of his work for *Wings*. It was most satisfactory telling Walder, the solicitor, that he no longer needed to draw on the family funds to support himself, nor did he need any capital to establish the business. A studio was set up in the house and although Mrs Wellibond complained of the mess, the arrangement was quite satisfactory. Every working day William would lunch with Hugh, whose business also seemed to be thriving and they would discuss art, technology and life in general, together. With his work, sailing expeditions and flying all going on at once, William was quite busy for the first time since his school days, and he enjoyed the experience. All good things, however, have a way of coming to an end. At the end of the second summer of these arrangements (it was in September 1931), William noticed that he had not been paid for five paintings supplied the month before to *Wings*. The following week he was busy with *Columba* so did not see any newspapers, but when he returned, a thunderbolt struck him. It was in the form of a letter from a London accounting practice informing him that *Wings* and Fosweight himself, had been declared bankrupt. It was unlikely that William, or any of the other unsecured creditors would ever see their money.

A more robust character would have shrugged off such a set back and found other outlets for his artistic talents. William had, by this time, gained a modest reputation in publishing circles for his cover designs, but he was somehow stumped by it. He felt that people were regarding him as an idler, spending his father's money and achieving nothing. He could not help comparing his own career with that of his father who had joined the Royal Navy as a cadet at fourteen, made a successful career as a naval officer, then played a major part in helping Parsons to develop the market for turbine engines, earning himself a fortune in the process. Thinking gloomily of his own prospects, William was well aware that there seemed to be no possibility now of following his father and joining the Royal Navy or the RAF. Both forces were in the grip of expenditure cut backs, and anyway he was now too old. Nor, as Walder had pointed out, had he qualifications or experience which might open the door to a business career. For several weeks he mooned about the house, feeling sorry for himself, then a casual remark made by one of his friends at the local flying club seemed to offer some slender hope.

"I hear," his friend had said, "that those air force auxiliaries get a lot of flying in these days, lucky beggars, they don't even have to pay for it."

The Auxiliary Air Force was very like the Territorial Army. It was a kind of half-trained reserve, consisting of pilots, observers and ground staff who trained on a part-time basis so as to be ready for any future emergency. The recruitment process was frankly snobbish, pilots being expected to come from a particular social class. William found that there was a squadron based near Newcastle and equipped with twin-engined Handley Page 0/400 bombers. The CO of the squadron, a Group Captain, received William in his rather grand office and immediately started talking about various distinguished local families. He became interested when he heard that William knew many of the local county set, and that his father had been a decorated naval officer in the Great War.

"Yes," he said, "I was Royal Naval Air Service myself you know. That was before they invented the RAF of course. Cracking good time we had trying to shoot down Jerry bombers at night. Never got one myself, but it was great sport. Some tricky landings in the dark; I nearly came to grief several times. Nothing like that in these times of course. Can't afford to lose the aircraft these days."

William told him about his own flying record, trying to conceal the rather dubious history of eighteen hours before his first solo. He need not have worried.

"What?" the Group Captain exclaimed. "You already have a licence? Normally we have to train you young fellows from scratch but you're already there. Capital. When can you join?"

A few weeks later William found himself at a regular RAF station for advanced flying training, using Hawker Hart biplane fighters. He was awarded his "wings" there and a few months later returned for a conversion course where he learnt to fly multi-engined aircraft. This was not too challenging; the aircraft were old bombers designed to harass German rear positions in Belgium during the war. They were steady, stable machines, slow, but easy to handle and the trainees were never expected to fly in anything but the most benign conditions. He passed the course with no difficulty and was now ready to join 444 Squadron AAF based just outside Newcastle. He found his colleagues were an assortment of young fellows like himself and one or two wartime veterans trying to keep their hands in. They assembled every Saturday and, if it was fine weather, would undertake a gentle cross-country flight or a simulated bombing mission. In the evenings the flyers would usually find themselves invited to drinks and dinner in one of the pilot's grand houses (three of them actually lived in castles) where there were always high jinks and often dancing and romancing far into the night. The Auxiliary Air Force was highly regarded as a pool of suitable young men by all the respectable mothers in the North East and their Saturday night invitations were much sought after by eligible young ladies. William enjoyed himself to the last degree. Handsome, if slightly "arty" in appearance, easy going and obviously well-connected (otherwise he wouldn't have been in the Auxiliaries) he was always a popular figure. He felt, however, no need for a long-term interest in any one particular girl. He was charming to all of them, dancing, laughing and dining with many, even kissing quite a few, but his romances never went any further.

The AAF was not, of course, a career. Although members were paid a little for each day served, this amounted only to pocket money. As the months went by, however, William found that the squadron took up more and more of his time. As he lived quite close by and was seldom busy except during the sailing season, he was often asked to do odd flying duties during weekdays and he was always happy to volunteer. As often as possible he took Hugh along with him on these occasions, as his friend seemed to have become very interested in aircraft, and especially how they found their way – or didn't – from place to place. Although not a member of the Air Force, Hugh had the necessary security clearance, and anyway, the squadron was relaxed and informal when it came to regulations. Flying the lumbering Handley Page bombers over the north of England and the North Sea, often in thick weather, presented all sorts of navigational challenges which the RAF in its wisdom chose to ignore during the blissful "Long Weekend" between the wars. They simply didn't fly if visibility was poor. William, however, became fascinated by the process of flying "blind" and finding his way, continually checking wind speed, airspeed and heading and making corrections based on diagrams which only he could understand. Hugh's quick and unconventional way of thinking devised all sorts of procedures and short cuts in the navigational process. Although he never became an ace pilot, William did establish quite a reputation being an excellent cross-country navigator, and his CO had no hesitation in reporting this to the Air Ministry.

One day, after a long and demanding flight to take part in an exercise over Scotland with some RAF fighters, William and Hugh were enjoying a quiet drink in the mess. Hugh looked carefully around him then asked, "Will, have you ever heard of RDF?"

"No, what does it stand for?"

"Well, it's a bit complicated, but I have been playing about with it for some time on an Air Ministry contract. Actually, I make up bits of kit for a fellow called Watson-Watt who works at Slough for the Department of Industrial and Scientific Research. He thinks, and I agree, that somehow we can use radio waves to detect incoming aircraft, bombers perhaps, and so direct our own fighters to them. It's all in the very early stages yet but I think I know how it might be made to work."

"Sounds fascinating, do tell me."

"Well, it's top secret of course, but I think this is the best way to explain it. You know that if we try to send a radio signal through a sheet of metal, we find it is very weak on the other side?"

"Yes."

"Well, the lost part of that signal must go somewhere, it can't just disappear. I think some of it may be bounced back towards the transmitter. Now if we fit a receiver next to the transmitter tuned to the same frequency, it might be able to pick up the returning signal."

"I can understand that but how much do we learn from it? All we can get is our own signal thrown back at us."

"Well, that's where it gets clever. You see, radio waves travel at the speed of light. If we send them in pulses and the receiver can pick up a pulse bounced off the target and detect the direction it's coming from, somehow, in theory at least, we can tell the bearing, height and range of an incoming target. But it's not easy as we have to deal with literally millionths of a second between transmitting the pulse and receiving the echo."

"Sounds wonderful but jolly difficult to do. How can you pulse signals that quickly and recognise the correct returning echo?"

"Yes, yes there are lots of unsolved problems, but Watson-Watt is convinced that it can be made to work, and I think he is right. I'm working on some bits and pieces for it now. I am so excited and it's wonderful to be able to tell someone. For heaven's sake, don't talk about it; it's top secret. We think the Germans are working along similar lines by the way."

"But, Hugh, why are you suddenly telling me all this?"

"Actually, that's what I was coming to. We need a large metal aircraft, a Heyford perhaps, to make some tests. I told Watson-Watt that I knew a fellow who could fly a Heyford quite accurately and was one hundred percent trustworthy and he said "go for it". If you agree, he'll clear it with the RAF and we'll have you and the Heyford for a week. Is that OK?"

Heyfords had just replaced the old Handley Page bombers of 444 Squadron. The Heyford was a machine that seemed somehow to have escaped from the First World War, although in fact the first one only flew in 1930. One experienced Heyford pilot put it well when he described the machine as "a steady aircraft, good for going to lunch in, not so good for going to war in". A biplane with its fuselage slung under the upper wing and a fixed undercarriage, on a good day it could achieve a maximum speed of one hundred and forty miles per hour. It was made partly of metal and partly of wood and fabric. It had two 575 HP engines and a massive wing area so that it could carry, in theory at least, almost four tons of bombs. The pilot sat behind a small windscreen on top of the fuselage, the top of his body exposed to the slipstream. He was over seventeen feet above the ground when the aircraft was parked. For defensive armament the Heyford had two gun positions in which the gunners were situated in the open air, and a third in a retractable "dustbin" which stuck out beneath the aircraft. Fortunately for RAF aircrews, Heyfords were withdrawn from front line service just before 1939; they would have made easy meat for the greenest German fighter pilot.

For Hugh's experiment, however, the clumsy old bird was perfectly adequate.

What William, with Hugh acting as a sort of amateur navigator, had to do was to fly accurately between the BBC broadcast transmitter at Daventry and a receiving station near to it. Flares had to be fired at specific points on the flight. The Air Ministry wanted proof that the plane would actually produce a detectable radar echo. After a couple of false starts due to weather and some technical problems, the experiment took place in February 1935, and the result was definitive. Navigation had been difficult due to strong north winds, but the Heyford had managed to do exactly what was asked of it. Even with a one-kilowatt transmitter (one hundred kilowatts was at the time considered to be ideal), the echo was readily detected. It was now a case of engineering a proper, serviceable RDF set. Hugh was ecstatic and set to work with Watson-Watt's team on circuit design. William returned, job done, to Newcastle and kept his mouth shut.

Hugh had been correct about developments in Germany. As early as 1904 the Germans had a set which would detect the presence of a ship by radio wave reflection, and in the early thirties they developed working pulse-modulated systems for ship detection and eventually for gun laying. Fortunately for Britain the development then got tied up in a morass of intercompany and inter service rivalry, and although technically their radar (as RDF came to be called) technology was at least as advanced as the British in1939, it was not deployed to its best advantage, and by the early 1940s had fallen far behind British developments.

Not long after the Daventry Experiment (as it came to be called) William was summoned into the CO's. office.

"Portman," he said, "I have some rather surprising news for you. This is a letter from the RAF inviting you to transfer from us to them on a short service commission. That's for five years. You would keep your existing rank of Flying Officer with one year's seniority. It seems that there was more to that week you took off on detachment than I realised. I won't ask you what it was, I know that's secret. It seems that they want you to continue to work in the same field. It's all Dutch to me, but I am told I have to have your decision by midday tomorrow. Make up your mind and give me a call. Seems they want to post you somewhere in East Anglia, by the way. We'll be sorry to lose you of course, but with the way things are looking in Europe, we may all be pressed into full-time operational work before long. Always said we could never trust the Huns."

William suspected that Hugh was behind this development in some roundabout way and he didn't like it. He determined to tell his friend that he had no right to involve himself in his affairs behind his back. As soon as he got home, he stalked across the lawn into Hugh's workshop. He was a little surprised to see a gangly youth with an adolescent, spotty face looking at some drawings on Hugh's bench.

"Ah, William," Hugh began, "I'd like you to meet Simon Keystone-Watts – Kilowatt we all call him" – the visitor blushed sheepishly – "Simon is from Cambridge and he will be working with me on RDF for a few months. I need to ask you if Mrs Wellibond will be happy for him to share my flat for a bit."

"Yes, I'll ask, I expect it will be all right, but we have another matter to discuss. Can we go outside?" On the lawn William told Hugh about his meeting that morning. "Are you at the bottom of this by any chance?" he asked.

"Well, not really, all I said to the Air Ministry fellows was that we needed a good pilot, used to large aircraft, and that the fewer people knew about our work the better. Maybe I did mention your name. I hope you don't mind."

William did mind. He still wasn't clear about what he wanted to do with his life. Of course the RAF would be the full-time job which he had been looking for ever since his work as an illustrator had come to an end, but did he really want it? How far could he hope to get in the Air Force after such an unconventional entry? Surely he would be an odd man out among officers who had trained together and known each other for years. Why should he give up his extremely comfortable life at Stonebeck House for a draughty officers' mess somewhere in East Anglia?

"At least you might have asked me before putting your nose into my affairs," he growled.

Determined to refuse the offer, he turned round and stalked back to the house. Half an hour later there came a knock at his door. He was not surprised to find Hugh waiting to apologise to him.

"Look here, old fellow, I am sorry I should not have even mentioned your name without talking to you first. But you see it's so urgent. We are on the verge of a real breakthrough. We've got a brilliant team together and the Ministry has given us full support and a generous budget. Young Kilowatt has been producing some brilliant work on pulsed transmissions. I did really hope you could be part of it. You see, you understand what we are trying to do, and it's so important that we have a pilot on the team who understands it properly. Please, please do think about it."

"Well, I have decided against. I'd be neither fish nor fowl in the regular air force, and I'm not really a military type anyway." Hugh's face fell.

"May I tell you something you don't know," he said. "With RDF we are close to being able to pick up intruders even before they cross our coasts. Light, darkness, fog or rain make no difference. You know the saying 'The bomber will always get through'? Baldwin said that I think. Well, it may not be true any more. We know that the Germans are building bombers which can make two hundred and fifty knots or more – that's as fast as our best fighters – but if we know they are coming at least we have a chance of doing something about it. Think what that means. Think of our cities being knocked to pieces and the hundreds of thousands of innocent deaths. Think of the horror of it. Our little team is the only way of preventing that and we need the very best people. Young Kilowatt, he's an example. He's one of the brightest physicists at Cambridge. Three-quarters through his PhD thesis he's broken off to join us because he hates the idea of our country being bombed, and he's not the only one. Let me give you just one phrase which Watson-Watt, our team leader used after Daventry. 'Britain has become an island once more'. That about sums it up."

This was quite a speech, coming from such an easy going fellow as Hugh. William had seen him excited before, but never so emotional. He had never before expressed the least patriotic fervour. Maybe, somehow, it was his duty to join. He thought for a minute about Flopsy and all he had done because of his sense of duty. Even of his father. He needed to reconsider his decision.

William's thinking took place in his local pub. Sitting in a corner by himself with a pint, he came to a conclusion. His life was going nowhere just now. If there was a war, his Auxiliary unit would be converted to a full-time operation anyway. He'd take the short service commission in the RAF to see how things went.

By the time William's transfer was completed the research team had moved to Orfordness where, in a little hut, the transmitters and receivers were set up. William found himself stationed at Duxford and attached to a Heyford squadron on the airfield. In practice, however, he worked directly under orders from Watson-Watt's team. William soon found out that he was by no means the only "odd ball" flying out of Duxford. There was a weather reconnaissance flight, a high-altitude test flight and several other special purpose units.

For members of the regular bomber squadrons who constituted the main part of Duxford's strength, service life in the 1930s was amazingly relaxed. Officers sat comfortably in leather chairs in the mess and chatted about women, sports cars, tennis and golf. They flew their machines only in fair weather and even then their evolutions were limited to gentle cross-country flights, landing perhaps at some friendly RAF station for a cup of tea before flying gently home. Navigation was strictly by means of map reading and compass. No one in the squadron knew anything about astro navigation or felt the need to. "Bradshawing" – the term used for navigation by following railway lines – was universally popular. William pointed out one day that as there are no railway lines over the sea, this would prove a problem if Bomber Command was to be called upon to attack a foreign country, surely that was its main purpose. The remark did not make him popular. Flights over the sea were avoided at all costs.

In contrast to the regular squadron, his fellow "odd balls" were a serious bunch. They were professional flyers, each dedicated to developing his particular sector of the science of aviation. William naturally gravitated to them and found himself in long discussions about the problems of navigation, blind flying, accurate bombing and what the aircraft of the future might be like. Many of them were older men who had experienced war in the air at first hand and who were appalled at the slow progress made by the RAF since 1918 and by the amateurism of many of its aircrew. Some had travelled to Germany and to the USA and seen some of the developments there which were far in advance of the peace time RAF. All agreed that war, if it came, would bring some nasty shocks and a drastic change of attitude.

Watson-Watt's team kept William busy. He had been assigned as navigator (then termed an "observer"), a rather eccentric ex-Royal Navy airman who had spent years, including the whole of the 1914-18 war, navigating flying boats and airships around the North Sea. Flight Lieutenant Pickles, or "Branston" as he was universally called, was almost fifty, incredibly old for his rank, but seemed to have no ambition or interest in promotion. Somehow his career had fallen into the gap between the Navy and the RAF, and neither seemed to want either to dispose of him or to do very much with him. Someone, however, had remembered that his navigational skills were outstanding and, as accurate flying was vital to the mission, had nominated him to fly with William. He just loved being in the air, looking down at the sea so as to judge drift and wind speed, looking at the clouds to predict a change in the weather, or spotting a tiny dot in the far distance and identifying it before anyone else had seen it. His particular interest was astro navigation, using the sun, stars or even the moon to fix his position. He had of course learnt the basics of the technique in the Navy, and had managed to acquire an American bubble sextant which was much more suitable than a standard naval sextant for use in aircraft, as it did not depend on the navigator being able to see the horizon. There is no horizon if you are above the clouds. He even persuaded William to buy one for himself.

William and Branston would get their orders by telephone every evening. At first light their Heyford would be trundled out of its hangar, fuelled up and off they would set, usually out over the North Sea, where they would fly a pattern over and around a spot determined by someone at Orfordness, or later Bawdsey, a few miles away, when it replaced Orford as the headquarters of the RDF project. The engineers on land would try to track the plane and use data collected to calibrate their radar. During these exercises it was vitally important that a careful log of the aircraft's actual position and movements was kept, and that navigation was spot on. This was Branston's main activity. They also carried a signaller, normally a sergeant, who would spend most of his time tapping away on his Morse key or dozing quietly, headphones abandoned on the desk in front of him. Often the three regular crew would be accompanied by someone from the engineering team, either checking incoming signal strength or just up for the ride. Hugh came whenever he got the chance. If there was some anomaly in the results, pilot and navigator would be invited to a meeting where all the observations would be brought to the table and some explanation worked out. Often the culprits were flocks of large birds, geese most often, giving off an aircraft-like echo. Occasionally it would be a stray aircraft somewhere near the target area. On one occasion the target being observed suddenly split into three and it turned out that Bawdsey had somehow been tracking a flight of Hawker Hart fighters instead of the Heyford.

There was a nasty incident early in the exercise which nearly brought an end to William's flying career. It was a grey day and they had been making some low-level passes along the east coast to see how easy it would be for an intruder to get in undetected, under the radar coverage. The wind had been strong when they set off, very nearly too strong for flying. In fact the flight had been cancelled once, then authorised again at the insistence of someone at Bawdsey. While they were in the air, however, the wind had unexpectedly increased to a full westerly gale. Flying low over the sea in these conditions resulted in an extremely bumpy afternoon's flying. It was cold and noisy in the open cockpit and, unaccountably, there was a constant smell of petrol which made life even more uncomfortable for the crew. Branston was peering down at the sea surface below, trying to estimate rate of drift, while William struggled with the controls, fighting to keep reasonably straight and level. Sergeant Weston, at the radio set, seemed to be restless. In fact the motion had made him feel terribly sick and he had migrated from his normal station into the unoccupied dorsal gun position, where his top half was exposed to the elements, to get a breath of fresh air and clear his head. Looking casually aft down the fuselage, suddenly he froze in his seat, horrified by what he saw. The rear part of the aircraft was fabric covered and somehow a whole section of the fabric had torn off the top of the rear fuselage and was flapping violently against the tail fins. He could also see that the panels covering the sides of the aircraft were bellying outwards due to the blast of the slipstream getting inside the fuselage. If they were to tear off they would obstruct the whole tail plane and make the machine totally unmanageable. The intercom was not connected so he had to clamber down and struggle forward to the cockpit to warn the rest of the crew. William had already noticed the controls becoming very heavy but thought it must be due to the violent weather. There was a hasty conference, shouted into the intercom above the roar of the two Kestrel engines. Obviously they must slow down as much as possible and fly straight back to base. Weston was told to return to the gun position and keep an eye on the tail while William slowed down to near stalling speed and made a gentle turn so as to head westward, towards the nearest land. By this time the fabric from the upper surface of the fuselage had wrapped itself right round the port hand rudder and the rudder bar was impossible to use, but the plane turned ponderously when William banked to port. Branston, still peering down at the grey sea a thousand feet beneath them tapped him on the shoulder. "We're almost going backwards!" he yelled. "Wind's up to fifty knots which is about the same as your airspeed. We'll never get there at this rate." He thought for a moment. "Look," he added, "I'll bet there is less wind nearer the sea surface. Give it a go." Down at sea level, with the wheels almost touching the angry-looking rollers, the wind was indeed a few knots less, but progress was still painfully slow. Cautiously, William opened the throttles a little and the airspeed built up to ninety. At this rate it would take half an hour to reach the coast and another hour to get to Duxford. As well as the danger of more of the fabric skin coming adrift, there was no possibility of flying this low over land. They would have to climb to at least three hundred feet, back into the full force of the wind. To make matters worse, Weston reported that the port hand panel was beginning to tear away. They must think of something else quickly.

Branston did a few calculations. "Look," he said. "If we steer west-southwest in this wind, our track will be almost due south. That'll take us onto the Norfolk coast in about fifteen minutes, I think it's our best chance." Skidding the machine round onto the new course, William thought about the terrain ahead. He knew the coastline well from his sailing, and in fact he had been there the previous weekend. Racking his brains, he worked out that it would have been low tide about midday. Perhaps if he could reach Holkham beach, he could put her down on the sands there; they were quite firm and would be dry until the next high tide. Weston was summoned and told to send an SOS to base, asking them to get the lifeboat crew to stand by. As he was working at this there was an ominous crack and the joystick jerked forward in William's hands. The loose panel had finally torn off its stitching and was snagging on the elevator. It took all his strength to stop the bomber diving straight into the sea. The windscreen was by now covered with salt spray and impossible to see through. He had to look round it with his head out in the slipstream. At last the grey sea turned yellow as it met the shallow sandbank extending from the coast, and the welcome sight of the beach came into view. With very little control left, he managed to keep just high enough to bank the machine to starboard so as to face into wind and shut the throttles in the hope that she would remain reasonably level as she landed. If the Heyford had one good point it was a very strong fixed undercarriage, and, headed into the gale, she was moving very slowly over the ground when she touched down bumpily but safely on the beach, scattering sea birds and throwing up a cloud of sand behind her.

With a prayer of thanks, the three of them clambered out of the aircraft and quickly shoved the chocks behind the wheel. William left the engines idling in the hope that he might be able to taxi up the beach, but the wheels were sinking into the sand and anyhow it would be impossible to taxi safely with a cross wind this strong. Just as they were about to give up hope and abandon her to the incoming tide, an astonishing procession came into view from amongst the pine trees at the top of the beach. The lifeboat crew from Wells had seen the plane come down and rushed to the spot in a borrowed lorry, recruiting as they came as many people, mostly farm workers, as they could. Among these were four horse-drawn plough teams who had been working nearby and were hastily unhitched from their ploughs. They trotted down towards the sea, the horses enjoying the change and the feel of the damp sand under their feet. William killed both engines and directed the men to steady the wings of the plane so that it wouldn't flip over, while the powerful animals were hitched to the rear fuselage. With much chaffing, joking and many "gee ups" the machine was hauled up away from the tide and parked in a sheltered clearing in the pine trees where it could be firmly roped down. Everyone involved, and a few who turned up too late, then invaded the Victoria pub in the village where William found himself spending the best part of a month's pay on beer.

The party in the Victoria was brought to an end by the arrival of a pair of Crossley Tenders, from Duxford, with a team of mechanics, to see what could be done with the aircraft, and with a guard detail to protect it over-night. In charge of this party was Flight Sergeant Ables, a fat, domineering, grumpy veteran who had seen more crashed aircraft than he cared to remember and had a low opinion of pilots. He spent half the night going over the Heyford with a torch and a ladder, accompanied by a pair of shivering, miserable aircraftsmen.

William had not been looking forward to meeting the fearsome Ables next morning, but it couldn't be avoided. They met under the pine trees, sheltered from the wind.

"Well, sir," began Ables. "She's not badly damaged apart from the fabric, and we can fix that here, but you'll have to fly her out. There's no other way of moving her except to take her apart and cart her away and the CO wouldn't like that, sir, not a bit."

"But how will we get her to take off on this wet sand? Surely she'll get stuck. She sunk right into the sand when we landed."

"You leave that to me, sir. Let my men get on with their work and then we'll see."

"Any idea how this all happened, Flight? The top panel just ripped off. I've never heard of that happening before, have you? It wasn't a bird strike or anything like that. If it hadn't been for Weston going up there to puke we would have been done for."

For a moment a flash of kindness seemed to appear in those piggy deep-set eyes.

"Matter of fact I have, sir, will you come this way where no one can hear?" They stepped out onto the sand. The gale had abated and now there was just a fresh breeze. "You know that new Irish boy we have, Aircraftsman Tuoy, sir, nice lad and keen, but a bit over eager if you take my meaning. Well, before we left yesterday, I found him crouched in the corner of the hangar sobbing his heart out. 'What's up, lad?' says I. Then it all came out, sir. Young Tuoy he loves to drive that tractor we use to move the machines in and out of the hangar. Well, yesterday morning we pulled them all out as we was ordered, then came the word that it was too windy, so quick as a flash Tuoy he jumps on the tractor and starts to put them back. Your plane, old Zebra we calls her, she is the last to go in and by that time all the lads, except Tuoy on the tractor, has gone off to the canteen. Now as he is putting Zebra away he manages to push her under the gantry we use to work on the engines. Ripped a good-sized tear in the fabric, he says. Well, he'd be on a serious charge for that so he don't want anyone to know. He thinks he'll come back in the afternoon with his mates and see if they can patch her up on the quiet like. So off he goes to his meal, not knowing that you had orders to take Zebra out after all. Well, someone else pulls her out and no one notices the tear. You know how tall those Heyfords stand, sir, so no one would see it. Young Tuoy goes back in the afternoon and finds her gone, then he hears on the grapevine that she's about to crash into the sea. All because of him, he thinks. No wonder the lad was blubbering."

"Well," said William, "there will be an enquiry of course. We'll have to see what we can do for Tuoy."

For the first time in his life he saw Ables smile broadly. The man was human after all.

Early the next morning everything was ready for the take-off. The plane had been emptied of all non-essential gear and fuel so that she was as light as possible, and the fabric had been patched up. Ables, who had recovered many a crashed aircraft from behind the trenches at night before the German guns had had a chance to smash it to pieces, had brought some rolls of wire netting with him and by stretching these out on the sand exactly in line with the wind and pegging them well down he had created usable runway about two hundred yards long. Much to the disappointment of the locals, the horses were not needed to take the plane to the start position. Instead the two Crossleys hauled her carefully over the soft sand. To save weight, Weston, to his relief, was left behind and only William and Branston were aboard. The engines started without too much trouble and William let them warm up for a good while before starting his run. "Keep on the netting, sir, and you'll be fine," Ables had said. "If you run off it she'll nose over and anything can happen." In the event the take-off was easy. With its light load and famously low wing loading, the Heyford was in the air well before the end of the netting and was able to make several low passes over the village, waggling its wings in thanks over the lifeboat house before turning towards Duxford where it was greeted with some merriment.

There *was* an enquiry of course. The CO, who disliked other people snooping into what went on on his station, tried to make it an internal affair, but the Air Ministry insisted on appointing one member of the board – an engineering officer – Group Captain Hassle. As pilot, William was examined first. His rather unconventional RAF career was examined in detail by Hassle who made copious notes and whispered comments from time to time to the CO. The enquiry then turned to the flight in question.

"Did you carry out the prescribed pre-flight inspection of the aircraft?"

"Yes, sir."

"What did you do?"

"The pre-flight inspection for the Heyford is in the book, sir. I carried it out exactly as prescribed. It is noted in my log."

"Indeed. Then how was it that you missed the fact that a large fabric panel was not properly secured?"

"With respect, sir, the Heyford's fuselage is seventeen feet above the ground. The top of the fuselage can only be inspected from a gantry. Gantries are not provided for pre-flight inspection."

"How do you explain the damage to the aircraft? Did it occur before take-off?"

"I've been asking myself the same question, sir. It could have been a manufacturing fault, or a bird strike, or some accidental damage on the ground. I certainly never witnessed an incident which might have caused it."

Next Weston and Pickles were questioned, then it was Ables' turn. William had to admire how the cunning old veteran covered up for his man, Tuoy. At no stage did he actually lie to the enquiry, but he didn't tell the whole truth either. Hassle clearly smelt a rat and dug as deeply as he could into Zebra's history and what went on that morning but it got him nowhere. The final report was inconclusive. No blame was attached to any of the aircraft's crew or the Duxford maintenance team. The accident was put down to "causes unknown".

After nine months of testing and calibrating, the scientists at Bawdsey were satisfied. At Kilowatt's suggestion, they had even had a try at mounting an RDF set in the Heyford itself. They found it was possible to pick up echoes from other aircraft and from the ground beneath them. This was a diversion however. Air Marshall Dowding, responsible for air defence of Britain, had watched the development of radar with an eagle eye. As soon as he was convinced it was a viable and reliable proposition, he was able to persuade the Treasury to sanction the building of the first five three hundred and fifty-foot steel towers which were eventually to form part of the "Chain Home" family of stations and to play a vital role in the protection of Britain four years later.

William's work at Duxford was now complete. He had learnt a lot and had gradually integrated himself into the life of the RAF.

Chapter 4

The existence of the Luftwaffe was not made public until 1935 but
it had become obvious that it existed long before that date. Anyone
who cared to study the various subterfuges, including the training
operations in Italy and Russia, the development of fast "mail
carrying" aircraft, which were in fact thinly disguised bombers,
and the selection and training of aircrew, could have no doubts of
its existence. As one of the chosen dive bomber pilots, Hans was
assigned to a unit based near his home in East Prussia flying the
new Henschel 123. The unit was known as the Immelmann
Gruppe. The Henschel was designed as a biplane fighter, but
Udet's enthusiasm for dive bombing led to some of the aircraft
being modified for dive bombing practice. In the early 1930s, quite
independently of Udet's experiences in America, the Germans had
conducted some dive bombing exercises in Sweden, using a frozen
lake as an airfield and developing the techniques needed to place a
bomb accurately from a steeply diving aircraft. What was the
optimal angle of dive? How to control the airspeed? What was the
ideal height to release the bomb? How to pull out and get away
safely? All this needed careful study and the issues were
approached with typical German thoroughness. By the time Hans
joined his squadron, a series of different approaches had been
developed for different types of target. All of them called for cool
nerves and considerable skill on the part of the pilot, but practice
dive bombing was the most superb experience. No one who has not
flown as one of an echelon of aircraft towards a target, peeled off
in his turn into a near vertical dive, seen the ground come rushing
ever faster towards him, heaved back on the stick at the last
moment and zoomed away, will ever understand the thrill and
exhilaration of the experience. The two years Hans spent there in
East Prussia learning to dive bomb were some of the happiest in

his life. Goering, who now was the Nazi chief in Prussia, as well as head of the nascent air force, took a special interest in the Immelmann Gruppe and he made sure that they lacked for nothing in the way of accommodation, food, comforts and occasions for sports or hunting in the forests. The other officers were mostly from similar social backgrounds to Hans and few of them cared a fig for politics, but they were all fanatical flyers and determined that the Luftwaffe should become the premier air force in the world.

Apart from flying, Hans was near his home, so he could escape with a few chosen friends for the occasional weekend break. The whole neighbourhood was intensely proud to have these young men in their midst. Invitations would flood in to hunt, to dine, to dance, to picnic. All great fun, but there was something about his home that worried the young airman. In the hall, there had appeared an ugly red flag in the centre of which was a white disc and a black swastika. The failure of the aristocrats supporting von Papen's government to contain Hitler's Nazi party had caused his father and many of his aristocratic friends to make a rapid revision of their political attachments. Hitler, whom they had considered an ignorant but useful fool, had turned out to be no fool at all. Clearly, to get on in the new Germany, one must be a Party member and an admirer of the upstarts and criminals who constituted the new rulers of the country. Albricht had never been slow to detect, and adapt to, a new political environment and soon it was difficult to imagine that he had ever been anything but a devoted Nazi. Hans' activities in the new air force of course enhanced his father's prestige in the party as did his wife's friendship with Goering. His contacts with the leaders of German industry and with international business made him extremely useful to the new regime and he was prospering. To Hans, however, the new political order remained unappealing. He resented the changes to his home and the uncivilised house guests his parents thought it necessary to entertain.

Hans first met Angela during one of his weekend leaves, at a picnic organised by a neighbour. Lively, handsome and intelligent, she was a distant relation of the neighbour's family. She had been brought up in England and had come to stay for a month in Prussia to perfect her already fluent German. She arrived at the picnic riding a dilapidated motorbike with a gigantic hamper strapped on the back. "Aunt's delayed," she explained, "and she asked me to come on ahead with the champagne and some oysters. The rest will be here in an hour or so." The four young pilots who had already arrived swarmed round her and competed to help her with the hamper, but she swung it down herself with great aplomb, got out a collapsible table and commenced expertly popping champagne corks. Hans had never seen a girl like this before, so confident, yet so beautiful, so strong, yet somehow underneath it he sensed a vulnerability which he found maddeningly attractive, not at all like the hard, glittering self-confidence of Sonia. By the end of the picnic he was completely smitten. There was to be a dance that evening in a nearby house, and Hans was terrified lest somehow this wonderful creature would be taken away from him during the evening. He even surreptitiously moved the place names at the dinner table so they could be together. His hostess noticed, winked at her husband, but said nothing. Apart from a few "duty" dances with relations, he was by her side all that evening. She seemed not to find this embarrassing. She always had something to say, some amusing remark, some little gesture. He even dared to hope that Angela found him at least a little attractive. And well she might. Hans was tall, blond and strongly built, with a kind, open face and the most piercing blue eyes. Except for a certain gentleness of manner he might have been a specimen of healthy Aryan youth out of a Nazi text book. In spite of his size he had a delicacy of movement which made him a natural in an aeroplane, and he spoke with an air of authority and decisiveness which was to make him an excellent officer. Above all he was a kind, caring man, in spite of his military profession. He hated to see people or even animals hurt or depressed and in this he differed markedly from most of his colleagues. Angela felt that this was a man she could truly trust and admire, and she felt safe and comfortable in his company.

Back at the aerodrome Hans could think of nothing all week except his new love and went about his duties in a dream. Luckily the weather was poor and there was no flying. The next weekend was to be Angela's last in Germany and it was arranged that she should spend it at the von Pilsen castle. Hans went eagerly home as early as possible. The two spent a blissful Sunday walking through the forests to a little village where they ate together at a country inn. Content to be in each other's company, they wondered at the majesty of the great trees and the stillness all around them. On the way home Hans told Angela a little about his love of flying and the excitement of life in the Immelmann Gruppe. She seemed interested and was impressed by his obvious love of his profession and asked many questions about his life and his friends. They felt so at home in each other's company that it seemed natural to stop at a little hut in the castle grounds, to kiss, to embrace... They had to almost run back to the castle for dinner, arriving slightly red-faced and muttering an unconvincing story about having been detained talking to a gamekeeper.

Then it was back to flying for Hans, and to England for Angela. She was studying for a doctorate at Cambridge. Promises had been made, however, and letters regularly crossed the North Sea: hers in German, his in his rather stilted English.

Hans' period of dive bomber training had now nearly finished, but there was a surprise in store for him. He, his friend Karl and one other excellent pilot, Ernst Fischer, were ordered to report to a special unit forming to introduce a new type of aircraft – the JU 87 Stuka. The Henschel had been a fighter adapted for dive bombing but the Stuka was a purpose-designed aircraft which was to strike terror into hearts right across Europe, from the Volga to the Ebro and from the banks of the Nile to the mountains of Norway. Early Stukas, like the one Hans first met, were, even by the standards of the time, pretty modest performers. Their 600 HP engine gave them a top speed of two hundred miles per hour and maximum range was six hundred and twenty miles with a bomb load of only a quarter of a ton. These bald figures belied the deadly efficiency of the aircraft. They were designed to dive almost vertically on a target and drop their bombs with a precision never equalled by high-level bombers. To enable them to do this, they required an incredibly robust airframe, able to sustain damage from defensive fire and to accept "g" forces, far beyond those which would wrench the wings of most fighters as they pulled out of a dive. To keep them controllable during steep dives, they had huge dive brakes which kept their speed within safe limits while still enabling them to be manoeuvred with precision. Any fighter trying to dive steeply enough to follow a Stuka down would find itself rushing past its intended victim and in danger of getting completely out of control. Stukas were two-seaters, with a pilot and a signaller/gunner seated behind him. For armament, apart from the bomb load, there was one fixed forward-firing machine gun and one machine gun on a flexible mounting facing aft. The primary roles of the aircraft were to provide close support for armour and infantry, and to attack shipping. The Stuka's effectiveness in these roles was witnessed by the sheer terror which the sight of a swarm of dive bombers struck into the hearts of their enemies. To make them yet more frightening, the machines were fitted with a wailing siren which was switched on during the dive and which terrorised all who heard it. Crews for this new breed of aircraft were carefully selected from the most daring and able members of the Luftwaffe; they were venerated in official propaganda and idolised by the public. It was to this select band that Hans and his two friends were to be introduced.

Like all new Stuka pilots, Hans was at first a little daunted by the very size of his new mount. However, once in the air, he found the big beast obedient and quite pleasant to fly. After a few hours of circuits and landings and some aerobatics, his instructor told him that it was time to try some dive bombing. He took off, climbed to cruising height, and flew off with a dummy bomb load of two hundred- and fifty-pound bombs towards the range where the target, a series of concentric rings of old tyres, was set up. He had no difficulty in finding the target, but the tricky part was to come. Pointing one's aircraft directly at the ground is a challenge in itself, but at the start of the dive a complex series of actions had to be performed – throttle back, close cooling gills, deploy dive brakes, switch prop to coarse pitch, switch supercharger to low-level setting – all with the aircraft rapidly gaining speed vertically downwards and while the pilot was trying to aim it at the target. Hans, normally a cool customer when at the controls, found himself getting confused and muddled – on the brink of panic in fact – as he hurtled towards the ground. The target grew steadily bigger in his sights as he grappled with the controls, trying to keep on target. Suddenly it seemed to rush upwards towards him so that he yanked the stick back in panic. Everything turned black before his eyes. Somehow he knew he was still flying but his limbs were paralysed and his brain fuddled. After what seemed a long time, but was actually about two seconds, his vision returned, but with black spots drifting before his eyes. He remembered that there were things he had to do. Mercifully, he was flying straight and level about two hundred feet above the ground but something was wrong. Quick! He must re-set the aircraft for level flight reversing the actions performed at the start of the dive. Throttle, cooling gills, brakes, prop, supercharger. At last he was back in control of himself and looked around. Maybe the dive had not been so bad after all. He wondered what his instructor, on the ground, would think. He couldn't talk to him as he was flying solo, early dive-bombing practice was too dangerous to risk the lives of useful signallers. Then, "Damned Fool," he yelled at himself. He had forgotten to release his first bomb! Trembling with frustration and fury he started to regain height to have another try. He found he was flying the aircraft downright badly, yanking at the controls and skidding unsteadily about the sky. "This won't do," he told himself. "Relax, settle down and fly properly." By the time he had to level off he had calmed down a bit and he turned off into his second dive. This time he was over-cautious, pulling out too high and too gently. He was able to see the bomb strike the ground well clear of the target. One more to go. The third time was a little better, the dive quite well-judged, but again the aim was poor, the bomb landing outside the outer circle.

Less than pleased with himself, Hans noticed that another machine was approaching the range. "That would be Ernst," he said to himself. He had plenty of fuel left and determined to watch his friend perform. Ernst muffed his first dive; it was too shallow and he overshot the target. His next effort, however, was excellent, and Hans saw the missile land within the outer ring. By the time Ernst had finished Karl, his friend from Italian days, was ready to go. His first dive was good. He had always been the best pilot of the three of them and Hans watched a little jealously as Karl soared up for his second attempt. Down screamed the Stuka directly at the tyres below. With her canted gull wings black against the bright sky and her claw-like undercarriage, she looked like an avenging bird of prey stooping on an innocent victim. Down and down she went, straight, fast but alas, a fraction too far. The horrified watchers saw her start to pull out but before she was in level flight, the belly of the aircraft smashed into the ground and she cartwheeled over, bursting into orange flames and billowing out an ugly pall of black smoke. An excellent comrade, who was at once rich and humble, a magnificent pilot and an irreplaceable friend, Karl was gone forever.

It normally took six months to train a Stuka pilot. Eventually Hans and Ernst were regularly hitting the centre of the inner circle almost every dive. As they completed their course, the Spanish civil war was looming and there were many rumours about deploying parts of the Luftwaffe to help Franco's army. The young flyers were aching to use their skills in real combat and anxiously awaited news of their next posting. Ernst went almost mad with joy when he found he was to join a regular squadron which he correctly guessed would lead to deployment in Spain. For Hans, however, a different sort of surprise was in store.

Chapter 5

William was released from his duties with the radar team after six months of hard and extremely valuable work. The essential testing and calibration were done. Now it was a question of learning how to use the system properly as an integral part of an air defence system. Dowding set about this with his usual efficiency and ruthlessly logical thinking, conducting exercises with whole wings of fighters and bombers. It soon became clear that keeping the radar sets operational was beyond the skills of regular RAF maintenance crews. Hugh's partner, Kilowatt, was set to work to identify ex-colleagues of his from academia, mostly, in fact, from Cambridge, who might be prepared to help out. He soon had a motley crew of physics graduates, armed with oscilloscopes, soldering irons and assorted valves and bits of wire, allocated to each radar station and available if needed in a national emergency.

William found himself relegated to the undemanding peace time role of a bomber pilot with his squadron. Although by now there seemed to be real danger of war in Europe, Bomber Command seemed totally unworried by the possibility of having to commit itself to battle against the might of the Luftwaffe. Training continued in the same old lackadaisical way. Under the uncertain and compromising leadership of the inter war governments, the strength of the RAF had been slashed again and again and budgets for training and equipment cut to the bone. Lord Londonderry, during his time as Secretary of State for Air, had actually evolved a theory that any increase in British air power should be avoided as it might upset relationships with Hitler. The poor old Heyfords continued to trundle about the skies on fine days, their crews blissfully ignoring the lessons which they might have gained from the air battles of the Spanish civil war. There were, however, rumours of changes to come. Someone caught a glimpse of a new bomber – a Wellington – which was almost one hundred miles per hour faster than the Heyford, and in which the crew actually sat in an enclosed cockpit, instead of having their heads poking out into the fresh air. One day maybe they might equip William's squadron. There was talk too of the new eight-gun monoplane fighters being developed for defence. Like spring coming to a shady corner of a chilly garden, the possibility of war was slowly awakening a somnolent Royal Air Force.

One corner of this garden was particularly late to feel the warmth of the coming spring. RAF Coastal Command had responsibility for giving air cover to British and allied naval and merchant shipping. This involved reconnaissance, bombing and torpedoing enemy shipping at sea, mine warfare and, most important of all, anti-U-boat operations. The Command was in a sorry state. After World War I the Royal Air Force had taken over all flying operations from the Navy and the unique skills which had been built up during the war had been almost lost in the process. Thus whilst, in 1918, Britain had had by far the most capable and the largest naval aviation force in the world, by 1938 this had withered into an ill-equipped Fleet Air Arm, restored to naval control, but unloved by the Admiralty, and RAF Coastal Command whose main role seems to have been to act as a bone of contention over which the two services could snarl at each other. The result of this was that its mission was never properly defined, its equipment was pitifully inadequate for what it had to do and, worst of all, its crews were untrained in long-range navigation over water. To add insult to injury, the Air Ministry had decreed that Coastal Command aircraft and their crews would be placed at the disposal of Bomber Command whenever a major bombing operation was to be undertaken. It was to this sorry force that William found himself posted soon after the notorious Munich Agreement of 1938.

William's squadron was equipped with Avro Ansons, a type which epitomised the muddled thinking which pervaded the Air Ministry. This was an aircraft designed specifically for Coastal Command and first flown as recently as 1935. From the start it was obviously pitifully inadequate for its task. Ansons were slow, clumsy, ill-defended and had a range of only six hundred and ninety miles. Their normal bomb load was a pathetic three hundred and ninety pounds. For defensive armament they had a single forward-facing machine gun and another in a dorsal turret. Their limited range made them unable to patrol any area except the English Channel and the western part of the North Sea; hence William's squadron, the "Ospreys" as they called themselves, were based at Lydd in Kent. William arrived there on a drizzly March afternoon and reported to the CO's office. Wing Commander Swan kept him waiting for fifteen minutes then consented to see him. He was a small, fat man with sharp blue eyes and a face which betrayed an aggressive nature. On his chest, below his pilot's wings, were rows of medal ribbons testifying to a distinguished war record. He greeted the new pilot without warmth.

"Well, Portman, I see that you joined us from the Auxiliaries. I don't remember any other aircrew doing that. Please explain."

William was immediately embarrassed. He could not say anything about his work on radar. It was top secret. He stuttered out something about Duxford's requirement for a Heyford pilot to undertake some special assignments.

"What sort of special assignments?"

"Sorry, sir, they are still hush hush."

"Oh! Well, I've no time for hush hush here. I need regular reliable pilots who tow the line. Is that clear?"

"Yes, sir."

"Why did the RAF, in its wisdom, select you for this "hush hush" assignment?"

"I think it was because I had more interest than most in long-range navigation, sir. It's almost become a hobby for me."

"Hobby? I don't want hobby pilots in my squadron and I don't want fancy ideas about navigation either. While you're here you will navigate by the book and you'd better come back safely and on time. Is that clearly understood?"

"Yes, sir."

"Now tell me about the accident you had and the enquiry into the damage to your aircraft."

William told him about the incident at Holkham.

"Well, I think you were lucky to get away without a serious reprimand. Imagine taking off with a rent in the fabric. I'm going to watch you closely, Portman. Any carelessness and you're out. Quick as a flash. Understood?"

"Yes, sir."

A crestfallen William went off to find his quarters and settle into the mess.

The CO's hostile attitude had clearly rubbed off on the other officers. Instead of the usual friendly introductions in the mess, all he got was a few nods and he found himself buying his own beer and sitting in solitary state in a corner reading a crumpled newspaper. He felt like a new boy at school.

The next morning he was taken to his aircraft and given a briefing by a flight sergeant. He had already had time to study the pilot's manual and there didn't seem to be anything too difficult about it, except for the fact that this was to be his first experience of a retractable undercarriage. In the afternoon he was introduced to his two regular crewmen: Sergeant Willis was to be his observer and Leading Aircraftsman Hopson radio operator/gunner. In contrast to the officers, these two had friendly faces and welcomed their new skipper warmly. William was given permission to make a brief familiarisation flight. He knew that Swan would be watching his performance critically and determined that nothing should go wrong. Once in the air the only peculiarity of the Anson was that the undercarriage had to be retracted manually by winding a handle a seemingly endless number of times. They flew sedately down the coast to Brighton, did a few gentle turns over the sea, then came safely back to Lydd. The Anson at least seemed to have no vices in the air, and the three-point landing was almost perfect. The crew stood together on the tarmac, chatting after the flight and Hopson, who was an inveterate joker, brought out a couple of his famous risky stories, making the other two roar with laughter. William slapped him on the back as the party split up and returned to their quarters. The moment he reached his room, an orderly appeared at William's door.

"The CO wants to see you, sir, says it's urgent."

The little man was red in the face with fury.

"Portman, I saw that. I saw you associating and joking with other ranks. I will not have it. You may be from the Auxiliaries but you're supposed to be an officer, and I expect you to behave like one. We have proper old-fashioned standards here, and within twenty-four hours of arriving here you are letting us down. Pull yourself together, man! Any more of your nonsense and I'll take you off flying altogether. Understood?"

William was getting quite used to understanding what the CO was saying.

"Yes, sir."

As soon as the Ospreys undertook reconnaissance patrols, the inadequacy of the Ansons became obvious. Assigned a patrol area just south of the Isle of Wight, they formed up over the aerodrome into four flights of three aircraft each. They then trundled off to their patrol areas; by the time they had reached them they had been in the air for almost an hour. They were now out of sight of land and in poor visibility; no one was quite sure where they were. However, they split up and patrolled as ordered, the crews looking down at the sea below them and making notes on the various ships sighted. The patrol lasted only just over an hour, then the aircraft had to turn north to pick up the coast and return to base. To William's surprise, the coastline they saw beneath them was not the Isle of Wight at all but Anvil Point, south of Poole Harbour. The east wind had been stronger than they had anticipated and they had clearly been patrolling the wrong bit of sea throughout their flight. The flight flew back low along the coast line, making hardly one hundred and twenty knots over the land against the headwind. The CO who had not been flying held a debriefing after the flight. He was disgusted at the report he heard, and demanded explanations. William then ventured a suggestion.

"Sir, I could have taken a sun sight several times during the flight down. I know they are not very accurate but it would at least have given us a clue that we were getting too far east. I've got a special type of sextant of my own and I am sure that if we all had them this sort of problem would be much less likely." The others turned to him in astonishment.

"Sun sight? Sextant? What are you talking about? They are not in the training manual and there's no astrodome in the Anson anyway."

"But I believe I could have used the dorsal turret."

"Rubbish, and it would take too long anyway."

"In the Heyford we were taking them all the time, they were invaluable."

The CO put a stop to the argument.

"My squadron is not going to have its pilots mucking about in the gun turret. Who's going to fly the aircraft while he's there? If Flying Officer Portman wants to do that sort of thing he can go somewhere else and do it. We work things by the book here. Understood?"

Once again William understood. But he never flew without his sextant.

That was as far as the debriefing got. Nothing had been learnt and nothing would be better next time.

And so it continued throughout 1939. Even the outbreak of the "phoney war" made little difference to the operations of the Ospreys. Bomber Command made some disastrous raids on German shipping in harbour, and on one occasion one of Ospreys Ansons saw a German flying boat, but nothing else was seen of the enemy. No German U-boat captain was stupid enough to sail down the Channel in daylight on the surface in good visibility and the Luftwaffe was too busy in Poland to give much trouble to the Coastal Command. William and his crew continued to "tow the line", as Swan had put it, so their flying duties became extremely boring. Their Anson droned over miles and miles of grey sea, its crew trying to keep alert but constantly looking at their watches and longing for the order to return to base. The one thing which gave William pleasure was the attitude of his regular crew. Willis was intelligent and keen and William was able to teach him most of what he knew about navigation. He passed on, not just the theory, but also the skills, learnt from Branston, of how to calculate wind strength and drift, where to find calmer air and how to scan a seemingly empty seascape so as to spot the smallest irregularity which might indicate a small vessel or a conning tower. Hopson was brilliant at keeping up morale with his cheeky humour delivered down the intercom. Gunners were allowed a short burst to test their weapons during each flight, and he always made the most of this, getting William to take them close to any floating debris or off-lying rock to test his aim. C-Charlie, as she was called, was a very happy aircraft and, in spite of his best efforts, Swan could find little to criticise.

Unknown to the Ospreys, however, there were happenings at the Air Ministry which were to bring about radical changes in their role and duties during the course of the war. Air Marshal Sir Frederick Bowhill had taken control of Coastal Command in 1937. He was perfectly qualified for the job: trained as a cadet in the Merchant Navy, he joined the Royal Naval Air Service and qualified as a pilot in 1912. During the Great War he was captain of a seaplane carrier which conducted a successful raid on German airship sheds. In the interwar period he had transferred to the RAF and commanded a squadron policing Iraq. He was thoroughly dissatisfied with the standard of training of his command and set about making drastic changes. The first of these was to fit radio direction finding to the aircraft in his charge. This proved a great boon to the navigators. The next was more difficult to achieve. He fought a running, and eventually successful, battle with Bomber Command and with the Air Ministry to get more up-to-date aircraft in place of the pathetic, frequently worn-out machines which had traditionally been issued to the coastal service.

Early in 1940 the Ospreys learnt that they were to lose their Ansons and would have to convert to an altogether more formidable and warlike aircraft, the Bristol Blenheim.

Although it had been in service since 1935 and was considered a bit of a death trap when used as a daylight bomber, the Blenheim was an exciting prospect for a squadron used to Ansons. William met his first Blenheim at Upwood Operational Training Unit. It was standing outside the hangar when he arrived at the unit and he couldn't resist a look over it. Just as he was climbing onto the wing, a bus carrying the squadron NCOs arrived, and his two crewmen scrambled to join him. The pilot's instruments and controls were not unlike the Anson's except for the variable pitch propeller controls. The observer/ bomb aimer had a seat beside the pilot and also a position in the nose of the aircraft into which he had to wriggle in order to get at the bomb sight and to operate the two forward-facing machine guns. The gunner/radio operator was in a separate dorsal turret with an excellent view upwards and astern, but very little downwards. The three men scrambled over the machine and were suitably impressed. They could hardly wait to see how she felt in the air.

The first week at Upwood was spent in the classroom learning the procedures and systems on the aircraft. William's colleagues from the Osprey squadron made a show of finding this boring and an insult to their many hours of flying experience. William himself did his best to pay attention, however, as mechanical things interested him and he liked to understand the details of the Bristol Mercury radial engines, the Claudel-Hobson carburettor, the variable pitch propeller and the workings of the Browning machine guns.

Then it was time to fly the beast. For initial training there were a number of Mark 1 Blenheims fitted with dual controls. William made his first flight sitting alongside a sergeant pilot instructor, one of the few who had survived attempts to raid German shipping in the early months of the war. He demonstrated a perfect circuit then handed the controls over to his pupil. William taxied unsteadily to the beginning of the runway then opened the throttles so as to run the engines up against the brakes. The machine shuddered and danced with the vibration of the engines, the spinning propellers shining in sunlight only a few inches from the cockpit windows. Brakes off, plus five boost, full power, and she started her take-off run, slowly at first, then, as he pushed the stick forward a little to lift the tail, she seemed to come alive and quickly built up to ninety miles per hour. Gently back on the stick and the rumble of the wheels on the tarmac faded and up came the undercarriage. Once in the air the Blenheim was remarkably handy and responsive, and the pilot had an excellent view. William made a quick circuit then came in to land. The machine seemed to be going awfully fast compared to the Anson, but it was not difficult. The instructor immediately climbed out onto the wing and told William to go round a couple of times solo. No problems. William's now considerable flying experience had enabled him to overcome his early clumsiness as a pilot and, although the Blenheim's top speed of two hundred and seventy miles per hour was almost a hundred miles per hour more than anything he had flown previously, he had little difficulty in mastering the aircraft.

Over the next three weeks the Ospreys practised the arts of close formation flying, an essential discipline in the Blenheims as their weak defensive armament made them easy meat for enemy fighters unless they flew closely grouped together. They made dummy bombing runs, practised air-to-air gunnery and honed their night-flying skills. The most exciting exercises of all were dummy attacks on shipping. Attempts to attack enemy ships using high-level bombing in the early months of the war had shown very clearly the inadequacy of existing bomb sights and bombing technique generally. Most of the missiles had landed too far away from the target to do the slightest damage. The RAF had no purpose-built dive bombers or torpedo carriers, so the only viable way to attack a ship was low-level bombing. For this, a force of several aircraft would attack the quarry from various directions, zooming low over the sea, releasing their bomb at the last minute, virtually hurling it onto the ship's side, then pull up violently, skim over the enemy at masthead height and escape at full speed. This was a highly risky business and even practising it was dangerous. Two aircraft were lost as a result of pilots getting too low and striking the sea's surface. William and his crew became quite adept at the technique although it was certainly a hair-raising experience for Willis, lying prone in the nose of the aircraft as it charged straight at the side of the target ship at over two hundred and fifty miles an hour.

Training completed, the Ospreys were sent, to their disgust, not back to Lydd, in civilised Kent, but up to a remote station in northern Scotland, noted chiefly for its high winds and prodigious rainfall. William, however, was not to accompany them. Just before he was due to fly a new Blenheim Mark IV up to Scotland a telegram summoned him to a meeting in the Air Ministry. Willis and Hopson were also ordered to remain at Upwood; perhaps they would be sticking with their skipper.

It was June 1940, German forces had stormed through Poland, Holland and Belgium. Norway and Denmark had fallen under Hitler's yoke. France was on the brink of collapse and German generals were planning for a massive air attack on Britain to be followed by a full-scale invasion. William had not yet seen an enemy or fired a shot in anger. Why was he being diverted from his squadron? What on earth could the Ministry want with him?

He had taken a stopping train to London and, as it paused at the stations on the way, something odd struck him. He could not fathom what it was but there was something familiar somewhere. On the underground the feeling was even stronger – strong enough to be even disturbing. Changing trains at Leicester Square, it suddenly struck him. It was the handsome face staring at him out of posters and billboards all over England. The face belonged to none other than his old friend from Chelsea days, Jacky. In the poster Jacky was dressed in a black leather jacket and wore a flying helmet with goggles pushed up over his forehead. A silk scarf flew elegantly from his neck. He was helping an impossibly beautiful young blonde into a racy-looking aeroplane. The film was showing in cinemas all over Britain and the United States.

Chapter 6

Hans was surprised and annoyed to find out that he did not have an appointment to an operational squadron, but to the Foreign Ministry in Berlin. He was briefly interviewed by a senior diplomat and then the thunderbolt struck: "Lieutenant von Pilsen, you are to take up the appointment as assistant air attaché in London. You are to report to Ambassador von Ribbentrop in London one week from today." Hans was furious. He suspected his father had had a hand in this, taking him away from his friends and denying him a chance to fly in combat in order to mince about playing the diplomat so as to further his father's career in some way. He stormed out of the ministry and made for the nearest bar to drown his sorrows. Slumped over a table with a pot of lager, he was struck by a new thought. Angela. Wasn't she studying at Cambridge? That wasn't far from London. His mood began to change. He downed his lager, stood up straight, glanced at himself in the mirror on the wall and strode off to prepare for his journey.

The German Embassy in London in 1937 was not a happy establishment. Joachim von Ribbentrop, the ambassador, was described as a man who one only had to know to dislike intensely. He was routinely rude and discouraging to his inferiors, dishonest and insulting to tradesmen and devious in his dealings with his equals. Only one thing really mattered to him and that was to find new ways of flattering and pleasing Hitler. If the news was bad from the German point of view, he didn't report it. If things were not as Hitler expected, he would twist the report until they were. Above all he would somehow bend the story so as to emphasise the brilliant insights of the Fuhrer. Ribbentrop also totally misunderstood British society and where power lay within it. He had fawned on King Edward VIII and is even rumoured to have had an affair with the odious Mrs Simpson. He tried to cultivate parliamentarians and peers simply because they were rich or titled. He wormed his way into endless dinners and impressed his fellow diners only with his arrogance and stupidity. All this did not prevent him from being highly influential in Nazi circles; indeed it was widely expected that he would at some point become Minister of Foreign Affairs. It was for this reason that Hans' father, Albricht, had sought to ingratiate himself with this loathsome being by getting his son, so handsome, so wholesome and so typically German, into the embassy.

On arrival Hans had a brief and unpleasant meeting with the ambassador, then reported to Major von Stokenbach, the air attaché. The major turned out to be a man much more to his liking. He had distinguished himself as a fighter pilot in1917 on the western front and had become an expert on all aspects of military aviation. His brief to Hans was simple:

"You have two missions. The first is get to know as many people in the upper ranks of English society as you can so as to understand their thinking, especially about relations with Germany. The second is to find out as much as possible about radio detection systems. We know they have been working on a system of some sort. We have people working in the same sphere, and although I don't know any details, I am sure that we are ahead in this, but we need to know how far they have got. It is reported that your English is perfect and I can see that you will have no difficulty in establishing yourself in the best circles. Keep your eyes and ears open and ask questions. Something is bound to emerge."

The brief suited him fine. Angela could possibly introduce him into society and as for the radar, well, he would just have to see.

He couldn't have picked a better time to call Angela. His hasty postcard from Berlin had just arrived and when he telephoned, she was delighted. "Oh, I'm so glad. How wonderful. Look, I know it's short notice but can you come to a May Ball at Trinity on Saturday as my partner, my wretched brother, can't make it and we will be such a jolly party. There's going to be Freddy, the Marquis of Blakeney, young George Alresford and Selina, you know I told you about her, her father owns half of Devonshire? Oh, it would be such fun if you came."

What could be a better introduction to British society? And all at the embassy's expense.

The May Ball lived up to expectations. Angela was sweet and affectionate but at the same time did not fail to be charming to all the rest of the party. She had been at Cambridge for five years now, first as an undergraduate and then studying for her PhD in history and had an enormous circle of friends. She made a great effort to introduce Hans to as many people as possible so that his poor brain became overloaded trying to remember names, titles and interesting titbits. They danced, dined, danced again and punted dreamily up the Cam for breakfast at Grantchester. Hans thought he had never in his life been happier, or in more civilised company. He just loved the casual yet elegant atmosphere, the magnificent buildings, the odd sort of way in which these strange British people seemed to communicate, almost wordlessly or with forms of words that only they could interpret. On his part he attracted plenty of attention for his good looks, his ready humour and his courteous manner. He made no attempt to pump anyone for their political views, although he got the impression that these people were mostly strongly anti-war, unsurprisingly anti-communist and had a sneaking admiration for National Socialism. When asked about German affairs, he never had any difficulty in dodging awkward questions and diverting the conversation by telling stories about flying or about hunting in the forests. This was not an occasion for serious politics.

The following day was given over to sleeping, Hans in his hotel and Angela in her college, then a wonderful intimate dinner together in the evening in a quiet restaurant. They talked about the people they had met at the ball and what they did, then wandered together down The Backs and then all the way to the gates of Girton College, forbidden to men, kissing discreetly outside the gates as they said goodnight.

Angela had to work on her thesis the next day, and Hans could spend it alone in Cambridge. Wandering aimlessly around, he arrived at the Pickerel pub just outside Magdalene College and dropped in for a pint. One thing which astonished him about England was the warm, bitter beer and he never managed to develop a taste for it. Listening idly to the chatter at the bar he was suddenly brought out of his reverie by a nearby conversation.

"Yes," said one young man to his friend. "I spend a lot of time at Bawdsey now. We're working on a system to pick up radio frequency echoes. There's lots of Air Force people involved, but they need physics specialists to do the technical stuff. We go to the site every weekend and in the vac. They pay your expenses of course. Bawdsey Manor is certainly worth the visit. There is the lab work, of course, but there are wonderful tennis courts, and you can swim in the sea or play jolly games of cricket in the afternoon. And I really think we are onto something there. You know we can pick up aircraft miles away out to sea. They are going to start building towers and a proper aerial soon, and the physics is fascinating. You remember Keystone-Watts who was up a couple of years ago? Well, he's a leading light there now. If you are interested, I'll have a word and we'll see if we can get you in."

The conversation then drifted off into megacycles and kilowatts which Hans couldn't understand. But he had heard enough. Bawdsey Manor was going to have a visitor.

Stokenbach and Hans planned the next move. It was decided that Hans should take a seaside cottage in Suffolk for a month and sniff around to see what he could find out. His chief warned him to be careful. "Remember," he said, "you are a diplomat not a spy. There must be no question of break-ins or anything like that. Just listen and report back, that is our role, nothing more."

Shoreside Cottage nestled at the end of the village of Bawdsey itself, just over a mile from Bawdsey Manor. It belonged to Mrs Smithers, a widow who lived next door and used Shoreside as a nice little source of income during the summer. She looked after the cottage herself and provided a cooked breakfast and evening meal when asked. The perfect spot for a gentle summer holiday. You could walk along the cliffs northwards towards Orford or south to the river Deben which wound through woodland and fields up towards Woodbridge. Everywhere you looked, there was history. Martello Towers had guarded the coast from the supposed danger of attack by the French in the days of Napoleon. In the river, fierce battles had been fought against invading forces of Vikings and Danes. A few miles inland, at Sutton Hoo, a marvellous treasury of ancient jewellery lay waiting to be unearthed and, underfoot, the red cliffs concealed relics of a far far older time in the form of the fossilised remains of terrible prehistoric beasts. You could enjoy seaside or country walks, bathe in the sea, sail in the river, or watch the myriads of sea birds wheeling and calling overhead. The manor was a frequent topic of local conversation. There were all sorts of rumours as to what went on there; the local consensus was that it was being used to train spies. Certainly car loads of strange unmilitary-looking young men went in and out, and could be seen swimming off the private beach, playing cricket, and strolling in the grounds. They seldom visited any local pubs or cafés, and when they did they were remarkably silent about their work.

Hans liked Shoreside as soon as he saw it. Not only would it suit his official purpose, but it could perhaps be used to further his relationship with Angela. In those days it was unthinkable that an unmarried couple should share a holiday cottage, but if her brother was able to come too…? It went like clockwork. Rory, her younger brother, was a keen sailor and jumped at the possibility of a few weeks on the Deben. Angela herself was still in college, trying to write her thesis, and it was easy to convince her that a change of scene would make the work go better. Hans promised her that he would leave her alone most of the day, either sailing with Rory or – here he invented a new hobby for himself – looking for fossils in the clay cliffs. Mrs Smithers would provide the meals and the German Embassy would be paying most of the bills as the fossil hunt was disguised as an attempt to further cultural relations.

Hans arrived a week before the other two and started immediately on his work. He tried every trick he could think of to see inside the manor, but every possible access or viewpoint was blocked.

Soldiers and police were posted at the only entrance. Wire on the beach made it impossible to approach that way, and even when he hired a rowing boat from near the Felixstowe ferry, he found that a motor boat was on constant patrol offshore to ensure that passing craft kept their distance. Visiting the local pubs, hotels and cafes proved equally fruitless. The manor and its works seemed completely cut off from the outside world. This was disheartening, but towards the end of the week his mind was concentrated on other, non-military affairs.

The house had to be made fit for Angela. A typical German, Hans had high standards in respect of tidiness, much higher than those of Mrs Smithers. Everything had to be taken down, dusted and polished. Flowers had to be bought and placed in her room. Bath towels and swimming towels had to be procured. A work room had to be designated and suitably furnished, an old writing desk had to be borrowed from the Smithers household. Hans nearly ruptured himself moving the thing into its place in the new study. He even insisted on replacing the bedroom curtains so that they matched the bedspread. There were long consultations as to the content of the welcoming meal. Eventually a freshly caught local sea bass was procured and prepared for the table.

The first evening was wonderful. A calm, gentle dusk replaced a wet and windy day, and the three sat outside after their meal, enjoying a glass of port provided by Rory and listening to the steady beat of the gentle breakers on the beach. The men enjoyed cigars, and Angela sat relaxed and contented beside them, enjoying the wine and the delightful seaside air. She tried not to think about her thesis, (the subject was the influence of the renaissance scholar Erasmus on the reformation in Scandinavia) which was not going well. Rather, she let herself enjoy to the full the company of her beloved younger brother and this wonderful German man whom she adored. He was no equal to her in education or in intellect, but he had something about him which made her feel complete, secure. His powerful body, strong face and commanding but gentle manner gave him a degree of manliness, of authority, which she had never seen before. For all his seriousness he still had a delightful touch of humour and an ability to laugh at himself as heartily as he laughed at others. What more could a girl ask? Rory and Hans soon found common ground between them. Like Hans, Rory had been thrust into a legal career by his parents (Father was a High Court judge) and found the training inexpressibly boring. He loved the outdoors, sailing, hunting in winter and rock climbing in Wales and in the Alps. He longed for an excuse to escape from the law and do something more suited to his active nature. By bedtime he and his host had formed the basis of a firm friendship.

The days which followed were blissful for the two men. Rory had arranged to borrow a half-decked sailing boat from an old school friend and there were glorious days spent sailing up to Orford Ness, exploring the Deben and the muddy waters of the Orwell and the Stour. They caught fish, drank beer in most of the local pubs and bathed in the chilly North Sea. In the evenings they would be back to the cottage tired and hungry, but ready to drag Angela away from her books and down for a bathe or a game of tennis on a grass court belonging to a local big house which Mrs Smithers "did for". The only shadow over these blissful days was Angela's mood. She was working hard all day and seemed to be progressing. She was loving and thoughtful with Hans and obviously adored her brother, but something was wrong. She spent an inordinate amount of time poring over the newspapers, and after the others had gone to bed they often heard her moving about in her room, still trying to work or fiddling with the radio. She seemed obsessed with listening to the BBC news bulletins. She was often silent and preoccupied at meals. Increasingly, she looked tired and distraught when the boys came home. What could be the matter?

Hans had not altogether forgotten the purpose of his mission. He was forcefully reminded of it by the sight of a strange structure being erected in the grounds of the manor. It looked like the beginnings of a tower of some sort; it was certainly too tall to conceal behind the defences of the manor grounds. Making the excuse that he really must do some fossil hunting, he arranged for a couple of days by himself while Rory sailed single-handedly. First of all he went to a little stall on the beach and bought a few fossils and a handbook in case anyone asked him what he had been up to. Next, he found a site near the approach road to the manor where he could see what went in and out. He settled in comfortably, pretending now to be a bird watcher, equipped as he was with powerful binoculars. Several anonymous cars drove up and a couple of RAF wagons, then he noticed a rather battered Bedford lorry with the name of a building contractor painted on the side. A few minutes later another similar vehicle pulled into the gates. It seemed to be loaded with steel girders. Maybe this had something to do with the mysterious new structure. Patiently, Hans watched the road all day. No one seemed to have noticed him and his main difficulty was keeping alert and awake. At about five thirty in the afternoon, both trucks pulled out of the gate. Out of boredom more than anything else, he ran to his car and followed the two Bedfords down the road. To his delight they both pulled into a pub car park a few miles away and the drivers got out and seemed to be waiting for opening time. Noting the name of the company, J Newheart of Lowestoft, Hans thought he had done enough for the day and returned to the cottage. The next evening he made a visit to the same pub at opening time. Sure enough, the two trucks were parked outside with the drivers enjoying a refreshing beer before setting off home.

"Excuse me," began Hans. "Would you two be from Newhearts?"

"Yes, sir, we just come from Bawdsey."

"Ah, I wanted to catch you, you see I am thinking of building a small observation tower in my woodlands near Thetford and I was hoping to talk to someone who had worked in that sort of thing. I was told you were the experts."

"Don't know about experts, sir, but we got this job in Bawdsey and seems they wants a few more of these towers, some down London way. All we does is we digs the foundations and delivers the steelwork; they does all the rest themselves. But we could build one for you shouldn't wonder."

"It sounds as if you would be too busy to bother about my little job, but tell me, how high are these towers going to be? Another beer?"

"Don't mind if we do, sir, but I can't help you about the towers, all hush hush, sir, and we don't know anyway but judging by the foundations could be two hundred feet or more."

"Good lord, two hundred feet, and what are they for?"

"They says it's something to do with rays or something like that, but they don't tell us nothing see."

"Ah well, I have your address and phone number. Have a good run back to Lowestoft, I'll call you in a few months if my scheme goes ahead. Good evening to you."

Hans had all the information he needed.

The final evening at the cottage was planned as a celebration. A special meal was promised by Mrs Smithers, Rory borrowed a gramophone and some records and Hans was at great trouble to procure an excellent claret. Somehow, however, the festive spirit was lacking. The problem started when Angela got into a worry about her thesis. It was almost finished but she had just read it over and concluded that it was shallow, unconvincing and lacking in originality. "This is two years' work," she said plaintively, "and it's a complete farce. Oh, what a waste, what a terrible, terrible waste of time!" The boys could do nothing to comfort her. Then she buried herself in a newspaper. This was worse still.

"Just look what your Hitler is doing in Czechoslovakia!" she cried. "It can't go on, there has to be a war coming and, oh, Hans, you are in the air force; it will be your job to come over and bomb us! Oh, I feel so useless! The world is falling to pieces and all I can do is write this stupid rubbish. I can't bear it! I should never have met you; it was bound to end in tears." With this she flung herself on him, sobbing. Hans tried to be rational. He explained that the Fuhrer had no quarrel with England. He had assured his officers of this, all he wanted to do was to win back for the German people the lands and peoples that had been so unjustly taken away in 1919. Most sensible people sympathised with this. He loved her and nothing could change that. The quarrel went on and on, Angela

100

getting more desperate and emotional by the minute. Rory tried to divert her with her favourite record, and Hans tried to get her to dance, but she was furious now and stormed off to her room. Hans had never seen her like this. He went miserably to bed, hoping the morning would bring on a better mood.

It didn't. Angela was calm now, subdued almost, but couldn't even smile at Hans. It would be better, she said, if they did not see each other for a time, at least until the news was a bit better. She could not deny that she loved him but circumstances made their relationship impossible. Rory had a few brief words of comfort.

"She gets like this sometimes, old boy. She'll calm down after a bit then we'll see."

Back at the embassy, the crestfallen Hans had a long conference with Stokenbach and with the other military attachés. He had to go over his findings again and again, trying to remember every word said and every detail. What were these towers for? Perhaps it was an audio-location system, but that did not correspond with the conversation Hans had heard in the Pickerel. Perhaps it was some new sort of ray? No, that was scientific nonsense. Perhaps it was a chain of direction-finding radio beacons, but surely those existed already, and there would be no need for so many of them so close together. It must be radio location, and this must be reported immediately to Berlin; meanwhile, all intelligence sources available must try to find out more.

Hans himself and Stokenbach were summoned to Berlin as soon as their report reached the Luftwaffe headquarters. By that time they had developed some firm conclusions between themselves. The meeting was to be with two generals in the air defence section, but it so happened that Goering himself and Milch, the technical chief of the Luftwaffe, were in the building and chose to sit in and listen. First Hans talked through his evidence then Stokenbach presented his conclusions.

"I believe," he concluded, "that the British have made great progress with this technology in recent years. The towers are being built to act as antennae for a network of radars which will cover the whole of south eastern England. Using signals from them, they will be able to identify a threatened attack well before the aircraft cross the Channel or the North Sea. They will then deploy their defensive fighters to meet the threat."

Fat, jovial and confident as ever, Goering laughed at the conclusion.

"Well done, Stokenbach," he chuckled. "You've only confirmed what we already know. The British are trying to keep pace with certain Luftwaffe developments, but don't worry, we are well ahead. Our radars will detect any aircraft which ever approaches our airspace and it will immediately be destroyed. As I have already said publically no enemy aircraft will ever intrude into the airspace of the Reich. We have nothing to fear from British radar. But well done, both of you. You confirm our beliefs."

Stokenbach was not satisfied. Goering obviously hadn't comprehended the whole scope of Chain Home, as the British system was called. He tried to argue, but Goering waved him away. He focused instead on Hans.

"Have we not met before, Von Pilsen?" Hans assented. "And I remember you were training as a Stuka pilot. Why are you not in a front-line unit today?"

Hans pretended not to know.

"Well, you have done a good job as a diplomat, now by my orders you are to return to your unit. We are going to need young men like you soon, especially in the Stuka squadrons. I will see that you are promoted to Oberleutnant immediately. Leave diplomacy to old soldiers like Stokenbach here. Dismiss."

Hans was not sorry to leave the embassy. Now that Angela was out of reach, at least for the time being, he relished the thought of joining his comrades again and doing some serious flying. If Goering was so blasé about his intelligence gathering, it was doubtless because he knew a lot more about the situation than Stokenbach. Forget all that and back to the squadron.

Goering had certainly been right about the Stuka squadrons. He was welcomed back to the Immelmann Groupe heartily. To his annoyance, they all had tales to tell about their exploits in Spain, and he was the only pilot who did not have operational experience. He had only stories of diplomatic parties and mixing with the English aristocracy. However, his flying skills were not as rusty as he had feared and he was soon established as leader of a schwarm of four aircraft. Most importantly, he had selected an excellent crewman Feldwebel Stokmann, a tough, reliable and unflappable colleague. The Gruppe had been issued with new aircraft since its return from Spain, the JU 87B-1 with twice the power and much better air-to-air armament than the original aircraft. With this mount they felt they could cope with any opposition.

And so it proved in Poland. When the war broke out in September 1939, the Polish air force was equipped with P11c fighters, obsolescent high-wing fixed undercarriage machines, which were no match for the Luftwaffe. They were soon shot out of the sky or destroyed on the ground. The Polish army put up a stout resistance, but whenever the Poles concentrated to repel an advance or to counter attack, in would scream the Stukas, smashing down with their bombs and their guns, destroying transport, disabling artillery and hurling tanks into the ditch. This was a concept evolved uniquely in Germany. They used aircraft as long-range artillery clearing the way for the blitzkrieg. It was horrifyingly effective. Hans' schwarm was especially busy, flying four or five missions every day, inflicting devastating blows on Polish armour and communications. This was far more like proper combat than the largely unopposed action which the Gruppe had known in Spain, where it had mostly been bombing infantry trenches or built-up areas. Here you could see great masses of enemy material disabled with each attack. Hans felt a savage elation after each successful sortie; this was what he had trained for and he knew he was good at it. He revelled in the comradeship of his schwarm and never failed to encourage and share his successes with the ground crews, who were working frantically all hours to keep the aircraft in the air. As for Angela, he tried not to think too much about her. He had been wrong about the possibility of war between Britain and Germany, but even so it seemed likely that the Fuhrer would find a way of making peace with Britain as soon as his objectives in Poland had been achieved. Soon relations would be restored and he could see her again. Thank God he had not had to bomb England, and there didn't seem to be much chance of his having to do so. Soon enough he would be able to see her again, and all her worries would be over. Letter writing was of course impossible while the war was on, but he was confident that she would be waiting for him.

Luftwaffe casualties in Poland were few and all objectives were achieved more rapidly than anyone had dared to hope. As Germany closed its jaws on western Poland, the Soviet Union, by arrangement with the Nazis, helped itself to the eastern provinces of that unhappy country. France and Britain took almost no part in the fighting.

The collapse of Poland in September gave Hans' Gruppe a chance to relax and take some winter leave at home. He found his parents rejoicing in the brilliant successes achieved by the Reich and in the wisdom and foresight of Hitler. As a front line pilot he found it rather pathetic to see his parents so uncritically devoted to the Fuhrer. Did they not remember that he had predicted no war with Britain? Why was any rational discussion with them now impossible? They were, of course, delighted to show their son off whenever possible, and constantly forced him to recite over and over again his account of his experiences at the front. He felt rather like a prize bull at a show, and soon became tired of playing the German hero. He was quite glad when it was time to return to his duties.

There was plenty to do. After his success in Poland, Hitler sought to secure his supplies of iron ore from northern Scandinavia. This precious war material travelled by ship through the Baltic during the summer months, and here it was reasonably safe, but in winter, when the Baltic was frozen over, it had to be taken by rail to terminals in Norway and then shipped down through the chain of islands known as the Norwegian Leads, to a port in Germany or in occupied Poland. There were signs that Britain and France were going to attempt to close this route and starve Germany of vital raw material. In a lightning stroke German forces occupied Denmark and then moved relentlessly on to occupy the whole of Norway, throwing aside the feeble resistance of the surprised Norwegian armed forces and hurling an ill-prepared Allied intervention force back whence it came. This bold move was accomplished with very little fighting, but the Stukas were on hand to harry enemy shipping and to soften up any military concentration which seemed likely to offer resistance. It was a brilliant campaign, skilfully executed. No sooner had it been successfully concluded than the might of the Luftwaffe was redeployed and ordered to ready itself for some serious fighting – the assault on France was about to begin.

Chapter 7

William simply had to see Jacky. He had some time to wait before his appointment at the Ministry and he spent it in a call box, trying to run his old pal to earth. He tried all the main hotels without success then remembered that the Garrick Club had always been something of a mecca for most of the young RADA folk. He got through and, after some annoying obstruction, he was put through to the star himself. A meeting was arranged for that evening in their old haunt, The Royal Dragoon. "Listen," Jacky had said. "There is this awful bore of fans all over the place. I'll have to come in a big hat with my face covered up somehow or we'll get no peace. I'm so glad you rang, I've so much to ask you."

At the Ministry William found himself shunted into a little meeting room which seemed to have been chosen for its airlessness and obscurity. It occurred to him that this might have something to do with another secret project. He sat there gloomily anticipating a long stint of boring test flights when Hugh Wesley, closely followed by Kilowatt, came bursting into the room. It was amusing to see that Hugh was now decked out in an RAF uniform – he was a Squadron Leader, no less – but he looked just as awkward and untidy in uniform as he had in civilian clothes. "They made me join up," he explained. "I think it was because they wanted to start ordering me about, and they knew I'd do my own thing in my own way if I was still a civilian." The three chatted about nothing much until they were joined by two senior officers, an Air Commodore and Group Captain. The Group Captain called the meeting to order.

"Mr Keystone-Watts," he said. "Will you please tell the meeting about your night vision project?"

"Ah," began Kilowatt. "In the early days of the radar development project we once tried fitting a radar into a Heyford bomber. You'll remember that, William? Good, well, we got it to work after a fashion, then shelved the project. Now, however, Fighter Command is convinced that Jerry is going to have a go at night bombing our cities. Perhaps not for a month or two, we expect it to start when the nights get longer – perhaps in October or November. We are afraid they will be able to do it quite accurately because we think that they have been developing a system which enables their bombers to fly along radio beams which tell them where they are and when to drop their loads. Now, it's almost impossible to intercept bombers at night using the Chain Home radar system. We've been trying for some time but so far only one has been shot down in this way. You see, Chain Home can only guide the fighter to a spot a few miles from the intruder, and he'll hardly ever see it in the dark. What we can now do is to use ground radars to feed information into a system we call a Plan Position Indicator which will get the fighter within three or four miles of the intruder. The difficult bit is the final stage of the interception. What we have been trying to do for this is to fit a radar set in the nose of a fighter so he can sniff out the enemy from a few miles away, get within range and destroy him. Of course, the radar has to be relatively low-powered so its range will be only five miles at best, and, as you will know, radar has a minimum range too, because the echo signal begins to get confused with the pulsed transmission if it's too close, so the last few seconds of the attack will require visual contact. Airborne intercept, as we call it, is not perfect, but it's the best chance we have of developing a useful night fighter. If we can't use fighters at night, there's really no other effective way of protecting our cities. Just think of the horror that would bring."

The Air Commodore broke in:

"We have given some thought to the aircraft we can use for radar-assisted night fighting. There are several new types under development, but for now there is only one machine readily available for use – the Blenheim. I know it's no faster than the German bombers and that's going to make interception difficult but it's Hobson's choice I'm afraid. I believe that you, Portman, have been trained on the Blenheim? Good, well, the fighter version is much the same as the bomber, but it has a four-gun pack under the nose, and of course the bits and pieces of radar gear. The reason why you are here, Portman," he went on, "is that you have experience in test flying, and I believe you understand radar, at least in outline. When Squadron Leader Wesley here suggested you to run some operational tests on the night fighter, and I saw that you were training on Blenheims, I had to agree with him. You will be based at Tangmere and will carry out trials of the new interception system. If it works, a new dedicated night fighter squadron will be formed, and I should imagine that you will be part of it. There is already a small night fighter development team operating there so you will be joining the team. Any questions?"

"Yes, sir, can I keep my existing crew? We've been together for six months now and trained together on the Blenheim."

There seemed to be some doubt about this. Radar-guided attacks would require an observer who understood the system and was intelligent enough to make use of it. Also the gunner, Hopson, would need to train as a dedicated radar operator. William sang Willis's praises as a navigator and explained how quick he had been to get to grips with the sextant and celestial navigation. As for Hopson, he was bright enough, but a radar operator? Well, at least no one else had much experience in the role, he might make a success of it. In the end William got his way. When the meeting broke up he was able to grab a quick lunch with Hugh and Kilowatt, although they both claimed that they were rushed off their feet by the demands of the war. His two friends could not tell William much about their work, but they were clearly enthusiastic about the night fighter project. William was slightly resentful that, once again, Hugh, in his muddled way, seemed to be calling the shots as regards his career, but there was hardly time to address the matter during their brief meal.

William's posting to Tangmere was dated three days after the meeting in the Ministry. He determined to spend the time in London rather than travel up to Tyneside on the crowded wartime trains. It was springtime and the city by day was decorated as usual by the blossom in the parks and the early green leaves on the trees.

There had been very little warlike activity at that stage, although the blackout was rigidly enforced during the hours of darkness, and uniforms were everywhere in the streets. Shops and cinemas were open as usual, although the goods available in shops were now strictly limited and rationed. Everyone carried a little haversack containing a gas mask. After an afternoon wandering around drinking in the atmosphere, William still had a couple of hours before his meeting with Jacky and to fill the time he decided to take a cup of tea in a Lyons Corner House. He took a table in a corner and sat down with his evening paper. He did not actually see the girls come in, but he could not miss their chattering as they took the table next to him. They were trainee nurses, all dressed in hospital uniform and looking incredibly lovely. He stood up and made a futile attempt to help them with their chairs, in the process dropping his uniform cap on the floor and recovering it, red-faced. The girls were delighted to find themselves involved with an RAF officer sporting a pilot's wings on his chest and begged him to join them. Introductions were quickly made. He found himself pressed into telling the girls what it was like to fly an aeroplane in wartime (mostly pretty boring), and they talked about their life in hospital. They were all educated, well-bred girls and had volunteered to train so as to become members of the QAIMNS, the Queen Alexandra's Imperial Military Nursing Service. Nurses in this service were all from upper-class backgrounds and once qualified they enjoyed officer status, but they were expected to work hard, doing menial tasks on the wards and supervising junior medical staff. The girls had almost completed their training and were eagerly awaiting their first postings. They had an evening off today and were planning to use it seeing a film. "You see," said the most talkative of them, whose name William discovered was Angela. "It has Jacky Simple in it and he's sooooo beautiful."

William nearly fell off his chair. Could he let them in on the details of his next appointment? Well, perhaps he could.

"I know Jacky well," he burst out. "We used to see a lot of each other in London years ago when I was at the Slade and he was at RADA. I haven't seen him for some time though."

"What? You know him? Oh, how I'd love to meet him. He's so attractive, and brave too; they say he does all his flying himself. Most actors they have stunt men to do that for them."

Angela was quite carried away, then suddenly she remembered Hans and his flying, and she looked at William's uniform.

"Oh God, what a tragedy it all is," she whimpered.

The remark froze the conversation. Not another word passed from her lips until it was time for them to go. She sat broodingly silent, thinking how things might have been if it wasn't for this bloody war. William sensed her unhappiness; at one moment she had been so lively and full of joy, but now so downcast. She was the most exciting, the most vibrant girl he had ever met, and so beautiful in her immaculate uniform, but there was something gnawing at her that he did not understand and he felt a longing to get closer. Leaving the Corner House, he seized a moment to confront her.

"Look, Angela, are you doing anything after the film? No? Then meet me in the theatre bar at the Odeon Leicester Square at ten. I may be able to arrange something. Come on, it'll be fun, but you'll have to come by yourself; it'll be impossible if you bring your friends."

Arriving at the Royal Dragoon William bought himself a pint and waited. The wait was not long. A bar waiter came over to him and whispered. "Mr Portman, sir? I have a message for you from a friend." He handed him a scrap of paper. "The Ritz, quick as you can, room 257." Taxis were still running and William sped to the Ritz.

"Room 257?" The desk clerk looked doubtfully at him. "Do you have an appointment?" For once William was rude and short-tempered.

"Yes, and what has that got to do with you?" he snapped.

"Mr Simple is not to be disturbed this evening."

"I'll disturb Mr Simple, all right, take me there right away."

"Your name, sir?"

A phone call later and William was ushered into the hallowed room. Jacky had put on weight since William had last seen him, but he was the same decent, direct fellow and still as amazingly handsome as ever, with slow, easy, graceful movements and a languid, but somehow watchful manner.

"William, wonderful to see you. Whisky? Good. So sorry about the change of venue but my bloody minders refused to let me out by myself in London. Said it would break my contract. You see, I have to put in an official appearance on the day after tomorrow at some "do" or other and I am supposed to have just stepped off the plane from the US. Take my tip, old boy, never get into films. Anyway, I desperately needed to see you, I heard you were in the RAF, but first tell me what you have been up to."

William filled him in as far as he could.

"Well, the thing is," went on Jacky, "I'm probably a fool, but I feel I have got to do something for my country, England, so I'm giving up this film business for a bit, and I've written to the RAF to see if they'll have me. They say 'Yes please'. The studio is furious, of course, but my attorney tells me that there is a clause in my contract which lets me pull out in the circumstances. I've got four hundred flying hours in my log book, mostly in the States and I'm sure I could be useful somehow. Also, with due modesty, I think my joining the fight may have some impact on public opinion in the States. Back there they all think you're beaten already, you know. What I really need now is someone who can fill me in about life in the RAF. Can you help?"

"I'll do what I can."

"Oh thanks, William, now how about some dinner? We have a special arrangement here so in spite of the rationing we can get quite a decent steak, how about it?"

The steak duly consumed, William began to wonder what he could do about the meeting with Angela, so hastily arranged. He was desperate to see her again and, what with the war and postings coming up, this might be the only chance. He shared the problem with his old friend.

"Hell, but we haven't finished talking yet," exclaimed Jacky, "and there you are after this girl you've only just met. Tell you what. Elmer here, my sort of sidekick, he'll run up to Leicester

Square and find her. He's good at that sort of thing, then she can join us here."

William was a bit anxious about the arrangement. Would she come? Would Jacky bowl her over to such an extent that he himself would be forgotten? Anyway, off Elmer set and Jacky started quizzing him in detail about life in the RAF. When did he have to salute? How should he address various ranks? How much free time would he get? Had William flown a Spitfire (he hadn't)? What training would he need before getting into combat? The two were still deep in conversation when a flustered Angela was ushered into the room. She was at first dumbstruck to be in the presence of the great film star himself, but he put her at her ease, and she was soon showing her usual gaiety and charm, quizzing him about Hollywood, his life, the various girls he had worked with and the films he had been in. William began to feel a bit out of the conversation but, to his delight, she flashed him the occasional smile and actually winked once or twice when Jacky said something outrageous. As the chatter went on and the drinks kept coming, a curious thought struck him. This was Jacky performing an act he had done many times before and he had perfected it. He wasn't really interested in Angela at all. Perhaps he wasn't interested in any girls ever. He was just an actor doing his stuff.

It was after midnight when the party broke up. William and Jacky arranged a lunch meeting the following day to talk further about service matters and William was left to escort Angela back to the grotty Bayswater hotel where she and her colleagues were billeted. There were almost no taxis left on the streets, but it was a fine warm night and they decided to walk the mile or so. William never forgot that walk. Angela was elated, walking on air, thrilled by the meeting with her hero. But there seemed to be something else. She was willing to laugh at some of the things he had said; but she was not infatuated by his personality. She seemed to regard William as her ally in the whole affair, the miraculous person who had arranged for her to meet him and whom she actually preferred to be with. Hands were held tightly as they sauntered along the deserted streets and talk came easily, naturally. Reaching the door of the hotel, nothing seemed more natural than an embrace and a long, gentle kiss which lifted William onto a plane of happiness and desire which he had never before experienced. This girl – he had only known her for a few hours – but she was now the most important thing in his life. How could he possibly wait until tea time tomorrow when they would meet again?

Jacky had had an early meeting with someone from the Air Ministry and had been told that he was to be posted to an advanced training unit in south Wales. It appeared that half a dozen other US recruits had turned up and they were to be trained together with some escapees from Poland, Czechoslovakia and France before being posted to operational squadrons. In spite of being over thirty years old, he would then be posted to a fighter squadron (most fighter pilots were in their teens or early twenties). It seemed that the RAF was going to try to make a propaganda success out of him. William was a little concerned that Jacky might have overstated his flying skills at his interview but he said nothing about it as the two friends talked over lunch. Then it was time to go to meet Angela again.

"Boy, that chick sure does something to you," said Jacky. He sure was right.

Tea with Angela was taken in a quiet café in Shepherd's Market. She was lovely as always and bursting with news. "We've had our postings! I have to leave for Southampton the day after tomorrow. No details but the rumour has it that I'll be on a Med bound hospital ship. Isn't it exciting!"

It was altogether too exciting for William's taste; he wanted this wonderful girl safe in England. Anything could happen to a hospital ship. But Angela was eager to talk. She told him all about her PhD, and how she had abandoned it for nursing. She was so much happier, she said, doing something really useful. The more she talked the more he loved her. He felt sympathy with all her aspirations and her worries. They sat and chatted regardless of time until the café closed and it was time to saunter off to find some dinner. Angela herself could not explain why she felt so at home with this RAF officer. He was calm, kind and somehow sympathetic, but she also detected a trace of vulnerability. He was a little hesitant when giving orders to the waiter, for example, and his slightly unsteady gaze seemed to suggest a man not entirely confident in himself, one who needed understanding, yes – and love.

Suddenly, over dinner, something went wrong. Maybe it was sparked by the far-off wail of an air raid siren. Perhaps it was the crisp note of a fighter zooming overhead. There was no air raid, but without warning, Angela started to sob quietly into her handkerchief. William bent anxiously towards her.

"No, I'm sorry. It's nothing," she gulped." It's just that…"

William seized her hand.

"What, my darling, what is it? There's nothing to be afraid of."

"No no, I'm not afraid of anything, it's just that… Oh well, I must tell you, you're bound to find out anyway. I had a boyfriend just before the war. Hans was his name and he was a German airman. Oh, he was sweet and kind, rather like you, darling, but I just couldn't go on with him. His job was to bomb this country. How could I possibly have got involved? But he seemed only a boy, so unsophisticated and innocent in a way. I'm supposed to be intelligent and yet I think I fell in love with him, for a time anyway. Him, a bomber pilot. Oh, how could I have been such a fool?"

In the days and months that were to come, William could not get this German out of his mind. How dare he intrude on his Angela? Who did he think he was, parading about in England? How could a Luftwaffe officer possibly be sweet and charming? He loathed this man he had never seen and raged inwardly against him. With luck, he consoled himself, he was at that very moment being shot out of the sky by some avenging Hurricane.

In spite of all this the meal finished pleasantly enough and there was another blissful walk home through the darkened streets. He could not see his love the next day, as he had arranged a visit to godfather Flopsy in the East End, but he would see her off on her train on the following day.

The platform at Waterloo was crowded with nursing officers and their families. William pushed his way through the crowd to find Angela talking to an elderly couple whom he took to be her parents. A young man was with them; he was in the uniform of a Second Lieutenant in the Hampshire Regiment. Who was he? Another ex-boyfriend? The matter was soon settled when he was introduced as her brother, Rory. He had come up on the train from Winchester to see Angela off. It was a little awkward meeting the family in these circumstances. He wished he had been alone with his love, but she was ebullient and excited, occasionally giving his hand a secret squeeze. The whistle went and the train pulled out of the station, leaving the four standing forlornly on the platform. "How strange," said Rory to William. "Here we are, trained to fight but standing safely in London while Angela, an academic and a nurse, is being whisked away into a war zone." It was not a tactful remark. His father, Sir Felix Pointer, a high court judge, swallowed hard and hid his face and Lady Pointer gave way to a fit of quiet, persistent sobbing. Rory had an hour to wait for his train and he and William repaired to a dingy station bar to wait.

"She told me that you had talked together about her German friend," Rory said over his beer.

"Yes, did you meet him?"

"I did, actually. Hans and I spent two weeks together and I have to say that I found him charming; although he was a Prussian, he was not at all the typical German officer. He was quite amusing and good company. Good sailor, too. The family lived in a castle somewhere near the Polish border, I think."

A strange thought came into William's head. A Prussian? Living in a castle? Called Hans?

"You don't know his surname, do you?"

"Yes, I remember it because it means something like mushroom, I believe. It was von Pilsen."

Von Pilsen! This must be his cousin, Albricht's son. William turned quite white. He had to make an excuse and leave the bar to recover. After two minutes he staggered back to his new friend.

"Are you feeling all right, old boy? Maybe this beer is a bit off. I thought it tasted funny."

"I'm OK, but I just remembered I have to be at a meeting in fifteen minutes, all the best, nice meeting you, take care." With that, William was off to brood over the horrific thought that Angela had been, perhaps even still was, in love with his first cousin.

Chapter 8

Jacky's career as an RAF officer started later that same week. His colleagues were a mixed bunch; some of the Czechs and Poles were already experienced pilots and only needed a brief introduction to British procedures and fighting technique. The Americans were mostly leisure flyers with only a few solo hours. He himself had handled all sorts of aircraft and performed mock battles and stunt flying in everything from World War One biplanes to modern Curtiss fighters, but almost all his experience had been in sunny California, mostly in cloudless skies, very different from the grey clouds and rainstorms of Wales. After a few circuits in a Harvard trainer, his instructor led him over to one of the Spitfires standing outside the hangar. He showed him the controls and talked for a few minutes about handling the machine. "You'll have no trouble with her in the air," he said, "but remember that you can't see in front of you when taxiing. You just have to weave from side to side to see where you are going. The undercarriage is narrow and not too strong. We lose more machines on the ground than in the air, but I can see you're a pretty fair pilot, just take it gently."

"He was certainly right about taxiing," thought Jacky as he wove his way unsteadily to the end of the runway. He felt more than a little scared as he got a green from the control tower and opened the throttle. The noise and power of the Merlin engine were terrifying as the plane accelerated bumpily down the runway. Then she was off. The sensation was fantastic. This aircraft was something much, much more than a machine. It seemed to know where he meant it to go before he even moved the controls. It responded eagerly and willingly to his every command with precise, elegant movements. He came in to land and put her down perfectly, exactly where he wanted. The instructor climbed up onto the wing.

"OK?" he asked.

"Great."

"Well, then, take her up again, throw her about a bit, try some aerobatics, see how you get on."

The love affair between man and machine blossomed. Jacky spent a glorious hour throwing the Spit about the sky, playing with the clouds, looping, rolling and pulling the tightest turns he had ever done. If this was life in the RAF give me more of it, he thought.

Before the terrible pilot losses of the Battle of Britain, the RAF thought it had enough fighter pilots and there was not much pressure on the advanced training units to rush men through their courses. Jacky and his colleagues spent ten weeks in Wales learning about the machines, their engines, their armament, practising air gunnery and combat tactics. During those ten weeks, German forces stormed through the Low Countries and Eastern France. The Dunkirk evacuation took place and Fighter Command found itself thrust into the position of the sole defender of Britain from the threatened onslaught of the Wehrmacht. Aircraft were now being produced in sufficient quantities but gradually losses over France and in the defensive battles over southern England drained away trained aircrew so quickly that the training establishments, including half-trained pilots, instructors, and administration staff, found themselves drafted into the front line. Sometimes poor fellows with only ten hours experience on single seaters found themselves trying to survive in front-line squadrons. Jacky's intake of assorted foreigners therefore turned out to be in better shape than many of the new British recruits to Fighter Command. He himself was posted to a squadron based near Salisbury, which was responsible for defence of Portland and Southampton. The mess of 609 Squadron was friendly and hospitable. Of course, Jacky's reputation as a film star was known to all and sundry but he had become adept at keeping a low profile, taking jokes about himself and not flashing his wealth around.

Though he was by far the oldest pilot officer in the squadron, he neither expected nor received any special treatment. His first three operational flights he flew as wing man to a twenty-year-old Flight Lieutenant, Arthur Wadkin. Wadkin had flown Hurricanes throughout the Battle of France and the Dunkirk evacuation. He was a steady, cautious pilot, that's how he had survived those terrible months, but he also had four confirmed kills to his credit. Jacky was wise enough to follow his lead closely. "Your job," said Arthur, "is to watch my tail and keep as close as possible. We'll lose each other as the scrap develops of course but try to keep close. If Jerry is around, two things are vital. Keep looking in your mirror and never, never, fly straight. An Me109 is faster than you at altitude and they come out of the sun at a rate of knots. Fly straight just for ten seconds and they'll have you on toast." The first three operations were uneventful. Radar vectored them onto some attacking bombers but in all three cases the enemy had dropped their load and turned for home long before 609 got anywhere near them.

The fourth sortie was different. Two formations of bombers were detected heading for Southampton and it seemed that above them there was a swarm of fighters. 609 scrambled and climbed on full power to intercept the bombers. Height is everything in air-to-air fighting. Jacky had to concentrate hard to keep close with Arthur's wing tip. It was far from easy to fly in tight formation and at the same time keep a good lookout for the enemy. After fifteen minutes Arthur spotted the little black dots ahead which were the Dorniers, flying impassively on towards their target in perfect order. They were a little above the Spitfires, and below them huge formations of white cloud were spread out in the sunlight like gigantic eiderdowns. The squadron went for a beam attack. "Stay close!" yelled Arthur as the ugly black crosses on the fuselages became visible, then even louder, "Pull out, dive like hell." His sharp eyes had spotted in his mirror fifty or so tiny dots directly behind him, an overwhelming number of enemy fighters screaming down on them and closing rapidly. Down plummeted the Spitfires into the clouds below pursued by bursts of gunfire from behind. Jacky lost sight of his leader as they both plunged into the safety of the cloud cover. He kept diving downwards, hoping to make contact again when he came out into clear air. In its dive the Spitfire's speed built up alarmingly. Four hundred, four hundred and fifty, four hundred and seventy miles per hour, the airframe began to shudder and the engine raced madly. He must pull out or he'd be into the ground. He burst out of cloud at about five hundred feet, hauling back on the joystick with all his strength. Such a pull out would have wrenched the wings off most aircraft, but the Spit levelled off gracefully. Jacky felt the blood drain from his upper body and saw nothing but blackness in front of his eyes for a few seconds, then he was again alert and speeding over the Hampshire countryside. Looking down, he saw an airfield below him and from it rose a column of ugly black smoke. He could see aircraft scattered over the ground and orange fires burning. Ahead of him two black dots were silhouetted against the green down land, flying low and fast southwards towards the Channel. The Spitfire was rapidly overhauling the dots ahead and they soon transformed themselves into ugly aircraft with sharply cranked wings and a single engine. Stukas!

The Stukas had attacked the airfield in a steep, screaming dive and hit it fair and square, cratering the runway and scattering aircraft and men with the blast. Now they were making for home, keeping low and hoping to avoid the ack-ack. The gunner in the hindmost machine had, like Jacky, lost consciousness as the aircraft pulled out of the dive and was still fuddled when he saw the menacing shape of Jacky's plane rapidly catching up. He yelled to his pilot and fired burst after burst towards his enemy, but his own aircraft was now swerving violently and his aim was wide. Jacky managed to get a long burst into the Stuka from close astern. He saw bits fly off the plane then it banked sharply and plunged downward onto a field below where it burst into flame. Madly excited by his success, Jacky looked ahead for the other machine. There she was, still hedge-hopping desperately towards the sea. This pilot was obviously more experienced than his colleague. His wheels were almost on the ground as he plunged over hedges and telegraph wires, hoping the Spitfire would be unable to follow him. If there was one aspect of flying that Hollywood had taught Jacky it was flying spectacularly close to the ground. He banked, turned and zoomed over obstructions, drawing ever closer to his quarry. The two shot over the coastline near Chichester, and now Jacky was able to fire a succession of short bursts each time the Stuka crossed his sights. A trail of black smoke began to sprout from the machine and it was clearly in trouble. Jacky was now close behind and had it firmly in his sights. He pressed the gun button. Nothing. He was out of ammo. Furious, he kept on its tail until the French coast was almost beneath him, cursing wildly at his guns, the Stuka, and life in general. At the last minute he glanced at his fuel gauges. Almost empty. One last glance towards his victim, and he saw it plunging towards the sea as he turned for home.

Oberleutnant von Pilsen never knew how he managed to put the stricken Stuka down on the surface of the Channel with a seized engine. Stukas trying to land on water normally tripped over their undercarriage and somersaulted. Somehow Hans splashed down safely and on an even keel. He climbed out onto the wing. Feldwebel Stokmann was bleeding profusely from a wound in the shoulder but he was still conscious, and Hans was able to get him out of the plane and into the tiny dinghy. The Luftwaffe had cleverly provided a line of brightly coloured rafts along the French coast for use in just such circumstances. Hans could see one a short distance from the wreck and paddled towards it, watching his aircraft sink gracelessly in the calm water. He was strangely sorry to see it go. This was the very machine which had carried him safely through the Battle of France, blasting enemy tank concentrations and supply convoys. A few miles to the east of his present position, he had hurled it down on a British destroyer trying to evacuate the broken British army from Dunkirk. The destroyer had filled the air with flak, but it is difficult for even the most experienced gunner to hit a target diving vertically from overhead, and Hans had seen his bomb crash through her deck just aft of the funnel, and watched her capsize, a burning wreck, in less than two minutes. This new assault on the south of England, he mused, was a different story. Hitherto the Stukas had been fighting in an environment where they had air superiority. Enemy fighters had been kept at bay by the devastating superiority of the Messerschmitts, but over England things were more difficult. Spitfires and Hurricanes appeared in alarming numbers and seemed undeterred by the fighters escorting the Stukas. Losses had been five, ten, fifteen percent on each raid and destruction at this rate was simply unsustainable. Better leave the bombing of England to the high-level machines and keep the Stukas for the time when the RAF had been grounded. That wouldn't take long. He had been assured by his commander that fifty to one hundred British fighters were being downed every day. As soon as they were all gone, his Gruppe could decimate what was left of the British army as they had the Poles and the French.

Sitting damp and dishevelled on the raft awaiting rescue by motorboat, Hans looked forward with enthusiasm to the day when the British would eventually see sense and come to terms. Then, perhaps there would be a chance to see Angela again.

Jacky returned to his squadron with two confirmed kills. Not bad for a beginner.

Exactly a week after his first triumph, Jacky and Hugo, a Fleet Air Arm pilot drafted into the battle from his aircraft carrier, took off to intercept bandits (enemy aircraft) approaching over the Isle of Wight. Radar guided them accurately towards the intruders, which seemed to consist of about twelve Dornier bombers escorted by Me109s flying high above them. The two Spitfires managed to work their way round behind the Dorniers before they were spotted by the fighters and were able to make a stern attack out of the sun. Just before Jacky opened fire, the rear gunner of a Dornier saw him and must have yelled at his pilot to take evasive action as he opened fire on Jacky's machine. Too late. As the Dornier began its last, desperate turn, fire from the Spitfire's eight machine guns poured into its belly and it rolled over on its side then blew up in a horrific sheet of orange flame. Jacky felt debris striking his aircraft and dived quickly for cloud to get some cover from the avenging Messerschmitts. In the relative safety of the cloud, he checked his aircraft for any damage caused by flying through the wreck of the Dornier. He noticed a rise in engine temperatures which gave warning of a coolant leak. Closing the throttle to reduce damage to the engine, he managed to slip away and land safely. His third kill was confirmed.

The very next day the whole squadron was scrambled to deal with a large enemy formation approaching Southampton. A squadron of Hurricanes was directed to attack the bombers while the faster, more agile, Spitfires kept the fighters at bay. Sure enough, as soon as 609's aircraft came in sight of the great aerial armada a flight of Me109s came streaking down on them from far above the bombers. A furious melee ensued with machines turning, diving, whirling and zooming upwards, desperately trying to get an enemy in their sights. Jacky was sweating and swearing in his cockpit, throwing his machine about the sky with abandon. This was the sort of fighting he had always hoped for, man against man in equal combat. Slamming in a violent turn towards an enemy who crossed his path, he got in a short burst which left it plunging downwards, pouring black smoke. Looking for another victim, he suddenly heard a voice in his headphones. "Jacky, break right break right!" Perhaps if he had been a younger man, his reactions would have been quick enough, but at thirty-two he was a fraction of a second too slow. Out of the sun roared four more 109s in a steep power dive. Two of them poured a deadly fire into Jacky's machine which broke clean in half with the impact of the blast. The front section careered downwards, engine screaming in its death throes. As it fell, bits and pieces of the fighter became mingled with those of a stricken Heinkel bomber, a victim of one of the Hurricanes. The two wrecks smashed together into the chalky hillside below, their structures bent and charred metal, their crews nothing but shredded and burnt flesh. Jacky, beautiful Jacky, was gone forever.

Gone but not forgotten. Dead, Jacky did more for the British cause than he could possibly have achieved alive. Newspapers, radio programmes and newsreels all over the US were soon fed with the story. The heroic deeds of the movie star turned fighter pilot were told time and again as every household in America was reminded of his handsome face, his daring deeds and his devotion to the cause of freedom. Americans, especially the women, who had been strenuously isolationist and anti-war, began to re-examine their sentiments. Gradually President Roosevelt was able to marshal public opinion onto the side of Britain. The end of Jacky's life, terrible as it was, was not in vain. Six months after his death the Lend-Lease Act passed through the Congress, giving Britain almost unlimited access to the mighty arsenal which was American industry, and nine months after that, the US was at war with Germany.

William was confronted by another tragedy even before he learnt of Jacky's death. Reunited with his crew before joining his new squadron, he found them in sombre mood. Their old squadron, the Ospreys, had been in action off the Dutch coast. An attack on a convoy had resulted in eight out of the ten aircraft involved being lost, two to defensive fire and six to attack by Messerschmitts, who, alerted by radar, had picked them up on their flight home. Sadly William, Willis and Hopson contemplated the fate of their erstwhile comrades. Although he himself had been somewhat cold-shouldered by the old-timers in the squadron, he felt their loss deeply. They had been sent into battle poorly trained and equipped with inadequate aircraft and with no support whatever from friendly fighters. It was criminal, murder. Britain needed every machine and trained pilot it could get and to throw them away like this was not the way to win a war.

William's Blenheim night fighter squadron had had a poor start to its operational career. Blenheims were too slow and too clumsy for the role; they were, however, the only machines available which could be fitted with radar for night fighting. The radar itself was a system known as the AI (airborne intercept) radar. It was extremely temperamental. It had a short antenna projecting from the nose of the aircraft and could pick up another aircraft at a range of two or three miles in good conditions, provided that the target was within its fairly narrow arc of acquisition. The job of William's new unit was to develop the procedures needed to make proper use of the system and to iron out any technical problems.

The development unit was commanded by a Squadron Leader. Although nominally based at Tangmere, it actually flew from Martlesham Heath. It worked in very close co-operation with Bawdsey Manor. To everyone's surprise, one of the first radar-equipped Blenheims had shot down a Heinkel as early as February 1940, but since then there had been no further successes until June when William joined the team. He found congenial company among the officers of his new squadron who were not unlike the "odd balls" he had worked with at Duxford. All the aircrews were aware of the vital importance of the work they were doing and were interested in the technology as well as the tactics involved. They would fly all night, struggling with the strange behaviour of their radars, stalking each other through cloud and darkness and making imaginary kills. Then they would sit for hours working out tactics with people from Bawdsey and the fighter controllers who operated with the Chain Home system. The unit was extraordinarily democratic, allowing the radar operators, often junior NCOs, equal say alongside quite senior officers. The radar sets went through many stages of development and modification to make them more suitable for operational use. William was delighted with the progress made by his own operator, Jimmy Hopson. He was now made up to flight sergeant, and scheduled to go on a navigator's course as soon as his operational duties allowed. His quick practical way of thinking allowed him to contribute useful ideas to the team. He had a natural inventiveness and feel for what an operator needed in his dark, cold cockpit. The brilliance of the set must be variable, the intercom microphone must not obstruct the operator's vision. All the instruments must glow dark red to assist night vision... there were hosts of other details.

As summer wore on, the squadron's routine became frequently interrupted by urgent operational requirements. The serious nocturnal blitz on Britain by the Luftwaffe had not yet started but there were frequent night time intrusions by bombers and the

Blenheims were called on to try to intercept them. Typically an aircraft would be scrambled and ordered to stand by over a selected location:

Control to Blenheim: "We have trade for you, bogy is at angels one eight (eighteen thousand feet) make course one eight zero."

The waiting machine would climb on full throttle towards the path of the intruder.

Control to Blenheim: "Target bears one three zero five thousand yards, do you have contact?"

Blenheim: "No contact."

Control to Blenheim: "Target bears one two zero. Steer one zero zero for beam attack."

Blenheim: "Have contact. Tallyho." This indicated that the radar operator had a trace on his screen and from now on the attack would be orchestrated by the aircraft's crew. Eventually the pilot might see the exhaust flames of the enemy and attempt to close the range. However, since the intruder was probably at least as fast as the Blenheim it was a frustrating business. Occasionally the pursuing pilot would catch a glimpse of the intruder, illuminated by the moon or see a tell-tale stream of sparks from his exhaust, but the fighters almost never managed to get close enough to open fire, and when they did, it was seldom effective. The Blenheim just wasn't up to the job. The team did achieve a few kills on unsuspecting bombers but nowhere near enough to justify the effort expended. William himself never once got a chance to open fire at all.

His first taste of serious fighting came in August, a few days before Jacky's death. The Battle of Britain was now raging and the RAF was in severe danger of losing control of the sky over southern England. Every available aircraft had to be thrown into the fray. A squadron of Blenheims was briefed to make a dawn bombing raid on airfields in northern France in an attempt to hinder the relentless pressure exerted by their skilled and ruthless enemy. The bombers were to be escorted by Blenheim long-range fighters, and, scraping the barrel for enough of these to go round, Fighter Command decreed that the radars should be temporarily removed from William's unit's machines to eliminate the danger of them falling into German hands, so that the aircraft could be pressed into service as daylight escorts. At first all went well, eighteen bombers and twelve fighters formed up over Selsey Bill and roared off across the Channel. William's flight were in the lead, and aimed to approach the target from the east so as to make their attack out of the rising sun. They rapidly identified the airfield, near Lille. Half a dozen Dorniers were standing near the hangars being readied for the day's operations. The leading Blenheims seemed to have caught the defenders napping and were able to make a high-speed pass over the aerodrome, guns blazing so as to soften up the defences a few seconds before the bombers struck. They then climbed away, gaining height as quickly as possible so as to be able to protect the bombers on their return run. From his turret, Jimmy Hopson was able to see the bomb bursts as the main attack went in and satisfactory plumes of black smoke rose from the hangars and surrounding aircraft. Now it was a question of getting back safely.

The Germans had woken up and flak was bursting all round the bombers. Jimmy saw two of them crashing earthwards, trailing smoke. Worse was to come. A swarm of little black dots appeared high overhead, and these soon turned into Me109s. The twelve Blenheim fighters turned towards the attackers but their chances of success were small. Using their superior speed and agility, the Messerschmitts easily slotted in astern and poured fire into the returning aircraft. Jimmy watched in horror as two of his companions plunged downwards. He had heard from a friend in the sergeant's mess that you could always tell when a pursuing single-seater was going to open fire as it would always lift its nose a fraction before opening up so that the pilot could align his sights. He watched a machine line up behind his Blenheim carefully. When it seemed to be about two hundred yards away, he saw the nose begin to rise as the pilot sighted his guns for an easy kill. "Break right now, skipper!" he yelled and saw the tracer whizz past them as William flung the aircraft into a steep turn. He tried to turn his gun onto the 109 as it flashed past, but missed behind. The fighter pulled up into a steep climbing turn to have another go.

William decided that his best chance was to get as low as possible and hope that he might lose his attacker by some high-speed hedge hopping. He went into a steep dive, only levelling out a few feet above the ground.

His assailant followed him down. It had now been joined by another fighter and they lined up one on each quarter of the Blenheim, waiting for a chance to pounce. William flew as he had never dreamed he would have to. Skimming houses, weaving over open fields and dodging round church towers, he fought desperately to keep his enemies so occupied with flying that they could not get in a shot. Afterwards he remembered a fraction of a second when he had seen a herd of cows, terrified by his approach, stampede through a hedge in panic. Right ahead he saw some high-tension pylons. If he pulled up to cross the cables, he would give the fighters an excellent chance of a shot. He must pass under them. Fighting the temptation to shut his eyes he aimed between two pylons and held his breath. The fighters behind decided to pull up over the obstruction and this gave Jimmy an opportunity. As the fleeing Blenheim passed beneath the wires, he had a clear shot at the bellies of the Me's and blazed away at the right-hand machine. A single .303 machine gun needed luck to strike a mortal blow to an aircraft, but he saw his fire striking the underside of the wing and the machine pulled up and climbed away. Perhaps he had actually damaged it. At the same moment the other fighter put in a long burst. Most of the fire passed over the top of the Blenheim, but the crew felt the judder of strikes on the wings and tail. William felt his aircraft trying hard to turn to port. He stamped on the rudder pedal and managed to keep her on an even keel. Ahead of him, he could see the sea and far, far away the cliffs of Dover. Perhaps, against all the odds, they might make it. The second attacker now seemed to be giving up the chase, probably he had used all his ammunition. He climbed and turned away leaving the damaged Blenheim to escape, still at zero altitude, across the Channel.

William had a chance now to check that his crew were OK. Willis, the observer, had been operating the gun pack in the nose. He was white and shaking with terror from the hedge-hopping but unharmed. Jimmy Hopson's voice came through from his turret. "Think I'm OK, skip," he answered. "But it's too bloody cold here to tell. That bastard's shot the roof off of me turret. I'm bleeding from somewhere but I don't know where." The machine itself was still pulling hard to port but the engines seemed OK and she could maintain height. William called Tangmere for emergency landing clearance. It was very difficult to line up correctly on approach, the machine seemed to insist on crabbing sideways when he reduced power for landing, but he managed to get her to bump down safely and the crew scrambled out. William, for the first time, noticed that he was sweating profusely, and when he tried to stand, his legs collapsed under him and he fell flat on the grass beside the plane. He was shaking all over after his terrifying escape and his teeth chattered. In a few seconds he was recovered enough to look round the damage to the aircraft. One side of the rudder and tail fin was shot away completely and, as Jimmy had said, the top part of the turret had been cut clean off, like the top of an egg. Jimmy's bleeding came from nothing worse than a severe nose bleed which, he improbably claimed afterwards, had been caused by "a bleeding Jerry bullet".

So ended William's first combat mission. Of the thirty Blenheims involved, four of the fighters and three bombers were lost. At least six enemy aircraft had been damaged or destroyed on the ground and fuel and ammunition dumps had been wrecked. A hangar containing parts and a workshop caught fire and burnt out. The Blenheim fighters had shown once again that they were totally outclassed by single-seaters, but their intervention certainly prevented much heavier losses among the returning bombers.

One of the casualties was an aircraft from the radar development team. News of this spread a cloud of gloom over the mess. The Blenheim crews were not like the young exuberant single-seater boys who charged around the local pubs in high spirits whatever horrors had occurred in the battle. They were older men, most of them married with families, and took an altogether more serious view of life. Theirs was a sombre, quiet mess that evening and the CO, who had been flying one of the fighters, took upon himself the daunting task of visiting a little family devastated by the loss of a beloved dad.

William could not sleep that night; he lay sweating in bed, trying to analyse his own performance in combat. Yes, he had done all the right things and got home safely. The intelligence officer who had de-briefed him had seemed impressed by his performance. Secretly, however, he knew the intense terror he had felt as he fled before the German fighters. This was what many other pilots had to face every day, it was part of being in the RAF, but he was now forced to doubt if he was up to it. He remembered the terror of that deadly chase, the sickly feeling of panic, the muttered prayers. Deep down he felt he was a coward, unworthy of his crew and his service. He lay there in the darkness, miserably aware of his own inadequacy. The night wore on, sleepless. Soon after dawn he dragged himself out of bed and looked at his image in the mirror. A typical RAF officer stared back at him, lean, clean shaven, with longish dark hair and a face already showing the strains brought on by too much night-time flying and the heavy load of responsibility he felt for his mission and his crew. His uniform was draped untidily on a chair nearby and he saw the wings sewn on below the left breast. He felt unworthy of them. His colleagues were flying combat missions in their Spitfires and Hurricanes, sometimes two or three times a day, and fighting against terrible odds, and yet here he was after his first taste of combat, proud only because he had successfully fled from the enemy and racked with terror by the experience. He must give up. He couldn't stand it. Somehow he must get out of this ghastly fight and convince the RAF that he was no combat pilot. He flopped down in a chair and reached for a cigarette. He had to open a new packet of twenty for the second time in twenty-four hours. His hands trembled as he opened it and inhaled the first puff of rank-tasting smoke. Stubbing it out, he sat miserably on the bed and contemplated the morning.

At breakfast a letter was handed to him. It was from Angela. It had been posted weeks ago in Gibraltar. Remembering the nagging fear that she was truly in love with his cousin, he tore open the envelope:

My darling,

It has been difficult to write to you as we have been at sea most of the time and terribly busy with the wounded every time we come into port, but at last I have a few moments to write.

I'm not allowed to tell you much about our voyage out here and through the Med, but it has certainly been exciting as our convoy has been attacked from the air and from under water. Don't worry, our ship has not been hit but we have had to take on sailors from other ships which were not so lucky. Everyone has been so brave and many have suffered so much but I am learning to understand how long-suffering and undaunted British people can be in adversity. It is such a privilege to feel that I am part of the struggle and am playing my own little role in bringing some comfort to our boys. Of course what I have to do is nothing compared to fighting men like you, my darling. I'm just proud to play my small part.

I pray every night that you are all right and not taking too many risks. You airmen are really in the front line now and you are setting such a wonderful example to us all. Please, please keep safe until we can meet again, the rumour is that we may be coming back to England soon with a ship-load of wounded and perhaps we will be able to meet up then and re-live those wonderful days of happiness we had together. I sometimes dream of them and feel you quite close to me and those are the best moments of my life.

Darling, I have no more time to write. I am on duty again tonight and have so much to do before we sail again.

I love you, darling, and feel that I just cannot live without the hope of being with you again.

With all my blessings and love.

Your Angela.

William stared at the letter, dumbfounded. Shaking, he left the mess table and hurried to his room. Over and over again he read it, and a new determination seemed to fill his whole body. He must somehow be worthy of this wonderful, brave girl. How could he snivel fearfully here in the safety of his room while she was at sea facing dangers and horrors that he could scarcely imagine? She assumed that he was fighting to defend his country, and here he was trying to find a way out of it. And what else was she saying? That she loved him, longed for him. Nothing about that bloody cousin. Pulling himself together, he got up and returned to his duties.

He walked over to the hangar to see what progress was being made on repairing his aircraft. To his surprise, it was pushed to the back of the hangar, looking damaged and forlorn with no one working on it. He called the flight sergeant who normally cared for it.

"Flight, why is no one working on P, Peter?"

"Orders, sir, we have to leave her as she is, don't know why, and we are getting the spare machine, B Baker ready for tonight."

"Tonight?"

"Yes, sir."

"But she can't do a night radar op, she has no radar fitted."

"Don't know about that, sir."

William hurried off to the ops room to see what was going on. Sure enough he and his crew, together with three others, were scheduled to attend a briefing that afternoon. Remembering his sleepless night, William slipped off for a nap, asking an orderly to be sure to wake him in time. Gone entirely was the gloom and self-doubt which had overcome him. Once again he was a confident, determined officer.

"Gentlemen," began the CO. "Yesterday morning we were fortunate enough to do some considerable damage to the enemy. We have been told that no fighters were able to use the base we hit, considerably weakening the German offensive," – muffled cheers from the assembled crews – "however, our own losses were unacceptably heavy. Tonight we are going to try a new tactic. We are going to make a night raid on one of the key airfields, only a few miles from our last target. Once again we will be escorting the bomber force but as well as shooting up the airfield before they arrive, it will be our job to drop flares so they can see the target.

There probably won't be any fighter opposition, but of course we must expect some flak. The great thing is that we have to find the target in the dark and hit it. Fighter Command seems to think that our night-flying experience makes us the best people for the job. Remember, our boys are knocking down Nazi bombers every day but their own losses are just not sustainable. If we can't do something to make it more difficult for the enemy to put up his mass attacks, the situation in this battle will become extremely serious. Good luck, chaps."

With that he handed over to the met officer and the intelligence specialist.

A night attack! So far night attacks by air had consisted mainly of leaflet dropping and the occasional brave venture over German territory. Accurate navigation by night was so difficult that most raids finished up miles from the intended target. This time the Blenheims were going to have to find and hit an airfield accurately. Time spent blundering about over enemy-held France looking for the target would be fatal as everything depended on achieving surprise and getting away before the defences were alerted. The weather was on their side; the met officer predicted light easterly winds and only about one tenth cloud. There was a half-moon which should make it reasonably easy to see major physical features on the ground such as rivers and, with luck, railways.

It was agreed that the best approach would be to come in low over the Channel at maximum speed. The bombers would then climb to five thousand feet while the fighters would keep low, trying to map read their way to the target. They would then drop flares to guide the bombers and attempt to silence some of the flak, then clear the target area before the bombers arrived. In daylight Blenheims would normally try to fly in close formation so as to maximise the effect of defensive fire, but as night fighter activity was not expected, the aircraft would split up on the way home so it would be each man for himself. To his horror, William was assigned to lead the fighter section. The aircrews huddled together over the latest maps of northern France to try identify landmarks which would be visible at night. The target was the headquarters of KG 1, one of the most important of the German bomber groups, situated between Beauvais and Amiens. To find it, the easiest route would be to find the mouth of the Somme, then follow the river as far as Amiens. Having identified Amiens, they could turn due south and follow a compass course which should bring them in sight of the airfield, provided the moon and clouds obliged. There would be plenty of flak on the course and around the target, but the distance to be covered over land was less than one hundred miles, and if they could identify the target quickly, they would be over enemy territory for less than forty-five minutes. The fighters would take off at about two a.m. (it was double summer time, so this was equivalent to midnight GMT). The moon would be up when they reached the target.

The crews all tried to rest during the afternoon and were served a late and unappetising supper of corned beef hash and vegetables. They waited in the crew room while the mechanics made final checks on the waiting Blenheims. A little after midnight the telephone rang in the crew room; the news was devastating. The operation was postponed. No reason was given. Men who had screwed up their courage, tense with anticipation and battling to control their nerves, were totally deflated. The language in the room was horrible, and the disgruntled flyers slunk angrily off to bed.

William felt some of his own self-doubt return. He had been ready to play the lead role assigned to him but as he lay tossing in bed he managed once more to convince himself that he was not up to the job. He just couldn't play a leading role when he might take his own crew and many others to their deaths. How could he? He would see the CO in the morning. If he was branded a coward so be it.

As he struggled out of bed the next morning, there was a knock on his door. Sammy Burtonwood, one of his closest friends in the squadron came in.

"William, you knew that film star Jacky Simple, didn't you?"

"Yes, why?"

"Well, look at this."

"This" was a morning paper; the front page carried a large picture of Jacky and a glorified story of his life, his RAF career, and his death in combat over England.

William sat heavily down on his bed. Jacky, his friend, brave Jacky who could have been earning millions in Hollywood, but chose to serve his country as a humble pilot. Jacky, so handsome, so confident, so splendid. Dead. Gone forever. He buried his face in his hands in despair, and his shoulders shook with sobbing.

"Oh, sorry, old boy," Sammy stammered, "I didn't know..." He slipped out of the room.

In less than a minute William stood up. His misery had somehow turned to rage. Who the hell did they think they were these Germans flying their ugly aeroplanes, covered with their disgusting heathen symbols, over England killing people? How dare they try to impose their revolting, cruel code on decent Englishmen? If he had to die to stop them, he would. He'd smash his plane into one of their filthy Dorniers if he could. Jacky and thousands of others would be avenged. Fired with a new and terrible determination, he faced the days of waiting.

Two days later came the news that the attack should take place that night. Once again there was expected to be little cloud over the target and the wind would be light easterly. The machines lined up, ready for take-off, their engines already warmed up and the crews once again enjoying what might be their last chat and cigarette in the crew room. Again the telephone. This time it was their own control tower. Emergency, a damaged Wellington, returning from a raid on the docks at Cherbourg, was trying to make Tangmere. She had been blundering about the English coast for half an hour, unsure of her position but now she seemed to have identified Tangmere and was coming in at exactly the time that the Blenheims should be going out. The dimmed airfield gooseneck lights were lit and the crews, waiting in the open now, heard the distant sound of engines. They could see nothing but they heard an engine throttle back and then a green light soared up from the tower. The wounded plane cut its motors and announced itself by a shower of sparks as its belly flopped down on the runway, wheels up. The fire engines and a host of mechanics rushed towards it. There was no holding the waiting aircrew, to a man they dashed towards the Wellington, hoping to be able to help. As it turned out they were not needed. The crew all scrambled out unaided, leaving the machine clear to be soused by the fire crews. The plane had been hard hit by heavy ack-ack fire and had lost one engine and half its tail plane. It was a miracle that it had got home, but here it was in the middle of the runway and until it was moved, the Blenheims could not take off. There was much pulling and shoving with tractors and eventually the carcass was heaved out of the way, but it was almost an hour after the designated take-off time before everything was clear. It was now three in the morning and the CO needed clearance from Group headquarters before allowing the attack to go ahead. As usual it took some time to raise anyone responsible at HQ and he had to hold further consultations, so it was not until almost four that the clearance for take-off was given. This was an act of severe irresponsibility at Group level. Had the staff officers studied the operational time table they would have realised that the Blenheims would have to return from their mission after dawn and this would make them easy meat for German fighters. The CO made this very clear but was told the mission must go ahead regardless. Apparently, Group was prepared to sacrifice a few aircraft and their crews for a successful raid.

A cold fury possessed William as he led the six fighters fast and low across the Channel. The waiting had given him time to brood, and as he brooded, his anger against the Germans, the war, and everything else, developed. He was short and ill-tempered with his crew, and he flew the aircraft coarsely, cruelly, as if the whole affair was its fault. Willis, his navigator remained calm and temperate, giving courses and corrections quietly as they sped over the sea. The aircraft following them were invisible, blacked out in the darkness, each showing a dim stern light to guide the pilot behind.

"Skipper," Willis said as they approached the French coast, "I don't believe the wind Met gave us is correct, I think we have a fresh easterly. I think we'll meet the coast at Dieppe, not at the mouth of the Somme."

"Well, stick on this course for now, we'll see it in a minute."

The coast came into view, a line of white surf breaking on the beach.

"Skipper, that's certainly Dieppe, I recognise the docks. Turn ninety degrees to port. We should pick up the Somme in a couple of minutes."

"OK."

"There it is, skip. Turn to starboard and follow it inland. I calculate we have fifteen to twenty knots of wind. That'll affect our course from Amiens, I'll re-calculate."

Thank God for Willis.

They flashed over Abbeville without provoking any defensive fire and roared on towards Amiens. The moonlight was now quite strong, the river glowing silver below them. Farms and villages, sleeping peacefully, flashed beneath the wings.

"OK, that's Amiens ahead, Skip, steer two three zero degrees from the town centre, we should be over the airfield in seven minutes. I'll go forward into the nose now, it's a question of keeping a lookout for the target."

"OK, Sarge, Jimmy, did you hear that? Keep your eyes skinned up there, remember that triangular-shaped wood we saw in the recce photos. That should give you a clue."

"Bloody hell, what was that?"

The defences of Amiens had woken up. a barrage of fire surged towards them. A shell bursting close astern threw the aircraft on her nose for an instant, but otherwise the aim was poor. They still could not see the following aircraft and were keeping radio silence. They saw tracer reaching out towards a point behind them but there was no sign of anyone being hit. The bombers now would be climbing hard to five thousand feet and looking out for their flares.

Seven minutes passed. No sign of anything in the blacked-out land below.

"We must have missed it. I'm going to circle this point so we get a better look; it must be somewhere near. Jimmy, break radio silence, Jerry knows we're here anyway and tell the others what we are doing."

"Roger."

Two big circles and nothing seen. Obviously the enemy were holding their fire so as not to give away their position.

"Skipper, quick, look down there, three o'clock left from the nose, something silver." It was Jimmy's voice, then Willis in the nose, saw it too. "It's an aeroplane on the ground, silver, big one, I think it's a Ju 52 transport."

Now clearly visible in the moonlight, the silver aircraft had been bringing a new draft of pilots to France. The Germans were normally masters of camouflage but for some reason this machine had not been painted and had been carelessly left out in the open at night.

"This is it, all right, I'm going to shoot up that machine and drop flares. Let's go for it."

Opening the throttles, William dived towards the Junkers as Willis dropped his flares and opened up with his machine guns. The parked plane was a sitting target and soon burst into flames. At the same time the defensive fire opened up, tracer seemed to arc slowly upwards from the ground then accelerate madly as it approached, whizzing above and below them. Angry balls of dirty-looking fire marked where heavy ack-ack shells were exploding. On each side they could see the other fighters blazing away at the gun emplacements. Their .303 machine-gun fire could do little to damage the bombers on the field, as they were carefully dispersed in protected pens, or to the AA guns in their armoured dug outs, but at least they distracted the defenders from the approaching high-level bombers. The flares lit up well and out of the corner of his eye, William saw a host of men running out of one of the buildings. They were in fact aircrew who had been assembled for an early morning briefing.

"I'm going round again!" he yelled to his crew and he flung the aircraft into a tight turn, so low that the wing nearly touched the trees below. Before the little figures on the airfield could reach shelter, the Blenheim's machine guns were on them as William made his second pass. Jimmy's rear turret followed up as the Blenheim climbed away, chased by furious tracer fire from the ground. No sooner had they reached a reasonably safe height than they saw the bombers begin their work and great dirty black clouds of smoke and dust rose from the airfield.

The raid seemed to have been a rare success for the Blenheims, but the difficult part was to come. In the east the rim of the sun was just appearing over the horizon, and gradually colour was returning to the landscape. Dark fields were turning to green grass and yellow stubble, and the midnight blue of the sky was lit up by orange and greenish light as the sun rose over northern France. Soon the sky would be full of venomous fighters, ready to avenge their comrades, and there was over one hundred and twenty miles to fly before they reached the English coast. Sure enough, Jimmy reported some suspicious-looking specks in the sky above them. To his horror, he saw two machines detach from the formation and dive towards them. It seemed that their quarry was one of the other Blenheims and soon an ugly pall of black smoke marked where it had been destroyed. William had been hugging the ground to try to avoid detection but it could only be a matter of minutes before he, too, was seen. With so many fighters around, he could not hope for the same luck as had saved him on his last foray over France.

The German plan for that day had been to dispatch four hundred high-level bombers to attack airfields in southern England. They would be escorted by two hundred fighters which would station themselves about five thousand feet above the bombers, and another one hundred and fifty which would keep close to the bombers, weaving about around their formations. The bombers would take off before dawn so as to reach their targets soon after first light. The fighters would not be airborne until half an hour later so as to conserve their fuel as much as possible. This plan had been disrupted by the Blenheim's raid. The German bombers' take-off had been delayed while damage was assessed. News of the delay had not got through to all the fighter formations, and the ones which attacked William's colleagues had taken off well before the first of the bombers. They had been looking for their charges when they spotted the unfortunate Blenheims below them.

Unaware of all this, William hedge-hopped towards home, trying to weave a course across country. Suddenly he saw a mass of dark-coloured shapes rising into the air ahead of him. Obviously these must be a formation of aircraft. He now could see that they were Junkers 88s, climbing away in front of him.

"I'm going to try to link up with those Jerries," he told his crew. "If we keep up sun of them, they won't be able to see us well and may mistake us for one of their stragglers. It's our best hope. Don't anyone for heaven's sake open fire or do anything stupid unless I say so, and keep a look out for the Me's."

"OK, skip, let's hope."

The Junkers, with their single tail fin, looked not unlike a Blenheim in the distance and with the sun in their eyes, the enemy crews did not pay much attention to the aircraft climbing alongside them and heading north towards the Channel. With a light fuel load and no bombs on board, the Blenheim could easily keep station to the east of, and slightly behind, the formation. The crew hardly dared to breathe as they crossed the French coastline, expecting the close escort to appear at any moment. There was a thick bank of white cloud on the English side; if they could reach that undetected they might be safe. It was not to be. Willis, still in his nose gun position spotted a shoal of little silvery shapes, at about their height, joining the formation. Me109s! They couldn't possibly miss the odd-shaped aircraft with RAF roundels on the flank of the bomber stream. For a few valuable minutes all went well, then two of the enemy seemed to see that something was wrong. They pulled a tight turn and worked round onto the tail of the Blenheim. There was only one thing William could do. Pushing the throttles to their emergency full-speed position, he steered centre of the German bomber fleet, aiming to pass close above them. The fighters couldn't possibly open fire while he was so close and perhaps the gunners in the Junkers would not realise what was going on. The Me's pulled out of their attack and shot past the Junkers. They seemed to have decided to have another go, this time attacking while climbing from below so as to have a clear field of fire. As they manoeuvred, William pushed the control column right forward, putting his machine into a steep dive. At the same time, Jimmy opened up from his turret, with the general idea of creating confusion. The aircraft shuddered and bumped about horribly as it passed through the slipstream of the enemy bombers, still progressing in perfect formation towards their target. The engine note rose to a howl as the speed built up. Surprised by the sudden move, the German fighters rolled into a dive to follow, but they also were thrown about the air by the wash of their own bombers and took several precious seconds to regain control. Too late they resumed their chase after the Blenheim which disappeared into the welcome cloud below. Panting and sweating, William pulled out of his dive and tried to keep inside the cloud by making tight circles.

They saw no more of their attackers. The main danger now was being shot down by their own fighters, mistaking them for a straggler from the German armada. Luckily they saw nothing of them. The Blenheim came out of the cloud just above Bognor Regis and broke radio silence again to report its position. In a few minutes they were over their home airfield and landed safely. This time William was not the trembling wreck who had tumbled out of his plane a few days earlier. He was elated, proud of his performance and of his crew. Willis and Hopson both looked shaken; they had certainly had a hair-raising ride, but neither was hurt and he overheard them telling the ground crew how their skipper had outwitted the Luftwaffe to get home. They were right to celebrate. Only two other aircraft limped back from that raid, both badly damaged. One other had been brought down by ground fire, the rest had been picked off by Me's.

This was to be the last time the radar development team was used to join in raids on Nazi airfields, and indeed the last such attack mounted by Blenheims. It was obvious that the loss rate was unacceptable. Also, during the following weeks it became clear that Goering had made a change of policy which was to be fatal to his objective of overwhelming the RAF. In retaliation for some raids by Bomber Command on Berlin, he turned the might of his bomber force against London. Here his bombers were operating beyond the range at which effective fighter escort could be provided and their losses were horrific. As autumn drew on, the Luftwaffe was forced to accept that it would have to give up its attempts to bomb Britain into submission. Instead they would try to demoralise the population by intensive night time attacks, just as Kilowatt had predicted.

The Martlesham Heath radar-equipped fighter unit was now reduced to three Blenheims, all now in barely serviceable condition. There was time for another meeting with the boffins from Bawdsey Manor while work on the aircraft progressed and replacements were provided. Hugh and Kilowatt arrived at the air station, looking utterly exhausted. For three months they had been rushing between Chain Home radar stations, helping to fix problems and improve performance. In the early stages of the Battle of Britain, Stukas had successfully been used to attack the radar masts, but somehow they had always been repaired and brought back into service in a few days, so that eventually the Germans gave up their attacks on them. Keeping the radars operational was only one of Hugh's tasks however. Early in 1940 a German bomber had been shot down, and among documents recovered from it was reference to a *"knickebein"* beacon. What on earth was that? Gradually evidence began to mount that the Germans had developed a system for generating a narrow radio beam which could be transmitted from a fixed point in the Low Countries and which could guide aircraft accurately to their targets in total darkness. This was the system which the Orfordness people had got wind of just before the war. There was some experience within the RAF of using radio beams to enable aircraft to land in poor visibility, but it had seemed to be impossible that such a system could be developed so as to guide bombers over a range of several hundred miles. With authorisation from Churchill himself, a project was launched to detect a German guidance beam and a flight of three Ansons had been assembled for the purpose. They were fitted with an astonishing assortment of radio sets in the hope that one of them might have the right characteristics to pick up the beam. One machine, using a set which had been borrowed from a US police establishment, was tuned to 31.5 megacycles. The crew picked up a narrow radio beam on this frequency and themselves used it briefly to hold a steady course towards a target selected by the enemy. This was devastating news. Using the *knickebein,* the Germans could accurately bomb any point in Britain in total darkness and they could fly so fast that no existing night fighter could get near them. "We are doing everything we can to find some way of interfering with these beams, but it's new science to us and it takes time and needs research specialists who are in short supply," said Hugh. "Also, Jerry isn't just standing still; there seems to be a further development on the way, *X-Gerat* we think they call it, which really gives pinpoint accuracy. They could easily knock out a chosen factory, Rolls-Royce in Derby for example, in a single night raid. We've got to stop them and you night fighter boys are the only effective defence we have."

At that moment the sound of an unfamiliar aircraft shook the table around which they were sitting, then another, then a third. A glance out of the window revealed three short-nosed, rather stubby-looking machines with enormous engines and propellers taxiing bumpily towards the hangar. Three Beaufighters.

Chapter 9

Hans was none the worse for his swim, but the return to his squadron brought bleak news. No less than eight Stukas from his station had failed to return from their mission. It was now obvious that, formidable as it was to harry and terrify ground forces and to sink enemy shipping, the Stuka simply could not operate in areas where the enemy had effective, modern fighters. The lesson of that day's disasters was well learnt, even in the top echelons of the Luftwaffe, and the aircraft were withdrawn from the battle. Hans and his colleagues wondered where their next posting might be. There were rumours that an attack was to be launched one day against Russia. No one really believed them; nevertheless, there was a lot of discussion about the part they could play, blasting a way for the Panzer divisions towards Moscow, or to the oil wells at the eastern end of the Black Sea.

The wing to which he was attached was re located to Germany, allowing him to take a few days' leave at home. He found that life in the castle was remarkably untroubled by war. There were still domestic servants and there seemed to be no shortages of food or household products. Only petrol was hard to obtain, and with his connections in the Luftwaffe, he found little difficulty in wangling even this when he needed it. He found himself feted wherever he went: his exploits in Poland and over France had been trumpeted all over the district by his mother who insisted on throwing numerous dinner parties so that people could admire her son. In particular she had a way of surrounding him with suitably attractive female company, especially seeking out girls from wealthy or noble families. "Hans," she said before one such event. "You need to forget that little English girl. You have the future and the family to consider and it's time that my hero made a proper marriage. The Fuhrer himself has said that Germans have a duty to produce large families of good Nordic stock. At least consider that delightful Countess of... so charming, and such a family! Or how about Gertrude... they say she'll have a career in films... then there's..." Hans was not generally an ill-tempered fellow but this he simply couldn't stand. He became almost rudely standoffish and cool, giving them all a wide berth. He still dreamed about Angela and what they would do together when Britain finally saw sense and ended the war. No one else would do. He was quite glad when he was recalled to his unit early.

By the end of September, it was clear that the attempt to smother the RAF and open the way to an invasion of southern England was not going to succeed. As the weather turned in October, units of the Luftwaffe were withdrawn and redeployed, mostly to the east where they rebuilt their damaged formations and trained new aircrews. 1/StG1, Hans' unit, however, found itself posted briefly to the Baltic so as to hone its anti-ship operation skills. In particular they practised endlessly bombing a wooden mock-up of a British aircraft carrier. Intelligence had discovered that the *Illustrious* class carriers had armoured decks and these could only be pierced by thousand-pound bombs which were just coming into service. Four thousand-pound hits would, it was believed, sink any carrier ever built. That winter they learnt that they were destined for the Mediterranean. They flew their machines by easy stages across the Reich and down the length of Italy to the beautiful island of Sicily. They were to be based on a well-defended aerodrome near Catania. Here they formed the core of a new and formidable formation known as "Fliegerkorps X". By early January their ground crews and equipment had caught up with them and they were ready to practise the deadly trade they had learnt that autumn.

The situation in the Mediterranean was at that point not looking good for the Axis powers. Italian troops were being heavily defeated in North Africa and the Greeks were holding off the Italian attempt to invade their country. Things were about to change, however. Released from northern Europe, German ground troops, armour and air force units were beginning to come onto the scene. In Libya the defeated remnants of the Italian army were soon to be reinforced by the superb troops of the Afrika Corps led by General Rommel, while at the same time Churchill made the disastrous decision to deprive the army in Africa of most of its air power and many of its best troops in a vain attempt to check the German forces who began to pour into Greece. In this situation the role of the Stuka squadrons in Sicily was simple. They had to deprive the Royal Navy of the ability to use the Mediterranean to supply its forces in Egypt and Greece, and to assist the Italians in forcing the surrender of the strategic island of Malta. They very soon made their presence felt.

Only a week after he had arrived, Hans found himself leading a flight of three machines forming part of a formation tasked to attack British warships approaching Malta. It was to be a memorable day. The target was a large section of the British Mediterranean Fleet consisting of two battleships, seven destroyers and the aircraft carrier *Illustrious* herself. This was no easy target. The British had plenty of experience in fighting off Italian high-level and torpedo bombers, and several of their ships, including *Illustrious*, were fitted with radar. *Illustrious* also carried a squadron of Fulmar fighters – slow and clumsy compared to land-based single-seaters but more than a match for a dive bomber. From the first, Fliegerkorps X had luck on their side. An Italian destroyer located the British at dawn. An abortive attack was made by a pair of Italian torpedo bombers. Their weapons missed the target but they distracted some patrolling Fulmars which chased them back to Sicily. Almost simultaneously *Illustrious's* radar picked up a large number of incoming aircraft. It was too late to launch more fighters. Hans looked down from his cockpit and saw the great ships like toys on the sea beneath him, white water breaking under their bows, and each sending out a pattern of ripples in her wake. This was exactly the situation they had been training for. There were forty-three Stukas in the attacking force and they formed a defensive ring over the warships. Anti-aircraft fire soared up towards them as they circled, but at twelve thousand feet they were too high for it to be effective. The obvious targets for the Stukas were the aircraft carrier and the two battleships. Some of the Stukas, each carrying two five hundred-pound bombs, would distract the defensive fire of the battleships while thirty of them, armed with the new thousand-pound weapon, would make straight for the carrier. One by one, with perfect precision, they pulled out of the circle, did a half role and plunged into a near vertical dive towards the speck on the water below. Hans saw great spouts of water erupt around the carrier as she wove and squirmed to avoid the terrible onslaught.

Accustomed to attack from Italian high-level bombers, the British gun crews had never seen anything like this assault from directly above and carried out with such immaculate precision. Although the gunners blazed away with everything they had, the waiting aircraft in the circle saw each of their comrades pull safely out of his dive and skim away over the sea. When it was Hans' turn, he felt the animal thrill of the chase pulsing through every fibre. As the dive commenced, he watched as the target began to grow, at first slowly, then suddenly with alarming speed as he steered straight downwards towards the flight deck. At the very last moment, he released his bomb and hauled the machine out of its dive. He was almost on the deck himself and the aircraft whizzed along the length of the carrier well below the level of the bridge structure, almost as if to land on her. "Hit!" yelled the faithful Stokmann, who saw the bomb plunge through the deck and a burst of smoke and steam spout upwards from the hole it made. Hans stayed at low level and was quickly joined by the other two aircraft of his flight. They sped home, job well done.

Illustrious was hit six times in this attack, and struck again by high-level bombs from a Heinkel 111 as she struggled on towards Malta. Her rudder was destroyed, and she was massively damaged below decks, but she managed to steer using her engines and limped into the dockyard for urgent repairs. The action was not without losses for Fliegerkorps X, the Fulmars eventually accounting for six of the attacking aircraft.

The Luftwaffe were not finished with *Illustrious*. Two days later Hans found himself briefed to attack her whilst she was under repair. With his two comrades, Hans took off before dawn so as to arrive over the island before the defending fighters were airborne. On schedule, they arrived at first light and had no difficulty locating *Illustrious*, dwarfing the other ships in the dockyard. Over the island the ack-ack was legendary for its ferocity and, as they plunged down towards their target, he saw one Stuka explode alongside him as a shell struck it, detonating one of its bombs. Undeterred, he thought he scored a hit on the flight deck. Pulling out of his dive, he wove from side to side to confuse the gunners close below him. He escaped undamaged out over the sea, closely followed by his remaining colleague. Out of range of the guns now, he went into a slow climb on a course for home. Suddenly Stokmann yelled over the intercom, "Enemy fighters behind us, closing fast. Two of them. Hurricanes!" Hans opened up to maximum power and dived for the sea, followed by the other Stuka. Glancing for a second over his shoulder, he could see the other pilot, young Oppermann, a newcomer to the squadron. Hans knew him to be a nice lad, shy and quiet but full of courage and happy to volunteer for any action going. Today he was replacing another pilot who was sick. Hans noticed that he was gradually pulling ahead of Oppermann's machine, and that the Hurricanes had seen them and were giving chase. If he stayed alongside Oppermann, then the two Stukas could perhaps put up some resistance, using both their tail guns; if he pulled ahead, the full fury would fall on his comrade and he himself might escape over the sea. There was low cloud ahead which would give him a chance. His choice was clear: he could run for it or support his comrade. He told himself that he was of more value to Germany than this young rookie. He doubted if even both tail gun turrets would put off the enemy. He remembered that Stokmann had a wife and baby. It took him less than a second to choose to save his own skin. The gap between his machine and the other steadily increased, and he watched as the Hurricanes both closed on Oppermann; alone the poor fellow had no chance at all, a long burst of fire from the leading Hurricane and his machine cartwheeled into the sea. The second Hurricane continued the chase, but now

Hans saw the cloud bank rushing towards him and he plunged into its protecting dampness. To shake off pursuit he made a violent turn, then another and hugged the sea surface, skimming back over the water towards Sicily and safety. From that day he began to despise himself as a coward.

Coward or not, he had to fight on. During the following eight weeks, Hans flew twenty-four combat missions against shipping targets and over Malta. *Illustrious* was eventually patched up enough to make her escape to Egypt, but there were plenty of other targets to go for on the island. It was the end of March, with spring coming to Sicily, that he took off on yet another sortie. Once again it was a pre-dawn departure and this time the target was an RAF station in the south of the island. The Stukas had the comfort of a BF109 escort, so defending Hurricanes should not be a problem. The station was heavily defended but the bombs were dropped, cratering the runway and damaging some hangars. The German aircrews had been instructed to shoot up the buildings around the airfield before heading for home, and Hans spotted a large block a little apart from the rest which he made his target. Approaching low from the airfield, he emptied his forward guns into the front of the building and turned sharply to give Stokmann a chance to use his weapons before they flew away. As he turned, Hans noticed a huge red cross painted on the side of the building. Outside he glimpsed a row of vehicles with red crosses on their sides. Pulling away he saw smoke billowing out of the windows from a fire which must have been caused by his tracer. A hospital! Clearly marked! And he had strafed it with everything he had. Feeling utterly sick and exhausted, he wrenched the aircraft into a turn for home. He was so shaken he could not even make a proper landing. He almost hurled the aircraft down onto the grass runway, got out leaving the engine running, vomited on the grass and stalked away back to his quarters.

Major von Kostler was a superb commanding officer: tough, professional and extremely brave; he never failed to be in the air when there was dangerous work to be done. At the same time he was an excellent and civilised leader of men, understanding their problems and praising their strengths. He was intolerant only of idleness and deliberate insubordination. Hans stood before him in his office, still pale and trembling with rage. Why had he not been told about the hospital? What sort of air force operated without proper reconnaissance and intelligence? How could he fly again after the incident with Oppermann and now the hospital? The major had seen this sort of thing many times in two world wars, and he knew how to deal with it.

"Oberleutnant, I order you to sit down and take this drink."

Hands trembling, Hans accepted a glass of local grappa.

"You are angry about the hospital, I understand that," von Kostler continued. "But let me tell you something. I have a report here on my desk from one of your colleagues, Schinder; he also made an attack on that building and he swears that it was not properly marked on the south side, from which you attacked, or on the roof. It seems that the building has only just been put to that use; it once served as a mess for NCOs. The British seem to have been careless about marking it properly. Any blame is down to them, not to you."

"Herr Major, thank you for that information," replied Hans. "But I fear that I have to report to you that I consider myself unfit to fly on combat missions." He recounted the Oppermann incident.

The major smiled at him, unruffled. "Hans, tell me how many guns a Hurricane has?"

"Eight, Herr Major."

"And how many were chasing you?"

"Two."

"And how many guns could you bring to bear on them?"

"Six, three on each aircraft."

"What is the top speed of a Hurricane?"

"About three hundred and twenty miles per hour."

"And a Stuka?"

"Two hundred and fifty."

"So do you really think the two of you together had any chance against those two British machines? Be sensible, Hans, and do yourself justice. You took the decision of a mature German officer to save at least something from disaster, not to make a foolish, useless gesture. Any fool can get himself killed. And, talking about being killed. I had this cable from the Red Cross this very afternoon. Oppermann and his gunner were not killed by their crash into the sea. They were picked up and are both prisoners in Malta."

Hans felt the fury drain out of him. He gulped his drink and just felt unbearably tired.

"Listen," said the major. "You are one of the best pilots we have and an excellent comrade, but we have been working you too hard and you need a rest. It is spring here in Sicily. I order you now to take one of the squadron motorbikes and take ten days rest away from the airfield. The Italians here are friendly and welcoming and their cooking and wines are superb. If I were you, I would try Enna, in the centre of the island; it's beautiful and peaceful. Then come back and sink some ships for us. Dismiss!"

"Ja, Herr Major!"

The tempestuous and violent history of Sicily has left the behind it a plethora of the most magnificent and impressive churches, castles and domestic architecture in Europe, dating from early pre-history to the recent past. The island's beauty, the richness of its products and its strategic position, poised between Europe and Africa, have attracted conquerors and immigrants for as long as man has been able to travel. Greeks, Romans, Arabs, Normans, Spaniards have fought over Sicily and left their distinctive marks behind them alongside traces of yet more ancient civilisations. In spite of all the conquests and colonisations, the people of the island have retained their distinctive dialect, independence and character. The fields and vineyards have continued to yield their riches, and the astonishing beauty of the countryside seems to have absorbed all the human activity around it. Hans began to fall in love with the island as he puttered his way along the dusty roads and up the tortuous mountain track towards Enna, poised on its mountain and dominating the plain below. Above the city he saw the enormous bulk of the castle, the Castello di Lombardia, frowning down on the narrow streets of the town. The crowded medieval buildings jostled together, some Norman, some Aragonese and some showing evidence of Arab design. He found a small hotel which seemed quite clean and modern and deposited his few belongings in a comfortable and airy room.

Resolving on a stroll before dinner, he walked out and down the cobbled Via Roma. There seemed to be few people about, but the sound of a bell some distance away and the murmur of human voices drifted upwards. Walking towards the sound, he came upon a strange procession wending its way slowly towards him. The procession took up the full width of the street, and Hans had to press himself into a doorway to let it pass. Men seemed to be organised into groups, each group distinctively dressed in its own extraordinary costume, hooded and with faces masked, and preceded by a banner. The sound had now ceased entirely as the procession moved slowly, deliberately, on its way. Hans saw that some of the men were carrying heavy wooden crosses and a few were flagellating themselves with whips. It was impossible not to be moved by the solemnity and dignity of the marchers. Following respectfully behind the procession were women, all dressed in black, their faces half hidden by their black scarves and headgear, eyes turned down, totally silent. Hans noticed that, sheltering in the doorway next to his, was a young woman, dressed soberly, but not hooded. She looked at the stranger and smiled shyly.

"I see you are a stranger in the town," she said, speaking, to Hans' surprise, in excellent French. "Have you come to see the Good Friday procession next week?"

"Certainly I am a stranger, but I know nothing of these processions. I was most surprised. What do they signify?"

"These are the guildsmen of the town. These days they are mostly charitable organisations, their members process through the town during Holy Week. What you have seen is a small procession in advance of Good Friday and Easter Day. That is really something to see."

"Well, I feel privileged to have been here. Thank you for your explanation. I can see that there is much here in Sicily which is strange to us Germans."

"Oh, yes, there is plenty to see in Enna, and the country around. Before the war there were tours and guides for visitors, but now, of course, that is all over."

"Yes yes, very sad. We Germans never wanted war, you know. If only they had listened. I suppose I will have to find my own way around."

"Sir, I have lived here all my life; if you would like a guide, I can show you the town tomorrow. I am at liberty."

Hans was rather surprised by the offer, but it would be stupid to refuse. He had nothing else to do. He thanked her and they arranged to meet in the morning. He was not to be disappointed. In place of her sober outfit worn the previous day, Ester (that was the girl's name) arrived in an attractive patterned dress and a fetching straw hat. She was clearly well versed on the attractions of the town and seemed well-respected by her fellow citizens. She knew who kept the keys of the duomo (which was locked up) and the crusty old custodian opened up for her quite readily; she was also greeted heartily by the gate keeper at the castle, and they climbed the towers together, Ester clambering up the rickety stairs daintily, holding her skirt against the breeze. She chattered gaily as they took in the sights and not only had a fund of amusing stories about several of the people she met but also showed a deep understanding of the history of the place.

"You see," she said, as they paused for a rest, "there have been, in the last fifteen hundred years or so, many conquerors of our island and all have left their mark, but nevertheless something unique has remained intact. The Arabs came here in the sixth century. They built their mosques and their minarets, but their most profound effect was in the countryside. They taught the people how to farm productively, making proper use of irrigation and building systems which survived for centuries. Then came the Normans. They were great fighters and came to dominate the island, but they liked to live in the towns and they built here the most wonderful churches and cathedrals. They were clever enough to see that the Arabs knew things about agriculture that they did not, so they left them alone to do their work, pay their taxes, of course, and even to practise their religion. They were tolerant rulers and intelligent. Under them the island prospered as it had never done before or since. Then came the Spanish. They were different: proud, narrow, cruel rulers who drove out anyone who did not accept their faith and they destroyed much of what the Normans had achieved. Nevertheless they built some glorious things, especially in the towns where you can see their ornate baroque streets and wonderful carving. Now of course we are a part of the united Italy, actually the first part to be freed by Garibaldi. It is too early to say what this will achieve, but as you can see we are now plunged into a war which has taken away most of our young men. We will see how it all ends."

"Don't worry, Mademoiselle, it will end soon and all will be well for Italy, our Fuhrer will see to that," broke in Hans. She looked at him quizzically.

After a hard day's sightseeing, Hans thought that the least he could do was to offer Ester dinner. She needed some persuasion but eventually agreed, and that evening they sat together at a table in a restaurant of her choice. In most of war-torn Europe, food was scarce and, even in Hans' mess, monotonous German-style canned or preserved foods were the rule, but here in rural Sicily the locals made sure that whatever else happened there would be plenty of their own products for their tables. They had a magical spaghetti dish with peppers, capers and other vegetables unknown to Hans, followed by sardines on a bed of spinach and seasoned so as to make the little fish almost come to life in the mouth. They finished with a delicious dessert made primarily of local oranges but sweetened and flavoured so as to make a perfect finish to the meal. Ester had insisted that they should drink the local wine, which was drawn from an ancient barrel and served in a porcelain jug. It was astonishingly cool and refreshing with not the least hint of sharpness. Hans felt he could drink it all night and feel not a bit the worse, but its alcohol loosened his tongue and he began to talk freely to this astonishing girl. The grace and sophistication she had shown during their tour was still apparent but there was something more, a kind of feral attractiveness which radiated from her as she sat at the dimly-lit table. All uncertainties and self-doubt forgotten, somehow he wanted to impress her with his manliness, to match her beauty with his own prowess. He told her about his unit's mission and about how proud he was to have fought in Poland, France, over England and in the Mediterranean, about the capabilities of the Stuka aircraft and the damage they were doing to British shipping, about his brave comrades and the skilled and daring leadership of the Luftwaffe. As he spoke she kept silent, and he could see that she was troubled.

"Hans," she said at last, calling him by his first name for the first time, "what is your opinion of the treatment of minority races within your Reich?"

He was nonplussed by the question.

"Well," he stammered. "The Fuhrer has indeed said some harsh things about parasites who eat away at the substance of the Reich, Jews for example, but that's nothing to do with us flyers."

Ester sat very still and looked at him closely.

"And have you wondered perhaps," she continued, "why I introduced myself to a stranger last night and took the trouble to show him round our town?"

She had turned pale and was staring at him, her eyes narrowing. He thought for a moment she was going to explode in the way that Sonia had years before, but she continued in an even tone.

"I will tell you why. The elders of my community had heard that there was a German officer in the town whose job it was to find any 'parasites' as you called them and prepare to deal with them. I was chosen to find and question this officer as I speak French and some German, and to discover if the story was true. I can tell by your remarks that you are not him. You are far too stupid for such a mission. You are no more than a donkey doing what he is told and asking no questions. Go back to your beloved Stuka and kill some more people. That's what you are here to do."

Hans dropped his glass and started to rise from the table. The outburst had terrified and astonished him and his only instinct was to get away, but she had not finished.

"Sit down!" she commanded. "Let me tell you this. I myself am one of your 'parasites'. My family came here with the Arabs and we prospered. We learnt to trade and to barter, to open banks, to become doctors and professors. Then the Spanish came and tried to expel us. We were too smart for them. We pretended to be Christians, "Conversos" they called us, but we were still the same faithful Jews in our hearts. Even now we control much of the commerce in the island. We know what your Fuhrer is doing to our people in Germany, in France and in Poland. We know all about the Crystal Night. I warn you, you will never drive us from this island." Her voice rose to a scream. "Never." She stormed out into the night.

Hans slunk back to his hotel.

What were his feelings towards this girl? He seemed, he thought, to have bad luck with girls, especially Italian ones. Those he liked he always seemed to upset. It had never occurred to him that Ester might have been Jewish. He had felt he could have developed a relationship with her just as he had with Angela. They had such a happy carefree day together and the meal had crowned it until the last moments. Glumly he ordered a grappa from the porter and made his way miserably to bed.

The next morning he met Ester's intended target. Obersturmfuhrer Feldman of the Allgemeine SS was a strikingly handsome young officer who was taking coffee in the breakfast room and looking benignly about him. He greeted Hans warmly. "Ah, so pleasant to meet another German officer so far from home. And a distinguished flyer too, I see. May I enquire the nature of your business here in Enna?" Hans told him. "Oh, so you are on a short vacation, how fortunate. I myself am here on business. We SS officers have so many duties these days, and there are so few of us." Hans knew a little about the Allgemeine SS. Unlike the Waffen SS, they were not fighters but were employed to retain an iron grip on subject peoples and had an evil reputation. It was surprising to find one operating in Italy, an allied country, but Ester's words had given Hans a clue as to his mission. He took an immediate disliking to his compatriot. Feldman, however, remained politeness itself. He asked Hans to tell him all he knew about the town and its inhabitants, and congratulated him on his knowledge of its history. He insisted that they should meet for dinner that evening, and offered him the use of an SS car and driver for a day's sightseeing. Hans refused, preferring his own company and his motorbike. He spent a confusing day trying to find the remains of a Roman villa nearby, which turned out to be closed, and got himself hopelessly lost in a maze of bumpy unmade roads. He was irritated and dusty by the time he met Feldman for dinner. The Obersturmfuhrer wanted to go to the same restaurant that Hans had visited the night before, but Hans dared not show his face there after being made to look such a fool the previous evening. Instead they found a more modern establishment where they ate worse but more expensively. Again the wine flowed freely.

Hans was poor company during the meal, replying in grumpy monosyllables to his host's questions, but as, once again, the wine started to have its effect, he became a little more talkative. The conversation had turned to the progress of the war in North Africa.

"You must be delighted, as a fighting man, at the progress General Rommel is starting to make in Libya, supported, of course, by your formidable Luftwaffe. It seems now that German soldiers are invincible everywhere."

"Yes, and Rommel impressed all of us with his bold advance in France, when he commanded 7 Panzer Division. He really understands how armoured forces and aircraft can work together."

"Especially your Stukas."

Hans continued in a whisper, "But not such good news on other fronts, Feldman. It seems that the British know something about using air power too. You have heard about the British sinking those three cruisers in the Aegean? My God, what a disaster. I don't think the Italian public have been told yet. A colleague called me with the news this morning."

"I had heard too, through SS channels. Tell me, Oberleutnant, what do you think of Italian forces? Your professional opinion please."

"Well, we have co-operated with them many times. I have to say that they are nowhere near as effective as we are. Their airmen certainly don't lack courage. I have often seen their formations press home attacks after terrible losses, but they seem not to have the skills or the correct leadership. As far as I know, it is the same at sea; the British keep making their navy look pretty silly. As for their soldiers, they seem to be mostly lacking in leadership and determination."

"Yes, can these really be the same people as formed the Roman legions of the past? I think not. I think that the good Roman blood has been too much diluted by immigration and contact with foreigners. My own mission here is not unconnected with this matter. Of course we can never make these people into Aryans like our German folk, but we can purge some of the worst elements. Unfortunately, our allies do not seem to grasp the importance of these purification operations. Sometimes they are even obstructive to my colleagues and myself."

At this point they were interrupted by a fearful wailing sound from the kitchen. Two young women came rushing out, clinging to each other and weeping. "Marco! Marco!" they screamed.

"Their brother," whispered a tearful waiter. "They just heard of his death in Eritrea – it's the second death in the family."

"Disgusting!" muttered Feldman. "Can you see German women behaving like that? Our women folk are proud to have a son or brother fall for the Fatherland."

Hans' dislike for the man, which had actually waned slightly during the meal, reached a new level of intensity. He could no longer stand being in the company of such a heartless, narrow-minded bigot. He invented a stomach ache and walked home alone.

He managed to avoid Feldman for the rest of his stay in Enna, and Ester seemed to have vanished into thin air. At least, he hoped, that would keep her out of the clutches of the SS. Hans' days were spent on lonely treks in the mountains, and quiet evenings in obscure rural villages. He gave the Easter processions a miss.

Certainly he was a refreshed man when he returned to the squadron, and the memory of the hospital bombing had faded into the back of his mind. He remained troubled by Ester. Had there been any deep feelings between them? Could he even have started to fall in love with her? He didn't think so, but never had a girl left such a strong impression on him. Her humour, her serious interest in the history she was trying to explain, her lithe, animated movements and, above all, that blazing anger, those furious flashing eyes; he just couldn't get them out of his mind. Jew or not, she had fascinated him. He had to see her again.

Hans flew three operations during the week of his return to the squadron, then poor weather intervened and the Stukas were stood down. One misty morning he was leaving the mess after breakfast when the battered truck which delivered vegetables to the air station stopped beside him. "Oberleutnant Hans?" The man thrust a screw of paper into his hand. The engine of the truck revved and it was gone into the mist.

Back in his room Hans examined the paper. It was dirty and roughly torn from a notepad. The scrawl was written in some rusty-coloured material. Perhaps blood. *Help me. SS lines Enna. E.* Hans froze. Those bastards. God know what they would be doing to his Ester. Anyone could see that that Feldman had a cruel streak. He must get there and sort it out. Not a second to lose.

He grabbed the motorbike, kicked it into life and thundered off into the fog.

The SS lines were just outside the town among some abandoned farm buildings. Tents were neatly laid out in a field and there was a sinister-looking barbed wire cage overlooked by a wooden watch tower a little way away. Hans pulled rank and demanded to see the senior man present. Oberscharfuhrer Otto Glock was a huge coarse man with a shaven head and the face of a street fighter. He had a way of addressing commissioned officers which was almost a sneer, concealed under exaggerated politeness. No, he was not aware of any prisoners in the camp, the Herr

Hauptmann could see for himself that the cage was empty. The Hauptmann looked tired, would he like a drink, a schnapps perhaps? Was there anyone particular he was looking for? Obersturmfuhrer Feldman? He would perhaps be in the hotel, would the Hauptmann like to telephone? Without returning the man's salute, Hans turned on his heel and sped off to the hotel.

Feldman was sitting on the terrace, enjoying a cigar. He waved Hans towards a chair.

"Ah! My friend, good to see you so soon. My Oberscharfuhrer telephoned to tell me that you might be heading in this direction. Can I offer you a drink?"

"Where is she? What have you done with Ester?"

"Oh, I think you must mean the little Jewess. Yes, I can understand your interest in her. I can tell you that my men, too, found her most attractive, although she was a Jew. Of course there are laws against any relationships between good Germans and those disgusting people, but here we can, of course, overlook a little indiscretion. Well, I can tell you that we put her on a train yesterday. She should be half way to Rome by now. So let's forget her. A drink? Brandy perhaps?"

Normally Hans was an even-tempered fellow, avoiding arguments and violence, but there was something about the SS officer which broke through his normal self-control. Like most German fighting officers, he knew little about the death camps and the gas chambers, but the sinister doings of the SS and its minions was not entirely secret and the thought of Ester in a camp run by creatures like Feldman and Glock drove him to a form of madness. His fist smashed into the face of the Obersturmfuhrer, leaving the man scrabbling on the floor, bleeding from the mouth and trying desperately to draw his pistol. Hans was wearing heavy motorcycling boots and his first kick jerked back Feldman's head. The man ceased to struggle and lay bleeding and moaning on the terrace. Hans turned away from his victim and was struck by a sudden panic. He charged down the hotel steps, leapt onto his machine and sped off towards the aerodrome with no idea in his head of what to do next.

The end for Obersturmfuhrer Feldman did not come as a result of Hans' assault. He had been stunned and had lost some teeth but was otherwise unharmed. One of the waiters saw him sprawled helpless and bleeding. He was well enough acquainted with the German's mission and, good communist as he was, decided to put an end to it. He grabbed the man's pistol, at the same time slitting his jugular vein with the wicked little dagger he always carried in his belt. The pistol was immediately hidden where no German would be able to find it. It came in useful later when the Allies invaded Sicily. When the SS investigation into the affair commenced, every staff member in the hotel swore that he had seen the Luftwaffe officer knock the victim over, slash his throat and then seize his pistol. They even produced a razor-sharp knife thrown into the bushes which they swore was the murder weapon. Not for nothing do the Sicilians have a reputation "managing" such affairs and keeping quiet.

When Hans reached the base it was a hive of activity. Once again a British convoy had been detected, heading for Malta and strongly escorted. It seemed that no word of the incident at Enna had reached Hans' squadron and he arrived just in time to listen to a rapid briefing by Major von Kostler. Struggling rapidly into his flying kit, he resolved that this must be an end to his life as a flyer and as a human being. He did not know if Feldman was dead or alive, either way his assault on him would mean death by firing squad or a long stretch in prison. He would end it now in the soldier's way, facing the enemy of the Reich. Climbing into his machine, he watched Stokmann settle into his seat. Before his faithful gunner had tightened his straps, he shouted into the intercom, "I think there is a fault with the bomb attachment under the port wing, and I can't get the ground crew to listen to me. Quick, go and check it yourself, Oberfeldwebel, but don't waste time, we will start taxiing in a few seconds". As soon as Stokmann was out of the plane, Hans opened up the engine and the Stuka moved forward, leaving its gunner yelling and waving on the grass. In the general confusion of the rushed take-off, no one in the attack formation noticed what had happened. As he led his section towards the enemy, Hans' mind was racing. The events of the day had rendered him incapable of sober, logical thought.

"I've killed that arrogant bastard, now I'm going to kill myself," he kept muttering. Thank God, he'd left his gunner behind: he did not deserve to die. He himself planned to smash his plane into one of the enemy ships. He did not want to hear his comrades and pulled out the plug of his headset. Waggling his wings to indicate to his section that he had a communications problem, he pulled out of the formation and dived away close to the sea surface. He would come in alone, fast and low, while the others were making their bombing attack and distracting the enemy fire. He would slam his machine into the side of the biggest ship he could find and that would be an end of it all. He reached down to the switch which armed the bombs.

For once this Luftwaffe strike was badly planned. The convoy had been reported by an Italian submarine which had sighted six large merchant ships and escorts heading east between Sardinia and Tunis. What the sub had failed to spot was the aircraft carrier *Rampant* steaming behind the convoy, screened by two destroyers, and a radar equipped anti-aircraft cruiser to the north. The convoy was out of range of British Malta-based fighters so Fliegerkorps X expected no opposition and decided to mount a dive bomber strike, without waiting for a fighter escort to be organised. After this decision had been taken, an Italian shadowing seaplane did spot *Rampant* but by then it was too late to recall the Stukas or to get any protective fighters into the air in time. The cruiser picked up the German strike force on its radar when it was still some fifty miles from the convoy, giving the carrier time to launch twelve Fleet Air Arm Sea Hurricanes.

Sub-lieutenant Billy Reeve RNVR was not the best pilot in his squadron; in fact, he only just managed to avoid being taken off flying altogether after a succession of bad landings and getting separated from his leader during fighter sweeps on two occasions. Today, however, as he climbed away from *Rampant* on full throttle, he felt things would be different. He clung to the starboard wing tip of his leader, keeping as close as he dared, eyes peeled for the enemy bombers. *Rampant* had been well to the west of the convoy so with luck the Hurricanes would be between the evening sun and their prey. The radio crackled in Billy's ears. The leading aircraft had spotted the Stukas, still slightly above them, in close formation. Swinging northwards so as to attack from behind, the Hurricanes deployed into a textbook attacking formation. Before they could reach the Stukas they were spotted. In these circumstances the best defensive move the Germans could make was to form into a big circle, following each other round and round. It would then be difficult for a fighter to pick on an individual aircraft and get on its tail. Approaching the circle would bring the attacker under fire from the rear guns of several aircraft at the same time. Undaunted, the Hurricanes charged at the defensive ring and the sky was full of zooming, shrieking aircraft.

Billy at first stuck like a limpet to his leader, gritting his teeth and hauling on the controls with all his strength. Twice he fired a short burst from his eight machine guns but both times he knew he had missed by a mile. Also, with all these machines in a terrifying, whirling melee, he was in constant fear of hitting a friendly aircraft. Suddenly he glimpsed a machine approaching him from his port side. In a fraction of a second he had to take evasive action; he hit the rudder hard and in panic hauled back on the stick. The Hurricane reared up, forcing him down into his seat and blacking him out completely, then the plane toppled over on one wing and plunged downward, out of control. By the time Billy recovered consciousness, his machine was in a steep, uncontrollable dive, the engine racing and the whole airframe shuddering and protesting as the speed crept up towards four hundred miles per hour. Forcing himself not to panic, Billy shut off the throttle and somehow regained control of his machine. He pulled out into a shallow dive, then looked around him. Nothing. No aircraft in sight anywhere, just a thin blanket of cloud overhead and a featureless sea beneath him. Once again he had lost his leader, and this time he might be accused of chickening out of the fight deliberately. He had used up more than half his fuel and could not possibly climb again to re-join the fight even if he could find it. Trembling with shame and rage and anticipating a frosty reception, he turned south towards where he expected the convoy to be. After ten minutes he glimpsed a freighter below him and soon picked up the bulk of *Rampant* way off to the west. Ahead of him, low down, another machine was heading towards her, and he swung onto its tail so as to follow it in to land on deck. Pray, pray for a decent landing at least, he kept saying to himself. Then he noticed something funny about the aeroplane ahead. It had curious gull like wings and it was much bigger than a Hurricane. A Fulmar? No. A Skua perhaps? No, wrong shape. A Roc? Impossible. For God's sake, wake up! It's a Stuka! Making straight for the carrier. Billy shoved the throttle forward. He'd have to be quick to catch the dreaded bomber before it could drop its load. But why didn't it try to avoid him? What was the rear gunner doing? Why the hell didn't he tell the pilot to take evasive action? It was an easy shot, even for |Billy. Straight ahead, no deflection, he watched his bullets knock pieces off the tail plane and flicker along the fuselage. The ugly black plane banked sharply, staggered and plunged into the sea. A raft of debris floated on the surface only twenty yards from the carrier. Billy had not a second to glance at it; he was careering towards the grey bulk of *Rampant* at full speed. For the second time in half an hour he blacked out as he hauled back the stick so as to skim over the carrier, then he had to join the circuit of returning Hurricanes to land on deck. For once a perfect landing! The celebration on board that evening was memorable. Six Stukas for certain, maybe a couple more, but the prize victory was Billy's, right alongside the ship so everyone could see. For the first time in his career, he was a hero to his colleagues and to the ship's crew. What a night it was!

No one in the officers' mess was particularly interested in the activities in the sick bay that evening. A rescue tug had pulled a German pilot out of the water alive. No sign of his gunner. The man was delirious and his right arm was shattered beyond repair. As the surgeons worked, the convoy steamed on eastward. By dawn they would be in the comparative safety provided by fighters from Malta.

Chapter 10

The Beaufighter ("Beau" as it was called) was deceptively similar to the Blenheim at first glance, but under the skin it was an entirely different beast. For a start it had seventy percent more power, and no dorsal turret to slow it down. It was thus some sixty miles per hour faster and far more agile. Almost as fast as a single-seater fighter, it had a range of over one thousand five hundred miles and could remain on patrol for five or six hours at a time. As a dedicated night fighter, it had a massive punch of four heavy cannons in the nose and six wing-mounted machine guns. But above all it had its radar, the unblinking eye which spied out intruders by night and brought the deadly firepower to bear. The AI Mark IV set fitted was similar to that which William had used in the Blenheim, but with greatly enhanced performance and reliability, and, thanks to the work done with the Blenheims, a procedure for working effectively at night with ground controllers was now in place. The Beau was poised to become the definitive answer to the German night raiders.

First, however, the crews had to sort themselves out and get to know how to master the beast. They were to be transferred from their experimental flight to the newly formed 223 squadron, generally known as the "Owls", based at Tangmere. The squadron had specialist ground crews, trained on the Beaufighter and on the Mark IV radar, allocated to it. It was commanded by Group Captain "Whiskers" Williams, a fiery Welshman and a superb pilot. Most of the squadron's pilots were career RAF men in their thirties, professional and cautious in their attitude to the new technology, quite unlike the boisterous single-seater heroes of the Battle of Britain.

The Beau was a two-man aircraft and so William had to say goodbye to one of his crew; Willis was transferred to a heavy bomber squadron, Jimmy remaining as his navigator/radar operator. The new aircraft proved quite a handful. It was heavy and had high wing loading so that it took off and landed very fast. The massive Bristol Hercules engines gave it terrific acceleration and an excellent rate of climb but if one of them were to fail, especially on take-off, the machine was virtually unmanageable.

Then there were the problems inherent in flying at night. The Beau was quite unstable in pitch – meaning it would start to climb or dive unexpectedly if the pilot lost concentration. These changes in pitch were easy to detect and correct in daylight, when there was normally a visible horizon, but in the dark they could easily go unnoticed, especially when climbing or descending through cloud. It was natural to want to keep staring ahead and trusting one's instincts to keep the plane straight and level, but instinct in these conditions is unreliable. Pilots had to learn to trust their instruments and fly by them. They either learnt to fly with eyes glued to the instrument panel or they didn't last long in Beaufighter squadrons.

Another persistent challenge was how to get home. At that time there were no effective landing aids, so the crews had to come home on a bearing given by their radar controller (always supposing that the radio link was working correctly) then look out for a familiar flare path. Judging height and drift correctly after a long night's flying in an ice-cold cockpit in the dark was always a challenge and the slightest mistake could be fatal.

Night fighter pilots went on standby as soon as it got dark, and had to sit uncomfortably in the dimly lit crew room in flying gear, wearing darkened goggles, waiting for the order to scramble. This would be given when ground radar detected enemy intruders at long range. The fighters would be instructed to take off and orbit a beacon until the course and height of the enemy were clearly determined. The ground controllers would then direct each individual aircraft to a selected target, guiding it to within a mile or so of its intended victim. By this time the fighter's own radar would be switched on and seeking to acquire the target. As soon as the radar operator, sitting beside the pilot, saw the target on his screen, he would direct the pilot towards it, closing it from astern. All this time the enemy would have no idea that he was being stalked. When the range was reduced to about two hundred yards, the pilot would, with luck, make visual contact with the enemy, probably at first making out the red glow of the exhausts or seeing a black form illuminated by the moon. He could then open fire with his massive armament. This would probably be the first indication the victim had of his presence. Unless the aim was good, the enemy might well be able to escape a second attack by diving away into cloud and evading the narrow beam of the airborne radar, then the whole process would have to be repeated, but the bomber would be alert and would weave around, becoming very difficult to find. A common error was to approach too fast, overshooting the enemy plane before seeing it. In this case the enemy would probably see the fighter as it drew close and could open fire himself, at the same time taking violent evasive action. As the experimental flight had found with the Blenheims, the key to success was good team work between the ground radar, radar operator in the aircraft and the pilot.

Whiskers was a stickler for good discipline in the air and on the ground. Crews were not listed as operational until they had proved to him that they could fly accurately and had total command of radio procedures, radar operation, and of how to handle the aircraft. Woe betide anyone found in the crew room not fully ready and wearing his darkened goggles.

"Fathead!" he would yell. "How are you going to fly in the dark, let alone see a bomber with your vision not adjusted? You'll kill yourself not the bloody Huns. Get the hell out of the crew room and stay out! See me in my office before breakfast in the morning."

Jimmy and William, thanks to their experimental work, were among the first aircrews to be declared operational. On a chilly March night, they found themselves listening to the crackle of the crew room radio. They had been there for three hours, bored by the incessant twaddle from the BBC and from cups of grey-coloured tea from the little kitchen in the hut. Just as William, blinded by those awful goggles, was clumsily stretching out his hand for yet another cup, the urgent clanging of the telephone bell exploded into the semi-darkness. "Number 3341 Scramble, Scramble". Tearing off their goggles as they stumbled into the darkness outside, the two men ran towards the dark form of their waiting machine. The ground crew – William already knew their names and recognised each man in the darkness – cranked the engines by hand and operated the Ki-gas priming pumps.

"Starter booster coils engaged! Starter engaged!"

The great engines stuttered, then burst into throbbing, trembling life. The ground crew stood ready to continue priming until both engines settled down to a steady roar. William methodically checked the engines and controls – his many years of flying had taught him never to rush this process, then, setting the flaps at fifteen degrees down, he flashed his navigation lights to tell the tower that he was ready and rumbled forward onto the runway.

"All set to go, Jimmy?"

"All set, skip."

The Beaufighter surged down the grass runway, gathering speed, so that the dim lights of the runway seemed to merge into one as the aircraft rushed past. They lifted off and soared away at one hundred and seventy miles per hour, then climbed quickly to sixteen thousand feet so as to orbit a beacon, flashing a green light, somewhere near Bognor Regis. Flying in circles round the beacon became almost as boring as sitting in the crew hut. There was nothing to see except the occasional flash of lights over Dover which they thought indicated bomb bursts. The moon was nearly full and occasionally it was possible to see it shining on the sea a little way to the south. Suddenly the radio burst out.

"3341 standby for trade."

"Roger, Magnet."

("Magnet" was the call sign of the fighter controller.)

"3341, make your course two two zero degrees, angels at two two thousand. Clear to smack."

("Clear to smack" meant that the target was positively identified as an enemy.)

"Roger."

The powerful fighter climbed and headed towards the intruder.

"3341, your target now climbing to angels two two twenty steer two three zero."

"Roger."

William forced himself to stay calm in this game of blind man's buff. All he could do was to fly as accurately as possible, following instructions. Ahead he could see searchlight beams still probing the darkness. It was probably these which had caused his quarry to climb.

"Your assigned target's range now thirty miles."

There was at least one hundred miles per hour speed difference between the Beau and the bomber; they should catch up in fifteen minutes or so. Time to check guns.

Magnet called again, a renewed note of urgency in his voice:

"Turn to port ninety degrees, range to target now fifteen miles."

The enemy plane seemed now to be flying southeast. Magnet was trying to bring the fighter round directly onto his tail.

Magnet, triumphantly:

"Your range now five miles, you are on the same heading as the bandit. You are closing rapidly. Clear to flash weapon."

Jimmy turned on his radar set. The screen showed all sorts of clutter. He tried desperately to pick out an echo from the enemy.

"You are closing rapidly, do not, do not overshoot."

William swore under his breath. The controller was right. He had been used to struggling to catch up with enemy bombers in the Blenheim. Now, idiot, remember you are much faster. If you overshoot, he'll see you and you'll lose him. He closed the throttles and pulled up the nose.

"Got him, skip," muttered Jimmy into his intercom. "Ten degrees off the bow range about nine hundred yards, just below us."

William closed the throttles further and pushed the stick forward.

"We're closing on him slowly now, skip, go port a little, more, more; OK, he's dead ahead now. Flying straight and level."

"Thanks, Jimmy. Range?"

"Five hundred yards now."

For what seemed minutes, William peered into the darkness ahead, then suddenly something reflected the moon's baleful glow above them. Yes, there it was just ahead, a long, narrow fuselage and two small tail fins, a Dornier 17. He could even make out the disgusting black crosses on the wings. How dare this foul thing come and bomb his peaceful country? William lined up the gun sight.

"Opening fire!"

Immediately the cannon shells ripped into the bomber and bits of metal seemed to fly off in all directions. Caught entirely unawares, the machine plunged down to smash itself onto the downs near Selsey Bill.

William reported to Magnet.

"Roger, 3341, return to base."

William's first call was on the squadron intelligence officer who wanted to know every fine detail of the encounter so as to use it as a model for training purposes. As he was leaving, a Flight Sergeant walked in and handed him a message. He stuffed it into his pocket and walked over to the mess, where bacon and eggs was being served to night-fighter crews. Exhausted by their night's work, the crews were delighted with the results of their first operation. Two other bombers had been brought down by the Owls and even Whiskers was in high spirits, slapping people on the back and promising a serious drinks party as soon as there was a break in the operational schedule.

It was almost midday when he remembered the note, tearing it open as he lay on his bed. It was from an east London hospital. The Reverend James Tullow (Flopsy's proper name) was in casualty, badly hurt, and was asking for him. Still in a buoyant mood the CO agreed to thirty-six hours compassionate leave, and William got ready to drive to Lambeth in the Lagonda. Just as he was leaving, Jimmy appeared.

170

"Skip, if you are going to London, can I cadge a lift? I got a thirty-six too."

"No problem, Sarge, but where exactly?"

"I'm off to see my old lady. She's at home in Camberwell, I hope."

"That's just near Lambeth, where I'm going, hop in."

It was still daylight when they started, and sped off, London bound. As darkness fell, the dimmed headlights gave barely enough light to drive, and slowly they progressed through dismal-looking suburbia. A steady rain made the roads glisten faintly under their masked lights and a bitter, probing wind found every gap in the old car's inadequate canvas roof. Not many people were about, and occasionally they saw searchlight beams stabbing the air over the capital, but there was no air raid warning.

"A bit stormy for Jerry tonight, I'd say, skip, especially after the licking we gave them last night," remarked Jimmy.

"Yes, they won't be flying tonight, thank God. We should be OK."

As they progressed, even in the dim lights of the car, the destruction around them became evident. Ugly gaps appeared between the rows of houses on each side of the road and many windows were covered with boarding or corrugated iron sheets. In a few places, orange flames still flickered, licking at fallen roof timbers, defying the steadily falling rain. There was no one much about, and the few figures in the streets hurried through the damp, huddled in heavy waterproofs. The blackout stifled any light which might try to shine from those houses which were still occupied, making the sensation of driving through the city eerily like entering a ghost town. Twice they had to stop where piles of rubble blocked their way so they had to weave round through side streets. Once a pale-looking policeman stopped the car, enquired their business, and diverted them round a street still being cleared by a bulldozer and a team of exhausted workmen. For the first time the two flyers were experiencing at first hand the havoc wrought by their ruthless enemy. The wreckage they saw being carted away must have been from a bomb dropped the previous night, the very night of their first operational sortie. As they approached Lambeth, Jimmy was getting into familiar territory and was able to guide them through the maze of streets to the hospital. He gave directions in his usual bantering manner, but William noticed a catch in his voice from time to time. These were his streets, his houses, his people, and they were being reduced to ruins.

The hospital was an ugly brick building which somehow had escaped the bombing. Inside, the walls were painted cream and chocolate brown and the floor was covered with worn yellowish linoleum. The staff looked tired and harassed, but a friendly enough receptionist, doubtless impressed by their RAF uniforms, found a cup of sugary tea for Jimmy and directed William to Flopsy's ward. He was sickened by what he found. A solitary nurse had charge of some twenty patients, all of them suffering from injuries caused by the bombing. Try as she would, the poor girl had no hope of bringing water, medicines, painkillers and bed pans to all her charges and the place stank of urine. Groans and cries, some angry, some despairing, made sleep impossible and gaunt eyes stared starkly at William as he walked in. Flopsy's bed was surrounded by screens. Pushing them aside, he looked at the frail figure on the mattress. The face was pale and drawn and the lips pulled back over the gums to give a skull-like appearance. He was breathing in short irregular gasps and could speak only in a hoarse, laboured whisper. He recognised his visitor, however, and attempted a smile.

"Silly me!" he wheezed. "Do you know what I was doing? Fire watching! At my age! In the church tower, then a bomb landed nearby. It seemed to suck all the oxygen out of the air and there was this terrific impact. Seems to have shaken the old frame up a bit. But good of you to come – they've been so kind to me here although they are so very busy but it's nice to see a familiar face."

He was convulsed with coughing and for several minutes could say nothing, then he started speaking again, this time more strongly.

"I want you to know, William, that your father was the finest, bravest man I ever knew. After your mother and brother and sister were lost in that terrible accident, I was so proud when he asked me to do what I could for you if he did not survive the war himself. Of course, I don't know exactly what you are doing in the RAF but I believe that you are proving yourself a worthy son to my dear friend. I have to tell you also that he felt especially bitter that the war had divided his own family and he longed for it to end so that he could bring the von Pilsens together again. It will be hard, but do try, dear William."

The effort of speaking seemed to have exhausted the poor man and he collapsed back onto his pillow in another fit of coughing.

William nodded, but his eyes filled with tears as he took hold of one of the withered hands on the bedspread and held it gently. The little figure in the bed seemed to relax and fell into a doze. William sat there with him for half an hour, trying to digest the burden these few words seemed to have placed upon him, then he tiptoed out of the ward to find a doctor. The young man on duty looked completely worn out, but with a sigh he took William into a small office. He knew Flopsy well as the clergyman had often visited the hospital in more peaceful times to see sick parishioners.

"I have to tell you," he said, "the poor reverend has suffered terrible internal injuries, bomb blast often damages internal organs, especially in old people, and I believe that his lungs were weak anyway due to gassing in the First War. Poor fellow! And he was trying to do his bit watching for fires in the tower – all by himself, in this weather! I am sorry but I can't see much hope for him. It's terrible to see such a good man go."

Jimmy was waiting in the lobby trying unsuccessfully to chat up one of the nurses.

"OK," said William, "I'll drop you off by your house now and collect you here about midday tomorrow. I don't think I'll be able to do anything for the old boy tonight."

"But where are you going to sleep, skip? Lord, you do look all shaken up."

William couldn't answer.

"Look, you've got yer ration card, haven't you? Come round to my old lady's place; she'll put you up for tonight, so you're nice and close to the hospital in the morning."

"But she won't be expecting me. Can't we phone her first?"

"Telephone! Do me a favour, skip, we ain't got no phone. Doubt there's one in the whole street."

William marvelled that this expert radar operator and competent navigator had lived all his life without a phone. He was worried about his own reception in what was obviously a working-class home. The RAF had taught him to get on with all sorts of people, but staying in an east London cockney household would be a new and daunting experience.

They pulled up outside one of a row of terraced houses. It was one of the few undamaged in the street but, even so, it looked gloomy in the blackout. Obviously relieved, Jimmy jumped out.

"'Ere we are, skip, number forty-three."

William followed him through the front door, which was not locked. The narrow hallway led into a fair-sized room in which Mrs Hopson was engaged in laying the fire. She half turned round then, let out a little scream as Jimmy scooped her up in his arms.

"Ullo, Mum."

"Lorks, Jimmy, you didn't 'arf gimme a turn."

"Sorry, ole girl." He turned towards William. "This 'ere is my skipper wot I told you about. 'Ee's come for the night. Where's Dad?"

"Eez on night shift, ain't 'ee. Sit down, Mr Skipper, this one's comfy."

William noticed a face which smiled all over and kind blue eyes. Mrs Hopson was a small person with large strong-looking hands, all black with coal and soot from the still unlit fire. In spite of this, she looked neat in her floral pinny over a day dress and slippered feet.

"Yer dad won't be back till eight in the morning I should think. Let me finish this and I'll see about some tea. Aizul!"

"Hazel's my brother's wife," explained Jimmy. "Bombed out they was so she's living 'ere for now, so you'll 'ave to 'ave the back bedroom where I used to sleep."

He showed William his room and when they returned both women were hard at work in the kitchen and a welcome fire was burning in the grate. Soon they were tucking into plates of sausage, mash and cabbage liberally covered with onion gravy. Mrs Hopson explained that she had three other sons, all away at the war. She herself worked in daytime at an aircraft parts factory and she and Hazel kept house for Mike, her husband, and any of the family who might come home on leave.

After supper and the radio news Jimmy went down the road to meet some old mates in the pub and show off his sergeant's stripes. William sensed that he would be out of place among Jimmy's pals and planned for an early night, but it was clear that Mrs Hopson was not going to let him escape too easily.

"Mr Skipper, my dear, I tell you I'm not 'alf glad to meet you, and to see that you're looking after my Jimmy. I wouldn't want to think of him up there in the air with any young tearaway, and you seem such a sensible man, but tell me is what you are doing very dangerous?"

William reassured her.

"Thank God for that, I'm not worried about Freddy and Joe, they're both in the Navy, in a big ship called *Hood* I think, they'll be safe enough there, my Mike he was a Navy man in the last war. In a battleship he was, and he said they never saw the enemy once. I was worried about Jimmy until I met you but I know he's all right now. Young George – I don't know what he's doing, he joined up in the Service Corps, sent him to Africa they did, driving lorries, but he's a wild one always getting into fights. I'm afraid he'll sign on for anything dangerous."

"Well," said William, "I don't know much about the fighting in Africa but I do know that in this war it's just as dangerous to be here at home as it is to be in the front line. Look at all the houses which have been hit around here."

"Strange, ain't it? Me and Mike has to spend most nights in the shelter down the playground at the end of the street. Right cold and damp it is in there and you should hear the language. Bad enough to make a cat blush. And you've got to keep an eye on everything. There's those in there would nick yer false teeth given half a chance! But I'll tell you one thing, we've never made money like we are now, what with the night shifts and both of us working. Coining it we are. But still I wish it was all over."

"Well, at least we're not in the shelter tonight; this is no weather for the bombers."

"Now tell me, Mr Skipper, you must know, being an officer and that, are we winning this war? They says we are on the radio and in the papers, but they would, wouldn't they? Are we winning?"

"Well, we got our men back from Dunkirk, that was important, and the fighter boys fought them off last summer and autumn. Now there's the night time blitz, but maybe we can put a stop to that by the summer, so I'd say we are holding our own now and perhaps the Americans will come in to help sometime. From what little I know it's the submarines we have to watch. If we can get on top of them we should be all right as I see it."

"Well thank you, Mr Skipper, you've talked a lot of sense, and thank you for looking after Jimmy, he worships you, you know. Now I can see you are tired, get you off to bed. I'll be gone by the time you are about in the morning. Good night."

In bed, William heard Jimmy come clumsily home from the pub, singing snatches of song. Although he had been flying the previous night and was terribly tired, he could not sleep. He thought of the destruction he had seen from the car, of Flopsy, terribly wounded while fire-watching on his own, up his church tower; of the brave woman he had been talking to, working in a factory, running the house, worrying about her boys and trying to make sense out of the war. Above all he felt humbled and inadequate to bear the responsibility of the trust she placed in him. This brave, hard-working woman seemed to represent the very core and backbone of the British people, but he himself was unworthy of them. He was no ace pilot. Even if he had been, he could not keep Jimmy safe. No one could ever guess at the terror he had felt during his bombing exploits. If only he could be carefree and easy going like Jimmy. Miserably he lay in the humble bedroom and at last fell into a troubled sleep.

Flopsy did not last that night. He passed away quietly, by himself, in his hospital bed dying, as he had lived, causing the least possible inconvenience to those around him. William looked at the grey, drawn face, peaceful now somehow in death. He thought of his bumbling, unworldly guardian, so brave and yet so gentle, now at peace. If there was such a thing as Heaven, surely he was there.

Two days later the weather changed and the squadron was active again. William and Jimmy flew eight operational missions during the next three weeks, two of them resulting in successful kills. The attrition rate of enemy bombers delivering the night time blitz on British cities was rising sharply as more Beaufighters came into operation and techniques for working with the ground control radars improved. The Luftwaffe were now suffering an attrition rate of over five percent of the bombers on each mission and they clearly could not sustain their assault for ever. That did not necessarily mean, however, that the interceptors were always free from risk, as William was to find out.

Oberleutnant Carl von Brunden of 100 Gruppe, was a highly experienced pilot. He had flown Messerschmitt Bf110 twin-engined two-seat escort fighters throughout the Battle of Britain. Bf110s had taken terrible losses when trying to escort heavy bombers in daylight to their targets, as they were no match in combat for the defending single-seaters. They were, however, quite formidable aircraft, faster and lighter than the Beaufighter, and heavily armed. The German high command decided to try to use 100 Gruppe's 110s to make deep penetration night time bombing raids on key British factories and airfields. As they could cruise at over three hundred miles per hour and reach over thirty thousand feet, perhaps they could safely avoid British night fighters and, guided by *X-Gerat* beams – the navigation system which Hugh and Kilowatt had described to William – make successful high-level attacks on strategic targets deep into enemy territory. Von Brunden was selected for one of the first of these ventures. His force consisted of six aircraft, each carrying two five hundred-pound bombs and the target was the Vickers factory at Bromsgrove, in the Midlands. To reach the target from their base in Holland, the aircraft were fitted with *Dackelbauch* long-range fuel tanks; these were rather unsatisfactory plywood tanks mounted under the fuselage. Von Brunden's regular rear gunner/signaller was off sick on the night of the raid and was replaced by a less experienced crewman, Feldwebel Hauser.

At first all went well for the raiders. All six aircraft took off and in spite of their heavy load of fuel and bombs, struggled up to twenty-five thousand feet as they crossed the North Sea. In the darkness the aircraft soon lost visual contact with each other and strict radio silence was enforced but it was somehow comforting to know that five friendly aircraft were at hand as they entered enemy airspace. They were navigating on the *X-Gerat* system which produced a wide radio beam along which the aircraft flew until they were within about twenty miles of their destination. Here they would pick up a narrow beam leading them directly to the target. A series of three cross beams, radiated from a separate transmitter, would time the aircraft as it moved along the narrow beam and signal the exact moment for the release of the bombs. The system was difficult to jam or bend as it operated in centimetric wave bands which could be changed each night and were extremely difficult to detect. The pilots, specially trained in the use of *X-Gerat,* listened attentively to the signals on their headsets – a constant hum meant they were on the beam, dots told them they were to the left of it and dashes to the right. A sharp "ping" sounded when they crossed the intersecting beams, telling them to drop their load. It was far from comfortable in the cockpit of the Messerschmitt. The crew were seated in tandem, back to back and encumbered in heavy sheepskin flying gear to keep out the cold. They were breathing oxygen from clumsy masks. During the outbound phase of the operation, von Brunden was fully occupied keeping the aircraft on the beam, but Hauser had little to do but keep a sharp lookout for any sign of enemy activity and occasionally retune his radio set. The stars shone brightly in the night sky, but below them nothing was visible through a blanket of thin low cloud. Beneath it, blacked-out Britain slumbered peacefully.

The six intruders were picked up on long-range radar well before they crossed the British coastline. In the darkness they had become quite widely separated but, as they were all on a similar course, it seemed likely that they were heading for the same target in the Midlands. Twelve Beaufighters, among them William's machine, were scrambled and instructed to orbit a beacon on Salisbury Plain. Soon Magnet had a target for William. This, however, was not like any intruder he had so far encountered. It was flying much higher than the bombers normally assigned to him and it seemed extraordinarily fast. As he climbed towards twenty-five thousand feet, to begin his stalking, he found that instead of closing the range, he was getting gradually further behind. Levelling off, he pushed the throttles forward to the emergency full-speed position. The engines could stand this setting for a maximum of ten minutes. The machine shook and trembled with the extra power and the controls felt heavy, but the speed built up rapidly and Magnet reported the range gradually closing.

At two miles Jimmy got a radar contact.

"He's dead ahead, skip, slightly below us. We're gaining on him slowly."

Three minutes later:

"Five degrees to port, we're catching him fast now, range five hundred yards."

William was afraid of overshooting his target. He was still on emergency full power and in a gentle dive, still gaining speed, he eased back the throttle. As he did so there was a loud report from the engines backfiring, and a sheet of flame from each exhaust. It happened that at that moment Hauser, in the Messerschmitt, was looking directly aft. He saw a vivid flash. He could not see what it came from, but he was certain it must be an enemy fighter. "Fighter astern!" he yelled and at the same time fired a burst from his

179

machine gun in the direction of the flash. "What the hell are you doing?" yelled Brunden. "How do you know you're not firing at one of our own planes?" This had not occurred to Hauser; anyway it seemed that he had missed his target, but for a few brief seconds, confusion reigned in the cockpit.

Hauser's burst of fire, however, had shown William exactly where to look for the target. Yes, there it was right ahead. He fired a two-second burst. Unfortunately, he had not remembered to correct for the swing of the aircraft as he made his last course alteration, and his shells whizzed past the target. Brunden knew now that Hauser had been right and that he had to get away fast. Jettisoning his bombs, he turned hard, pushed the nose down and made for the cloud layer beneath. As he turned, Jimmy's radar lost contact but for a critical moment William caught sight of his exhaust flames and followed him down. In normal circumstances the Me 110 could have outrun the Beaufighter but Brunden's machine was encumbered with the long-range fuel tank. He wove from side to side to try to put off the aim of his pursuer and Hauser kept up intermittent bursts of machine gun fire. In reality a small calibre machine gun was unlikely to do serious damage to a big machine like a Beaufighter but the fire was uncomfortably close and certainly disconcerting. Twice more William fired three second bursts but the swerving enemy was undamaged. Ammunition was beginning to run low. At last the Messerschmitt reached the clouds and disappeared into their welcome downy dampness. Brunden, now, as he thought, invisible, resumed a steady course, still at full speed. Unfortunately for him, he had reckoned without Jimmy's radar set. Entering the cloud a few seconds after the enemy, William levelled off and swung the nose of the aircraft gently from side to side, hoping to capture the enemy in his beam, like a hound sniffing for scent.

"Got him!" yelled Jimmy. "Turn to port... more... more... roll out now. Starboard... starboard. That's it he's dead ahead range four hundred yards."

"Can't see," said William. "Now don't lose him, tell me as soon as he turns."

"Going straight now, skip, running for it I guess."

The chase continued through the blanket of cloud, Brunden unaware of his pursuer, William unable to see to take a shot.

At last there was a gap in the cloud and a pale moon shone dimly on the wings of the quarry. William finished his ammunition in one short burst. He saw the shells pass below the belly of the Messerschmitt then suddenly the air ahead of him turned brilliant orange. The Beaufighter was hurled upwards and sideways with tremendous force and great chunks of metal whizzed past. William felt the impact of something hitting the lower fuselage and a hail of metal peppered the wing surfaces. Of the Messerschmitt there was no sign at all. A cannon shell had punctured the empty long-range fuel tank, detonating the petrol vapour inside and blowing the machine completely to pieces. No part of the airframe of the Messerschmitt or of its unfortunate crew was ever found, but two massive Vee-12 engines ploughed into the garden of a farmhouse near Coventry, scaring the farmer and his wife half to death. The engines buried themselves deep in the moist, damp soil and rested there, smoking and hissing, until morning. The two bombs buried themselves deep in the ground. They are probably still there.

But the victors had problems of their own. Caught in the blast of the explosion, the Beaufighter reared up, rolled over on one wing, then plunged downwards. William fought to regain control. "For God's sake, don't let her spin," he said to himself. "Gentle control movements, don't rush." Thankfully he found that the controls seemed to be undamaged. He could see nothing through the windscreen but he was used to flying entirely on instruments and managed to settle the machine into a controlled dive, but something was wrong. There was no response to the throttles; both engines had quit. Desperately he tried to remember the emergency re-start procedure. The best practice was to call it out aloud so that the navigator could double check:

"Stand by for emergency re start drills. Both throttles closed. Ignitions are both on. Feathering push button pressed. Release at six to eight hundred rpm."

He watched the rev counter as the props windmilled in the slipstream. "Releasing now." He watched the engine instruments. Not a flicker. He pushed the throttles gently forward. Nothing. Without power the Beaufighter glided like a brick. They were losing height fast, seven thousand… six thousand… five thousand feet.

"Trying again."

"Skipper, I think we're meant to let the revs get up to over eight hundred or they won't start."

Jimmy's voice was urgent. He was plainly frightened, but thank God, he was still thinking clearly.

"OK, Jimmy, but we're running out of height."

It was true; they were descending uncomfortably fast. William refused to look at the altimeter. If they tried to crash land without power in the dark they would almost certainly be killed. He kept his eyes solely on the rev counter. It inched up maddeningly slowly. There would not be a third chance. Seven hundred… eight hundred… nine hundred… one thousand.

"Releasing feathering button!"

There was no change of sound in the cockpit, the rush of air and the roar of the windmilling propellers drowned out any other noise, but William noticed the engine oil pressure gauge needles begin to tremble, then rise to normal idling levels. Muttering a prayer of thanks, he moved the throttles slowly forward. Both engines responded. They were flying again. Easing back the stick William glanced at the altimeter. Five hundred feet! That had been close. He climbed steadily on a southerly heading towards Tangmere.

"Bloody hell, skip, you had me scared there," said Jimmy.

"Not half as scared as I was. Thank God you remembered the critical rev number."

"It was drummed into us on our training course, but I never thought I'd need to use it. Let's hope that's the first and last time – I swear I could see the ground under us when you began to pull up."

Magnet gave them a course to return to base. When they landed, William was surprised to find himself quite calm and unshaken. His experience of the results of the London blitz had hardened his attitude towards German flyers, and that night's experience had taught him how risky his own job really was. But there was something else. Jimmy had shown that night that he was more than just a cocky, lively crew. He was made of strong stuff, cool and resourceful in an emergency with a brain that was razor-sharp when it was most needed.

All the drama would not have happened, of course, if the engines had not cut out for no apparent reason. A new Flight Sergeant had taken over the care of their aircraft. He had just completed a specialist's course at Bristol's so after breakfast Jimmy and William walked over to talk to him. Somehow he looked familiar to William but at first he couldn't place him, then the Irish accent gave him away. It was Tuoy, the aircraftsman who had ripped the fabric of the Heyford four years ago.

"Good morning, sir, and you're the very man who saved my bacon back in the Duxford days," he began. "Well, it's a real pleasure to see you again, if I may say so, sir, a real pleasure indeed."

Many Irishmen have an uncanny affinity with horses or dogs. Tuoy, on the other hand, had an almost psychic relationship with radial aircraft engines. He would stand and watch his flight take off, listening intently for the slightest hint of roughness, watching the exhausts for any hint of oil leaks or incorrect mixture. He knew where a cigarette paper would give just the right clearance between sliding parts in a fuel pump, or a single tap with a copper hammer would ensure that a cylinder liner seated right home in its sleeve. He had heard of unexplained cut outs before and hinted that there might be a solution. Possibly, he thought, the violent turn caused by the explosion of the enemy close ahead had caused an interruption of the fuel supply, or perhaps the sudden blast had sucked the oxygen out of the air. Maybe he could work out an unofficial fix for the problem.

"What I'd advise also, sir," he said, smiling, "is to shoot them down a bit further away in future. You'd be much safer. And by the way, sir, do try not to run into things, I've never seen so many holes in the wings of an aircraft."

As William and Jimmy left the hangar, Tuoy made an excuse to call William back alone.

"Sir," he said, "I've not forgotten what you did at that enquiry. I can never repay you but you have my word that the boys and I will not leave a stone unturned to make sure you have the best, most reliable Beau in the whole RAF, you have my word on it, sir."

He was to prove as good as his word; not only was the cutting-out problem dealt with by a minute adjustment to fuel pump settings, but engineering standards in William's flight became superb.

As winter turned to spring and the nights grew shorter, German night-time raids on the British mainland became infrequent. The Owls kept up their night-time patrols but enemy encounters were rare. William and Jimmy achieved only one more kill, bringing their total to five. The reduced level of activity suited William well as he had another matter on which to focus his attention. It must be almost time for Angela to arrive home.

The Owls continued to patrol throughout spring and summer 1941. Night-time hit-and-run raids in their sector were becoming less common, but there were some particularly damaging mass attacks. Two heavy raids on Plymouth carried out by over six hundred bombers in April cost seven hundred and fifty civilian lives and determined attacks were also made on Belfast, Liverpool and Bristol. On 10th May a final massive assault on London marked the end of the night-time offensive, and the Luftwaffe bombers found themselves being diverted to prepare for the ferocious Barbarossa campaign against Soviet Russia. Bombing had killed some forty thousand people and seriously injured as many more, but British morale remained high. Although there was heavy damage to property and infrastructure, the bombing did not seriously affect war production or the will of the people to fight on.

Successes by the night-fighter force did much to sustain civilian morale so their activities were given all possible publicity, but William himself was somehow dissatisfied with his role. Jumping enemy bombers at night was neither easy nor, as he had discovered, without risk, but somehow he felt he had had enough of it. He did not like the constant late nights, hanging around in the crew room in the darkness waiting to be summoned, circling the beacon, sometimes for hours waiting to be allocated a target, or increasingly often, to be sent home; the dull days hanging around the airfield, unable to sleep and with nothing much to do. In particular, he was beginning to feel rather like a footpad, jumping out on unsuspecting victims in the dark and smashing them up before they even knew that they were under attack. True, the enemy were killing innocent civilians and causing horrific scenes such as those he had seen himself in east London, but they were skilled, brave fellow flyers and creeping up on them in the dark seemed somehow unsporting.

He was feeling particularly sorry for himself one rainy summer afternoon when a letter at last arrived from Angela. It had been rapidly scribbled in Southampton where she had just arrived, and it begged him to get the weekend off so as to be able to meet at her parents' house in Hampshire. He knew he was scheduled to fly on Sunday, but another pilot owed him a favour and he lost no time in arranging a swap and clearing it with Whiskers. "Oh by the way," said the CO, as William was leaving his office, "I believe there may be a change of scene on the way for you – drop into my office on Monday morning and I may be able to put you in the picture." A change of scene! Normally this would have put William into a fever of excitement and speculation, but he had no time for that. He could think only of Angela. He dug out her last letter. Yes, yes, he had remembered correctly, she had signed herself *Your Angela*. His hand shook as he held the precious bit of paper. He got out his best uniform, gave it to his batman to press, and paid a young aircraftsman two shillings to clean up his car. Ample petrol was scrounged from the motor transport officer. No flowers were available anywhere for sale, but he knew where there were bluebells still in flower, wild, just off the aerodrome, and he surreptitiously slipped off to pick a large bunch, hoping not to be seen by any of his colleagues.

He was all nerves in the mess that evening, so much so that someone asked him if he was flying a special detail that night and he shut them up with an uncharacteristically sharp reply. Even Jimmy, who came round to consult him about a problem with the radar set, found him tense and curt. He set off early in the morning, glad to be away from Air Force life at last and revelled in the drive through the May countryside, feeling that every moment took him farther from the sordid world of war.

Exton Grange was a fine brick-built Queen Anne house set back from a small country lane in the beautiful Meon Valley. Behind it, a fine stand of beech trees clothed a low chalky hill and, as William drove up to the front door, a pair of insolent cock pheasants strutted across the lawn and through a wrought-iron gate into a walled vegetable garden. Immediately there was a sharp crack from a small-bore rifle and a cry of, "Got you, you bugger." Sir Felix Pointer appeared from the garden, rifle in one hand, pheasant in the other. He greeted William heartily.

"Are you any good at plucking pheasants, old boy? We could do with this fellow for lunch or it'll be a bit sparse, but you'll have to be quick, we'll be eating in a couple of hours. Angela and her mother are off down the village on their bikes, back soon, I should think, so you'd better make a start."

Trying to hide his disappointment at not seeing his love immediately, William went round to the garden shed and dealt with the pheasant, the judge chatting to him as he worked. The family had adapted to wartime conditions with the sort of amateur fortitude characteristic of British families of their kind. Lady Pointer, typical of her class, had not so much as boiled an egg until 1939, but now she was without a cook or any help in the house and was coping single-handed, learning her cooking from the Ministry of Food leaflets and her housekeeping from the local Women's Institute. She also worked three days a week for a local hostel for distressed sailors. Sir Felix, although now in his late seventies, had

186

volunteered for a job in Whitehall, vaguely connected with the oversight of the various military courts. He spent four nights a week in London, at his club, in the midst of the bombing. Rory, Angela's brother, was with his regiment in North Africa. William detected a note of unease in the judge's comments about the fighting there and the latest German advances, but as far as anyone knew, Rory was safe. At weekends the two old people helped Watkins, the ancient gardener, in the vegetable patch "Digging for Victory" as the posters put it, and tended their flock of twelve fat brown hens. "Instead of an egg ration the Ministry gives us an issue of chicken meal and of course we keep all our scraps," the judge explained.

"And how about you, William? I hear you are now in a night fighter unit. Is that exciting?"

"Well, sir, not really, quite routine mostly, but we have seen a little action in the last few months."

"You certainly seem to have had. A Jerry, a Junkers I think they said, came down just the other side of the road in the middle of the night last week."

"Do you remember which day that was?"

"Yes, the eighteenth, I think."

William knew about this one. Peewee Brown, newly posted to the Owls, had got a JU88 over the Meon Valley on the eighteenth. He did not like to tell the judge of how Peewee had misjudged his landing at four a.m. after his first and only victory, dug a wing into the ground, turned his machine over and caught fire. He could not tell of the screams coming from the burning wreck as he, with half a dozen other aircrew and firemen, tried fruitlessly to tackle the blazing petrol. It had been criminal to put such an inexperienced officer in charge of an operational night fighter. He bit his lip and plucked savagely at the pheasant.

Peewee and everything else was forgotten five minutes later, when two ancient bicycles wheezed up the drive. Angela was looking lovely in a bright floral dress and a wide hat, the very picture of a pretty English rose in the summer time. William could not help himself; he swept her off her feet, and carried her laughing and protesting to the door. Then, remembering his manners, he turned round to greet her mother. Retrieving the bluebells from the car, he shyly presented them to her, feeling embarrassed by his over enthusiastic greeting of his lady love. Lady Pointer immediately put him at his ease, admiring the flowers and saying how much the family had been looking forward to his visit. He could not help noticing how well and vigorous both the old Pointers looked. Hard work, fresh air and a reduced diet obviously suited them. As for Angela, she was delightfully brown from the Mediterranean sun and her happiness at being home and, he prayed, at seeing him, blotted out the cares and traumas of life caring for the sick and terribly wounded on the hospital ship. The pheasant was roasted and enjoyed, together with fresh vegetables and followed by fruit from the garden. It made a wonderful change from spam fritters and canned beans in the mess, and the conversation flowed freely. There was a lot the two young people could not discuss openly for security reasons but both had funds of funny stories about things they had seen and done and had the parents in stitches. After lunch, as the women worked in the kitchen, Sir Felix took William into the study and, with the subtlety which could only have been learnt over many years in the courts, began to question him about his family and ambitions. Obviously he had detected that this was the man his daughter loved and was determined to find out more about him. William was afraid that his answers, especially as regards what he intended to do after the war, were far from reassuring, but the old man seemed happy enough, and at long last he was released to take a walk through the country lanes with his love.

The English countryside had been dramatically changed by the war. Where once had been woodland and old pasture the "War Ag", as the department charged with maximising home-grown food production was called, had been at work grubbing out trees and ploughing up grassland. A host of tractors had taken the place of many of the old plough horses and they ground their way slowly across the fields tugging reaper and binders as men, women and boys collected the sheaves and built hundreds of little stooks.

Away on the hill behind the village a yellow bulldozer was at work clearing more land for food production. Women and girls had replaced men in many of the jobs on the farms, tractor driving, milking, harvesting and working with animals, their brown arms made strong by the heavy work and their faces ripened rosy by the summer sun. It was an idyllic walk in the warm sun, up a chalky track to a clump of beeches on top of a low hill. Talk came easily and they swapped war experiences, not the frightening kind, but funny or ridiculous things which had happened to them and their colleagues. Angela was especially interested in the visit to Flopsy in London and William's description of the blitz. She had seen something similar in Southampton a few days earlier and she felt a terrible anxiety that Hans might have had a hand in it. In fact, most bad things about the war reminded her of Hans. Though this didn't seem the time to mention it to William, Hans was lurking at the back of her consciousness like a grumbling cancer deep inside her which she could not ignore or forget. Somehow, however, not even Hans could spoil that day, the companionship of the walk, the warm feeling of his body against her as they sat together, hidden by the friendly beech leaves, the delightful excitement of his kisses, the boyish sincerity of his declarations of love. He was still the simple, sensitive, kindly man she had dreamed of in her little bunk in the hospital ship. How would she ever be able to let him out of her sight?

It was actually William who introduced the unwelcome guest to the party, asking Angela, rather surprisingly what her German friend had looked like.

"You see," he said, "your brother Rory told me his name at Waterloo Station. I think he may be my first cousin. My father's name was von Pilsen; he changed it during the First War."

"Oh, darling, he didn't really look like you, he was taller and blond. Darling, I never loved him, all that happened is that he, Rory and I had a little holiday in Essex together while I was working on my thesis. Yes, he was fun to be with, but as soon as I thought about what might happen if there was a war, I couldn't stop myself from hating him."

"Essex, where in Essex?"

"Near a place called Bawdsey it was, wonderful for birds and for sailing."

William's heart froze, his own Angela, staying near Bawdsey, with a German!

"Why so worried, darling? It was completely innocent and Rory was with us all the time?"

William had no choice but to believe his lovely girl, and after all, anything that bloody German might have learnt at Bawdsey would be way out of date by now. Both the lovers made an unspoken resolution to put Hans out of their minds (though neither actually managed it).

Chapter 11

Hans awoke from a long sleep which had been interrupted occasionally by odd sensations and distant, mumbling voices. He somehow felt detached from the world, floating above it on a cloud of something slightly wet but downy and soft. Waking, he saw a greenish room all round him and somewhere near, but out of focus, two faces peering down. Was he in heaven? Where was he? He remembered something about a motorbike ride, leaving someone behind, a fight… Then something brought him sharply back to reality. Someone was speaking to him. How clever! This someone spoke perfect English. "Hello," he said. "Do you speak any English?" Hans felt himself nodding.

"What is your name?" Hans thought for a moment. "Hans, Hans, von Pilsen, Hauptmann von Pilsen, Luftwaffe." Then somehow he seemed to drift off again onto his cloud, looking down on the greenish world around and the two white-clad figures who had been near him. A little later he awoke again. This time it was less pleasant; he felt a throbbing pain, somewhere in his body, and a sense that something was wrong. One of the white figures reappeared. This time what he said was clear and precise.

"Hauptmann, you have been severely wounded and you are in a British military hospital on Malta. As soon as you are well enough you will be taken away from here and transferred to a military hospital in a safe place. I have to tell you now that we could not save your right arm; when your plane crashed, it was torn off above the elbow. The stump may give you some pain at first, but you'll soon be right as rain."

"Right as rain."

Somehow the words echoed and re-echoed through Hans' brain in the days which followed. He saw them somehow written on all the walls, slowly rotating and changing colour. He wanted to reach out and touch them but somehow he couldn't. What did it mean? Pain – that meant something, he felt it every waking moment in his hospital bed, the nagging pain of a lost limb, the pain as the orderly none too gently removed his bandages and replaced them, the pain as the events of the day before his crash slowly gained form and reality in his head. But rain "right as rain", what was that? Slowly, slowly the reality of his predicament floated to the top of his consciousness. Dimly he heard the familiar roar and scream of engines and felt the shudder of explosions as the island was shaken by attacking aircraft. Somehow, however, he didn't care too much about any of this. Morphine was keeping him on a gentle "high" in which nothing really mattered as long as he was left to long solitary dozes, undisturbed and safe in his own little cocoon of drug-induced contentment.

All this changed when he eventually arrived, still bedridden, in a hospital ship, at Gibraltar. Still unable to walk or stand, he was transferred to the hospital section of a prisoner-of-war camp and deposited alongside a sorry rank of wounded soldiers and airmen. Little by little the implications of his new circumstances had been coming home to him. Though his treatment at the hands of British medical staff had been reasonably efficient, he was a prisoner and could expect little in the way of comforts, at least, he thought, until Germany won the war. But lack of comforts was nothing compared to the terrible wound which kept him in debilitating pain all day, his missing arm, calling out to the rest of his body that it needed attention. But it was during the nights that a chilling, terrible reality gripped him, seized him with a terror he could not subdue. His arm! His arm gone! He remembered an old man who used to stumble about the estate at his home, grinning, simpering, appealing, showing his stump where once had been a strong limb and begging for pence. How could he ever do anything worthwhile, take any pleasure in life now? He, a poor cripple, useless, a thing to be pitied? Hans would cover his face and try to sob himself into some sort of sleep.

He had been a few weeks in Gibraltar when a fresh detail of prisoners arrived. Fliegerkorps X had suffered another day of severe losses, this time because it had attempted a raid on Malta just when a new formation of British fighters became available and made mincemeat of a weakly escorted formation of Stukas. Numerous German aircrew officers had been fished out of the sea, six of them more or less severely burnt or wounded, and these were shipped to Gibraltar to await transfer to Britain. It so happened that all of these six were younger than Hans and were dedicated, fanatical, Nazis. News of the fate of Obersturmfuhrer Feldman had reached the aircrews soon after the attack on *Rampant's* convoy and the SS had put their own gloss on it. According to them, Hans had fallen in love with a Jewess, murdered Feldman and betrayed the attack on the convoy to the British. He had then escaped from the ensuing air battle and given himself up to the enemy. It did not take these six long to make it clear to their erstwhile colleague that an ugly fate awaited him as soon as he was out of hospital and came within the clutches of the Nazi POW camp administration system. "You traitor aristocrats are all the same," one of them hissed as he limped past Hans' bed. "Jew lover, be careful when you come among us true Germans; we know how to deal with traitors."

The ex-German liner *Minden* embarked a sorry load of passengers for the voyage home to England. There were injured British, Allied and German stretcher cases, and three hundred lightly wounded Italian troops captured in North Africa. Among the Luftwaffe officer prisoners were the six who had been threatening Hans. Allied and enemy wounded were in separate but adjoining wards, the enemy casualties being rather casually guarded by a Pioneer Corps corporal and six men. There were two Royal Army Medical Corps doctors on board and a dozen QAIMNS nurses tried to make them all as comfortable as possible; they were assisted by a handful of male medical orderlies. Although she was painted dazzling white with huge red crosses all over her, *Minden* was far from safe as she steamed alone and unescorted up the Portuguese coast and across the Bay of Biscay. U-boats and enemy aircraft did not always respect the red crosses and mines were of course entirely blind to them. It was now autumn, but to everyone's relief the weather was kind and the voyage started smoothly. At one point a German Condor aircraft flew close and took a careful look at the ship – she was cheered by any of the Luftwaffe men who could see her – but she flew away apparently satisfied that *Minden* was the genuine article.

It was not until after this incident that Angela, who had been looking after some terribly burnt British tank crews, happened to walk through Hans' ward. He glimpsed her as she passed. Immediately he felt something leap inside him.

Could it be? Impossible?

She did not see him but hurried on her mission. Hans waved his good arm and called to the soldier who was on duty in the ward.

"That nurse, quick, I must see her."

"Why, what's the matter, mate? She's on another ward."

"Yes, but I must see her. I knew her before the war, in England."

"Don't know nothing about that, anyway she's busy. Tell you what though, you tell me her name and I'll see if I can catch her when she next passes."

Impatient, Hans had to be content. Strangely, from that moment on, his condition began to improve rapidly. That very day, for the first time, he managed to get up and walk carefully about the ward, steadying himself with his one good arm. He kept a good eye on the guard and tried to get into conversation with him so as to be sure he wouldn't forget his promise. The man proved uncommunicative. He was as good as his word, however, and when he met Angela in a corridor the following day, he spoke to her.

"Excuse me, Miss, but there's a Jerry patient, Mr von Pilsen, 'ee says as 'ee knows you back in Blighty. Seemed a nice enough bloke and quiet, so I says I'd let you know."

Angela almost dropped the bed pan she was carrying.

"What! Not Hans! What's he doing here? Is he badly wounded? I must go to him! Where is he?"

Hans was sitting on his bed, trying to write with his left hand; he had suddenly realised that he should write to his parents, via the Red Cross, and to several other people in Germany. He was sure it would be allowed, but first of all there was a note for the guard to take to Angela. He struggled with the pencil, ashamed of the misshapen, ugly letters scrawled across the paper. Then there she was, running, yes, running towards his bed. He felt himself flush red in the face as he struggled to his feet. He tried pathetically to open both arms to embrace her and found himself off-balance, staggering to compensate for the gentle movement of the ship. Before he could fall, two strong brown arms were round him, gently lowering him onto the bed. This could only be Angela and her touch was still somehow familiar and reassuring. They sat side by side, unable to speak, each totally overcome by the other's presence.

Angela broke the silence.

"Hans, oh, Hans, what happened? How badly are you hurt? Who is looking after you?"

He did not answer, but sat still trembling with emotion. Eventually he looked at her, prim in her nurse's uniform.

"Oh, my love, what are you doing on this ship? This is war, this is dangerous, you should be safely at home. How can they have let you go to Gibraltar, to a war zone? You could get killed."

"Well, you seem to be the one who got closest to being killed. Tell me, what injuries do you have? How did it happen?"

Hans told her about his crash, though not the reason for it, and, little by little, conversation started to flow more easily. War was a taboo subject; they remembered Cambridge, Shoreside Cottage, the dances they had had, their first meeting in Germany, then the tannoy summoned Angela away and off she hurried to another ward, not forgetting a swift kiss on his forehead and a promise to be back in the evening.

Unfortunately, this encounter was not unobserved. Kurt Gronsen, the most senior of Hans' fellow Luftwaffe casualties and the most fervent Nazi, had slipped into the ward to find his traitorous fellow officer obviously closely involved with an English girl, dressed as a nurse, but probably an intelligence agent, talking in fluent English. He was almost certainly telling her secret information about German forces at that very minute. As soon as the ship docked, von Pilsen would surely be snatched away by

British intelligence and doubtless sent out on some other mission of betrayal. This must be stopped and he was the man who must do it. The problem was how? He had no weapon, and was himself suffering from an amputation, a foot removed when he was being cut out of his wrecked Stuka which had crashed on Malta. His injury, however, earned him permission to walk on deck for an hour or so each evening so as to get used to using crutches. Maybe he could put this short period of relative freedom to find some sort of weapon. That very afternoon he struck lucky. When no one was looking, he managed to get hold of a small hand axe which was stowed in a cabinet on deck, ready to be used to cut away the lines securing the lifeboats in case it was necessary to release them in a hurry. He managed to slip it into the leg of his trousers and, limping rather more painfully than usual, returned to his bed space and slipped the axe under his mattress. He made himself scarce that evening when Angela returned to see Hans. She had brought with her a much-prized can of Californian peaches which the two shared, sitting on the bunk. She had spoken to the medical officer in charge of Hans' case and learnt from him of the loss of blood, the depression and the generally low morale of his charge.

"Seemed a lot better this evening though, I thought," he concluded. "Why are you interested?"

"Oh, we met in England before the war," she replied. "Nice boy, friend of my brother's, so I couldn't really ignore him when I saw him here."

"Well, I'll tell you what I think he needs," said the MO, "more fresh air. I've got an idea which might be helpful. Seeing as he's a friend of yours we'll move him up to Cabin 34B on the upper deck, it has a porthole open to the sea, and the poor Polish guy who was in there died last night so it's empty. Get one of the orderlies to help and move him tonight if you like."

Angela told Hans about the spare cabin, saying that she thought that he ought to grab it at once before anyone else got wind of the possibility. Hans had no objection, so they moved his few things that evening and sat briefly together in the dark, close but not holding hands, watching the smooth sea rush past the sides of the ship as the moon looked benignly down on the water.

Being a hospital ship sailing alone, *Minden* was not darkened but it was difficult to see in the ward where Hans' old berth had been so that when Kurt got to his own bed that night he did not realise that his intended victim was not there. Just after midnight he retrieved the axe and crawled on all fours silently past the row of wounded sleepers. One blow to the forehead would put an end to the traitor, but he had to see clearly to do the deed. Heaving himself upright near the bedhead, he struck a match and looked down at the bed, axe at the ready. Empty! He swore under his breath; he must have the wrong bed. He looked at the sleepers on each side. Yes, they were the same as ever, only Hans had gone. Furious and confused, he heaved himself back to his own bed and passed the night sleepless and angry.

In the morning he held a secret conference with his comrades. News of Hans' move had by now percolated down the grapevine and it was clear that it was going to be less easy to reach him in his new abode. None of the plotters had any doubt that Germany was soon going to win the war, so whoever did the deed would return home as a Nazi hero long before British justice got round to punishing the murderer. Nevertheless, it would obviously be better if they could make Hans' death seem like an accident. Several ingenious ideas were suggested but the best came from a young air gunner named Pilch. Pilch had noticed that the medicine trolley which came round each evening was easily accessible and not well guarded. He had also noticed that Hans was issued with a few grains of morphine each evening to help him to sleep. If somehow the dose could be increased to a lethal level, the job would be done, and could be blamed on a careless medical orderly. It would be quite easy to get at the dose as the various patients' prescriptions were laid out on the trolley, each with a name tag. He and Kurt would watch the procedure with the trolley carefully that evening and do the deed the following day.

It was dead easy. The nurse with the tray, Julia, was accompanied by a soldier who was supposed to keep order, but he was much more interested in "chatting up" Julia. Pilch, who spoke reasonable English, joined in a gentle tease of Julia while Kurt had a good look at the drugs on issue. Each patient's envelope was sealed and contained his dose, details of which were written on the outside. He noticed that Hans was supposed to have twelve milligrams. of morphine. Jars containing the various drugs in use were kept on the bottom shelf of the trolley together with a weighing machine and various paraphernalia for making up the prescriptions. Kurt had no idea what a lethal dose of morphine might be but thought that if the dose was increased by a factor of ten it might be lethal. He would have to find some way of spiking Hans' dose with copious extra morphine from the jars on the trolley. He practised sidling up to it while Julia was talking to a patient and found that he could quite easily lift the jar off the trolley without attracting attention. While doing this he also discovered that a stack of blank envelopes was stored in an open box on the bottom shelf. Seizing the moment, he snaffled two of these and hid them in his pocket. That night the conspirators worked on the envelopes and managed to make a passable forgery of the writing on the outside. It was now only a question of filling the forged envelope and substituting it for the proper one. The job had to be done that night. The prisoners had no way of knowing the ship's position, but it was getting distinctly cooler so they guessed that they must be approaching the English Channel. If they waited much longer, the ship would have docked and Hans would be removed from their clutches for ever.

The next evening, when the trolley came round, all was ready. Kurt had the trolley to himself for over a minute while the others contrived to drop someone's dose on the floor and get the whole ward, including the nurse and the guard, on hands and knees, looking for it. Pilch tried to follow the party out of the ward and along to the cabin where Hans was confined to see that the job was fully carried through, but one of the guards stopped him, so he had to return to his comrades and spend the night hoping for some commotion which might indicate that a death had taken place. They were not disappointed. At about three in the morning there was some muffled conversation in the corridor and the sound of wheels told them that a corpse was being taken to the ship's mortuary. In the morning it was confirmed. Prisoner von Pilsen had died from unknown causes during the night. There would be no time for a post mortem and the *Minden* could not stop for a formal burial at sea; a simple ceremony would take place with the ship under way. Prisoners were allowed on deck to watch the body being consigned to the deep, a bugler sounded a rather shaky last post and the weighted corpse plunged into the water. There was some surprise among the ship's crew when a party of German prisoners broke into a hearty chorus of the Horst Wessel song and gave three cheers for the Fuhrer.

The Nazis never guessed that their celebrations were premature. Hans was not a fool and had guessed that the threats made in Gibraltar were real and some attempt would be made to carry them out in the relatively relaxed atmosphere of the hospital ship. As soon as his health and morale began to improve on the ship, he started to try to work out a way of outwitting the clique of Nazi officers. He discussed the situation with Angela and they both agreed that they would need to attempt to outwit the plotters, and that the transfer to Cabin 34B gave them an excellent opportunity to do so. It was Angela who came up with the best scheme.

Stanislas Potoski was a Polish corporal who had been terribly wounded by a mortar bomb which burst in his trench just outside Tobruk. His survival seemed so unlikely that there was some dispute as to whether it was worth shipping him to hospital in England at all, but eventually he was loaded onto *Minden* where he received intensive nursing during the first part of the voyage. On the day before the attempted murder, his luck ran out. A blood vessel burst and he died peacefully in his bed in the intensive care ward, with Angela and a colleague tenderly holding his hand. It wasn't difficult for Angela to arrange for his body to be moved into 34B, while Hans moved quietly into the corporal's place in the intensive care ward and pretended to be in far worse shape than he actually was. Luckily there were no other Polish speakers in the ward and no one except two of Angela's colleagues, who were sworn to secrecy, noticed that the figure in the bed in the corner was no longer that of the suffering Pole but of a rapidly recovering German. As for Kurt's carefully prepared morphine dose, it was delivered to cabin 34B occupied by the corpse and disposed of down the drain. For now, anyway, Hans was safe.

Thinking about it later, Hans tried to recall what his relationship with Angela had been during those critical two days. Certainly she had been extraordinarily attentive to him, attending to his bandages herself and somehow bringing that spark of homeliness and comfort to his surroundings, which only a woman can bring. He was also flattered that she had believed his account of the threat from his fellow Luftwaffe officers immediately and, at some risk to herself, taken such imaginative and effective action. But had she shown love? Had the old magic returned now that he was no longer going to be bombing England? He simply didn't know. He only remembered the gentle touch of her hand on his body, the chaste, sweet goodnight kisses, the warmth of the smile. His own feelings for her left no room for doubt. He was now more than ever deeply, dangerously, in love.

As *Minden* entered the Channel, Angela was in total confusion about her own feelings. She remembered the dashing young German officer whom she had so admired in her Cambridge days, and seeing him wounded and distressed had awoken in her every protective instinct. Often before she had felt a deep, almost motherly love for wounded soldiers in her care, but this was different. This was a man she had loved, dreamed about, idolised and she could tell that he still loved her. They were able to communicate at a deeper level than speech or touch could convey and it was with a special tender gentleness that she changed the dressings on his wounds, plumped up his pillows and settled him in bed. But there was something wrong. Looking into his strong, sad face, she could not help looking for features, movements, mannerisms that reminded her of William. If she studied him closely, it was plain to see a family resemblance, but there were differences too. Here was a harder, simpler man with nothing in him of the artist who lurked deep in William's psyche, none of the gentleness, of the self-doubt which made William so irresistibly attractive to her. Did she love him? She did not know, but she would nurse him with all her loving kindness, and protect him with all her might.

At Southampton the wounded were sent to various local military hospitals, Hans ending up at Netley on the Solent. He was still masquerading under the name of Stanislas Potoski, and was relieved to find that he was the only "Pole" in the hospital, most of the others being British or Canadian seamen, with a handful of Free French soldiers. He was interviewed by a senior naval medical officer. The doctor was surprised to find that his charge spoke fluent English and could converse readily in French too. Hans explained this by making up a story about being brought up near Danzig, a free city in western Poland and a hub of international trade, and of frequent trips to England connected with his father's business. Luckily his knowledge of the country enabled him to make his story reasonably credible. The MO was also surprised to find his charge in better shape than the paperwork sent from Gibraltar had led him to expect, and told "Stanislas" that he seemed to be recovering amazingly well from his wounds and would soon be ready for discharge. Apart from the loss of his limb, he should be perfectly fit and able to work. "I expect that you'll be wanting to get back to your Free Polish Army pretty soon" he said encouragingly. "I'm sure they will have a good use for you, arm or no arm, you'll be able to get some of your own back on the Jerries."

For Hans, of course, this was a problem to be overcome. It wouldn't take the Polish Army people in London long to find out that he was no Pole and the consequences would be disastrous. Once again his salvation would have to depend on the goodwill of Angela.

Luckily for him, *Minden's* nursing crew had been granted two weeks' leave after the voyage from Gibraltar and Hans managed to get a phone call through to Exton Grange. A visit to Netley was arranged.

201

Chapter 12

William had returned in a haze of happiness from his weekend leave with Angela. There was no formal engagement as yet, but there hardly seemed to be any need. The two were so deeply, so obviously in love. Hans had not been mentioned since the brief, uncomfortable reference to him on the first day of the visit and both hoped that he had vanished forever. As he drove, blissfully happy, back to camp, William's mind was occupied thinking of weddings, of bringing his love to his Tyneside home, and of an idyllic life together after the war.

He had entirely forgotten the hint from Whiskers that his role might be about to change and was brought up with a bump when he was summoned to the squadron office. He was a little less surprised to find Hugh Wesley sitting in the office waiting for him. Hugh always seemed to turn up when change was afoot.

After some pleasantries, Whiskers opened the conversation.

"William, you and I are both aware that with the Beaus and our radar we seem to be more or less on top of the night bombers now. Yes, they make the occasional stealthy raid to keep us on our toes, but they seem to be too busy in Russia and in the Med to give us much trouble, and I guess the high levels of losses when they do raid us are pretty off-putting for them. Our masters in the War Office have another plan for us, however, and you and I are the lucky fellows they seem to have selected to carry it out. Squadron Leader Wesley here will explain."

Hugh started by outlining the situation regarding night-time interception as he saw it.

"The fact is," he concluded, "that we have cracked the problem to all intents and purposes, and the Germans seem to have almost given up the game. I can tell you fellows also that we have further improvements in radar coming along and, as you probably know, an even better night fighter than the Beau, I think it's called the "Mosquito", will soon be available. That should make things better still. However, there is one aspect of this war which we are not winning, and if we don't start to make progress soon it could be the end of us."

As his friend spoke, William could not help marvelling in how this man – a bit of a buffoon before the war – had grown into his role under the pressure of war. He now had a kind of natural authority born of his passionate belief in the importance of his task. William could now envisage him taking on government scientists at the highest level, forcing them to support his practical vigorous approach to problems and to recognise his infinite capacity for innovation and hard work.

Hugh continued.

"Do either of you know how much shipping we lost during the last twelve months in the Atlantic?"

Both shook their heads.

"Well, it's about six million tons, five hundred thousand a month – far more than we can possibly build. In return we think we sank about a hundred U-boats and we know the Germans built at least two hundred, so it's going to get worse and worse unless we can find some way of turning the situation round. Now, we've been working on an idea which may help, but we need aircrew who are familiar with radar and with flying long distances over water to develop the system and the procedures for operating it. The Air Ministry worked out that you two would fit the bill. What do you say?"

"Well, it sounds very much like an order to me," said Whiskers. I wouldn't mind having another go at test-flying. I did some before I came to the Owls. What is the set-up?"

"There's an experimental squadron based at Ford. You'll be part of that. They test all sorts of weird and wonderful things there. It actually belongs to Bomber Command, but you'll be working with Coastal Command of course."

Winter had set in by the time they arrived at Ford. William was delighted to have been posted to a station within easy reach of

Angela's home in Hampshire, although she herself was off again to Gibraltar in a hospital ship. Both he and Whiskers were much less pleased when they found that all their flying was to be in Wellington bombers, about the most unglamorous machine in the RAF's inventory. Wellingtons ("Wimpeys" they were universally called) were twin-engine bombers and these Mark 1 machines were old, slow, clumsy and underpowered. Coastal Command was allocated them mainly because their brethren in Bomber Command had decided they were obsolescent and were phasing them out in favour of the more powerful Mark IIIs, and of course the new generation of four-engined "heavies". The fuselage of the Wellington was fabric-covered and the whole structure could bend in flight, often resulting in alarming movements of the control column. Wellingtons did have some virtues however. They were able to sustain an astonishing amount of damage and remain airborne and they were considered to be extremely reliable.

The RAF had allowed the two pilots to bring a few chosen crew with them to Ford, so William was able to keep hold of Jimmy and Flight Sergeant Tuoy. At least Wellingtons had a Bristol engine, like the Beaufighter, so Tuoy felt at home with them immediately. After a brief period of familiarisation with the aircraft, the crews were grounded while a team of technicians worked on them to fit the special equipment with which to enable them to start on their test-flying.

During this brief lay off, William had hoped to take a few days' leave but it was not to be. Bomber Command was determined to make a massive raid on Dortmund in the Ruhr, the heart of German industry. From the start of the war, it had been decreed that crews from training establishments, experimental units and from Coastal Command itself, could be drafted into the bomber force when a major operation was in the offing, and as there were some spare aircraft at Ford, William and Whiskers were ordered to prepare one of them and get together a scratch crew. A Wellington on a bombing mission normally had a crew of five: Pilot, (Whiskers) Navigator (William), Radio Operator/Flight Engineer, and Front Gunner/Bomb Aimer (Jimmy) and Rear Gunner. Joe Isaacs, another Beaufighter crewman from Tangmere stood in as Radio Operator, the other place was filled by Sergeant Phillips a spare air gunner from Ford. William was more than happy to act as navigator instead of pilot. He knew that Whiskers was a far better pilot than he would ever be and was secretly pleased not to have the daunting responsibility of skippering the Wellington over enemy territory.

By winter of 1941 and 1942 the RAF had given up daylight raids on Germany, as the losses were horrific and was beginning to adopt the strategy of "area bombing" by night. The aim was to demoralise the industrial workforce so that production of war material would grind to a halt. In reality it was the only way in which Britain could make use of its massive bomber force, as accurate night-time navigation was impossible to achieve with the systems then available. As it was impossible for bombers to strike accurately at a specific industrial target, they had to blast a whole city, killing in the process thousands of civilians. The policy was ruthless in the extreme but it was to be the backbone of the Allied bombing strategy until the end of the war. The Dortmund raid was intended to be one such attack.

Whiskers got his scratch crew together and managed to find time to give them a couple of short flights together so as to weld them into some sort of team. It was not easy. The Wimpey was noisy, cold and extremely uncomfortable at the best of times, and the spare machine provided by Ford was a poor example of the breed. Tuoy and his team worked their magic on the engines, but the instruments were unreliable and secondary systems, like the radios, were decidedly shaky. In these conditions everyone on board was tense and nervous. Whiskers himself set an excellent example of skill and professionalism, making a point of trying to talk to each man in the crew during the flight, telling them what he intended to do and drumming into everyone the vital importance of the success of the mission and the part they had to play in it. There was no trouble with Jimmy or Isaacs, but the rear gunner was a different kettle of fish. He didn't want to fly operationally and, though a qualified air gunner, he had no experience in night flying. He was continually looking for faults in the aircraft (known as "P-Peter") in the hope of it being pronounced as un-airworthy. Twice, Whiskers had to threaten disciplinary action to stop him complaining.

P-Peter was allocated to reinforce a Wellington squadron based in Norfolk, so she flew up there on a chilly, grey March day, Whiskers putting her down, perfectly as usual, just before sunset. The crew split up, three officers reporting to the officers' mess, the rest to their respective billets. No one much seemed to want to see Whiskers and his party, and they huddled together round a dreary-looking bar, waiting to be shown their quarters. Eventually a Squadron Leader joined them, announcing himself as the adjutant.

"Are you the crew from Ford?" he began. "Well, briefing in half an hour, you've missed the navigator's briefing, so you'll have to pick up the charts later, hope you've settled in all right. Sorry, I can't wait," and with that he was off into another room which seemed to contain a billiards table.

The crews filed into the briefing room, which was set out, rather dramatically, with a stage and curtain at one end. There was a roll call, closely watched by an RAF policeman to ensure no one was missing or had sneaked in with no business to be there, then a tired-looking Wing Commander unveiled a map of North Germany and the target. The Bomber force was to form up over the Thames Estuary and pass south of Antwerp before making a turn for the Ruhr. The Wellingtons, constituting over half the bombing force, being a little slower than the four-engined machines, would set off fifteen minutes ahead of them. Heavy flak was to be expected over Belgium and over the target and, if visibility was good, there might be night fighters.

"Good luck, everyone!" he concluded, and left the stage to a met. officer, followed by a navigation specialist who rather vaguely pointed out the way points they should look out for.

"You can't miss the Ruhr," he concluded. "It's all lit up by blast furnaces."

"And f... ing searchlights!" shouted a man in the audience.

"Bloody flak too!" yelled another.

Takeoff was scheduled for 22.00 hours. that evening, and the crews were told to have their dinner at 20.00 and be ready to start engines at 21.30. There was a rush for the respective messes, each man being checked off as he entered so as to keep out any possible intruders. Whiskers' crew were held up at the door.

"Sorry, sir, your names are not on the list."

"F… that we've just been briefed we are flying tonight."

"Can't help that, sir, you'll have to see the adjutant."

The adjutant, of course, was nowhere to be found. Whiskers by now was red with fury and starting to shout. He attracted sniggering glances from the men eating their dinner. The shouting match with the policeman on the door became more and more heated.

After a few minutes Whiskers pushed past the sergeant who was denying them entry and stormed into the dining hall.

"Right!" he announced. "My crew are getting their meal NOW! And they are sitting HERE" – pointing to a table by the door, laden with documents – "to eat it."

His arm swept over the table, depositing neatly piled paperwork on the floor.

By this time all eyes in the room were focused on this fiery Welshman. With great composure he sat down, spread out a napkin and beckoned his crew to do likewise. A mess waiter sheepishly started to lay the table; this provoked a round of cheers from the aircrew in the room which redoubled when plates of food arrived. Whiskers maintained perfect composure throughout the meal and his influence forced the others to do likewise. When the meal was almost finished, the adjutant belatedly appeared in the room and strode over to the table.

"What's this I hear about trouble over dinner?" he demanded.

Whiskers stood up and addressed him loudly, so all the room could hear.

"Air crew about to risk their lives are having their dinner here, Squadron Leader," he said icily, "and it's obvious that you desk pilots can't organise something as simple as dinner so you'd better bugger off back to your desk and see if you can't get yourselves properly sorted out, or next time you'll get something uncomfortable up your backside. Now piss off, I'm eating."

The adjutant had never been spoken to like this before. With a feeble "You'll hear more of this" he fled out of the room to the laughter and applause of the diners.

As it happened, none of them flew that night. The weather clamped down at the last minute and the operation was postponed. Whiskers and his crew found themselves hanging around the airfield for another three days before they finally took off. They suffered no more trouble from the station establishment.

At last the Wellingtons were bombed up, fuelled and trundled down the runway into the darkness of the winter night. They were supposed to form up over the Thames Estuary and fly in some sort of formation towards their target, but it was too dark for the aircraft to see each other, and after a few minutes aimlessly circling around, they blundered off on their mission. Behind them thundered the brand new four-engine "heavies", hoping to strike a devastating blow at the heart of German industry.

Accustomed as he was to long hours of night flying, William at first found it quite relaxing to be occupying the navigator's seat, leaving ultimate responsibility for the aircraft to Whiskers. He could see nothing but the stars above him, thick cloud blotted out the earth as P-Peter droned steadily on. Over the North Sea he struggled up into the astrodome and took a star sight. They seemed to be well south of their correct course; the wind must be stronger and more northerly than the Met. had forecast. He gave Whiskers a new course. The navigator in a Wellington had very little view outside the aircraft except from the astrodome on top, so the front gunner/bomb aimer in the nose had to do all the "map reading". Sure enough, Jimmy reported the Scheldt away to port, visible through a gap in the clouds.

At that time German night fighters were only experimenting with airborne radar, but there were excellent radar-directed searchlights located on the likely paths of attacking bombers and heavy anti-aircraft guns. There were also lighter guns to deal with low-flying targets. Great concentrations of such gun batteries also covered prime target areas such as the Ruhr and Berlin itself. As a further hazard, even without on-board radar, the night fighters were often highly effective. The German border areas were divided into "boxes", each box being the responsibility of a ground radar station and an orbiting fighter. The station would identify a target and guide its designated fighter towards it by radio. The pilot would have to make the final stages of his attack using the "Mark one eyeball" to spot its silhouette against the moon, or its exhaust flames. German night-fighter pilots were highly trained experts and often proved deadly opponents, especially to lame aircraft, perhaps damaged and with tired crews, returning from a bombing operation. Slow twin-engine bombers like the Wellington depended entirely on the alertness of the crew and especially the tail gunner to spot an attacking fighter before it could open fire and drive it off with machine gun fire or warn the pilot to take violent evasive action.

P-Peter's crew soon saw the menacing fingers of searchlights probing the night sky in front of them and then the bursts of shell fire exploding ahead. Twice they saw a glowing meteor of fire plunging to earth to mark the last resting place of an unfortunate colleague. Oddly William felt strangely detached from this part of the action. The aircraft droned steadily on, weaving gently from side to side in an attempt to confuse enemy radar. The ruse seemed to work and the machine crossed what appeared to be a barrier of searchlights and ack-ack without attracting the attention of the defenders. William was concentrating hard on his navigation and managed to get another star sight to confirm his course. Somehow he had shut out of his mind the terrible danger he was facing, or indeed the suffering the raid was likely to inflict on innocent German civilians. At the briefing it had been made clear that the aim of the operation was to destroy not just industrial sites but also the homes and lives of the people working in them. He managed to shut the horror of all this out of his mind and concentrate on his own technical responsibility for making the mission a success. Somehow the steady engine note, and the sight of Whiskers sitting there confident and calm at the controls lulled him into a state of well-being which was far detached from reality. He knew very well how his own morale would collapse if he let his mind dwell on anything but the technical aspects of his mission. He need hardly have bothered with the second star sight – by now Jimmy, in the nose, could see the glow of the industrial heart of Germany dead ahead and already there seemed to be fires breaking out on the ground to the west of what seemed to be the target area.

"Ignore those," ordered Whiskers. "Jerry often lights them in the open country hoping that we will go for them instead of the target. Bomb aimer, look out for the canal; it leads to the heart of the city. Navigator, time to target, please."

His voice was calm, reassuring, familiar.

"Twelve minutes, skipper."

"Thank you, we are going to make this a perfect approach. Everyone OK?"

Everyone was not OK. William heard a strange sobbing sound over the intercom. Jimmy and Isaacs seemed fine, so it must have come from the rear turret.

"Navigator, go aft and see what's happened to him."

Whiskers as cool as ever.

William crawled back down the fuselage. It shook alarmingly and blasts of cold air spurted at him through hundreds of leaks and joints. The tail gunner, Philips, was leaning forward over his guns, oxygen mask removed, slumped in his seat. William took him by the shoulders, looking to see if he had been hurt. He could see no sign of a wound but the man was rigid and did not react to William's attempt to unbuckle his harness and drag him from his seat. It was bitter cold in the turret – cold enough to make anyone turn stiff, but there was something about Philips which could not be explained by mere cold. William kicked him off his seat and half carried, half dragged him forward. He had almost reached the navigator's compartment when the screaming started. It was high-pitched, like a woman's wailing, but louder and more insistent. "I have to get out, I have to get out," he screamed. William was not normally a violent man but the sight of this pathetic fellow revolted him. He smashed a fist into the pale face. The man shut up, whimpering quietly to himself. William fumbled for the medicine bag under his desk and found morphine. A double dose was soon pulsing through Philips and he became quiet and limp. William reported to Whiskers.

"OK, leave him, Navigator, Bomb Aimer, can you identify target?"

"Yes, dead ahead, skipper."

The clouds and industrial smog seemed to be thinning in the strong wind, revealing the centre of the city circled by an impenetrable ring of searchlights. Suddenly the aircraft was bathed in a powerful bluish light which seemed to grip it like a menacing presence from another world. Whiskers swore under his breath but held a steady course. William found that he was crouching down behind his navigation desk as if that might give him some protection from the shells which would surely come. P-Peter was suddenly shaken by an explosion right beneath her. Splinters of metal came whizzing through the cabin and there was a foul stink of burning. The burst seemed to have lifted the machine vertically upwards, straining every part of the structure, but miraculously she remained on an even keel and the blessed drone of the engines kept on uninterrupted. That Wellington was a tough old bird.

Jimmy's voice came over the intercom. "Blimey, skipper, this is bloody dangerous. Target still dead ahead."

William chipped in. "One minute to target."

The flash of the explosion below seemed to have put off the searchlight which had been holding them, but all around, the horrid, deadly fingers kept on probing into the night.

Jimmy kept calling out directions. "Steady, steady, left, steady, left again…" then at last, "Bombs gone." Shedding her deadly load, P-Peter surged upwards, and William quickly gave the pilot a course for home. Whiskers started to organise his crew for the return. Jimmy was sent crawling to the rear turret to keep a lookout for fighters. Isaacs was ordered to monitor the engines carefully, paying special attention to the fuel situation in case a tank had been punctured. William was to keep an eye on Philips, prostrate on the floor, and give him another shot if he showed signs of life. The

211

calm voice of the skipper making practical, sensible arrangements steadied everyone's nerves as they set off on the dangerous path for home.

Behind them the "heavies" were now over the target and great spurts of flame erupted as the bombs hit home. From his rear turret, Jimmy kept up a running commentary as he saw the bursts, the rising flak and the occasional terrible sight of a bomber plunging to earth. P-Peter seemed none the worse for her ordeal by fire, and her depleted crew settled down to their tasks. William had detected on the way out that the wind was stronger and had more north in it than the met officer had predicted. He therefore gave Whiskers a course of three three zero degrees and aimed to cross the English coast somewhere near Cromer. He was in the astrodome trying to get a further star sight when he heard Jimmy yell into the intercom.

"Break left, break left, fighter on our tail!"

In a moment all was chaos on board. The procedure for avoiding a fighter was the corkscrew turn. This meant throwing the machine violently into a steep dive, at the same time turning sharply in one direction then pulling up into a climb, turning the opposite way. An aircraft flying as erratically as this was almost impossible for a night fighter to aim at accurately. The corkscrew was not an easy trick to perform in a battered old Wellington, but Whiskers did it perfectly. Maps, instruments, mugs, torches and all kinds of clutter flew about the cabin as he savagely dived, banked and climbed, every man hanging on and praying that the wings would not be torn off. Jimmy tried to see what happened to the attacker but it was lost somewhere in the darkness, unable to take a shot. Eventually Whiskers levelled out and resumed his course. Everyone scrambled to recover their possessions, strewn about the aircraft.

Calmly from Whiskers:

"Everyone OK? Any sign of him, tail gunner?"

Just as he was about to answer, Jimmy saw a darker patch in the sky astern. Could it be the fighter again?

"Skipper, he's still with us, closing from behind."

.

Whiskers was himself a highly experienced night fighter pilot. He knew very well that his opponent must be an expert to have kept on his tail through the corkscrew procedure but he also knew from his own experience that the easiest mistake for a night fighter to make was to close up on the victim too quickly and overshoot before being able to open fire. He slammed both throttles shut and at the same time pulled up the nose and lowered the flaps. The Wellington groaned and staggered under the strain of the flaps being lowered at speed and floated upwards as she slowed down. Jimmy, surprised by the manoeuvre, was forced back in his seat. He saw the fighter flash past beneath him and tried to give it a burst from his guns but saw his tracer pass well behind. Once again, Whiskers put the machine into a tight turn, raised the flaps and dived towards what seemed to be a cloud bank.

There was no more sign of the fighter, but all this action had taken the plane a long way off course and the strengthening north wind, which William had observed on the outward journey, was a further complication. They remained circling in the safety of the cloud bank for a further ten minutes, then emerged into clear air, finding themselves over an angry-looking sea. Where the hell were they? Isaacs tried to raise a directional radio station without success. The radio didn't seem to have survived the violent treatment suffered at the hands of Whiskers. The sky above them was covered by broken high cloud which gave only occasional glimpses of the moon and stars so there was no hope of an astro fix. William looked down at the sea and wished that his old navigator, Branston, had been on board. He could accurately estimate wind speed and direction by looking at wave tops and calculating drift – a vital skill for naval flyers in World War One, now almost lost.

Pilot to navigator:

"Where are we?"

Navigator to pilot:

"Working on it, skipper."

"Well, work quickly, Wellingtons don't fly on fresh air, you know, we have only fuel for another forty-five minutes."

William was at a loss. The temptation was to head due west and expect to cross the English coast somewhere over Kent, well south of his original course. But suppose they were being blown even farther south? They could be over the Dover Strait already. If they flew west they might blunder down the Channel, seeing no land until fuel ran out. So should they try a course of northwest? That was dangerous too, if the wind had backed- westerly, as the Met. had forecast, and they had passed over northern Holland, a course of northwest in a westerly wind would carry them on forever over the North Sea. He must think. He must not be interrupted, even by Whiskers. He pulled out the intercom plug and stared down at the sea now dimly illuminated by a pale moon. The white caps were certainly daunting, indicating a strong wind. Somehow, he thought, a little to the north of them, the sea seemed to look different. Maybe that meant something.

Navigator to pilot:

"Skipper, can you come down low, turn on the landing lights and look at the sea there to starboard?"

"OK, but it better be good. We've no fuel to waste blundering about looking at the sea."

Sure enough, the landing lights showed a yellowish patch where there should be sea; it seemed to be a sandbank running north and south. Waves were breaking heavily around it.

"Skipper, that can only be the Goodwins. I've sailed past them often enough to be sure of that. We seem to be somewhere over the south tip of the bank. I'll give you a course for Manston. We must have at least thirty knots of north wind."

"Roger, navigator, hope you're right. And let's hope some bright spark at Manston with an AA gun doesn't think we're a Junkers. Radio Operator, have the colours of the day ready."

William was right. P-Peter landed safely on the windswept airfield with five minutes of fuel left on board. As the aircraft slowed down, William thought again of Philips, still prostrate on the cabin floor. He took him by the shoulders and tried to sit him up. There was something warm and sticky in the middle of the man's back and the body was limp. A strange burning smell filled the cabin, and as the body slumped forward, it revealed a large hole in the floor of the aircraft. It was immediately obvious what had happened. A hot splinter from the bursting shell beneath them had come through to floor and buried itself in poor Philips's body, killing him instantly and scorching his flesh. Isaacs pointed out that had the splinter continued on its way it would have smashed through the crew compartment, killing him and probably disabling the aeroplane. Idle, cowardly and incompetent, in the end Philips had saved them all.

That night forty of the attacking bombers were lost; about twenty of these fell to German guns or fighters. The rest either had mechanical trouble or got lost and crashed into the sea. One such crew was rescued having blundered on down Channel and luckily ditched near a British destroyer which had been on a mine-laying expedition off Le Havre. The Dortmund raid was one of Bomber Command's disasters: forty aircraft lost out of a force of six hundred, and, worst of all, a high-flying Spitfire reconnoitring the target the next day noted locomotives shunting trucks on the railways and barges moving on the canal. All industrial buildings seemed to be intact and the blast furnaces were working as usual. There was some damage to residential areas but most of the bombs seemed to have fallen on open countryside some way from the city. A poor return for the loss of life and of aircraft.

P-Peter struggled back to Norfolk for debriefing by the intelligence staff.

Yes, they had certainly bombed the target. They had seen the canal clearly and the huge inland port. Jimmy was certain he had identified the massive Dortmund Union Building, a skyscraper by European standards. No, they had not bombed the diversionary fires. No, they had not been carried south of their course by the wind; they had correctly observed it and recalculated their course.

"Well done, boys," said a tired-looking Group Captain, and that was that. They flew back to Ford to resume their work.

Whiskers took William, Jimmy and Isaacs into his office the next morning.

"Look," he said, sounding more Welsh than ever. "We made a damned good crew over Dortmund. I'm sure lots of those others will have said they hit the target but they were miles away. We four know that we did a good job and that's what matters. Tell it to your grandchildren one day if you have any. Thank you, boys."

Whiskers did not remain much longer at Ford. He was posted to Norfolk to take command of a newly formed Lancaster squadron, leaving William to carry on the experimental work. It was a slow, frustrating process. The idea was to fit a new centimetric radar in an aircraft. This would perform much better than the longer wavelength radars previously used and enable the aircraft to pick out the echo from a U-boat up to twenty miles away, even in rough seas. No radar however could work if it was very close to the target as the return time of the radar echo was too short to measure. Thus the final stages of the attack had to be made visually. A bit of enterprising private development by Wing Commander Leigh, a serving RAF officer, produced an immensely powerful searchlight which could be mounted under a Wellington fitted with either a battery bank or a separate engine and generator. This would allow the pilot to illuminate the target in the final stages of his attack and sink it with bombs or depth charges. It all seemed quite simple, but getting everything to work correctly and developing an effective technique for attack all took time, and was not made easier by the continued sniping at the project by interested parties with rival systems. Endless dummy attacks had to be made on target floats or British submarines, and the aircraft themselves had to be modified, removing the forward gun position to make way for the radar and mounting the searchlight on a retractable "dustbin" underneath the belly. By early summer the first Leigh Light Wellingtons were operational and immediately changed the course of the Battle of the Atlantic.

William never got to fly one of the new machines operationally. In June, once again, Bomber Command called on Ford for two Wellingtons to make up numbers on a further raid deep into Germany. William was to pilot one machine and he chose Jimmy as his navigator. Isaacs was pressed into service again as radio operator and two leading aircraftsmen, Henry and Oliver, were to act as gunner and bomb aimer. Neither had been on operations before, but, unlike poor Philips, they both seemed keen and the crew appeared to work well together. They were allocated Z-Zebra, the newest and best of the Wellingtons on the base. Zebra was one of the new Mark III Wellingtons fitted with the more powerful Bristol Hercules engines, and she was hurriedly stripped of most of her anti-submarine gear and made ready for action as a bomber. Tuoy took a particular interest in her preparation. He was certain that he had worked out a way to get more range out of the Wellington than was standard by subtly juggling with the fuel/air mixture.

"Well, sir," he said to William, "provided you keep her on lean mix on the way out, you'll have ten minutes or more of juice on the way home. Just in case, sir. You remember what happened last time."

William didn't need reminding.

His crew received a more welcoming reception on this occasion. They were attached to a squadron based at Blackbushe in Hampshire. The crews had been well fed and cared for when they trooped into the station briefing room. Twenty Wellingtons had been rounded up from various operational training units and experimental stations to join the big four engine machines which were to make up the bulk of the force flying out of Blackbushe. The Wellington crews sat together and waited apprehensively for the Commanding Officer to uncover the map which would reveal their destination. He appeared, dapper and brisk, looking like a city gent about to announce a steep rise in profits. No one would have guessed that he himself was to pilot the leading aircraft in the bomber force and that very night would be fighting for his life, deep over Germany.

"Well," he started confidently. "Here's tonight's target." A dreadful hush fell over the room. His pointer indicated Ulm, a city on the Danube in the very south of Germany.

"Now this is a vital target," he continued, "It's the home of one of the biggest engine plants in Germany, and we believe it's quite lightly defended. We'll take off just before dusk and so we'll be in darkness for the whole of the run there and back – it's about seven hundred miles each way. The target will be marked by Mosquitos so that will be a good help for accurate bombing. The Wimpeys will take off first and the 'heavies' will overtake them before we reach Ulm. We should meet some friendly fighters on the way back so don't go shooting them down. Now..." The briefing continued in this half-jokey mode but the pilots could only think of one thing. Ulm. Seven hours flying over enemy territory, on a summer night with dawn breaking as they approached home. It would be murder. And as for the fighters meeting them... Poppycock. They had heard that one before and no one had once seen a friendly aircraft on the homeward leg. The CO droned on, then the met man – at least there was no moon and cloud cover most of the way – but William couldn't take his mind off the horror which awaited him. For a moment he felt his knees trembling, knocking together. With an effort he controlled them but he could not stop the blood draining from his face or the awful, sickening tightness in his stomach. Whatever happened, he kept telling himself, he must not let the others in Z-Zebra see how scared he was.

Briefing over, the crews were confined to barracks until it was time for takeoff. William couldn't eat or drink anything and just mooned about the mess, trying to listen to the radio. A loud voice interrupted his thoughts.

"Is there a bloke called William Portman in the mess?" William looked up. "Well there's a call for you on the public phone box outside. It should have been disconnected with tonight's raid on but obviously it wasn't. Sounds like a girl, want to take it, you lucky sod?"

Angela's sweet voice on the phone was unmistakable.

"Darling, never mind how I got through to you, we girls have ways, and I know not to ask you what you are doing but I have something important I must tell you now. Darling, I love you. Please don't be angry whatever I say. Promise."

William was so taken aback that he could only stutter.

"Darling, what is it?"

"You know I spoke about your cousin Hans, well, he's here in our house, yes, yes here but he's wounded, we must take care of him. Oh, William, on the ship…"

There was a click and the line went dead. At the same moment a call came through to the mess, summoning the crews for action. For a moment William was unable to remember where he was; the news was so devastating. He dialled furiously for the operator but got only a series of clicks. He yelled into the mouthpiece.

"Angela! Angela!" No response.

William beat on the sides of the kiosk with his fists. At that moment Jimmy came past at the run. Seeing his boss, he opened the door.

"Hey, skip, they've called us to get going. You OK, skip?"

"Yes, Jimmy, OK, just had a bit of a shock."

He didn't look OK. He was still trembling with rage at what he had heard, trying to recall every word Angela had said, trying to understand what might have happened, trying to make sense of it. That odious Hun bastard. In Droxford? With Angela? As he and his faithful crewman stood there, they heard a new sound, the clanging of a bell which could only have been mounted on an RAF police car. Someone had traced an outside connection to William's phone box.

Whoever was talking on an outside line would be in deep trouble. So would the operator who put him through.

"Quick, skip, we'd better run!" yelled Jimmy and he and William disappeared round a corner just as the police Morris screeched to a stop beside the phone box. William followed Jimmy in a daze, scrambled into a waiting truck and found himself stumbling up the steps of the aircraft into his seat. He had now flown the Wellington so many times that he went through the drills without thinking and soon they were trundling towards the runway. The faithful Bristol Hercules engines gave a reassuring, throaty roar and Z-Zebra moved steadily towards the end of the runway. For now he forced himself to put all thoughts of Angela out of his head and concentrate on the daunting task set before him.

Once again the invading force formed up over the Thames and thundered off into the darkness ahead. While they were still over the North Sea, German radar had them in its deadly gaze. Over Holland, Belgium and Germany itself, fighters were armed, crews briefed and engines warmed up. The great anti-aircraft guns around industrial towns and key strategic locations were readied and the Third Reich prepared to receive its visitors.

Chapter 13

Hans (alias Stanislas) was sitting on his bed when Angela appeared at Netley. It hadn't been hard for her to talk her way into the place, and she immediately saw that the patient's recovery had continued apace. She suggested a walk, and was delighted to see that he accepted readily and seemed quite strong enough to take her arm and stroll across the lawn to the wire which guarded the sea shore. Beyond the wire was a blue sparkling Solent into which Netley Pier projected. They sat together well away from prying eyes or flapping ears.

Hans began.

"Angela, it's so wonderful to see you, but I am afraid that I have bad news and we need to put together a story which will keep you, at least, out of trouble. You see, I have just heard that a Polish officer from London will be visiting the hospital next week to discuss my future and that of three genuine Poles just arrived here. I have managed to keep away from those three up to now but that can't last and I am certain that I will be found out as soon as this fellow arrives from London, so I am going to have to give myself up and I've decided to do so before he arrives. Questions are going to be asked about how I swapped identities on the *Minden* and we've got to concoct a story which keeps you out of it. Then, if for some reason you do get questioned about the affair, our stories will agree."

"But what will happen to you, Hans?"

"I don't know. Possibly if I come clean now I'll just be transferred to a POW camp, but if the Poles get me, well, I don't know what will happen…"

"Hans, that's terrible. You could be treated as a spy or anything. You could be shot! Even if you go to a camp, those horrible men who wanted to kill you on the ship will try to get you again. No! I won't let it happen! We must think of a plan. We must do it now."

Her eyes blazed and her face showed a fierce, animal determination like a mother defending a small child. If Hans had not been in love with her on *Minden*, he certainly was now. He felt her strength and somehow knew he himself could never match it, but he couldn't let her become endangered by his own predicament.

"Angela, it's no use, and anyway, I can look after myself in a POW camp. There will be other decent Germans there who will help. Anyway, you can't involve yourself; the work you do is too valuable for that. The important thing is to make up a sensible story. Now, I've been thinking…"

"Well, stop your thinking, you stupid man. We're going to get you out of here before that Polish officer gets anywhere near you. Shut up! Don't dare argue with me! I know the people and the system here and we'll have you safe in no time. Now get yourself ready, and I'll be here again on Thursday at four o'clock. No, don't speak to me, just do as I say and keep away from those other three Poles."

With that she got up and marched determinedly out of the hospital. Hans simply didn't know what to think. Why was this girl seemingly determined to save him? What could she do anyway? The whole thing was unbelievable, ridiculous. But then he knew that he loved her. She had saved him once and seemed to be prepared to do so again. Did that mean that she loved him too? Could he dare to hope that, cripple as he was, this girl really cared for him? If so then there was still something to live for, and perhaps he would be able to help her too when Germany eventually won the war. If there was the very least chance of this, he must at least try to survive. He would see what sort of scheme she devised.

As it turned out, escape from the hospital was absurdly easy. Angela had a friend who drove one of the ambulances which were constantly toing and froing between Netley and the docks. The sentries seldom checked them; after all, the hospital was for wounded British and allied casualties only, so Hans was smuggled out without difficulty. Angela borrowed some petrol from a farmer near Droxford and took the family Rover to Southampton, recovered an astonished Hans from the ambulance by the roadside, and drove him safely home to Exton Grange. It was not until two days later that the hospital discovered that it had lost a patient. The police were ordered to keep a lookout for a wounded, one-armed Pole but naturally nothing was found and the case remained open, but dormant, on their files. Probably, they thought, the stupid fellow had managed to fall off the pier at Netley into the sea. He was well known to be subject to fits of depression.

Reception at Exton proved to be the difficult bit. Angela had fought shy of telling Sir Felix anything about the affair, but her mother knew and had no option but to agree to put Angela's friend up, at least for a time. He was accommodated in a spare bedroom and allowed to walk about in the walled garden, where no one could see him. The master of the house would have to decide what to do with him when he returned from London on Saturday. Lady Pointer could not help being charmed by her guest's impeccable manners, and his pallid, tortured face and wounded body could only arouse sympathy, but she was aware that the situation was fraught with danger. Aiding an escaped enemy was a severe crime, and anyway, how could she know that he was not still a dangerous enemy spy? Angela was due back on her ship soon. What would happen then? Even if he did stay, how would she feed him, with no ration card? Hans must be got rid of. That was clear and Sir Felix was the one who would have to sort it out. More perplexing still was the question of Angela's feelings for this man. Of course, her mother knew about the holiday near Bawdsey before the war, and obviously the two had been close at that time, but now surely William was her daughter's sweetheart? Why, then, was she risking a long prison sentence and implicating her parents in her crime, for the sake of this wounded German officer?

Sir Felix duly returned and went straight to his study, fortified by a glass of claret. He had been an officer in the Royal Naval Volunteer Reserve in the First World War, navigating fast destroyers in the North Sea and the Western Approaches. He thus knew something about war but he had never encountered a situation anything like this. First he summoned his daughter to see him. She recounted the whole story of her rescue of Hans, her father listening in silence. He asked only one question.

"Angela, tell me honestly, are you in love with this man?"

"Oh, Daddy, how could you ask that? You have met William and surely you saw what I felt about him. No, I don't feel anything for Hans, except that he is in danger and in my care. If we sent him back it would be just like murdering a friend."

Hans was then ushered into the room. Twenty years in the law courts had taught Sir Felix a thing or two about interviewing people. He was immediately impressed by the bearing and stature of the young man before him. Even wearing an old pair of Rory's pyjamas and a dressing gown, he looked impressive and his handshake, even with his left hand, was firm and solid. He started by trying to thank his host, but Sir Felix cut him short.

"Young man, I will ask the questions and you will answer. Understood? Good. Then tell me from the beginning how you had your accident, and what happened on the hospital ship."

Hans' story exactly confirmed what Angela had told him.

"And why were your colleagues trying to kill you? Had you betrayed them or did they just not like you?"

Hans saw that this man would get at the whole truth eventually. He might as well come up with the whole story now. He explained about Ester and his quarrel with the SS Officer.

"You see, sir," he concluded, "I simply couldn't go on fighting for a regime where men like that can do such things. I am sure the Fuhrer knows nothing of this or he would stop it, but I just couldn't go on. I think I must have been going mad. I resolved to kill myself and strike a blow for Germany at the same time, but I failed. Your lovely daughter saved me, and here I am."

"And what do *you* think should happen to you now?"

"Sir, I have been considering this for days and there is only one way. I must go into town and give myself up to the military police. I will pretend to have become delirious in hospital and somehow wandered out. I will be sent to a POW camp for

Luftwaffe officers and I am sure I will find friends there and be able to explain myself. Whatever happens, I cannot put your family in danger. When this war is over and Germany and England are friends again, I hope to meet you all and thank you. I promise I will say nothing to your police about how Angela helped me."

"Very well, please go to your room now, I have to consider."

The Pointer family held a conference.

"At first I was inclined to do what he says," said Sir Felix. "But think of this. No one is going to believe the story about a delirium, and Angela is sure to be implicated in his escape. Also, what about this sudden assumption of Polish nationality? Technically, at least, that makes him a spy and we have aided him. We all know what happens to spies and their helpers, and like it or not, he's stayed concealed in this house so we are all implicated. There's no getting away from it."

"Rubbish!" retorted his wife. "How do you know he's not actually a spy anyway? We can explain to the police how Angela got involved. We need him out of this house at once. It's what he wants and what we want. You're supposed to be a lawyer; you can explain it all. Let's do it now."

"Mummy," replied Angela, close to tears. "How can you say that? Hans is a guest in our house, in distress. By all the rules of civilisation we must help and protect him. I saw those horrible men. No doubt they will kill him in the camp, that is, if our people don't shoot him as a spy first. You know him now. He is a nice, civilised young man. How can you talk like that?"

"Civilised be damned! He's a Nazi airman. He's probably bombed our country and he'll drag us all down too. Get him out of my house! Now!"

"Never!" shouted Angela. "I won't let you!"

Very occasionally Sir Felix had to assert his authority in the family. This was one of those occasions.

"Wait," he said, "I have a germ of an idea. If we do what either of you suggest, we put both that young man and ourselves, all of us, in danger. I'm away back to London on Monday and I may need to call in some favours. Maybe there's a way out of this which will

225

see us all safe. Angela, you must be off on Monday as if nothing had happened. Darling, keep that young man out of sight and feed him for another week. I'll see if I can bag another pheasant this afternoon. I promise it won't be more than a week. Now I have to fix some meetings. See you both at dinner."

Ten days after this family conference, two civilian policemen arrived and escorted Hans to a POW transit camp near Southampton. At the same time lorry loads of German prisoners arrived from various camps in the south of England; most of them were naval personnel, rescued U-boat officers and a few were soldiers picked up in the western desert. Many, like Hans, had been wounded and were struggling with artificial legs and missing arms or hands. Two days later they were herded onto a liner which, as they guessed correctly, was Canada bound.

Chapter 14

As Z-Zebra steadied herself on course, William had time to think more about his situation. This was a long-range flight, almost seven hundred miles each way, and over four hundred of those over enemy-held territory. He had to go through with it, there was no way out, but he dreaded what he might find when he reached home even more than the horrors awaiting him over Germany. Angela and that bloody Hun! It couldn't be, he couldn't let it happen, he must think of something quickly. "Enemy coast ahead, skip!" called Oliver in the nose. "Looks hot too." It did indeed. The searchlights were feeling for their prey in the darkness and already heavy shells were bursting ahead. William managed to get a hold of himself and spoke calmly to the crew. "Right, I'm going to start weaving. Now all keep a good lookout, there'll be fighters about, and we need to be careful not to ram one of our own machines." Zebra banked gently and seemed to slide like an eel between the hideous columns of light, groping blindly for them. Undamaged, they thundered on southward, eyes skinned for any trace of avenging fighters.

Luckily for them the Luftwaffe had been fooled that night into thinking that the attack would be directed elsewhere and defences concentrated way to the west of their route. Once through the coastal flak, the bombers had a surprisingly undisturbed two hours flying southwards towards their target. William had by now managed to force the thought of Angela out of his mind; he forgot everything except the one daunting task of getting to the target. He remembered how on his last bombing raid he had been comforted by the sight of Whiskers solidly ensconced in his seat, acting and speaking calmly just as if it had been a routine training flight. Forcing himself to act and sound like an intelligent robot, he constantly checked on every aspect of the flight, their course, fuel consumption, speed, height, the alertness of his crew, the weather ahead. Oliver was the first to see the brilliant green flares marking where the Mosquitoes had dropped their target markers. That must be Ulm, blacked out and sleeping in the darkness.

A little way northwest of them in the darkness, Hauptmann Heinz-Erick Stillmann was part of a team evaluating a new airborne interception technique. Just as the British had used the Blenheim as a "heavy fighter" the Luftwaffe adapted some of its bombers to a night-fighting role. However, unlike the poor Blenheims which the RAF had used in this role, the JU88 which the Major was flying was well suited to the task. Capable of over three hundred miles per hour in level flight and with five hours endurance, it had a crew of three and carried very heavy offensive armament consisting of three machine guns and one heavy twenty millimetre-cannon. The plan was to loiter close to the city being attacked, keeping a lookout for any bomber illuminated by a ground-based searchlight, then to attack it while it was still over the target. The obvious danger was being hit by "friendly" flak, so good communication with the ground was essential. The best targets were expected to be the last bombers to arrive, by which time the AA guns could be ordered to cease fire while the fighters moved in and attacked the raiders. That night Stillmann's force of three JU88s had initially been directed to Mannheim, which they had circled for an hour, waiting for a bomber stream which never arrived; only at the last minute were they informed that Ulm, forty minutes flying to the southeast, was under heavy attack. The three machines sped south eastwards towards the action.

William could not help feeling awestruck by the scene of the small town under bombardment by over a thousand tons of deadly bombs. Great red and yellow splashes of colour appeared, burned, then smouldered angrily. Thin, intense pencils of light probed the darkness, looking for the town's tormentors and the air was filled with tracer arching up, slowly it seemed at first, then heading at a terrific speed towards them. Heavy flak shells were bursting among the first wave of attackers. Oliver, prone in the bomb aimer's position, started calling out directions, guiding the aircraft to the green flares.

"Straight as she goes... left a bit, skip. Steady... Steady... Left again. Bomb doors open. Wow! What's that?"

The Wellington reared up and turned sharply to port, sending maps, pencils and bits of flying gear whizzing about the cabin. At the same time there was a roar and the whole machine shuddered and seemed to lose her grip on the air. Sitting beside William, Jimmy saw a huge shape plunging past them, little flowers of orange flame streaming from its wings. William pushed the control column forward, recovering from the incipient stall, swearing at the top of his voice into his oxygen mask. After a few minutes he was back on a steady course.

Skipper to crew:

"That was a close one. Stirling, I think, and she'd been hit. Maybe the crew had bailed out. She damned near took us with her. Bomb aimer, can you still see the target?"

"No, skip, we've lost it, and we'll be past it by now. What do you want to do?"

"We'll go round again. After flying all this way we're not going to waste these bombs. Navigator, take us back to just north of the target, I've lost orientation."

Going round again was a bold decision. Most of the bombers would be on their way home, and Z-Zebra would be among the stragglers, the focus of the almost undivided attention of the defenders. But William was determined. The events of the last few hours had ignited a bitter fury, a compulsion to hit out at something and that something was at hand – the unfortunate city of Ulm. His crew sensed his mood and said nothing.

The second approach run became a nightmare. It seemed that every searchlight on the ground was concentrating on the lonely Wellington, and the sinister bluish light bathed them in its evil glare. Strangely, however, over the target, the gunfire seemed less intense, then stopped altogether, just as Oliver released his bombs and took the obligatory photograph through the bomb sight. Bombs away, the Wellington surged upward and, at the same time,

William swung her to port and climbed hard, spiralling upward and successfully shaking off the glare of those foul searchlights. Jimmy called out a course for home. For a moment there was a feeling of relief aboard Z-Zebra. They had done their job and, still undamaged as they were, there was a good chance of a safe return.

Stillmann, however, had other plans. He had seen the lonely Wellington from a distance as he belatedly arrived over the city. He guessed that she would climb and head for home. He circled to the north of the burning city and saw his quarry silhouetted against the fires she had helped to start. How dare that bastard Tommy destroy his historic city? How could he be killing innocent German women and children, then expect to fly safely home over the soil of the Fatherland?

Cold and alone in the rear turret of the Wellington, Leading Aircraftsman Henry had been struggling to keep alert on the long flight south, but the excitement over the target had shaken him wide awake and he was the first to spot the sinister shape astern and a little below them, silhouetted against the glow of the burning city.

"Enemy fighter astern, skip! Coming up fast!"

"OK, Gunner, keep him in view but don't fire yet, he may not have seen us."

But he had seen them. Stillmann was famous for his keen eyesight; the night was clear and the two little tell-tale points of red light from the Wellington's exhaust had appeared exactly where he expected them, about a mile away. William was trying to decide what to do. The spiral turn as performed by Whiskers was an option, but if he tried it at this juncture he might give himself away and the enemy might not have spied him; instead he climbed gently, at the same time weaving from side to side. Stillmann watched the manoeuvre carefully. Probably it meant that the enemy had seen him, but that was not a problem. He could out climb and catch any British bomber except a Mosquito easily and he was fairly sure the machine he had seen in the beam of the searchlight was a Wellington. He would attack from below and astern. If he was quick he might get a chance to turn back and find another victim.

Henry tried to keep his eye on the deadly predator astern. This was his first operational flight and he was determined to do his best not to let the crew down. As the distance from the fires of Ulm increased, however, it became more and more difficult to be certain of where the enemy was. Although his turret was freezing cold, he was sweating profusely in his flying suit. He must, *must* keep his head and let the captain know what was happening.

Pilot to Rear Gunner:

"Can you still see him?"

"I think so, skip. Closing slowly, he must have seen us. No! I see him plainly now, below us and catching fast. Hell, he's close!"

Gripped by a sudden terror, he waited for no further orders and sent a long burst from his guns towards the enemy below him. At precisely the same moment, the Junkers opened up with its battery of nose-mounted artillery. For once Stillmann's aim seemed less than perfect. Henry plainly saw tracer from the machine guns whizz past the starboard side of the machine and disappear over the top of the wing. His own burst had passed well above the target. As Stillmann had been careful not to overshoot the Wellington he had the possibility of a second burst before he overtook her, but William immediately started a violent downward spiral, flashing past the nose of the Junkers and disappearing towards the ground before his enemy could take aim. Undeterred, the German pilot went into a shallow dive. The Wellington was sure to head north for home and he would catch her again and finish the job.

All was not well aboard Z-Zebra however. It was Jimmy first who noticed the smell of petrol in the cabin. From his position behind the pilot, he could look out over the starboard wing and to his horror he saw a plume of red flame streaming from the wing from a point just outboard of the engine. One stray round from the Junkers' heavy cannon had exploded inside the fuel tank. The tanks were supposed to be leak proof, but such a big shell was too much for the self-sealing membrane. The Wellington was equipped with a fire extinguisher system, but William knew that the only way to deal with a serious petrol fire was to blow it out by diving at maximum speed. He forgot his hunter for a moment and went into a violent power dive. Zebra shuddered as the speed built up and seemed likely to shake herself to pieces as she approached four hundred miles per hour, nose down, engines racing. Stillmann watched her plight, wondering whether she would plunge straight into the ground or if he needed to attack again to finish her off. Seeing the flames diminish, he decided to go in close to deliver a coup de grace. Unfortunately for him, he had not reckoned with Henry, hunched over his guns in the rear turret, terrified by the plane's violent manoeuvres, but still alert and determined to do the best he could. As the Wellington began to pull out of her dive, he felt the blood drain from his upper parts and for a moment blacked out completely. An extraordinary effort of willpower forced him into consciousness and although his eyes were still clouded with black specks, he managed to focus them on the gunsight in front of him. There was the Junkers dead astern, looming ever larger and more threatening by the second. A long burst somehow found its mark, shattering the glasshouse cockpit and blinding the pilot. The big fighter plunged past Z-Zebra and smashed into the ground below.

William levelled off and took stock of the situation. All control systems seemed to be working normally and both engines were running. The fire seemed to be out. All crew members reported OK, except that Henry's voice was quavering with excitement and fear. The problem was fuel state. The ruptured fuel tank was isolated, but half the fuel needed for the return trip was gone. There was no way the aircraft could make the journey home, and the route was all over hostile territory. William and Jimmy searched desperately for maps and finding a suitable small-scale chart, Jimmy drew a circle around their position, now a little to the north-west of Ulm and another showing the distance they might be able to fly on what remained of their fuel. There was only one way to avoid coming down in enemy territory. William strained to make his voice sound confident and calm over the intercom.

"Right, crew, we've dropped our bombs and Henry back there has shot down a Junkers. Not bad for a night's work but we haven't enough fuel to get home. I'm going to try to make it to Switzerland which is neutral. It's about half an hour's flying and we'll have to find a place to do a wheels-up landing. Everyone, remember the drill for that. As soon as we are out of the aircraft we'll have to set her on fire, in case Jerry gets hold of her. Jimmy, you see to that while I muster the rest of the crew. Meantime everyone keep alert, there may still be fighters around."

Flying south westwards, keeping close to the ground, William thanked God for the dim moonlight which he hoped would enable them to see the Alpine foothills before they ran into them. At first navigation was quite easy, following the course of the Upper Danube as it wound gently south westwards. At Sigmaringen, William turned south and began a gentle climb, seeing Lake Constance shimmering ahead in the moonlight. There was no sign of hostile action en route. British bombers seldom penetrated so far into southern Germany. Some light flak arched towards them from the north shore of the lake, guarding perhaps, some military installation on the water's edge. The last German town on their route, Konstanz, they left well to starboard, then made towards the lights which distinguished the neutral Swiss settlements from the Germans. William switched on his landing lights. A road and railway seemed to run along the lake shore. "Best put her down there," said William, "if we go further into Switzerland we'll probably get among mountains and we haven't enough fuel left anyway."

"Crew, brace for wheels-up landing!"

It would have been a good landing if there had not been a series of concrete posts along the roadside. The tip of the port wing touched one of these, breaking off and slewing the machine round so that she skidded sideways down the road in a shower of sparks. The tail then snagged another post and broke clean off the aircraft, finishing up upside down in a roadside ditch. The main part of the aircraft then brought up short against a tree and lay there making strange creaking noises, emitting a spiral of evil-looking smoke.

William woke up in a daze of white, white walls, white sheets, white ceiling, white…

"How's you, skip?".

A voice spoke from beside the bed, somehow familiar; who was it?

"Cor, it ain't half warm in 'ere don't know how you stands it, but you are looking better I must say."

Of course, it was Jimmy! A great lump seemed to be shifting slowly in William's brain. Jimmy! Had he destroyed the plane? Was he all right? How about the others? Where the hell were they? William tried to sit up in bed but a firm hand restrained him.

"Now don't you fret, skip, we're both safe in Switzerland. Thought you were a gonner when we hit that lamp post but it seems that your head was 'arder than the instrument panel. Came right up towards you it did. But me and Oliver we gets you out then, whoosh, up she went, Jerry won't learn much from that pile of ashes. Pity about the others tho'…"

Things were falling into place.

"Jimmy," he said weakly. "What happened? How about the rest of the crew?"

"Well, I'd better tell you now, skip. Poor little Henry in the tail, he was smashed against that post, finished up fifty yards from the rest of the plane, dead when we got there. He was a good 'un too. Remember that JU he shot down? Good man. Isaacs, well, he bought it too, we didn't see what happened, they took him off in an ambulance, but we could see he was finished. I've never seen so much blood… Now I'm going to leave you, skip. The doc here said you'd been concussed and I could only have five minutes, but I'll be back tomorrow."

William lay in bed trying to piece together what he had heard, but he couldn't keep awake. He plunged into a deep sleep. Somehow Angela was in the Wellington, sitting in the rear gunner's seat. She was smiling at him but he couldn't get at her, and something was pulling her out of the aircraft. He slept.

Two days later William was released from hospital. His injuries were not nearly as severe as they had at first looked. His face was covered with cuts and bruises and little pieces of glass and Perspex were embedded in his forehead and around his eyes. He had thus been a ghastly, bloody sight when Jimmy and Oliver had dragged him from his seat but the damage was short-lived. He had two broken ribs and severe concussion, both of which time would cure. Switzerland at that time found itself being used as a refuge by quite a number of combatants: German airmen who had got lost, Italians who had somehow blundered over the border, a few British soldiers who had escaped from France in 1940, escaped Allied POWs and quite a number of RAF aircrew like the crew of Z-Zebra. Their internment conditions depended mainly on the attitude of the particular canton in which they were held and on the whim of the local security and police bosses.

Zebra's crew were interned near Winterthur, in the German-speaking part of the country where most of the inhabitants were inclined to have German sympathies. Conditions of internment were not strict however. Airmen were accommodated in an old school building which was modestly comfortable, officers occupied the top floor, other ranks the ground floor and basement. Inmates, there were twenty of them altogether, were allowed to roam about the area within twenty kilometres of their base in daytime, provided they were present for nigh-time roll call. But it was boring. Wandering aimlessly about the little town, now busy manufacturing armaments which were sold indiscriminately to both sides, was a tedious and dispiriting occupation and yielded plenty of time for fits of depression and general gloom to take hold. William spent hours thinking ruefully about Angela, The Red Cross operated a mail service enabling internees to send and receive letters but somehow he found endless excuses for not writing to her, telling himself that she was probably posted to some remote spot, or at sea so there was no point in sending a letter. Instead he mooned about, thinking of what his loathed cousin and rival might be up to. In fact, Angela was indeed on active service again, this time on a hospital ship bound for the Far East. She did manage a few scribbled notes from Cape Town and from Calcutta, but the censors prohibited any mention of her ship's name or its whereabouts, and her father had impressed on her the vital importance of not saying anything about Hans or his escape in case someone in the censorship office might start asking awkward questions. The scanty and restrained communications with his love, combined with boredom and enforced idleness, turned William into a morose, self-centred figure, whom his fellow internees left well alone.

Jimmy, however, was not content to idle around all day. The loss of his two brothers when their ship, HMS Hood, was sunk by the battleship Bismarck had led him to hate anything German with a zeal which he soon passed on to his colleague, Oliver. Oliver had spent some of his boyhood in France and was a fluent French speaker. Many of the locals were bi-lingual so he could find out a little about what went on in the neighbourhood and it soon transpired that there was a camp for German detainees, mostly airmen who had crashed in Switzerland, housed in an abandoned ski resort the other side of Zurich. The two resolved to break the rules and pay a visit. It did not prove difficult. Pretending to be visitors from Geneva, they arrived at Arosa and had no difficulty in finding the billet occupied by German aircrew. Unlike their British counterparts, the Germans had established a military regime in their camp with regular parades and exercises in the mountains. Pretending to wander casually around the ski resort, closed on account of the war, the two truants observed their counterparts drilling, marching and singing patriotic songs for most of the morning. In the afternoon they hiked into the mountains following what seemed to be a regular circuit which ended up in crossing a plank bridge running across a deep ravine just outside the village. A close inspection of the bridge showed that its strength depended on two longitudinal beams supporting the whole structure. Jimmy became extremely interested.

Among the duties of the internees at Winterthur was the preparation of their own firewood. A few days after the pair's first expedition to Arosa the saw allocated for the purpose mysteriously disappeared. That same evening Jimmy and Oliver contracted a nasty bug and took to their beds so that they were excused from morning roll call next day. Next morning early the two visitors from Geneva appeared again in Arosa. They took coffee and croissants for breakfast in the only restaurant which remained open, then set off, seemingly for a stroll in the valley. Early that afternoon, after watching the Germans begin their customary hike, the pair from Geneva disappeared. That evening Oliver and Hopson, seemed to have made a full recovery and no one else caught the bug.

The Swiss newspapers next day were full of it. Two Luftwaffe internees had been killed and six badly hurt in a bridge collapse. How could it have happened? Were there too many men on the bridge? Was it in dangerous condition? Could it have been sabotage? Next day the German press took up the story but their line was more ominous. Dr Goebbels himself dictated the theme. Treacherous, cowardly Switzerland held unfortunate Germans in foul conditions illegally and refused to return them. Now they allowed them to be killed in absurd accidents. Or were they accidents? Dark hints were dropped about French or British assassins stalking German internees and of sinister Jewish-inspired gangs of murderers hiding in Switzerland. Finally, there was a demand that German police should investigate the affair and produce a "True" report. The affair now reached the highest levels in the Swiss government who were desperate not to provoke their powerful neighbour but at the same time staunchly defended their nation's independence and neutrality. Eventually it was agreed that a top-level meeting of diplomatic officials should convene in Zurich and thrash the matter out. William had studied this affair in the local German-language papers with desultory interest until he noticed a picture of the proposed German delegation. At its head was a figure he immediately recognised as his own Uncle Albricht.

Chapter 15

Albricht was the natural choice to lead the delegation. Throughout the war, there had been meetings in Switzerland in which British, German and later American diplomats would meet and discuss financial, humanitarian and diplomatic issues, with the Swiss acting as go-betweens. Among the functions of these meetings was the occasional internee exchange, usually involving wounded men, swapped for similarly damaged personnel on the other side. With his diplomatic and business expertise, Albricht had been a key figure in the German team at these negotiations whilst at the same time using his position to smuggle valuable items of art and even currency out of Germany on behalf of some of his Nazi bigwig friends who felt that some investments outside their own country might prove a useful insurance policy. In spite of his elevated position in the hierarchy, Albricht was not a happy man. The fate of his only offspring, Hans, had shaken him deeply. Once he had been a source of enormous pride to the family then suddenly some strange things seemed to be happening. There was a telegram from the Red Cross suggesting that he had been wounded and captured. A little later another message stated that he had died on a British hospital ship. Strangely no letter of condolence was received from his Luftwaffe unit, but his commanding officer, von Kostler did write, promising to visit the family in Berlin and explain the details of Hans' last flight to the family. Von Kostler's letter hinted that there was more to the story than he was prepared to put on paper. In the meantime Albricht was acutely aware of rumours circulating about his son's last days. Bitterly he and the Countess, his wife, mourned the death of their boy. Now the only survivor of the next generation of the von Pilsen family was that odd arty nephew in England. William, wasn't it? Heaven knew what had happened to him.

On one of his visits to Switzerland, Albricht had occasion to study a list of internees recently arrived in the country. He noticed the name Portman among them. William Portman? Wasn't that the name his nephew had used when he had visited before the war? He demanded to see a photograph held by the Swiss police. Yes, that was him, crashed his aircraft in Switzerland and reported to speak excellent German. Quickly he penned a note to his nephew. It would be quite improper for the two to meet, but did William by any chance have any news of his cousin Hans. Surely, if he had been captured, as some reports suggested, some news might have reached the extended family in England. No reply was received from his nephew.

Sir Felix's friends at the War Office had in fact ensured that there was no way Albricht, or anyone else, could trace Hans. Before boarding the ship to Canada, he had been given a new identity, "Oberleutnant Kurt Prim", in fact the name of a Stuka pilot who had been killed in a recent attack on a British warship. Hans was strictly forbidden to try to communicate with his true family. Letters which he addressed to the Prim household in order to maintain the deception were destroyed by the censor and dummy replies were fabricated to add an air of authenticity. As he was the only Luftwaffe officer in his camp, there was no danger of running into anyone who knew the real Kurt Prim.

The life of a POW in Canada, where food was plentiful and the inhabitants were not embittered by war, was comfortable in comparison to that in Britain and indeed luxurious compared to Germany, where a combination of shortages and the terrible effects of bombing made everyone's existence harsh. Prisoners in Canada were accommodated in comfortable, warm buildings with space for sports and classrooms in which a series of lectures and courses were arranged, initially by the inmates themselves. Soon various universities and schools in the locality got involved in the regime, sending lecturers and tutors to help with studies. Almost everyone learnt English and French and some undertook degree and even master's courses in law, history, mathematics and economics. A few hardened Nazis spurned the Canadian hospitality. These fanatics were termed "Blacks" by the camp staff, and eventually moved away to a separate establishment with a stricter regime. The majority of the officer prisoners forgot about politics and set about improving their post-war career prospects, keeping any political discussion to a minimum. Most still believed in ultimate German triumph over Russia and an eventual accommodation with the US and the British Empire. Used to being fed Nazi propaganda at home, they were unmoved by the news of the war they picked up in the camp, believing that most of it consisted of lies, although as time went on, new arrivals in the camp told disturbing stories of mass U-boat sinkings and ever more appalling devastation wrought by British and American bombers. Slowly confidence in victory began to wane.

Hans had concluded that after the war he would have to resume his legal training, and enrolled on a course given by a professor from Ottawa. He worked hard and managed to make the required grade finishing up with a degree in law acquired over his two-and-a-half-year stay in the camp. Apart from his studies, however, he found camp life lonely and frustrating. Being barred from contacting his family was bad enough, and he hated making up stories to tell his friends about the imaginary Prims, but being unable to contact Angela was worse. She must love him. Why else risk her life and family on his behalf. He remembered the happy days in Cambridge before the war, the soft touch on his pillow as she settled him down on *Minden,* the fierce, protective presence at Netley Hospital. In his mind he composed hundreds of letters, even a handful of clumsy poems, which never got written down. He thought of that RAF officer whose picture he had seen in Exton Grange. Was he a cousin or something? The thought made him wince and look down at his pathetic stump of an arm. Nothing he had seen of the war had made him doubt the ultimate superiority of the Luftwaffe so with any luck this rival (if rival he was) would meet his end at the hands of the Third Reich. But this was cold comfort. Sad, lonely and consumed by doubt and jealousy, he struggled on with his studies. At least a career in law would make him able to provide for Angela after the war.

March 1946 saw a depressed and anxious Hans deposited from a liner in Liverpool and taken to a transit camp for prisoners about to be released, near Newcastle.

Chapter 16

The Swiss had little option but to comply with the Nazi request to be involved in the inquiry into the accident at Arosa, but the business got off to a bad start. The three German detectives allocated from the Gestapo and the Abwehr (the military intelligence arm) booked into a hotel in the village, looked at the wrecked bridge for a day then waited to meet their Swiss colleagues, scheduled to arrive the next morning. Already the Swiss had taken away various exhibits and taken some statements from locals but even without these the three Germans had reached the conclusion that this was a case of deliberate sabotage. Saw marks were visible on some wooden beams lying in the ravine and the remaining timbers were substantial and in good condition. They could not possibly have given way under the weight of a small party of men. Now it was only a question of finding the culprits. That should be easy enough in a small and remote community.

The three were actually planning how they could drag the affair out for three or four weeks, during which they would be living, all expenses paid by the Swiss, in a comfortable and well-supplied neutral country, when the arrival of their Swiss colleague was announced – Colonel Isaac Schonbloomer of the Swiss. Isaac? Isaac? Could it be? They looked at each other in horror. When the colonel himself appeared, there was no possible doubt. His intelligent face and strong features were distinctly Jewish, and to make double sure a small silver Star of David was inserted in his buttonhole. There was nothing for it. With one accord the Germans got to their feet, turned their backs on the new arrival and stormed out of the hotel.

Telephoning his boss from the hotel, Schonbloomer had difficulty in avoiding dying of laughter. His name was not Isaac at all, but Thomas and he was certainly not a practising Jew.

"That will teach the bastards to come interfering in my case," he roared. The little phone booth trembled with his guffaws.

When the Germans were well out of the way, he continued his enquiries in the village and at all the local bus and railway stations. What did anyone know about the two visitors from Geneva who had been in Arosa recently?

It didn't take him long to learn that one of the pair was silent most of the time, but a waiter had heard one of them whispering something to his colleague – in English, or so the waiter thought. The other spoke fluent French but didn't seem to understand German. Yes, they both looked young, fit men but they never took their overcoats off and it was impossible to see what they were wearing underneath. No, they had not returned since the day of the accident. Schonbloomer easily narrowed down the field. Either this was the work of some French resistance group, or could it be someone from one of the internment camps? His colleagues from Geneva knew nothing about a resistance cell operating in Switzerland. Why should there be? There were plenty of Germans to kill at home in France. He resolved to call on all the internment camps for Allied soldiers anywhere near Arosa. Winterthur was the last call he made. The first thing he looked at was the attendance record for 6th May 1943. Interestingly, two internees had not answered that evening's roll call, being marked down as too sick to attend. On the evening of the 7th, however, they both appeared. There was no record of a doctor's visit, and no one else in the camp seemed to have suffered from the same bug. The detective summoned internees Hopson and Oliver. Yes, they had caught a strange bug that day, remembered it well, must have been in the food they thought.

"A day close to the bathroom," said Oliver. "And we were both fine. Right, Jimmy?"

"Yeah, right as rain, guv."

They both burst out laughing.

Schonbloomer didn't believe them. He went wandering round the building and soon found the wood saw, hanging up waiting for the autumn.

"A qui est cette scie?" he asked loudly.

"C'est a nous, pour l'hiver," Oliver replied, then turned red as a beetroot.

"Vous parlez Francais, Monsieur Oliver?"

"Juste un peu."

The saw disappeared into the police car and the investigation was over for the day.

That evening a crestfallen pair appeared in William's room.

"We've done it this time, skip," began Jimmy, and the whole story of the escapade came out. William saw immediately that this was real trouble; probably the pair would be extradited to Germany and shot. It would not take the police long to prove their case, but he couldn't let it happen. These fellows were his crew. His responsibility. He was supposed to be an officer and besides, that brave mother of Jimmy's had virtually entrusted her son to him. He sent the pair away and spent a restless night. Early the next morning he found a phone booth and managed to get a call through to Schonbloomer. A meeting was arranged in a quiet local bar.

"Herr Colonel," William began, surprising the man by his fluent German, "I understand that you have questioned two of my men about the affair in Arosa. Will you be kind enough to put me in the picture? These men are of course my responsibility and I had understood that this enquiry was in the hands of the German police."

Schonbloomer took a liking to this quiet-spoken English officer at once.

"German police," he replied. "Well, we'll see about that. I seem to have got on the wrong side of them." He chuckled to himself, remembering the incident in the hotel. "But you are correct; they have asked to be involved, but I can tell you we don't like it. Arrogant idiots that's what they are. As it happens we have a meeting with their negotiator this week and we will have to try to thrash out some sort of agreement. My boss will fight hard to keep German policemen out of our country, I can tell you. However, we have made our own investigation and it doesn't look good for your two men. You see, we have matched the saw in your wood store with the one used on the bridge…" William interrupted him. The word "negotiator" had given him an idea.

"Inspector, would the negotiator be Count Albricht von Pilsen, by any chance?"

"Yes, how did you guess that?"

"I saw his name in the paper, but let me tell you, I am his nephew. My father was half German; that's why I speak the language. I believe perhaps if you could arrange for me to meet him privately, I could help to resolve this affair."

"Well, if you can persuade him to keep his goons out of Switzerland, good luck to you. I'll try to arrange something but at the same time I will have to pursue the case against Oliver and Hopson."

"Colonel, let me put this idea to you. At this stage the Germans have no idea who committed this act. If either you or some German team find it was the work of British internees, supposedly under Swiss control, it won't look good for Switzerland, will it? There will be all sorts of allegations and demands from Germany, and you know how close they have come to invading your country already. This could be the spark which starts a war. Just supposing you could point the finger at someone else, perhaps French resistance fighters who have fled back over the border back to France, wouldn't that save Switzerland a lot of trouble? But you will have to arrange it before any German investigators arrive. That's where my uncle comes in. I believe that if I can see him privately, we can make time to defuse this matter."

The colonel got up from the table. He looked away from William towards the distant mountains.

"I can promise nothing," he said. "But there is some truth in what you say. I will call you tomorrow morning. In the meantime those two flyers will be taken into police custody on suspicion of murder, but you have my word that no other action will be

245

undertaken until we have met with the negotiator. Goodbye for now." He walked out to the waiting Citroen."

That afternoon a police detail arrested the two suspects on a charge of murder.

Raymond Ponsonby, the first secretary at the embassy in Bern, was fed up with hearing requests for release from British internees. All he could do for them was to tell them to wait patiently and that was exactly what they didn't want to hear. Repatriation could only be allowed for gravely injured cases or by some special arrangement with the Germans in exchange for Axis POWs in Britain. William was a bit different from most because all he wanted was to telephone England but even that wasn't allowed. Only the Red Cross could handle communications for internees. Ponsonby looked bored and unconvinced by this persistent Air Force officer wanting to communicate with a retired judge in England. In the end, to save further argument, he agreed to a brief exchange of telegrams.

William to Sir Felix:

Urgent urgent must know status and whereabouts of Hans von Pilsen. Understand was at Exton where now?

Sir Felix thought he knew his daughter's friend pretty well. Two "Urgents". There must be some reason for that, but was the telegram some German trick? He decided to reply not to the sender but by diplomatic telegram direct to the ambassador in Switzerland, who happened to be an old university friend.

Reference Portman telegram subject now POW in Canada alias Prim. Swiss embassy can confirm.

The telegram was a lifeline if only William could get access to Albricht. He decided that the only way was to take Schonbloomer into his full confidence. Another meeting was arranged in the bar and a plan was hatched.

At Albricht's next meeting in Switzerland, the colonel was summoned to fill the participants in on the status of his enquiry. He announced that two British internees had been arrested on suspicion of murder, but he himself had grave doubts about their involvement, hinting darkly at a conspiracy perpetrated by French

246

resistance. A suspicious saw had been recovered on a train at the terminus in Geneva. Two shady characters, one of them a French speaker, had been visiting the village. Further enquiries were being made; meanwhile the British suspects were being held "in humane conditions" nearby.

"Humane conditions!" stormed the Germans. "These murderers. They should be in one of our camps. We demand to see them immediately." This was exactly the reaction which William and Schonbloomer had expected. Just as the party from the delegation arrived at the prison, William himself was admitted on the pretext of giving moral support to his men. He was therefore the first person Albricht met on his arrival. The old diplomat could hardly contain himself.

"Nephew William," he called. "Do you not recognise your old uncle? Indeed we meet in strange circumstances, but we must talk." Leaving his colleagues to inspect the prisoners, he took William aside and commandeered an interview room in the prison block.

Albricht got directly to the point, asking William if he had received his note about his son, Hans. William denied having received it and asked exactly what it was that his uncle wished to know about Hans. Impatiently his uncle explained his predicament. When the explanation was over, William was silent for a while then replied.

"My dear uncle, as you no doubt know, I and my surviving crew members are interned here after an accident in which two of my men were killed and I myself was wounded. Now two of my crew are facing a charge for a serious crime which I believe is being investigated by your police. I am not satisfied that they will get a fair trial and I am responsible, as their captain, for their safety. Furthermore, we find internment here in Switzerland dull, disagreeable and very hard to bear. You are asking me to disclose information about Hans which, for some reason, the British government seems not to have, or wishes to keep secret. Now, I have contacts in the highest echelons of the British security establishment (Sir Felix would have enjoyed hearing him say that) and I may be able to obtain some information so maybe we can help each other. You want information from me: I want repatriation for my crew and myself. I am aware that you are in a position to arrange prisoner exchanges. What do you say?"

Albricht was taken aback by this blunt proposal coming as it did from the nephew he had written off as a vaguely arty, ineffective young man. He asked for time to consider and arranged a further, private meeting with William the next day. There were obvious difficulties. How could he be sure that what his nephew would tell him was correct? Suppose the truth was that Hans was dead, what use to him was that information? On the other hand, there was no real cost for Germany or for him personally in arranging an exchange of three rather unimportant prisoners. They could be swapped for Germans held in England or some neutral country. It would save a lot of trouble if the affair could be pinned on French "terrorists". After all, that police colonel seemed to think that it was nothing to do with the British airmen. He himself was getting old. Very privately he was now certain that Germany could not win the war now that America was involved and the Russian front was collapsing. All he wanted was to get his son safely back into the bosom of the family. Then he could end his life in contentment. In the morning he had an idea.

The next meeting with William took place in a police office. Albricht asked the obvious question about how any information William might get could be verified. The answer to this was simple; verification would come from either the Red Cross or the Swiss embassy, wherever Hans, if he was still alive, was being held. Written confirmation would be handed to the Swiss police and passed to Albricht as soon as the three British were on their way home. This he rejected immediately and came up with a counter proposal. If Hans was still alive, why not a straight swap with his cousin? Once this was settled, perhaps some arrangement could be made for the other two airmen. William saw some immediate advantages in this idea. Hans would be back in Germany, well away from Angela and he himself would be free, but he didn't like the rather vague agreement regarding his crew.

He would never consider leaving Switzerland without them. The meeting broke up with William promising to try to get information about Hans while Albricht came up with a more acceptable proposal for the other two. He had to return to Germany the next day, but would be in Switzerland again the following week.

Nothing could have prepared the old fixer for the visitor who appeared in his office on the morning of his return to Berlin. The SS officer was correct but forceful.

"I have come to question you in regard to your son, Hauptmann Hans von Pilsen. Do you know, sir, where he is?"

"No, I myself am trying to find what has become of him."

"Are you aware that he has been declared a traitor and an enemy of the Reich?"

Albricht was dumbfounded; his son a traitor? Impossible.

"I have to inform you that he has also been found guilty in his absence of the cold-blooded murder of an SS officer, Horst Feldman, in Sicily."

"I know nothing of this. Impossible," replied Albricht.

"Then I must inform you of these painful facts, Herr Count."

There followed an account of the events in Enna.

"I must tell you, sir, that we have no information regarding your son's movements on that last day. His aircraft was never found. We had a report that he might have been in a British military hospital in Gibraltar, but these are not confirmed. I do not have to tell you that should you or your wife have any contact with this traitor it is your duty to report it at once to the SS. We are of course aware of the vital work you are doing for the Reich in the diplomatic sphere (Albricht immediately thought of the two million dollars in gold coins he had recently transferred to a Swiss bank on behalf of Himmler, the head of the SS). Possibly you may be able to help us by making enquiries of the Red Cross in Switzerland. Rest assured, we will find the traitor and bring him to justice. Heil Hitler!" He strode out of the room.

Albricht collapsed into his chair, dumbfounded. His son, a traitor and murderer. Impossible! But what of this hint of his being in the hands of the British in Gibraltar?

He must get back to Switzerland as soon as possible. His young nephew, claiming contacts in the "British security establishment" was the best hope he had.

William himself had been busy trying to get as much information as possible about his cousin in order to strengthen his bargaining position. Communication with London was difficult and made more so by the obstructive Ponsonby at the embassy, but Schonbloomer had now become an enthusiastic supporter of his scheme to outwit the German police and was on good terms with senior personnel in the Swiss diplomatic service. A letter from William to Sir Felix was smuggled into a diplomatic bag and five days later a reply came from London. Reading the extraordinary story of Hans' escape, William almost got to like his cousin in spite of the burning jealousy he felt when he read of the risks Angela had taken on his behalf. God, how he longed for Angela, her soft, yielding body, her own special smell, her bubbly irrepressible humour, even occasionally her domineering certainty. Thank the Lord that bloody Hun was well away in Canada. He must get home. He must see her.

Another meeting with Albricht was arranged. William began:

"Uncle, I now have a report from England with all the information which you asked for, but the terms remain as I stated. You get the information: my crew and I return to England."

"I am astonished William that you put such a heavy price on simply letting me know what has happened to my son. Are we not family?"

"Family indeed, sir, but the lives of two of my men are at stake. Please do not think that I am unaware of the fate awaiting them at the hands of your police. Of course they are not guilty but our confidence in your judicial system is not high. I am afraid they will be made scapegoats to satisfy German public opinion. Either they are released and sent home or we have no deal."

"The leaders of our Reich will not permit it."

"Uncle, I am aware of your position of trust within your hierarchy. I believe that the British government would sanction the release of three German internees in exchange for my crew and myself. It would be a triumphant negotiation for you, besides the information which I know is foremost in your mind."

"But how will I know that the information you offer is accurate?"

"I will provide information from the Swiss embassy or the Red Cross in whichever country your son is held to confirm that what I say is true. This evidence will be handed to you as soon as my men and I are on the way to England."

It took a month for the Swiss consulate in Ottawa to take a photograph of Hans, authenticate it and send it to Switzerland, where it was held in safe keeping by Schonbloomer.

The Swissair DC 3 stood ready to depart for Barcelona, engines ticking over evenly while the Diplomatic Service Mercedes drew up near the control tower and Albricht examined the photographs. Yes, this was truly his son. With the pictures there was a brief report from the consulate and an affidavit signed by some English judge he had never heard of setting out the circumstances which had led to the concealment of his identity. His driver gave a signal to the control tower and the aircraft on the runway opened up its engines and headed west for Spain.

Albricht was not accustomed to thanking God for anything, but now he had to do so. His son was alive and safe in a country out of reach of the war. He no longer believed in ultimate German victory so maybe there would never be a trial for the killing of the SS officer. Perhaps Hans could one day return from Canada and become a leader of a new Germany under a different regime. He spent the rest of the day with Schonbloomer concocting a story about the Arosa incident which would satisfy the Nazi police.

The crew's journey home was not pleasant or easy. The Spanish authorities made life as unpleasant as possible for the three airmen, and then there was an uncomfortable and noisy flight from Gibraltar home as passengers in a Lancaster which had somehow managed to fetch up in north Africa. The flight was cramped, noisy and uncomfortable. William clambered stiffly out of the plane and made for the truck waiting to take the crew to the officers' mess.

Suddenly he caught the smell of freshly cut grass, and from somewhere in the distance the sounds of *Workers' Playtime* on the BBC drifted towards him from a hangar. From further away he could hear another sound, the unmistakable putter of a motor mower making its dark green and light green stripes on the squadron lawn. He took a deep breath. Yes, he was really home. Now he must find his Angela.

The next day a friendly bomber pilot gave him a lift to Ford, where he was ordered to take two weeks' leave, then report to the Air Ministry in London. "By the way, Portman," the CO remarked. "I think you'll find all your things in order; we didn't send them home as Flight Sergeant Tuoy said he'd care for them; he seemed to be certain that you would get back." Not only had the faithful Tuoy looked after the few possessions William had left behind, he had used his spare time to overhaul the Lagonda, and it stood gleaming outside the mess, full of petrol and running as sweetly as silk, waiting for his return. William lost no time in setting off for Hampshire.

The judge was in London, but would be home the next day. Lady Pointer made her unexpected guest welcome, but he felt that he was poor company that evening. His hostess brushed off all questions about Hans, saying that he must wait until Sir Felix returned. Angela, she said, was at sea again but she suspected that she might arrive back in England soon, as she had been away for almost three months. William went to bed imagining the very worst. Angela was keeping away on purpose so as not to see him. She was in love with that Nazi bastard. He had taken advantage of her in Exton while he himself was fighting. Perhaps she was even pregnant. Why was Lady Pointer being so uncommunicative? He passed a troubled, sleepless night.

The next day he was put to work in the vegetable garden after breakfast and spent the day weeding, planting out leeks, lettuces and cabbage seedlings. The solitary physical work did him good and the time passed quickly until Lady Pointer asked him to collect Sir Felix from the railway station at Alton. "He does hate that bus," she said. "And he gets exhausted after a week in London. He's almost eighty, you know, but he *will* not stop work at least until the war is over." William found himself quite shy and embarrassed to meet the man who had saved his two crew and probably himself from the clutches of the Gestapo, but the old fellow seemed cheerful enough and brushed aside all William's thanks.

"No trouble, old boy, when you are my age you have a pretty good idea of how things are done. Cost me a couple of dinners at Brooks's that's all."

Sir Felix went to bed early, so it was not until the next morning that William was able to question him about Hans.

"Well, I found your cousin a nice enough young man," he said. "Very shaken though, which is not surprising after what he had been through. I really think Angela saved his life on that troop ship you know – or perhaps you haven't heard that story? I'll tell you about it." He explained Hans' injuries and about the swapped identity with the Polish soldier. "Pretty plucky that, wasn't it? She could have got into no end of trouble, you know. But I must say I'm proud of her for it."

This was not at all what William wanted to hear. He slunk off to the vegetable garden, dug ferociously for a few hours, then invented an excuse to leave for his old home on Tyneside.

As ever Mrs Wellibond was delighted to see him and made a tremendous fuss of making him as comfortable as possible. Part of the house had been taken over as a nurses' hostel, but William's own room was intact and at last he was able to relax and remember his happy boyhood here in Stonebeck House. He had long talks with Freddy Seal. Freddy had been doing pretty well out of his inshore fishing activities, selling shellfish and freshly caught codling and mackerel to households longing for a bit of a treat. *Columba*, like most private yachts, was ashore, immobilised following navy orders to deny any possible means of escape to German POWs.

"Twenty-four hours and she'll be ready for sea again," said Freddy with a wink. "I reckon you'll be wanting to get to sea as soon as it's over."

Freddy was right. After all this dashing about in aeroplanes and the noise, smell and sheer brutishness of service life, William could hardly wait to be under sail again, At Stonebeck he began to sleep better than he had since the first days of the war. Everything took on a new, different dimension. Angela remained at the very centre of his thinking, but other things, aeroplanes, the RAF, the war and even Hans seemed to vanish behind a veil of foggy irrelevance. Instead he would calculate the state of tide at the river mouth, look up to see how the clouds were flying and pay close attention to anything which helped to forecast the weather. He felt in his sleep the jerk of flapping canvas, and under his feet the heel of the deck as his imaginary ship surged forward, washing her foredeck with clean seawater.

His next trip to London brought a sharp new focus. He was briefed by a Group Captain concerning the role which he was to play for the rest of the war. "You see, Portman," he said. "We never use chaps who have been released from detention in front line roles – security, you see, it's policy and we can make no exceptions; however, we do have something in mind which will suit you. We find ourselves in dire need of artists and your papers here suggest that was your work in civilian life." He went on to outline the situation.

The Allies had landed in Normandy and after a brief pause were about to overrun Paris, and drive a battered German army back out of France towards the Rhine. The Luftwaffe was concentrating what force it had left on intercepting the relentless stream of British and American bombers which were at last beginning to overwhelm the powerhouse of the enemy war industry. Only occasionally would a bold formation of fast bombers attempt to strike at British airfields, and few of these sorties were successful. Another threat, however, was developing in the hellish cauldron of the doomed German war machine. V-1 "Doodlebugs", unmanned flying bombs, rapidly followed by V-2 ballistic missiles were being launched from European sites with the object of striking terror into the hearts of the civilian population, especially the people of London. V-1s could occasionally be brought down by the fastest fighter planes or by ack-ack, but there was no defence at all against ballistic missiles, thousands of which were being built by slave labour in the depths of the Reich and smuggled to their launch sites in France, Holland and Belgium. Somehow they had to be stopped.

With almost complete control of the air over Germany and its occupied territories, the RAF was constantly using high-flying aircraft to photograph potential missile launch sites and to track the V-weapons as they moved, by road, rail or water, from their factories to the front line. Interpreting the thousands of photographs taken required an artist's eye which might be able to distinguish between a natural feature, an innocent quarry or an uncompleted bit of civilian groundwork, from a well-camouflaged launch site. Did that railway siding really hold a row of dilapidated cattle trucks, or were these innocent-looking bits of rolling stock actually cunningly hidden missiles on their way to a launch site in Belgium? Is that a haystack, or a camouflaged V-weapon? Why is part of the roof of that barn a different shape from the rest of it? Much of this painstaking analysis of photographic data was done by specially trained WAAFs (female RAF personnel). William's role was to be to head up one of the photo interpretation teams.

A week later he found himself in charge of a team of twenty-five keen-eyed young ladies, working in a disused and uncomfortable factory building in Hampshire. Photographs would be taken from first light until dusk, speedily developed and delivered to one of a number of such teams, each one specialising in a defined geographic area on the Continent. The teams would work until midnight on the day's pictures and recommend areas for further attention or for immediate attack.

To his surprise, William found the work congenial and interesting. His team of WAAFs would show him anything they deemed suspicious, and he soon found that his artist's eye was remarkably successful in translating fizzy photographs into three-dimensional pictures of the area and would give him a good idea of what was lurking in the shadows or underground. Often he felt he could even recognise the work of individual enemy camouflage officers, disguising a tunnel entrance here, a launch vehicle there or a transporter cunningly concealed by tree branches or by a haystack. Working as a solitary male officer among a large party of WAAFs obviously had its dangers and temptations, but William was deaf to every invitation and blind to all alluring glances. In fact, the girls began to speculate widely and not always kindly about his sexual orientation. He didn't mind. Being close to Angela's home, he spent any spare time he had there, helping Sir Felix in the garden and mooning about thinking of her, wondering morbidly what might have passed between her and his bitter rival – Hans. He was always a welcome visitor as Sir Felix loved having contact with young people. His son, Rory, was far away fighting his way up Italy and Angela on her hospital ship was now with the British Pacific Fleet somewhere near Australia, so William's company was welcome. Although security prevented him from saying much about what he did in the field of photo intelligence, he could talk freely about his operations with Bomber Command and in Switzerland, and made the old boy roar with laughter with his accounts of outwitting the Gestapo with the help of the Swiss police. The judge for his part talked about his political contacts, his rows with the various service chiefs (which were frequent) and his conviction that after the war a very different Britain would emerge.

Chapter 17

Ikari Samasido had lived his early years under a dismal, grey cloud. His grandfather, once a Vice Admiral in the Imperial Japanese Navy, had served his country well, including a glorious episode as commander of a destroyer in the great Battle of Tsushima in 1905 and a fine performance as a squadron commander in the Mediterranean in 1917-18. Intelligent, charming and a fluent English speaker, he had seemed to be bound for the highest positions in the Japanese military hierarchy. Then something went wrong. An avid reader of British and American news media, he saw that the world was not favourably impressed by the conduct of his country in the post-war period. Unwisely, he wrote an article for an American magazine entitled *An Alternative Future for Japan* which came to the notice of the government. The nationalistic clique then in power lost no time in interpreting this as a criticism of themselves and, worse still, of the Emperor. Deprived of his offices and honours, the old man had sunk into gloomy obscurity, dragging his family with him. His son, Ikari's father, just managed to hold onto his post as a local manager in the Post Office Department but was clearly barred from any further advancement. His earnings were barely enough to support his wife, son and two daughters. The family no longer received official invitations, were shunned by upwardly mobile acquaintances and had to endure countless minor insults.

Brought up in such miserable circumstances, Ikari nevertheless retained limitless love and respect for his grandfather and delighted to spend hours in the old man's company, learning about his exploits in the navy and imbibing much of his deep love for his country, his family and the truth.

No favours were granted to the young man at school, some of the teachers going out of their way to give him the hardest time possible; nevertheless, he passed into a prestigious private university, his fees being paid out of his grandfather's pension payments which the Imperial Navy had unaccountably forgotten to suspend after his disgrace. Whilst still at university, Ikari volunteered to become a "gakuto" or soldier-student. Gakuto students transferred directly into the forces when their studies were completed. They were often considered as somewhat "wet" by students from regular military academies and generally received a particularly hard time in their basic military training. Japanese forces were incredibly tough and cadets had to endure beatings, insults and humiliation from their officers and NCOs. Ikari got his share of all this but his boyhood tribulations had made him resilient and he had developed within himself a powerful resolve. He, Ikari Samasido, would restore the honour of his family. Once again they would be proud and the injustice of his grandfather's treatment would be righted. He was allowed a day's home leave at the end of his basic training and a family dinner was arranged for the occasion. Food was scarce in Japan in 1944, but his mother made a supreme effort and seven family members sat around the low table to enjoy a traditional Japanese meal. As was the custom, Grandfather Samasido got to his feet and made a short speech in which he praised the armed forces for their heroic struggle and celebrated the fact that Ikari would have the honour of joining the gallant Imperial Navy, serving the Emperor as he himself had. Ikari himself then stood up. He saluted his grandfather and his father dutifully then astonished his listeners with this devastating statement.

"For many years we have been aware of a cloud hanging over our family, a cloud undeserved but real nonetheless. As the first of my generation I can no longer endure the injustice which has brought shame on our name. For this reason I have volunteered for the Special Attack Force which our commanders are convinced will finally bring defeat on our enemies. I salute you all. I salute especially our ancestors. We are all one in our reverence and love of our country and our Emperor."

He sat down to the sound of weeping from his mother and his sisters and cries of admiration and astonishment from the men. The Special Attack Force! Young men resolved to destroy the enemy by crashing aircraft laden with explosives into enemy ships. The Kamikaze! The Divine Wind! No one knew what to say. This young man's actions would certainly restore the honour of the family. He was a saint, a martyr, but he was also their Ikari, their beloved boy and he was to give away his life deliberately for country and for family. Only the old admiral seemed to know what to do. He rose from the table, embraced the young man briefly, and walked slowly to his room. Closing the door, he went to the chest where he kept his old uniforms and drew out his razor-sharp sword. Unhurriedly, he penned a few lines of poetry:

Why must the young die for the sake of the ancient.
Why must an old man's pride bring innocent slaughter.

Leaving this brief farewell on the chest, he strode through the house into the little courtyard and did the terrible deed slowly, deliberately and with infinite dignity.

Ikari proved to be a truly natural pilot. Young men volunteering for the Kamikaze were revered, almost worshipped, as soon as they joined their training unit. The Emperor was a god and these were his angels, ready to hurl themselves to a most horrible death in the service of their country and for the honour of their families. Normally they were given only the most rudimentary flying training, enough only to take off, land and follow a leader to their assigned victim, the leader being an experienced navy flyer. Ikari was different. He was ready for his first solo flight after only four hours in training. His instructors noticed that every landing was perfect, every manoeuvre precise and crisply performed. Also, it emerged that his eyesight was truly exceptional. He could spot and identify birds flying in the mountains miles away from the base. He could read the identification number of each aircraft long before it commenced its final approach to the airfield. Often he could even see who was flying it, helmeted and goggled as they were, by their attitude in the cockpit and by their handling of the machine. One morning the commander of the unit took him aside. Normally juniors were expected to treat such senior officers with exaggerated respect, speaking only when spoken to and then only to agree with what had been said to them or to answer a direct question. This time the young pilot sensed that it would be different. The older man somehow looked concerned, even kindly.

"I have had reports of your progress and I myself have observed your flying," he began. "It is not to many that talents like yours are given. Tell me about your reasons for volunteering to join the Special Attack Force."

"Commander San, I joined this force because I love my country and its heroic struggle with injustice and also I vowed to bring honour onto my family. I wish to make the ultimate sacrifice in the name of the Emperor."

"Yes, yes, every young man who comes here gives such an answer. You, Ikari, are an exceptional young man. Have you thought that the Emperor might be better served if you applied your special talents in some other way? As a fighter pilot perhaps, defending our poor islands from the evil bombers who set fire to our cities and slaughter our women and children. Few people have abilities like yours; thousands have the courage and dedication to be Kamikaze pilots. You should think about how you could render the Emperor the greatest service. Go to your quarters now and think about what I have said. Report to me tomorrow morning."

Ikari could not sleep. He knew the commander was right; he had special skills as a flyer, and Japan had lost so many of its expert pilots that few were left with the skills to take on the monstrous American B 29s that were mercilessly pounding the home islands. He was almost sure to die in battle anyway; why not do so in a way which would best use his special talents in the service of the Emperor? He had given his word to his family and his old grandfather, but the commander had shown him another way. He must have the courage to follow his commander's advice. He strode to the headquarters' building the next morning, resolved.

It was a beautiful spring morning, the sky blue and crystal clear. He noticed that the cherry trees in front of the building had burst into flower. Cherry blossom, the very symbol of Japan! Some deep unconscious memory stirred in his mind and he heard the voice of his grandfather quite clearly as if he was beside him. "Stand by your oath, Ikari! You must be noble as your ancestors have been noble. You have given your word."

He gave his decision to the commander. There could be no turning back.

Kamakize pilots were being rushed through their flying training, mostly getting only about forty hours at the controls before being declared fit for service. Even this took several months due to the chaotic situation in the home islands and the shortage of aviation fuel, so it was not until May 1945 that Ikari and his comrades were able to take off for Kagoshima on the southern tip of Japan, which was to be their base. After that the wait was not a long one. Loaded with five hundred-pound bombs, six Zeke single-engine fighters, led by a single red-painted guide aircraft, set off on their suicide mission towards Okinawa. Above them six protective fighters would attempt to ward off defending US aircraft and return to report on the success of the raid. Each suicide aircraft was immaculately clean and polished to a mirror finish, the ground crews believing that as it was to be the pilot's coffin, it should be perfect, following ancient Japanese tradition. In his cockpit, Ikari had a strange feeling of elation. He was wearing a shimmering green silk scarf meticulously embroidered by his oldest sister and among the maps and paraphernalia behind his seat was a photograph of his grandfather, immaculate in his naval uniform. He tried to remember his training. *Look out for a worthy target, a battleship or, better still, a carrier. If it is a carrier, dive vertically down, aiming for the aircraft lift on deck. Never fly straight, veer from side to side so that the enemy won't know which ship you are aiming for. Strike at maximum speed!*

At first the machines flew peacefully over a deep-blue Pacific, keeping station carefully on their red leader. The lead pilot was in fact the only fully trained flyer among the suicide squad. A natural pilot like Ikari could fly easily in formation; the others had to concentrate hard to keep straight and level and could not let their minds wander onto higher things or dream about home, family and honour. Ikari even endeavoured to compose a poem as he flew:

How high the green young seedlings grow
While shines the sun and waters flow.
But they must fall to blade or hoe
When ancestors will bid them go.

The peaceful progress to suicide could not continue. Out of the clear blue Pacific sky, a line of tiny dots quickly materialised into a flight of large, fast fighters coming out of the sun at over four hundred miles per hour. In a few seconds the Corsairs had blasted four of the attackers out of the sky and were coming round for a second shot at the remainder. The protecting fighters were nowhere to be seen. Ikari saw the American machines clearly as they forged past him, great powerful monsters, heavily armed and skilfully flown. Instinctively he broke formation and hauled his little Zeke over into a half loop, rolled off the top so that the enemy were below and ahead of him. For a moment he thought that he could outfight these fearsome opponents using the amazing agility and acceleration of the Zeke, but his training kicked in. He was after a bigger prize than a single enemy fighter. Alone now, he dived into a cloud bank and flew on towards the point where he knew the enemy ships must be concentrating.

There they were! Straight ahead was what seemed like a swarm of little dots on the sea surface – the American fleet! He knew that there would be anti-aircraft destroyers guarding the outer perimeter of the fleet, with the carriers and battleships in the centre. Swerving and dodging from side to side, he soon passed over the outer screen and set his eyes on a fat carrier dead ahead. Suddenly huge volumes of smoke emerged from the ships below, making a hideous blackish cloud, hiding them from attackers. Ikari had learnt that the only way to avoid a smokescreen was to dive close to the surface of the sea, identify a victim while below the smoke, then pull up sharply, before diving onto its deck. He skimmed the surface of the sea. Several times he saw tracer probing towards him and once he felt his machine stagger as shells exploded close to its frail wings. Undeterred, he charged on to where he believed his quarry to be. Suddenly a white shape appeared right in front of him. He heaved back on the joystick but he was a fraction of a second too late. *City of Derry*, a British hospital ship, had been detached from the Royal Navy's force in the Pacific and sent to assist American medical teams with the horrific number of severely burnt servicemen who were victims of Kamikaze attacks. She had been transferring casualties from the carrier *South Fork* when the attack took place. The Zeke crashed bodily through her unarmoured sides and its deadly cargo exploded in the bowels of the old ship, wrenching her apart. Fuel from the aircraft ignited filling the interior with blazing petrol, consuming everything in its path. A few survivors, mostly from the upper decks were hurled into the sea but almost all the medical staff below, together with all the patients were blown to pieces.

As Senior Nursing Officer, Angela Pointer, had been supervising the transfer of casualties, standing on the foredeck. She was hurled into the water, splashing down on the side furthest from the carrier. After a brief blackout she found herself swimming amid a chaotic shambles of people, body parts and bits of ship's gear. Amazingly, only a few yards away floated a raft, blown from the deck of the hospital ship. She found that she could swim adequately and managed to reach the raft and scramble on board. Exhausted and trembling with shock, she looked around her. *South Fork* was already forging away from the scene. There were strict orders that capital ships must keep on the move when the fleet was under attack, whatever the circumstances, leaving destroyers and auxiliaries to collect survivors. All around the raft, among the flotsam, she could see heads belonging perhaps to survivors and perhaps to corpses, supported by their life jackets. She started to shout and wave her arms and saw some heads turning towards her. There was no way of propelling the raft, but there was about fifty yards of stout rope, which had been used to secure it on deck,

263

trailing in the water. There was nothing for it but to scramble back into the sea with the rope's end and swim to the nearest survivor. He turned out to be a young British hospital orderly. He was jabbering and trembling with fright, but finding him seemed to give Angela more strength and together they hauled in the line so that the raft was again alongside them. Getting onto the raft seemed to give Billy, the survivor, more courage. He would not re-enter the water but did locate six more survivors, three of them wounded, and helped Angela haul them onto the raft, which was now full and dangerously low in the water. There was no sign of a rescue ship, but Billy said he heard an engine, and after about half an hour a seaplane appeared and landed on the water beside them. Two crewmen got out a dinghy and paddled round the scene of the wreck, looking for survivors, then doing the grisly work of cutting the dog tags off floating corpses while two others helped the contingent on the raft into the big plane. Angela never forgot the hot, petrol-scented smell of that seaplane, the loud, confident American voices or the taste of the warm coffee brewed aboard. She was in fact quite unhurt and the rush of adrenaline which had sustained her on the raft seemed to continue as she examined her fellow survivors aboard the plane. Apart from Billy, everyone had suffered some damage. None of the aircrew had medical training, but the plane did carry an extensive first-aid kit and the two of them worked together to try to settle the casualties as the plane prepared for take-off. One poor fellow had lost so much blood that he died before the machine was airborne. The rest were settled down with morphine for the four-hour flight to Wake Island.

Chapter 18

The war was over, but in Britain austerity was still the watchword. Food, clothing and petrol were still rationed and the country, victorious though it was, had a grey, exhausted look about it. A Labour government was busily pushing forward a socialist programme for the country, while at the same time maintaining massively powerful armed forces, policing its defeated enemies and keeping a wary eye on the colossal Soviet armies which were poised to establish the Communist empire in eastern Europe over the coming three years. In defeated Germany appalling hardships were in store for the remaining population. Many fled westwards to avoid the cruel grip of Russian occupiers, only to starve to death on their travels. Railway, postal systems, telecommunications, gas, the electrical grid and food production and distribution were all in ruins. As the horrors of the extermination camps were revealed by occupying forces, any pity for German civilians caught up in the disaster befalling their country quickly evaporated.

Angela, fresh from being feted as a heroine in America for her bravery during the rescue, arrived in London in a US Air Force transport just before the first atomic bomb was dropped on Hiroshima, in time to be at home in Hampshire for VE day. To her delight, William had wangled some leave from his unit so the two could spend a few precious days together as the nation celebrated total victory. They worked together each morning in the Pointer vegetable garden, now famous for its delicious new potatoes and crunchy lettuces, cleaned out the chickens and mowed the lawns with the ancient family Atco. It should have been a delightful interlude together, but a monstrous elephant lurked in the room. An elephant named Hans. He was barely mentioned, even in their most intimate conversations, but William's jealousy smouldered, unquenched. He did not dare to question his love directly about their relationship, and she herself avoided any but the briefest mention of her encounters with him either before or during the war. Her parents followed suit, avoiding any reference to his brief stay in their house.

As William was preparing to leave, the news came that Angela was to be presented with the George Medal in recognition of her bravery after the sinking of the *City of Derry*. This kept everyone in a state of great excitement and sent the two Pointer ladies into agonies of indecision and torment over where they would find any clothes suitable for a visit to the Palace. William was doing everything he could to get his demobilisation from the RAF as soon as possible, but as Sir Felix warned him, the forces were reluctant to let go of useful officers when there were mammoth administrative tasks to perform, not least the repatriation of thousands of enemy prisoners. Now that his photo interpretation skills were no longer required, he had found himself drafted into a role in a camp which received POWs who had been held in Canada and arranged for their return to the wreckage of their own country. His fluent German had made him an obvious choice for such a job. Although he made a show of protesting, he was actually quite pleased because he thought he might be able to come across his German cousin in the course of his duties. That might enable him to settle matters.

The procedure for returning POWs was lengthy. Officers and men held in the US and Canada were returned to the UK where most of them were accommodated in camps operating a very relaxed regime. Only incorrigible Nazis were confined behind barbed wire. Each officer's political opinions were assessed to see if there was any danger of his joining undesirable political movements once he returned home. This process might take six months or a year, depending on the political opinions of the prisoner and the unit in which he had served. Once selected for release prisoners were shipped home, given some pocket money and finally released. William's job was to be one of the assessors, interviewing Luftwaffe prisoners held in a camp near Haltwhistle in Northumberland. As he had half expected, one of the first prisoners allocated to him for assessment was Oberleutnant Kurt Prim.

The two cousins prepared for the meeting in their individual ways. William simply wanted to get this fellow out of the country as soon as possible. Get him away from Angela. He had lost an arm and had no political black marks against his name so the repatriation guidelines suggested that he could be released early. Of course he might starve to death in Germany – thousands were starving every day. William was too decent a man to wish that on his cousin but he did want him as far away as possible. Hans, for his part, had almost given up hope of Angela. It had been almost four years since he last saw her and since then she had made no attempt, as far as he knew, to communicate. Why should she? How could she want a poor, wounded man? He could not, however, entirely kill his longing for that lovely, strong, courageous girl. The newspapers had been full of the story of her rescuing survivors from *City of Derry*; he had taken cuttings and kept them safely among his papers. Besides worrying about Angela, Hans was deeply concerned for his parents. The family seat in Prussia was in the hands of the Russians and he had no way of knowing if his mother and father were still there or had escaped into the relative security of the west. He had to maintain his false identity as Prim and so could not risk trying to contact his home, and he imagined that his parents would think that he had either been killed in the attack on *Rampant* or had died on the hospital ship *Minden*. He knew nothing of the communication which his father had received from Canada. Both his parents were now old, over sixty, and he had a duty to find them and offer what protection he could. In fact, he need not have worried on his parents' account. Albricht had seen the end of Nazi Germany coming and had been able to slip across the border into Switzerland where he and his wife were able to claim diplomatic status. Furthermore, not all the treasure entrusted to him by the Nazis had ended up exactly where they had intended. The von Pilsens ended the war with their fortune richly enhanced. Albricht did, however, worry desperately about his son. Since the communication from Canada reporting that he was safely in a POW camp, there had been no word from him, and for all his deviousness and cunning, Albricht was sincerely devoted to his son and concerned for the continuation of the family line. Also, there was that nagging worry caused by the visit of the SS officer who had suggested that his son was a traitor. He had heard nothing more about this, and it was not like the SS to let such matters drop. Almost all Hans' colleagues in his unit, including his commanding officer, had been killed so no information could be expected from that quarter. Somehow he must find his son and learn the truth. William was the only obvious source of information.

It took some time for Albricht's letter from Switzerland to find its way to Northumberland, and when it reached its destination it plunged William into a fit of indecision. He had postponed calling his cousin in for the first of his pre-release interviews, unsure how he would handle the situation. Now he could stall no longer. He called Hans to the interview room. Immediately, the situation turned awkward. There was an embarrassing fumble as they tried to shake hands, William unsettled by his cousin's empty sleeve. William went through the formal questioning process methodically, still using Hans' assumed identity as Kurt Prim. The farce could not continue for long, however; after fifteen minutes Hans broke the deadlock. "Squadron Leader," he said, "I think we both know each other's identity; perhaps I should explain my position to you clearly." He then briefly described the events in Sicily, his faked death on board *Minden,* his false identity and how Angela had saved him from discovery in Netley Hospital. Hearing him speak of Angela made William wince but he kept a straight face.

"And, Cousin Hans, if I may call you that, what do you want to do now?"

"I believe you have met my father before the war. You are aware that he and my mother are now old people. I do not know where they are – perhaps you can help me there – but they need my protection, then, when affairs in Germany settle down, I mean to resume my career as a lawyer. I have studied hard in Canada and have all the required qualifications, but Cousin, once again I have to call upon your family to help me. I must get to my parents quickly; I fear for their safety."

"Well, you can relax on that score anyway. I have a letter here from your father which was sent to me from Switzerland. Your parents will be safe enough there. I have replied to your father's letter to say that you are safe in England and will be returning to Germany as soon as certain formalities are complete."

Now that the two had broken the ice, conversation became quite easy and they actually found that they had things in common; the discussion turned to sailing and they discovered a common love of boats and the sea. They chatted quite amicably together for half an hour and it was arranged that they would meet again in a week's time. |Neither man had had the courage to mention Angela.

During the week that followed, the George Medal presentation was to take place at Buckingham Palace. William grabbed two days' leave and took the train down to London to join the Pointer family for the ceremony and her brother Rory just arrived back from Italy in time so that, besides her parents, Angela thus had the support of two decorated war veterans. The family made such a fine sight arriving at the palace that their picture appeared in the following day's *Times*. After the ceremony they had dinner together in Sir Felix's club, and over the meal it was arranged that they would all meet together at Stonebeck House in two weeks' time, William determined to show them his beloved home and the break would be good for the Pointers, who, like most Britons, had had no holiday since 1939.

When Hans and William met again in the camp interview room, William noticed that Hans had a copy of the newspaper in his hand. The subject could no longer be ignored. Hans, indeed had prepared a little speech.

"Cousin," he began. "I believe we both have the pleasure of knowing Miss Angela Pointer. I see from the newspaper here that you accompanied her to receive a decoration last week. I congratulate you both. William, if I may call you so, I cannot deny that I developed a strong affection for Angela when I was posted to London and that I had hopes that she had similar feelings towards me. Twice subsequently she saved my life and my gratitude to her and my respect for her is unbounded. I desire her happiness even beyond my own. I therefore have to consider how I can best make her happy. I do not believe that living in poor war-torn Germany with a cripple like myself would be a good life for her."

William didn't know what to do after this astonishingly formal, rather stilted speech. Should he say "Thank you", walk away or try some formal reply? He fumbled the papers on his desk, went red in the face and tried to clear his throat. Luckily at that point an orderly came into the room bringing mugs of tea. The hot, sweet liquid gave him time to recover. An idea began to take shape in his mind.

"Hans," he said, almost choking on the name. "I was with Angela last week as you know. She and her parents have the fondest feelings for you, and her brother Rory warmly remembers the time you spent together at Orford. What you have just said shows me that you are a man of principle and honour. I know that both Angela and her family would like to meet you again, and it happens that we are all going to meet together in my house on Tyneside next week. I have authority to grant you leave from this place. Will you join us?"

Thus it was arranged. Mrs Wellibond was able to clear most of the mess left behind by the nurses and managed to get two locals to tidy up outside. Rationing in Britain was still stringently enforced, but that didn't stop her from gathering together prime vegetables from the garden, fresh eggs from the hen house and best of all, four superb lobsters and a giant turbot from Freddy Seal.

Friday night's dinner, in spite of the splendid spread, began uncomfortably. Hans, who owed his life to both Sir Felix and to his daughter, could hardly feel relaxed in their company, and his feelings for Angela welled to the surface of his consciousness as soon as he saw her radiating health, energy and her own special brand of charm when she appeared for drinks before dinner. His upbringing before the war had taught him to manage most social situations, but somehow his lost arm seemed to have taken with it his self-confidence and his experiences with Sonia and Ester hardly made him feel at ease dining with pretty girls. Gradually however he became almost possessed by the charm and the radiance of that wonderful girl. They sat side by side and he found himself feeling almost physically lifted out of all the fear and horrors he had been through since that terrible day of the attack on *Rampant*. She laughed at him and the little jokes he managed. She helped him extract the last bits of delicious flesh from his lobster without making him feel embarrassed by his missing arm. She enquired so sweetly about his parents and how they had survived. By the time the coffee arrived he was a different man. Almost the fine fellow who had first gone so bravely, so carelessly, to war.

William could not help noticing the transformation being wrought on his guest, but he was not disturbed by it. He knew (or thought he knew) Angela too well. He had seen her exercise her charm on her parents' friends and on people they had met casually together. Hans was only getting the same treatment as they had. There was no need for jealousy or concern. He himself was acting as the attentive host to Lady Pointer, telling her about Tyneside before the war, the history of the house, and the miracles wrought by Mrs Wellibond in keeping everything in order during the war. He revelled in showing off his beloved home to his guests and felt impossibly happy and proud to think that soon he would be bringing Angela to it as his wife. What he did not see was the swift encounter between his love and his cousin on the staircase later that evening, the swift, one-armed embrace, the stolen kiss.

Although it was still early spring, the next day dawned fine and warm. Freddy had readied *Columba* for a gentle shake down sail. It was resolved that William, Hans and Rory would take her a little way down river on the tide to make sure everything was in working order while Angela and her parents took a gentle tour of the area in the old Morris belonging to Mrs Wellibond. *Columba* had been built in 1910 but under Freddy's care she still looked sleek and beautiful as she nosed her way down river, steering carefully round the clutter of naval and civilian shipping anchored in the estuary. Hans, at the tiller, soon showed that he had lost none of his skill as a helmsman. He watched as the other two brought sail bags on deck and hanked on the largest foresail for the leg along Entrance Reach towards the end of the two great piers. Soon they were past the lighthouses and out to sea, the boat heeling and seeming to enjoy the little waves which lifted her gently and occasionally left a little splash of salt water on deck. All too soon it was time to turn round and catch the start of the flood tide carrying them back, close-hauled in the southerly wind. Hans brought them neatly up to their mooring off North Shields.

Hans found himself happier that evening than he could ever remember. The short sail had shown him that even with only one arm he could still handle a boat as well as ever, and he had lost none of his skill. He was astonished at the easy, friendly relationship he now had with these two men, who not long ago he would be trying to kill, one of whom was, even now, his jailor. Above all there was Angela, the sweet smile she gave him when they got home, her excitement at their visit to Whitley Bay, the beach and the lighthouse, her enthusiasm for everything she did. On a cloud of happiness he sat down to enjoy his dinner, oblivious of the grim fact that he himself had solemnly renounced his love for her only a few days ago, and must return to a prison camp and thence to his defeated, disgraced and suffering country. He spent most of that evening in conversation with Sir Felix who had plenty to say about the future ahead of a new, democratic Germany, that he hoped would rise from the ashes and prove to be a bulwark against Soviet westward expansion. Occasionally he stole a glance at Angela who seemed to be happily chatting with Rory and William. Once or twice she met his glances and gave a little, private smile which made his whole body fizz with excitement.

On the next day, Sunday, it was the village church for all then, after a cold lunch, William and Hans had to set off back to the camp. It was less than an hour's drive in the Lagonda. Hans didn't know what to say about his feeling for Angela and it seemed that William had noticed nothing unusual in their relationship. Hans found, on his return, that his accommodation in the camp had been changed. His new Nissen hut had some unfamiliar names on the board outside, one SS Obersturmfuhrer Gluck caught his attention. It was rare for SS officers to be accommodated in the relaxed, low-security, camp at Haltwhistle. This Gluck must be a reformed character or a very good actor. Hans found him sitting on his bed reading a newspaper. Gluck got to his feet and introduced himself politely. Hans was still walking on air after his weekend away. With William's family he had been using his proper family name – von Pilsen and for one critical moment, elated as he was after his weekend, he forgot, for that critical moment, his disguise, and introduced himself as von Pilsen – his proper name.

"Excuse me," said Gluck. "There seems to be a mistake, this bed is for Oberleutenant Prim, it must be some confusion – typically British – maybe you should go to the administration hut and get it changed." For a moment Hans was unable to speak, totally paralysed by the situation. He could not stop himself from turning bright red in the face, bending down to fumble with the catch on his suitcase in an attempt to hide his embarrassment. "Oh, don't worry I will see Prim this evening and we will make a swap," he blurted out. "I have given up on getting any sense out of the administration clerks." Gluck returned to his newspaper but Hans already knew there was trouble in store. He skipped supper that evening and went to bed early, pretending to have a headache. But there was no escape. The next morning Gluck lost no time in getting back to the subject. "You said you knew this Prim last night. Forgive me, I have only just arrived here: could you kindly introduce me?" There was a long series of excuses, Prim was sick, Prim was at an interview, Prim was being investigated about an incident in Italy when some children were apparently massacred. Eventually Prim was "unexpectedly transferred to another camp", but Gluck had not been an SS officer for nothing. Hans' story was obviously false – all his friends in the camp called him Prim and also somewhere the name von Pilsen rang a bell. There were three other ex-SS officers in the camp and |Gluck called a furtive meeting. Someone remembered an incident in Sicily – an officer maybe on one of the projects looking for Jews and gypsies – was murdered. There had been a general alert but the murderer got away. A Luftwaffe officer was suspected. The story got more and more intriguing. Then Helmut Weiser, who had been a member of an SS unit posted to Sicily, remembered. It was Feldman. Murdered by a Luftwaffe officer who then deserted. Certainly that was why the name von Pilsen was familiar – this fellow with one arm in their midst was obviously the murderer and traitor in disguise. Probably he was actually working for the British as a "stool pigeon" in their midst. Ha! The SS knew how to deal with such people, even when the war was lost. By the end of the day a plan to punish the bastard was hatched.

Hans had smelt danger from the beginning of the episode. He must get away at once, before the SS got to work. He decided that his only choice was to place the problem before William. The two cousins were on the best of terms and a plan quickly evolved. The four SS men were confined to the cells on the pretext of claiming to have been officers in the Waffen SS – the fighting branch of the organisation – not the murderous Allgemeine squads to which they had, in fact, all belonged. That would take care of them, but the story might still get out somehow so it was essential to move Hans away as soon as possible. William would work on getting a quick release back to Germany while Hans would keep his head down and hope no one outside the little SS circle would hear the story.

Hans still could not keep his mind off Angela. He was more convinced now that in spite of everything she loved him and he became more and more determined that somehow she would be his. He poured out his feelings in a letter to his father, Albricht. This was the girl he would somehow win and marry. His love was too strong, too complete, to be denied. He posted the letter, confident that it would reach its destination in Switzerland.

The following weekend William wanted to get on the water again. The weather forecast was good and the *Columba* would be ready for him, although Freddy Seal had left word that he would be at a family funeral so he could not go sailing. The visitors had all left Stonebeck House and Angela had gone home with her parents, but Mrs Wellibond would be there looking after things and William saw no reason for not asking his cousin, useful in the boat in spite of having only one arm, to come with him. Also the less time Hans spent in the camp just now the better.

They had a fair breeze to take them out of the river, but once they got past the lighthouse, they found the wind much fresher than had been expected. The sky darkened and began to look menacing; the wind veered round to the north and blew cold and in savage gusts. The old boat was clearly over canvassed so William took in two reefs in the mainsail and changed to the smallest jib. The waves grew bigger and spray made it increasingly difficult to see, but, like the hero she was, *Columba* shouldered them aside and forged ahead. This was what she had been built for. This was her element. Hans, at the tiller while William worked on the deck, felt a strange sense of power as he drove her to windward into the rising gale. He remembered snatches of song, learnt in the old days before the war and, for the first time since that terrible day in Enna, began to sing lustily at the top of his voice.

He could not possibly have seen that sinister, grey shape lurking close to the surface, its horns choked with weed and its decayed mooring chain streaming beneath it. Mines were supposed to deactivate themselves if they came adrift, but on this one the mechanism was defective and the deadly monster was floating, ready to pounce. *Columba's* bow struck one of the horns fair and square. Made of lead, the horn crumpled, as it was designed to, and in a fraction of a second broke a glass tube within it, allowing acid to contact two electrodes and generate an electrical current, detonating the deadly weapon. The mine was powerful enough to destroy an armoured warship and the explosion was so violent that poor little wooden *Columba* was reduced to nothing more than splinters. Not a trace of her crew was left behind.

Chapter 19

It was 1957. Jimmy watched his car being loaded onto the ferry for The Hook of Holland. He was not looking forward to the next few days, but his wife had insisted they go, besides there were rumours of a legacy and he needed to get the close to the action. His fortunes had flourished since the war. He and Tuoy had set up their used car business in 1946, their first sale being William's Lagonda which the executors had insisted should go to his faithful mechanic and his air gunner. Tuoy's mechanical expertise and Jimmy's salesmanship had become the foundation of a very successful enterprise, but a little unexpected legacy would not come amiss as the family now needed a larger house and soon there would be school fees to think about.

It did not take them long to drive from The Hook to Munster, where the funeral was to take place. The "German Economic Miracle" had already restored much of the ravaged countryside which they drove through, and everywhere there was refurbishment, reconstruction and evidence of a buzzing industrial revival. Jimmy could not help marvelling that the country he had been trying to smash to pieces twelve years ago could have achieved such a thorough recovery. The couple had a quiet dinner in the hotel and an early night.

At nine o'clock the next morning, they were summoned from their room to meet Dr Franz von Grubben. It was he who had alerted them to the fact that Albricht von Pilsen had died and suggested they might like to attend the funeral. Grubben had been the old man's lawyer; he spoke perfect English and he set about explaining the provisions of his will. "You see," he said, "the Countess, his wife, died in 1945, and he had only one son, Hans. You are entirely familiar with his sad fate and that of his cousin, William. That leaves no living relative of the count's family. I discussed his affairs with him at great length and he eventually determined to leave the bulk of his assets, after expenses and taxes, to the lady his son was determined to marry. That Frau Hopson, I understand, is you. The Count kept a letter from Hans which must have been written only a day or so before his sad death.

Angela was staggered. She knew Hans was fond of her and she herself had risked her life for him. But marriage...? She didn't know what to with herself. Feeling dizzy and sick she fled from the room sobbing.

The lawyer rounded off his report to Jimmy. The family castle and lands were in East Germany, there was no chance of retrieving them and there were heavy taxes to pay and exchange control regulations to be dealt with on the Count's assets in Berlin, but the strange thing was that Albricht seemed to have been able to acquire a considerable fortune which was lodged in various Swiss banks. When the formalities were complete this would become the undisputed property of Frau Hopson – Angela. He believed the assets would be in total about $850,000. No sooner had he mentioned this staggering sum than Angela, recovered from her shock, re-entered the room. She still had fluent German and addressed the lawyer in his own language.

"Sir, this affair is based on a misunderstanding. I liked and felt sorry for Hans, yes, but we never even thought of marriage. I was halfway to getting engaged to his cousin, William, before the accident. I cannot accept this money. It would be dishonest. I cannot do it."

"Allow me, dear lady, to explain the rules which will apply to this affair. The money is held in the bank's accounts. It can only be released on production of certain documents which I possess and placed into your own hands when you provide proof of your identity. There is no other way. If these formalities are not completed the money will, after a number of years depending on local regulations and on the bank's own rules, simply be added to their assets. Is that what you want?"

"But I cannot accept money to which I have no moral entitlement."

"Madame, there is nothing here which says what you must do with the money when you have it. You could give it all to the Red Cross or some other charity if you wish. Surely there are more worthy homes for it than the pockets of Swiss bankers? May I suggest Madame that I accompany you and Herr Hopson to the Apostlekirche where the funeral service is to be held. I will then leave you and you can make your decision and perhaps you would be kind enough to visit my office in the morning. That would be convenient as there are some bulky and detailed documents to complete."

Angela's relationship with Jimmy was an astonishing one. They had met a few times while William had been serving in the RAF but they seemed to have nothing whatever in common; Angela could hardly be expected to take much notice of a cheeky young NCO from an East End background. It was tragedy which brought the two together. Jimmy had rushed to Newcastle when the tragic news of William's death reached him and had shown an unexpected, deep vein of sympathy and understanding. Also being the practical, savvy fellow he was, he set about making all the complicated arrangements about winding up William's affairs and the disposal of Stonebeck House, standing no nonsense from lawyers, estate agents or other such parasites. Just as the end of this ordeal seemed to be in sight tragedy had struck the Hopson family also. The little family house in Camberwell was destroyed when a German land mine, which had been lying in the foundations of a wrecked building opposite, was detonated by some building work. Mr and Mrs Hopson and their youngest son, George, just demobbed from the Royal Army Service Corps, were killed outright, Jimmy's two other brothers had gone down with the *Hood* in 1941. Angela, caring and kindly as ever, tried to repay to the some of the kindness she had received from Jimmy, doing hundreds of little time-consuming jobs while he worked hard to set up his business. The two had worked so well together, in defiance of social class or upbringing, that the friendship had gradually developed. Old Sir Felix and his son Rory could see that Jimmy made Angela happy and made no objection to the relationship.

Lady Pointer tried hard to "talk sense" into her daughter but, not for the first time, Angela stuck to her guns and the marriage was celebrated quietly in the parish church. Jimmy had proved a kind and attentive husband and gradually even Her Ladyship began to understand that he was exactly the man her daughter needed to make her happy. He was practical, cheerful and unfailing kind and his Cockney sense of humour often had the whole family in stitches. Two years in an RAF officers' mess had knocked some of the Cockney corners off him and his self-confidence and good nature made him acceptable in any company. Also, he knew exactly how to deal with Angela, forceful and headstrong though she was.

Albricht's funeral had been tedious and crowded with ancient pillars of various German regimes, some probably decent folk, many, doubtless, otherwise. Grubben, the lawyer made some introductions but conversations soon fizzled out and Angela could see that Jimmy was bored and uncomfortable. The two slipped off as soon as they could and drove out of Munster, wandering along minor roads until they came to a village with a little restaurant which looked promising. They ordered beer and omelettes and sat in the open air to discuss the legacy. At first Angela was adamant that she could not touch the money, but Jimmy had a brainwave.

"Look, love," he said, "there is sense in what the geezer said – you shouldn't let it all go to some rotten Swiss banker."

"No, I see that but there must be some way I can get out of it. I don't want to touch that money, most of it was probably stolen anyway, from Jews perhaps. William told me a bit about his uncle once, and my father, who had some dealings with him when you were in custody in Switzerland, said he didn't trust him an inch."

"Yes, that's what I was thinking, but wasn't your William interested in some old charity in London – my part of the world actually. There was an old vicar fellow. Can't remember his name. Saw him once in hospital just before he died."

"Oh yes! William often talked of him; he was his guardian, I think. Great friend of his father."

"Well, I think William would have liked any spare cash to go to something he was doing – I remember his name now, Flopsy wasn't it? Let's think about it."

It didn't take much research back in London to learn about Flopsy's work in the East End. Angela devoted all her drive and energy to the foundation of a children's charity and boy's clubs attached to what had been Flopsy's parish. The place soon became famous for community development in one of the most deprived parts of London and enhanced the lives of thousands of young people. In a twist of irony, many of them were Jewish or descended from the "Untermensch" folk from whose ranks the money had been stolen by the Nazis. The project was appropriately named *The William and Angela Foundation*.